WHAT PEOPLE ARE SAYING . . .

I could not put it down. Katie Schuermann is definitely on to something, with her continuing tale of everyday Lutherans captured by the Gospel and engaging the world around them. If you grew up in a small town, you have definitely known people like this—real people, with real sorrows, real struggles, and a very real Savior!

—Rev. Jon D. Vieker, PhD, Senior Assistant to the President, LCMS

It's rare that a sequel outshines its predecessor, but Katie Schuermann has accomplished that with *The Choir Immortal*. Katie captures life's complicated mix of sorrow and joy, grief and hope with the same warm narrative and delightful humor she gave us in *House of Living Stones*. She brings her characters to such life you weep with them in their sorrow, you belly-laugh at their antics, and you share the healing comfort of the sweet promises we have in our Lord Jesus Christ right along with them. Katie invites us to share the ups and downs of life with the people of Zion Lutheran Church, reminding us we are not alone in all we encounter and endure while answering each trial with the sweet truth of God's Word, grace, and redemption in Christ. A truly edifying delight of a novel.

—Vanessa Rasanen, wife, mom, and writer

The Choir Immortal describes the elating heights and sorrowful depths of our experiences in this fallen world with a careful balance of honesty and grace. Drawing from the riches of Lutheran hymnody, Katie Schuermann finds expression for what every congregation and individual Christian has faced. With an unswerving focus on the Gospel of Christ crucified, we're reminded of the Lord's promises through every season of grief and joy.

—Tony Oliphant, pastor

Something about Katie Schuermann's *The Choir Immortal* is very familiar. Anyone who has spent time in the rhythm of a Lutheran parish—a rhythm of sin and forgiveness, heartbreak and comfort, loss and enduring love—will find *The Choir Immortal* a familiar home. It is real sinners in need of the real Jesus, bearing one another's burdens as Christ bore them all on the cross. As a pastor, fifteen years out of full-time parish ministry, it made me long to return.

—Todd Wilken, host of Issues, Etc.

Retaining the engaging style which captivated *House of Living Stones* readers, *The Choir Immortal* positively sings with Mrs. Schuermann's sweet and distinctly Christian voice. Each page is liberally strewn with gems to discover—delightful turns of phrase, poignant moments, and archly-made insights by characters facing true challenges in an authentic way. Mrs. Schuermann's vignettes allow the reader to experience the gamut of human emotion: hilarity, awkwardness, heartbreak, catharsis, and more—oftentimes all on the same page. Once you pick it up, you will not want to put it down, and once you finish it you will immediately want to read it again!

—Heidi Poyer, wife, mother, attorney

Mrs. Schuermann is fantastic at developing characters which engage your imagination, allowing you to share in the lives of the people of Bradbury. These characters feel real, they experience real-life situations, and they fail in their handling of life issues as do we all. This is not sugar-coated storytelling. Life is represented accurately, both the good and the bad. Humor and faith make this book a complete gem. You will want to buy one for all your friends, it is that good!

—Sheryl Eby, wife and mother

Katie Schuermann once again draws the reader into the heart and soul of Zion Lutheran Church. She captures the raw emotions—both high and low—of each character and then delivers to the reader comfort, joy, and peace through hymnody, the Lord's words, and her own wit and wisdom. And, if one listens carefully when reading a hymn, one can almost hear Schuermann's sweet, angelic voice singing the hymn, bidding the reader to join her voice with hers.

—Teresa Becker, pastor's wife and registered nurse

You will laugh and cry with the people of Bradbury as Katie Schuermann weaves a story of real life that you won't be able to put down. In the most beautiful combination of character development, storytelling, Scripture, poetry, and hymnody, Schuermann acknowledges our own great joys and deep sorrows, pointing us again and again to Christ—His gifts of mercy, hope, and true peace for the choir immortal. Schuermann is a gift to the Body of Christ.

—Julie Habrecht, wife, godmother, Lutheran school headmaster

The Choir Immortal

KATIE SCHUERMANN

CONCORDIA PUBLISHING HOUSE • SAINT LOUIS

For my dad, Bob Roley, who raised me to
believe I could do anything, even write a book.

Published by Concordia Publishing House
3558 S. Jefferson Avenue, St. Louis, MO 63118-3968
1-800-325-3040 · www.cph.org

Library of Congress Cataloging-in-Publication Data

Schuermann, Katie.
  The Choir Immortal / Katie Schuermann.

1 2 3 4 5 6 7 8 9 10   24 23 22 21 20 19 18 17 16 15

Now let all the heav'ns adore Thee,

Let saints and angels sing before Thee

> *With harp and cymbals' clearest tone.*

Of one pearl each shining portal,

Where, joining with the choir immortal,

> *We gather round Thy radiant throne.*

No eye has seen the light,

No ear has heard the might

> *Of Thy glory;*

Therefore will we

Eternally

Sing hymns of praise and joy to Thee!

(LSB 516:3)

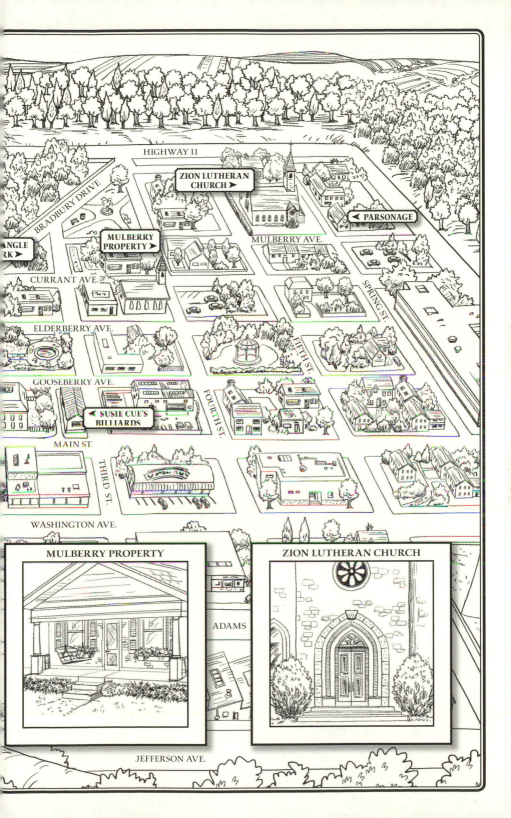

CONTENTS

CHAPTER ONE: THE BIG DAY

Zion Lutheran Church roasted in the late August sunshine like a crock in a convection oven. Ripples of hot, humid air rose from the asphalt parking lot in waves, and Beverly Davis, dressed in her favorite cobalt-blue frock with the embroidered portrait collar, heaved her sticky frame out of her Buick and onto the sweltering pavement. She fanned herself frantically, shaking out her pleated skirt in a desperate attempt to create wind where there was none, but her efforts were to no avail. Beads of sweat sprouted on her powdered forehead and threatened to stream down her temples in erosive rills as she crossed the black, oily expanse and entered the church office door. Irv, her husband and Zion's faithful trustee, was waiting for her there.

"Here," Bev panted, shoving a metal tool into his hand while dabbing at her face with a clean hankie. "I found it in the shed like you said. It was hiding under those bags of fertilizer we bought on sale last week at Big R."

Irv simply nodded his thanks before quickly disappearing down the hall with his adjustable wrench. The stoic man had never been one to waste words, and the present crisis called for

all brevity and efficiency. In less than one hour, Zion was hosting Bradbury's wedding of the century, and the church's air conditioning was a bust.

It was an ecclesiastical comedy of errors, really. Irv had been
urging the congregation for years to replace the five rusting
air-conditioning units currently baking on a concrete slab outside the fellowship hall, but his advice went unheeded. As Don
Kull had put it at last March's voters' meeting, "I don't see no
good reason to fix what ain't broke."

Irv had shrugged at the time, mumbling something like
"They're on their ninth life, that's all," but he didn't push the
matter any further. He wasn't much for speaking in public, let
alone arguing.

Some of the voters in attendance, however, rarely turned
down an opportunity to speak.

Candice Bradbury stood before the gathered assembly like
Eris on Mount Olympus condescending to address the lowly
humans below. "If there's a concern about longevity, we should
protect our investment by working the units less. I move we run
the air only on Sundays, when the majority of the congregation
is present, and let the church staff enjoy the residual air the rest
of the week."

Mrs. Arlene Scheinberg, Zion's crusty secretary of thirty-
seven years and exactly one-half of the church staff who would
be enjoying the proposed weekly leftovers, proceeded to turn the
office thermostat down an extra three degrees every Monday
through Friday for the entire month of June—in commemora-
tion of Candice's thoughtful benevolence, of course.

The situation worsened when two of the units began leak-
ing refrigerant in early July.

"Seems ta me we could jus' patch 'em up with some duct tape," Don Kull suggested to his fellow members on the Board of Trustees.

"The copper tubing's damaged," Irv explained. "Needs to be soldered or replaced."

"Well, then," Harold Schmidt sighed, doing his best to appear put out by the notion, "I guess we'd better get to it." Secretly, the retired appliance salesman was beyond pleased. He had a high-temperature torch sitting in his garage, waiting for an opportunity such as this.

Pastor Fletcher quickly intervened, both for Irv's sake as well as for that of the seventy-three-year-old stained glass windows rising above the fellowship hall. "How about we hire a technician for this job?"

Harold grunted and Don shrugged, but Irv gave his pastor a grateful nod.

When a fan on one of the units gave out exactly two weeks before the wedding, heat began to rise among the ladies in the quilting circle.

"I'm telling you, it's only a matter of time," Mrs. Scheinberg ruminated aloud to the other quilters one Tuesday morning in August. "Those units need replacing."

"I simply don't agree, Arlene," Candice quipped, setting down her needle to adjust the amethyst brooch pinned to her lavender top. She fingered it reverently as if it were a medal of honor and not her latest purchase from lia sophia. "Four of the units are still working perfectly fine."

"Candice makes a good point," said Nettie Schmidt, Harold's sweet-natured but rather dim-witted bride of fifty-two years, nodding from her corner of the quilt. "It's like that time I bought a turkey breast at full price at IGA when I already had cube steak thawing in the fridge. Harold nearly got sick from eating both for supper."

"Why didn't you just—?" Bev began to ask, but Mrs. Scheinberg laid a silencing hand on Bev's arm and shook her head. The church secretary had learned years ago not to follow the pied piper—however tempting his tune—through the meandering maze of Nettie's mind. That's how people got lost.

Candice, on the other hand, hummed an affirmative as if Nettie's carnivorous comparison had made perfect sense. "All I'm saying is that it's offensive. We shouldn't be spending money on something so opulent as replacing working air-conditioning units when there are children starving in Africa."

Mrs. Scheinberg snorted. "So says the woman flashing costume jewelry while sitting comfortably in seventy-two degrees Fahrenheit." She lifted her wattled chin, ruffled her feathers, and clucked at the purple peacock splaying her colors across the quilt. "Wait until it feels as hot as Africa in here, and then we'll see who thinks good stewardship is opulent and offensive."

Mrs. Scheinberg, it turned out, had not been too far off from the truth in her prediction that morning with the quilters, for it really did feel like the Congo in the church the afternoon of the wedding. Bev patted at her face, nervous that all of her foundation would be wiped clean away before the ceremony even started. Not that it mattered. It was the bride everyone would be looking at—and oh, what a sweet bride! How she had blushed a pretty pink when the women of the congregation had offered to throw her a wedding reception.

"Now, please, don't go to any trouble," she had pleaded. "All I want is a simple ceremony."

Simple, however, was not a word the women of Zion understood. Marge Johnson proceeded to make exquisite invitations by hand, using pressed, dried flowers from her own garden; Phyllis Bingley worked all of June and July quilting individual coasters for wedding favors; the Koelster sisters promised biscuits from scratch and fried chicken for the meal; and Candice, not to be outdone, baked and frosted fourteen fluffy, white twinkie cakes for the dessert.

Even Yvonne Roe, Zion's disapproving misanthrope, descended from her castle to offer to sew the bridal gown.

"What color should I make it? She's not exactly a virgin, you know."

Bev had colored five different shades of red at Yvonne's brash assertion, but Mrs. Scheinberg simply poured a look of hot contempt over her gold-rimmed glasses onto the wrinkled, priggish woman.

"Oh, for heaven's sake, Yvonne. She's a widow, not a whore. It's not her fault her husband up and died on her." Mrs. Scheinberg knew about such things. Her own husband had up and died nearly forty-one years before in a farming accident.

"The dress will be white." This final directive came from Rebecca Jones, a pretty, spirited mother of five, counting the one currently growing in her womb. She also happened to be the matron of honor for the wedding. "We already picked out the dress last weekend in Fairview Heights. So, thank you, Yvonne, but no thanks."

"Well, call me when your own dress needs letting out." Yvonne eyed Rebecca's expanding abdomen meaningfully. "I can't stand the way women flaunt their pregnancies in tight clothes these days. It's indecent."

Rebecca, who stood to be a full eight months pregnant the day of the wedding, fought against hormones, human nature, and the powers of hell to offer the sour woman even one civilized word, but charity turned out to be too tall an order for the moment. The expectant mother simply bit her lip and turned, red-faced, away.

In the beginning, Bev had felt left out of the wedding planning festivities. She had no special skills to offer the creative team, and Sunday after Sunday, everyone chattered and exchanged ideas around her as if she weren't there. But when three of the five air-conditioning units blew out the morning of the wedding, it was Bev who sprang into action. She knew her way around a pressure cooker, after all: keep the steam regulating properly and watch the clock. She cheerfully corralled the bridal party safely across the street to the parsonage to keep cool, fresh, and dry while Irv performed mechanical surgery on the busted units. Then, braving the heat, she returned to the stuffy church to look in on things while everyone else was away. She busied herself with centerpieces and mints and napkins in the fellowship hall, touching up an arrangement here and patting down a tablecloth there, fussing over every little detail like the good Lutheran girl she was. She wanted everything to be just perfect. Zion was her church, after all. She had been baptized, confirmed, and married here, and, as she was not one to leave any project unfinished, she fully intended to be buried here. If this wedding didn't come off as a complete success, she would feel personally responsible.

Having fetched Irv his trusted wrench, there was now nothing left for Bev to do but wait and pray for cool air to once again rush through those eerily silent vents. It was so blasted hot! She dabbed at her face one last time before tucking her soiled hankie into her purse and walking resolutely over to the cherry-wood desk sitting in the middle of the front office. She switched on the tiny oscillating fan clipped to its edge. Normally, she would never dare lay a finger on anything sitting within five yards of Arlene Scheinberg's sacred surface—the crotchety woman could be touchy about such things—but the heat was making fast work of Bev's carefully painted visage. One more minute in this stagnant air and what little remained of her makeup would slide down her face in a pink-and-blue avalanche. She threw all caution to the electric-powered wind and leaned her face into the delicious breeze.

"That's more like it," Bev breathed. She tossed a daring, side-long glance toward the darkened hallway through which her husband had disappeared. Not a single soul was in sight, so she lifted the edge of her skirt over the fan to dry out her intimates.

"Beverly Davis, what on earth are you doing?"

Bev jumped at the sound of the familiar voice, her hem catching on the plastic casing of the fan and ripping its precarious grip right off the desk. The fan crashed, still oscillating, onto the floor, and Bev bent over as quickly as her one hundred ninety-five pounds would allow to power off the contraption and secure it back onto the desk's edge. She patted the silenced fan meekly before turning around to face her accuser.

There, frowning like an orangutan in a lemon sherbet-colored muumuu, stood Mrs. Scheinberg, one husky hip propped against the outside door while the other supported a box of folded bulletins.

Bev cleared her throat apologetically. "I-I was just trying to keep fresh."

"By flashing my stapler?" Mrs. Scheinberg waddled on into the office, letting the outside door close behind her.

"The air conditioning's down."

"Of course it is. Those units needed replacing five years ago." Mrs. Scheinberg sighed contemptuously and dropped the heavy box onto the seat of her mid-back leather chair. She then bent over to remove a can of Lysol from the bottom drawer of her desk. "You do realize, don't you, that this is how *certain* diseases spread?"

Mrs. Scheinberg proceeded to generously spray the can's contents over the surface of her desk, hovering a few seconds longer over the violated fan.

Bev was naturally too genial and happy a woman to be more than mildly shamed by Mrs. Scheinberg's scorn. Besides, a much greater concern was pressing upon her conscience. "Oh, Arlene, what are we going to do? It's too hot in here for a beach party let alone a wedding. Irv's working as fast as he can, but Don Kull borrowed the toolbox from the janitor's closet last month so I had to go home to fetch Irv a wrench and then I couldn't find it. Well, I *did* find it, but not where I thought. Thank God we bought those cell phones last year! Those things really are amazing. Did you know we can call each other for free from anywhere in the country, even Canada? Not that we'll ever get to Canada, but still. It's amazing what technology can do these days. Anyway, all I had to do was call Irv, and he walked me through...."

Mrs. Scheinberg sighed. After forty-five years of friendship, she was used to Bev's roving rambles, but in this wretched heat, even her patience was tried.

"Why is it so hot in here?" a prissy voice interrupted.

Bev and Mrs. Scheinberg turned around to find Candice Bradbury glaring from just inside the office's front door. The self-proclaimed first lady of Bradbury was wearing a purple crêpe blouse, a white linen skirt, and two large, white gardenias pinned to her right shoulder. Apparently, the bride's decision not to order special flowers for the occasion hadn't kept Candice from ordering her own.

"The heat?" Candice insisted again, looking like a bobble-head figurine with her sand-colored wig bouncing from side to side in search of the sultry air's source.

"The air conditioning's broken," Bev explained.

"What?" Candice's eyes grew large, her pencil-drawn eye-brows pushing up into her forehead in an unattractive way. "Broken? For how long?"

"Since eleven."

"My cakes!" Candice immediately threw her abundant frame across the office and down the hall, griping the entire way. "Why did no one *tell* me? I brought the cakes in this morning and set them out on the table already. The temperature was *perfect* then, but the cream'll melt in this heat! Why does no one think of these things? Seriously, is it too much to ask that the church staff *think*, for once?"

Bev, who was scurrying after Candice, bowed her head like a penitent servant, though she had no reason to feel guilty. She was not church staff. Mrs. Scheinberg, however, following at a much more leisurely pace, rolled her eyes. If meteors fell from the sky, crashed through the fellowship hall roof, and landed directly on the cake table, Candice would find a way to blame it on the church staff.

"Oh, nooo!" Candice wailed as she entered the fellowship hall, loping like a tented elephant in her purple blouse. There, arranged in the shape of a melting heart on a circular table in the northwest corner of the room, were fourteen magnificent, three-layer twinkie cakes whose top two layers were slipping and sliding off their bases under their plastic-wrap covers.

Bev felt a sharp pang of regret. In all of her running around, she had never thought to refrigerate the cakes. They had looked fine before she'd left to run Irv's errand, but then, that had been almost an hour ago. "Now, Candice. It's not too bad," she soothed.

"Of course it is!" Candice snapped, looking as if she were about to burst into tears. "This is a disaster!"

"One that could have been prevented," Mrs. Scheinberg tut-tutted, a tiny but powerful glint of victory twinkling in her eye.

"We'll simply slide the top layers back into place and anchor them with some toothpicks," Bev suggested.

"Don't you *dare* touch my cakes!" Candice spat, holding out her right arm as if to guard her confections from a terrorist.

"Candice, be reasonable." Mrs. Scheinberg had little patience for Candice's foolish antics, but she was also cool in a crisis. "You need some help. Now, you do the sliding and arranging, I'll do the anchoring, and Bev can move them to the refrigerator. They'll firm up in no time."

Candice really did start crying. "I've never had holes in my cakes before."

"Maybe you'll find that you like them that way," Bev cheered. "Remember the time Dr. Duke's chicken breasts turned blue and green from the colored toothpicks she used for her tea party? She was pretty upset about it at the time, but we all laugh about it now. Mistakes can be kind of fun, see? At least, they make good stories afterward. Why, I don't think I ever told you about the time IGA was out of green bell peppers last summer, and I picked up one of those Hatch peppers instead. 'They're both green,' I thought to myself. Well, they're *not* the same, let me tell you. You should've heard Irv's stomach—"

"C'mon, now," Mrs. Scheinberg interrupted, moving toward the kitchen in search of toothpicks. "The wedding's in forty minutes. Let's get these cakes in the fridge before the guests arrive."

"I wanted everything to be perfect," Candice whimpered.

"So did the Pharisees, and look where that got them." Mrs. Scheinberg, with all of her confidence and wit, sometimes failed in the area of consolation.

The Koelster sisters arrived just then, pushing a cart laden with insulated food containers into the kitchen through the outside door.

"Good gracious!" Janet Koelster hollered, hefting a big tub of fried chicken onto the kitchen counter and waving a hand frantically at her neck. "Am I having a hot flash or did someone leave the ovens on overnight again?"

"Neither," Bev said, walking into the kitchen to assist with the unloading. "Air conditioning's down."

"Lord, have mercy. It's got to be over a hundred out there, and it's not much cooler in here. What a misery! Oh, well." Janet was never one to dwell on that which couldn't be helped. She clapped her hands decisively. "I hate to be the one to toll the bell of doom, ladies, but we've got to crank these ovens for a bit. Dot and I promised biscuits for the wedding."

Dorothy Koelster, who was currently swooning under the weight of a stainless steel bowl of biscuit dough, moaned softly from the kitchen doorway.

"Oh, here, honey," Janet cooed, taking the bowl from her sister's arms and motioning for Bev to bring a chair into the kitchen. "Sit down, now. That's it. Easy does it. Heat always makes it worse, doesn't it?"

Mrs. Scheinberg shook her head, baffled. How a woman with vertigo managed to work in a hot kitchen her entire life and never once fall face-first into a pan of hot grease was beyond her. "C'mon, Candice, the cakes aren't getting any cooler. And Bev, after you help us get the cakes into the fridge, I need you to set out the bulletins in the narthex. Guests'll be arriving any minute."

"Oh, ladies! Ladies!" Nettie Schmidt called, bustling into the fellowship hall and waving her hands before her face like sparklers on the Fourth of July. Her eyes were wide with child-like excitement. "She's here! She's here!"

"Who's here?" Candice asked, confused as to why the arrival of anyone but herself would cause Nettie to go all aflutter.

At that moment, a delicate woman wearing a smart orange skirt and matching suit jacket stepped through the eastern doorway of the fellowship hall. Her tiny hands were clothed in white gloves, and her hair was attractively pinned back from her cheeks. A sprig of fresh baby's breath and three white baby roses were arranged behind her right ear in place of a veil. Despite the atrocious heat, the petite woman looked as fresh and rosy as any bride on her wedding day. "Well," she blushed prettily, clearly embarrassed to have so many eyes focusing on her at once. "What do you think?" She shyly twirled around for a proper inspection.

"I thought you were wearing white." Candice's brow furrowed. She was thinking of the special-ordered white gardenias currently pinned to her shoulder—and the fact that she no longer matched the bride.

"Oh, well, I just thought . . ."

"You look lovely," Mrs. Scheinberg reassured.

"Like an orange rainbow," Nettie sighed.

"Yes, of course," Candice quickly recovered, pasting on a too-bright smile and singing, "practically perfect in every way!"

For once, Bev was at a loss for words. She had seen that orange suit many times before in a photograph hanging on a wall in the bride's home. The sight of it now, in person, unleashed a flood of bittersweet memories, particularly those of a beloved, sainted pastor now waiting in Zion's cemetery for the

Resurrection Day. Weddings had a strange way of being happy and sad all at the same time.

Bev stepped forward, took the gloved hands in her own, and blinked back a sting of tears. She did her best to muster a smile of encouragement, for she understood the bride's choice of dress perfectly. "You look beautiful, Alice."

"Thank you, dear."

Chapter Two: Here Comes the Bride

|||||||||||||||||||||||||||||||||||||||||||||||||||||||

Sweet Alice Gardner had married the love of her life nearly forty-five years before on a wintry New Year's Eve. The wedding had been a grand affair, complete with floor-length veil, red gladiola bouquets, six bridesmaids dressed in green satin, and a tall, handsome scholar of a man for a groom. Not once since that fairy-tale day when she had said "I do" to the Reverend David Gardner had Alice ever imagined that she would someday walk down the aisle again to marry another. In fact, on the morning of her second wedding, the idea still twisted and tied her heartstrings into a messy knot.

"I simply can't do it," Alice confessed, fingering the satin hem of the white midlength gown she and her daughter had purchased the month before.

"Do what?" Rebecca Jones asked, standing behind her seated mother and brushing out her shoulder-length white tresses.

"I can't wear white again."

Rebecca held the brush in midair and eyed her mother's reflection in the vanity's mirror. They had been through this before. Many times.

"I wore white when I married your father," Alice sniveled, tears threatening to spill down her wrinkled cheeks for the third time that morning. "It just feels wrong to do it again. Like I'm cheating."

"You're not cheating. Dad's been dead for seven years."

Alice thought Rebecca was acting remarkably calm for a girl whose mother was about to marry someone other than her father, but then, Alice thought Rebecca was remarkable, period. Ever since she had been a little girl, her daughter's pixie-like frame had reverberated with a life force that could fill an entire room, and even now, as an adult, her blue eyes crackled and popped as if charged from some internal socket. She was a tireless, devoted wife and mother who woke each morning to live her life in service to others, so it was no surprise that she was steady as a rock on her mother's wedding day. Alice reached over her shoulder to take her only child's hand affectionately in her own. "You're always offering me comfort when it should be the other way around."

"Well," Rebecca said, gently squeezing her mother's hand before letting it go to resume her brushing, "'It's not good that man should be alone,' is it?"

A fresh wave of tears—these of the grateful variety—gushed from Alice's blue eyes.

"Now, Mother, really!" Rebecca set down the brush and grabbed a tissue. "This has got to stop. You've cried off practically all of your mascara again. We've only got one tube to share between us, remember?"

"I know, I know," Alice moaned, half crying, half laughing at the ridiculousness of it all. She just felt so grateful. She didn't need permission from her daughter to remarry, but she was thankful for it all the same. "I'll never love Evan the way I loved your father, you know."

"I do know," Rebecca said matter-of-factly, reaching for the spray of flowers resting on the vanity. She gently clipped the posy in her mother's hair, just above her right ear. "No one expects you to, but Evan's your best friend. Besides, it'll save all of us a fortune in gas money if you both just go ahead and get married and live under the same roof, already."

Truth be told, it was a bit of a miracle that Alice and Evan were friendly toward each other at all, let alone getting married. It had not been too long ago that she and her groom-to-be had been at odds with each other. Well, *she* had never harbored any ill will toward him, but Evan had stubbornly held a sixteen-year grudge against her for the fact that his then-wife, Shirley, ran away with a younger man. Granted, Alice had played no part in Shirley's adulterous schemes, but her position as Shirley's closest friend at the time had made her guilty—at least in Evan's eyes—by association.

The whole ordeal had been quite the scandal in Bradbury, especially considering the fact that Evan was Zion's organist and Shirley's seducer happened to be Zion's choir director at the time. It took years for Evan to be able to think past his own pain and humiliation and see Alice's friendship as true; but thankfully, the two old chums had reconciled back in January and had been doing their best to make up for lost time ever since.

Alice smiled now, the memory of Evan's simple, tender proposal a bright stamp of joy in the scrapbook of her mind. He had walked her to her front step one soft evening after the Bradbury Municipal Band's Memorial Day concert.

"I'm getting tired of saying good-bye to you each night, Al."

He'd just started calling her that affectionately whenever they were alone.

"If you married me," he continued, "we wouldn't have to say good-bye to each other anymore. We could just say good night."

Alice hadn't needed much convincing. David was still the love of her life—always would be—but Evan was her boon companion, and he was right. It had gotten old, saying good-bye all of the time.

"C'mon," Rebecca interrupted her mother's reverie. "Maybe we did make a mistake at the boutique last month. White is so forty-five years ago. You should wear a different color today."

"Oh?" Alice sensed an adventure in the making. "I do still need 'something blue.'"

"I think your eyes count for that already."

"How about 'something borrowed'? I could wear that pretty black dress you wore for Jeremy's company party last year."

"Nope." Rebecca's blue eyes were firecrackers. "You're already borrowing my earrings. Besides, I'm thinking more along the lines of 'something old' for your dress."

"Don't you think the bride and groom have that category covered?" Alice and Evan shared more than 130 years of life between them.

Rebecca slid back her closet doors and started digging through the back corner where she stored her mother's older dresses that she no longer wore but couldn't quite bring herself to give away. Rebecca let out a victorious cry and reappeared holding a two-piece, polyester orange suit.

Alice sucked in her breath. It was her going-away dress from her wedding to David. Her own mother had sewed the skirt and matching jacket. They had argued about the color at the time—her mother had wanted the outfit to be pink—but orange had been David's favorite color. "You don't think—?"

"What?" Rebecca started taking the jacket off the hanger.

"You don't think it's, well, kind of morbid?"

"I think it's perfect." Rebecca motioned for her mother to turn around to be unzipped. Her voice was gentle but resolute. "Daddy should be the one to give you away, don't you think?"

That settled it. Besides, Alice knew that Evan would understand. In fact, he would undoubtedly approve. David had been Evan's best friend before colon cancer had taken him, too soon, from their midst.

"There," Rebecca announced triumphantly, standing back to admire her mother's slender frame in the orange suit. She tossed a quick glance down at her own protruding belly. "You know, not every woman can fit so easily into a dress she wore nearly half a century ago."

Alice fiddled nervously with the top button of her jacket. She was thankful the darted seams hid how loosely the skirt fit around her waist. No doubt, she had lost a few pounds in the excitement of planning and anticipating the wedding.

"Now, Mother, before we go over to the church," Rebecca said, walking around to the side of the bed, where she pulled a small package from a drawer in the bedside table, "I want to give you this."

"What is it?"

"Your wedding present."

"Oh, Rebecca, I told you not to get me anything—"

"Now, don't get too excited. Jeremy and I talked, and we want you to have this. It'll make both of us feel better about your driving around on all of those country roads. I know Evan's house is just a few miles out of town, but still. It won't be the same as having you just a few streets away in town."

The package Rebecca placed in her hands was small but surprisingly heavy. It felt almost as heavy as the royal blue velvet box David had given her on their thirtieth wedding anniversary, but surely her daughter and son-in-law weren't giving her sapphires. Alice pulled back the white bow and broke the bonds of the Scotch tape on the silver paper. She felt her heart quicken with anticipation. She opened the crisp, white cardboard box with an apple on the front, but she had to bite her lip to hide her immediate disappointment. "Oh. An e-phone."

"An iPhone," Rebecca corrected, quickly taking the computerized white rectangle from her mother's hands and powering it on. "Look. Jeremy already has it programmed with all of our phone numbers on it and everything. And if you press this top button, a picture of the kids comes up. Isn't that cute? And he took a picture of your old house and used it for your wallpaper. See? Robbie insisted that we put Angry Birds on your phone, though Words with Friends is going to be your favorite, I'm sure. Now, I know you get overwhelmed by technology, but really, Mother, it's all quite sensible. You'll be shocked at how much this little thing'll simplify your life."

Alice had her doubts. Rebecca's own phone had made the Joneses' life anything but simple. She took the slender apparatus unceremoniously from her daughter's hand and put it back in its box, gathering the wrapping paper and bow from the bed and stuffing everything in her purse. "Well, dear, how nice of you. I'm sure this thing will come in handy. I'll have to study it after things settle down a bit."

"Don't you want me to show you how to use it?"

"No, no. Don't you bother yourself with such things today. I'll read the manual later when I'm home and figure it out. Now," she said, turning around, a smaller package extended in her own hand, "I have something for you. Go ahead. Open it."

Rebecca accepted the gift and untied the white ribbon around the red velvet box. Her breath caught in her throat as she opened the flip-top lid. Staring back at her was the pearl engagement ring her father had given her mother.

This time, it was Rebecca's turn to cry.

"There, there, dear," Alice soothed, wrapping her arms around her daughter and whispering sweet words of comfort that only a widow and mother whose hope is in the resurrection of the dead can think to say.

When all eyes in the room had been properly dried and another coat of mascara applied, Rebecca opened her purse and threw the tube in determinedly. "Okay, you and I are done with the tears, do you hear me? We've been given so much in the last year." She touched her pregnant belly with the hand that was now bearing her mother's pearl ring. "More than any one family deserves. I'm tired of crying. Let's just be happy for the rest of the day."

But Alice had one final misgiving as they climbed into Rebecca's SUV. "Are you sure I won't get too hot in this thing, dear? It is a winter suit, you know."

Rebecca dismissed the question with a wave of her hand and shifted the vehicle into reverse. "With the way Mrs. Scheinberg's been cranking down the air conditioning all summer long? Trust me. You'll thank me later for the long sleeves."

CHAPTER THREE: TIMBER!

Dr. Emily Duke lifted an octavo from her music stand and fanned her flushed face with hummingbird-like speed. She liked to joke with members of her sanctuary choir that singing in the balcony brought them all a little closer to heaven, but the withering heat rising from the nave the afternoon of the wedding made the balcony feel a little too close to the opposite. At least she had been able to find a couple of loose hairpins hiding in the bottom of her purse, or her blonde ringlets might still be plastered miserably to her damp forehead and neck.

The young man seated at the organ console, however, was having no such coiffured luck. His own black hair, shaved to five o'clock–shadow length, was too short to absorb any of the beads of sweat forming on his head, so they all ran in slick rivers down the back of his neck and pooled in a dark spot at the top of his collar.

"I chose the wrong month to cut off my hair, huh?" He wiped his face and hands with the floral hand towel Emily had snagged for him from the church kitchen. She smiled sympathetically but didn't say a word. Blaine Maler was a student at Bradbury College where she was a professor of music history, and Emily made it a rule never to comment on the appearance of a student—especially when that student moonlighted as the accompanist for her church choir.

Not everyone at Zion handled the matter of Blaine's appearance with such discretion. The young man had sported three dramatically different hairdos since Emily had first met and hired him last summer—each one more shocking than the last—and his ever-changing hair was a point of perpetual fascination with the other musicians in the choir.

First was Blaine's "Sleeping Bear 'Do" as Marge Johnson, a native of northern Michigan and a soprano in the choir, liked to call it. Blaine's hair had hung in long, sleek locks all the way to his waist, like a Native American warrior's.

Then, Blaine had cut and styled his hair to look like a tsunami wave rolling onto his forehead.

"Do you suppose I might hear the roar of the ocean if I leaned in a little closer to the piano?" Janet Koelster had whispered rather loudly to the other altos one Sunday morning last spring.

"I think you could ride a surfboard to Hamburg on that wave," Dot returned. The entire alto section, Mrs. Scheinberg excluded, had proceeded to flood the balcony with giggles.

That second hairstyle had definitely stretched the comfort zones of Zion's eldest matriarchs, but it was Blaine's latest 'do that hit the ladies of the choir like a punch to the gut.

"He looks like a skinhead," Candice had announced decidedly at last Tuesday's quilting circle.

Bev was shocked into silence, though she happened to agree.

Mrs. Scheinberg did not. She was fond of that sensitive, misunderstood boy, and as his self-appointed guardian angel, she snapped her wings to attention in preparation for an attack.

"Now, dear," Alice tempered before Mrs. Scheinberg could speak a word, "it could be worse. Much, much worse."

"I don't see how," Candice frowned.

"He could wear a wig," Mrs. Scheinberg fired point-blank at the toast of Bradbury. Candice's hand flew self-consciously to her own head of borrowed hair, and the ladies let the topic rest in peace after that.

Still, Candice was justified in her observation, for Blaine's close shave, when combined with his left eyebrow ring and black eyeliner, gave a certain appearance of aggression to the average Bradbury beholder; but Blaine's manners were always perfectly respectful and professional. In fact, everyone in the choir loved him. It didn't hurt any that he was the best pianist Zion Lutheran Church had ever heard, a point driven home by the fact that he, despite having no official training as an organist, was covering for Evan at the console the afternoon of the wedding. Granted, his chops were nowhere near Sowerby's *Pageant* level, but he could at least render a simple prelude with basic pedaling so that Zion's faithful organist of the past twenty-six years could stand before the altar with his bride.

"Is there anything else I can get you?" Emily asked.

"A working air conditioner."

"We're fresh out of those, I'm afraid. How about a glass of water?"

"Nah, I'll manage. It's the organ I'm worried about." Blaine demonstrated his concern by simultaneously playing a C in four separate octaves.

Emily winced at the sour tuning. "Well, I guess it kind of fits with today's forecast. We're miserable in the balcony. Why shouldn't the pipes be, too?"

Blaine gave a wry smile.

"It's quarter to one. Ready?"

Blaine wiped his head and hands one last time on his towel and gave a bald nod. "Let's do this thing."

||||||||||||||||||||||||||||||||||||||||||||||||

Downstairs in the narthex, Bev was trying not to panic. The thermostat in the nave read almost as high as her basal body temperature, and the humidity level in the church was downright oppressive. If the air conditioning didn't kick on soon, she'd have to start wringing out people's hair into buckets to save the wood floors. At least the bride's grandchildren seemed oblivious to the sweltering oppression.

"I a princess," three-year-old Alison Jones proudly announced as she spun around in the narthex for Bev to admire her white satin dress with the yellow ribbon sash.

"You're a flower girl," Rebecca corrected, leaning down to rearrange the daisies that had fallen from the wreath pinned atop her daughter's strawberry-blonde head. "Now, hold still."

"She thinks it's her crown," Frankie Jones explained to Bev.

Bev turned to face the serious seven-year-old boy dressed in black pants and a white, short-sleeved dress shirt. His red hair was parted and combed neatly to the side, and a black bow tie stuck out from beneath his chin. Of Jeremy and Rebecca Jones's four children, Frankie was the third—a difficult spot for a child to occupy in any family.

"And what are you doing today in the wedding?" Bev asked cheerfully.

"Go ahead, Frodo," Davie, the eldest Jones boy, teased from behind. "Tell her."

Frankie looked up at Bev with world-weary eyes. "I'm the ring bearer."

Davie snorted obnoxiously.

"That's enough, Boromir," Rebecca reprimanded, silencing her eldest son with a pointed look before giving Alison's bangs a final fluff. She straightened up and rubbed the small of her back with her right hand.

Bev eyed Rebecca's distended belly and swollen ankles with concern. "Are you going to make it in this heat?"

"Do I have a choice?" Rebecca smiled bravely and held out a basket of orange and pink zinnias to Alison. "Come here, Cinderella. Take your basket. You, me, and Frankie are going to wait this out in the nursery."

"Anything I can do for you?" Bev asked their retreating backs.

"Make sure Robbie doesn't make paper airplanes out of the bulletins?" Rebecca tossed ruefully over her shoulder.

Robbie Jones, Rebecca's second-eldest and most freckled son, was already standing at his post next to the door to the nave. His bright red hair blazed like a fiery torch against the mahogany wood. He was quite proud to be serving as the bulletin boy for the wedding, although what he really wanted was to be an usher and escort guests to their pews. He sighed. Davie always got to do all of the fun stuff.

"Young man," Bev instructed, nodding with the authority of a general, "there's a box of bulletins sitting on Mrs. Scheinberg's chair in the office. It's too heavy for me to carry. Can you bring it here for me?"

Robbie grinned to be given such a manly task. "Yes, ma'am."

"And you, David." Bev made certain to pull out the ornery boy's given name for the occasion. "My husband is working on the air-conditioning units outside the fellowship hall. I believe he could use a drink of cold water."

Davie frowned, less than thrilled with his assignment. Yet, even at eleven years old, he knew better than to cross a woman at a wedding. He slumped his shoulders and trudged off toward the kitchen to fetch a glass. Bev smiled in secret triumph. That ought to give those younger boys a leg up.

Guests were arriving in full throttle now. Robbie, having successfully retrieved the heavy box of bulletins, took up his post again by the door, and a rather flushed Davie made it back in time to begin escorting guests to their appropriate pews. The opening strains of J. S. Bach's "Wachet auf" floated over the balcony railing and drifted across the sanctuary, the gentle bass *ostinato* in the organ pedals pulsing in anticipation of a joy yet to come. Bev smiled. It wouldn't be long now. If only it weren't so hot!

She felt a light touch at her elbow. Irv stood just behind the nave door, out of sight, his eyes tired and his red face streaked with sweat.

"Oh, no," Bev moaned. "You couldn't get it fixed?"

He shook his head.

"And Alvin doesn't answer his phone on Saturdays, does he?" That ridiculous man! What good was having a mechanic in town if he never worked on weekends? Bev began to pace back and forth. "We should've called Hank Schmidt from the very beginning, that's what! And now there isn't time to call in a repairman from Hamburg. What about that new guy at Dusselbach's Elevator? Surely he knows something about air conditioners. Oh, but he doesn't live in town, does he? I don't suppose Don or Harold know anything about this kind of thing?"

Irv shook his head resolutely.

"What're we going to do, Irv? Anyone on blood pressure medicine'll keel right over in this sauna as soon as they stand up to see the bride. And someone'll need to sit next to Althea. Why, she's been an absolute mess on her new meds. You know, I don't think that fancy doctor in Champaign got her cocktail quite right. What's the point in seeing a specialist if he doesn't do anything special? And just watch. Yvonne'll sue the church for everything it's got, just for ruining her permanent. Honestly, Irv, I don't think I can handle that woman today, not in this heat. Oh, and you should've seen Rebecca earlier! Her cheeks were so flushed, even with her hair pulled back in that pretty knot. What if she goes into labor right in the middle of—"

"Now," Irv spoke for the first time, his deep voice an immediate tranquilizer to his wife's agitations, "I've called the Kulls and the Johnsons. They're bringing over as many fans as they can get their hands on. In the meantime, I need to change."

"Of course, of course," Bev nodded, fighting for control. "I've got a clean shirt and change of pants for you hanging on the coatrack in the front office. Don't bother with the tie. It's simply too hot for such things." She stopped long enough to deliver a quick kiss on her husband's salty lips. He was such a hard worker, and he hadn't complained one bit this whole time. No doubt about it, Irvin Davis was her knight in shining armor and always would be.

The women of the church were making their exodus from the kitchen to the nave. Candice looked a little red-faced and worse for the wear, but Mrs. Scheinberg appeared remarkably fresh in her muumuu. Bev made a mental note to go shopping on Monday for some clothes that breathed. The Kulls arrived just then, and Don and Lois got busy setting up fans along the back wall and up each side aisle of the nave. No one would be able to hear Alice and Evan exchange vows over that din, but at least everyone would be able to breathe.

"Here, Mrs. Shinebug."

Bev looked over just in time to see Robbie hand Mrs. Scheinberg a bulletin folded into a peculiar shape. *What did he—?*

"Robbie Jones! Set those bulletins down at once." Bev felt an irritating drop of sweat trickle between her shoulder blades.

She maniacally reached behind her back to scratch at it. "You're not to be folding your grandmother's wedding programs into airplanes, do you hear me?"

"Huh?"

"I said, those bulletins are for reading, not for flying, young man. Your mom strictly forbade any paper airplanes—"

"These aren't planes, Mrs. Beverly. See?" Robbie held up a folded bulletin for inspection. It had been pressed back and forth to resemble an accordion. "They're fans. I thought they'd help cool ever'body off."

Mrs. Scheinberg let out a slow, rumbly chuckle. "Why, you clever boy!"

Bev sighed. At least it wasn't a plane. Rebecca couldn't fault her for that. All things considered, really, it wasn't such a bad idea. "I'll take two, please," she said.

Irv appeared, looking fresh in a blue button-down shirt and pressed dress pants, and followed a respectful few steps behind as Davie proudly delivered Bev to the fifth pew from the front on the pulpit side, right next to Althea. There was at least one lady in the church who wasn't going down during the service, not on Bev's watch, anyway. She patted Althea's arm and looked over her shoulder, making note of the most vulnerable attendees currently sitting in the pews—Ed Schwirmer with his cane, Curly Storm with his John Deere–green walker, Hilda Latch in her support hose—and planned exit routes, should any of them go down.

Blaine craftily modulated down a minor third on the organ for the processional hymn, and Emily Duke's sweet soprano voice could be heard resonating from the balcony.

"Wake, awake, for night is flying,"
The watchmen on the heights are crying;
"Awake, Jerusalem, arise!"

Bev teared up—or was that sweat in her eye?—as Pastor Fletcher led Evan and his best man, Jeremy Jones, from the sacristy to their places at the head of the aisle. Evan's face, crowned with a thick, meticulously combed mane of white hair that would make even the likes of Blaine Maler jealous, glowed from something other than the heat.

Midnight hears the welcome voices
And at the thrilling cry rejoices:
"Oh, where are ye, ye virgins wise?

Rebecca Jones came up the aisle. A few wisps of her blonde hair had loosened from the knot at the base of her neck, and they billowed whimsically in the circular breeze created by the choir of singing fans. Bev thought Rebecca looked prettier than ever with her rosy cheeks glowing and her zinnia bouquet resting on her baby belly. Little Alison followed closely behind her mother, skipping and swinging her basket of flowers, and a mortified Frankie brought up the rear.

The Bridegroom comes, awake!
Your lamps with gladness take! Alleluia!
With bridal care
Yourselves prepare
To meet the Bridegroom, who is near." (LSB 516:1)

Bev held her breath as Althea, Curly, and all of the other potentially heatstroking guests in the nave stood as one body to turn and face the bride. Although she couldn't really see Alice for Irv's tall frame, Bev followed her friend's progression up the aisle by monitoring the pitch of everyone's posture, catching only a fleeting glimpse of her profile as she came alongside their pew. Bev sniffed. Yes, those were definitely tears. She reached toward the floor to grab a tissue out of her purse, then thought better of it. What was the point? She'd already sweated off all of her makeup. What was a little more salt water on her cheeks? She straightened back up and sighed joyfully. This was a happy day, heat and all. Her dear friend was getting married, Irv was standing at her side, and all of her Life Alert attendees had made it safely back down to their seats with no major incident.

Well, except for one.

The bride was lying in an orange pile at the groom's feet.

Chapter Four: Abide with Me

"Someone get me a wet rag and a bowl of ice from the freezer! Quickly, now!"

Bev was kneeling on the floor beside Alice before anyone else even realized what had happened.

"Evan, help me roll her onto her back. Slowly, now—that's right. Sit at her feet and elevate them. Try resting them in your lap." Bev was relieved to see that Alice had crumpled to her right and landed on her side rather than falling face-first on the hard floor. None of her bones appeared to be broken, but who really knew? It didn't take much to break a hip at Alice's age. She patted her friend's stone-white cheek. "Alice, honey, can you hear me? Rebecca, help me loosen her jacket. And someone call 911!"

"Done." Jeremy put his phone back into his coat pocket and knelt to the floor. "Pastor's getting the ice."

Bev leaned down and hovered her ear directly above Alice's nose and mouth. "She's breathing."

Rebecca's own breath started coming a little too fast.

"Jeremy, get your wife over to a pew, please, and stay with her." Bev took over loosening Alice's jacket.

"Grammy?" Frankie whimpered, standing over his grandmother, frozen with fear. He looked like one of those precious garden statues with his bow tie and shiny eyes, but his face was stricken with horror. Bev quickly grabbed one of Robbie's genius fan-bulletins from a nearby congregant. "Here, Frankie. Fan your grandmother's face for me, please. She's all right."

Pastor Fletcher came running up the aisle with a plastic bucket of ice and a wet rag as well as a bottle of water from the refrigerator.

"Good thinking." Bev took the wet rag, doused it with more cool water, and laid it across Alice's forehead. Next, she tucked a couple of ice cubes into each of her friend's armpits. Alice stirred a bit. "That's right, honey. Come back to us."

Alice's eyes fluttered open just as the sound of sirens could be heard over the din of the fans. "W-what happened?" she whispered, attempting to sit up, but her head immediately fell backward.

"No, no," Bev warned, gently pushing her friend back to the floor. "Lie back, now. You just fainted, that's all. It's this stupid heat."

"Where's Evan?"

"I'm here." Evan scooted on his knees toward Alice's head and took her left hand in both of his own. "Trying to get out of marrying me, are you?"

Alice tried to smile, but she winced at some unseen pain.

"Your head probably hurts," Bev soothed. "Just relax. Help is here."

Two EMTs came running up the aisle with a stretcher, and Bev stood and backed out of their way. She wanted to do more for her friend, but the professionals were there now to take care of her. It didn't take them long to assess the situation and take Alice out on the stretcher. Evan went with his betrothed in the ambulance, and Rebecca and Jeremy followed in their SUV. Bev insisted the kids stay behind with her and Irv.

"Attention! Everyone!" Mrs. Scheinberg hollered from amidst the melee, waving her hands in the air. She had stepped out into the middle aisle from her usual pew on the lectern side. Bev couldn't help but think that she looked a bit like a traffic director in that yellow muumuu. "I'm sure we're all concerned about Alice, but—oh, good grief! Don! Can we *please* turn off some of those fans? A lady can't get a word in edgewise."

Don and a few helpful men jumped up and turned off the fans standing guard in the side aisles of the nave.

"That's better," Mrs. Scheinberg muttered, clearing her throat and trying again. "Now. What just happened was unfortunate, but I'm sure Alice is in good hands with Rodney and Lewis. If it's anything like when Althea fainted last month at the county fair, then it'll be hours before she's even released from the hospital. Am I right, Althea?"

Althea nodded from her seat in the pews.

"Right. I think we can all agree that the wedding's most likely not going to happen today, so there's nothing more for us to do other than pray and wait for someone to call us from the hospital." Mrs. Scheinberg lumbered to the front of the church, grabbed the open water bottle sitting on the floor, and took a generous swig before continuing. "The way I see it, we might as well do our praying and waiting while eating Janet's fried chicken and biscuits. Food like that can't wait too long, or it'll all go to waste. Alice wouldn't want that. So Pastor, if you'd be so good as to lead us all in prayer, we can scoot on into the fellowship hall. Unless, is there any kind of sacred tradition we're breaking by eating the wedding meal before the actual ceremony? You know, like the bride seeing the groom before the wedding and all? Does anyone even keep track of those kinds of silly things anymore? Candice?"

Candice, who was still sitting straight-backed in her pew, nostrils flared from the snub of her cakes getting no mention in Mrs. Scheinberg's speech, shook her head authoritatively.

"Right, then. That settles it. Pastor, how about that prayer?"

It was the first time anyone had really looked at Pastor Fletcher all day, what with the excitement of the bride and groom and all. The poor man. His face was red as a plum, and his black, curly hair was soaked with sweat. His clerical shirt, pants, cassock, and surplice apparently didn't breathe as easily as Mrs. Scheinberg's muumuu.

"Oh, for heaven's sake, man, take a swig of this." Mrs. Scheinberg held out the community water bottle, and Pastor didn't refuse it. When he had downed what was left, he held out his hands in an invitation for everyone to bow their heads.

"Let us pray. Lord Jesus, You are the great Physician. Please, heal Your servant Alice and bring her back to full health according to Your will. Guide the hands of the physicians and medical assistants as they care for her needs, and thank You for caring for our needs fully on the cross, that we might hope and trust in You, even in the face of illness and hardship. Thank You for the hands that prepared today's meal, and we pray that You would 'Come, Lord Jesus . . .'" The congregation joined in, "'be our guest, and let these gifts to us be blessed; and may there be a goodly share on every table everywhere. Amen.'"

Despite the awkwardness of the bride and groom being in absentia for their own wedding meal, their guests did their best to stay positive while they ate.

"You suppose she's seein' the same doctor as me?" Althea asked, her mouth around a biscuit. "I've been fallin' ever since I met him."

"Nah," Curly said, waving a chicken leg in the air. "This ain't arthritis. It's a problem with her heart. I'm sure of it."

"It's prob'ly an arrhythmia," Hilda surmised. "That's what finally got my sister."

Bev's face blanched as she cleared some plates off a nearby table. She couldn't help but overhear the morbid conversation. "Can I get you more to drink, Hilda? Curly?"

"No, thank you, honey," Hilda smiled. "But I sure would like a piece o' that pretty cake."

"That's it!" Curly spat, back on the subject of Alice. "She's got low blood sugar, I jus' know it. Anyone can see she's too skinny."

Bev escaped to the cake table, but the conversation there wasn't much better.

"What if it's cancer?" Candice ruminated aloud as she sliced her mended cakes into triangular pieces.

"It's not cancer," Bev insisted. Why were none of these people putting the best construction on the situation?

"You don't suppose she's pregnant?" Nettie asked with a confounding degree of sincerity.

"Good grief, Nettie!" Bev cried. "No!"

The phone in the kitchen began to ring just then, and, to everyone's horror, Nettie got to it first.

"Hello? . . . Uh-huh? . . . Yes, of course, Jeremy." The entire room went silent as a morgue. Only the sound of the coffee percolating at the drink station could be heard, for nothing—not snow, not rain, not sauna-like heat—could keep these Lutherans from sipping a cup of coffee in the fellowship hall.

"Of course, I can take a message," Nettie continued. "Uh-huh . . . Yes . . . Yes . . . Oh, no!"

Everyone held their breath.

"Oh, dear . . . Yes . . . Yes, I will . . . Of course we'll keep praying. You just hold tight and tell that pretty wife of yours to keep that baby baking in the oven as long as possible, you hear?"

Bev visibly cringed.

"Okay now . . . Yes . . . You too . . . Bye-bye now." Nettie hung up the phone and walked back out into the fellowship hall to resume her station as a server at the cake table. The whole room watched her with bated breath.

"Well?" Candice prompted.

"Oh! Yes. Well," Nettie said, "the good news is that she's still alive!"

Bev hung her head in silent despair. This was not going to go well, she just knew it.

"And?" Mrs. Scheinberg asked.

"And she is *not* pregnant like I thought."

Everyone stared at her, first in confusion, then in an uncomfortable silence.

"Rebecca *is* pregnant, though," Nettie continued, "and, I'm happy to say, she is *still* pregnant."

Bev considered the consequences of putting her hand over Nettie's mouth and sequestering her to one of the open Sunday School rooms. Surely it would be better for all involved if this conversation didn't go down in public. Arlene could be the inquisitor. She was good at that kind of thing. And Pastor Fletcher could be the interpreter. Yes, he was gentle and kind. He would do his best not to ruin anyone's reputation in this whole mess— but he wasn't there to help. He and Dr. Duke had driven off to the hospital shortly after the prayer to offer support to Evan and the Joneses.

"What was the diagnosis?" Curly hollered.

Nettie nodded her head like a statesman taking a question from the floor. "Jeremy said it was most likely a stroke."

A few of the ladies cried out in dismay. Bev covered her mouth with both of her hands. She thought she was going to be sick.

"Now, don't you worry!" Nettie held out her arms as if trying to shush a herd of bellowing cattle. "Alice is walking around and feeling good. She just needed some fluids, that's all."

"Wait a minute, Nettie," Mrs. Scheinberg's brow was furrowed. "Do you mean that Alice had a *heat*stroke?"

"Yes, that's what I told you," Nettie nodded. "A stroke. But she's going to be fine, Jeremy said. Just fine. No one needs to worry. Everyone can just relax and enjoy their food. Who else wants a piece of cake?"

〃〃〃〃〃〃〃〃〃〃〃〃〃〃〃〃〃〃〃〃〃〃〃〃〃〃〃〃〃〃〃〃〃〃〃

The meal, despite the day's various and sundry complications, was a success. Even Candice's wilted cakes, if not visually perfect, tasted divine.

"I've got to hand it to you, Candice," Mrs. Scheinberg admitted, her chipmunk cheeks bulging with cake and cream. "Even a little melting and sliding couldn't mess up this perfection. Your baking is flawless."

Candice smiled with pleasure. Compliments from Arlene were a rare species, indeed.

All the ladies were sitting at a table with four electric fans on high pointed straight at it. They were the only ones left in the fellowship hall, and they were enjoying a leisurely bite of dessert before tackling the dishes soaking in the hot kitchen.

"It's just too bad the bride and groom didn't get to enjoy any of it," Bev sighed.

Candice practically beamed. "I saved one whole cake in the refrigerator for them. I had to cut the first ten cakes into eleven slices each to be able to do it, but Alice and Evan'll be eating wedding cake on their honeymoon, after all."

Mrs. Scheinberg smiled. Even a cloud such as Candice had a silver lining.

"If there *is* a honeymoon," Janet said.

"Oh, there will be." Mrs. Scheinberg scraped the last bit of frosting off her plate and forked it into her mouth. "Pastor texted me a couple of minutes ago. Alice has been released from the hospital, and she and Evan are going to say their vows tomorrow morning during the church service."

"Oh, how lovely!" Bev said.

Candice immediately stood, unpinned her corsage, sprinkled it with some water from the faucet, wrapped it in a plastic sandwich bag, and put it in the fridge.

"What're you doing?" Janet asked.

"Alice'll need some flowers to wear tomorrow. She fell on her roses today. I'm guessing they won't be any good in the morning."

Mrs. Scheinberg kept smiling. There was even a pretty rainbow hiding behind that cloud.

"I've got some good news, too." Bev was all lit up like a Christmas tree. "Irv got ahold of Nettie's son, Hank. Well, he just got back in town from the tractor pull around four, and he talked to Arlene's brother, Larry, in Hamburg. Turns out, Larry doesn't have the right parts in his store to fix the air-conditioning units, but he *does* have five new units in stock and ready to install. He's bringing them over right now—as we speak—and he, Hank, and Irv're all going to install them tonight—"

"All five?" Candice protested from the kitchen. "I thought only three were broken."

"Now, Candice," Mrs. Scheinberg's bright sun threatened to vanish behind a dark, ominous cloud. "Don't even start."

Candice wisely kept her distance, and her silence, in the kitchen.

"Everything's board-approved already," Bev quickly continued. "Seems no one's messing around after Alice's fall. We should have cool air again tomorrow, just in time for the wedding. Well, the *real* wedding. Isn't that a blessing?"

"Yes, it is!" Janet stood up and stretched her back. "Okay, as much as I'd rather soak my feet in ice water than my hands in hot dishwater, it's that time, ladies."

Bev rose from her chair to follow Janet into the kitchen, but Mrs. Scheinberg held her back with a quick question. "Where'd you learn to do that?"

"Do what?"

"Take care of Alice that way."

"Oh." Bev wiped her sweaty brow with the back of her hand. She looked tired. "Remember that emergency responder course the hospital offered at last year's county fair? Irv and I both took it, you know, just in case something happens on the farm."

Mrs. Scheinberg's face blanched for a split second, but she quickly recovered. She had forty years of practice in her favor, after all. She flared her nostrils determinedly and pushed her chair away from the table as if nothing were wrong. "Well, you did great, kiddo."

She stayed long enough to help the ladies clean up the kitchen, but she didn't linger. As soon as she could politely get away, Mrs. Scheinberg climbed into her Grand Marquis, turned the AC on high, and drove straight home. Her stomach was upset, and it wasn't from the heat or from Candice's creamy confections. It was from the dizzying sound of Bev's voice reverberating in her head like a chastising echo: "in case something happens on the farm."

Bev hadn't meant anything by it, of course, but her innocent comment had ripped open an old wound that had never completely healed. The image of her husband's limp body lying next to their auger flashed before her eyes, and Mrs. Scheinberg pushed the gas pedal a little harder. If only she'd been smarter all of those years ago and taken an emergency responder course like Bev, then maybe Dean might still be—

"No!" Mrs. Scheinberg reprimanded herself aloud in the car. She gripped the steering wheel tighter and watched in her rearview mirror as the dusty road billowed into clouds behind her spinning wheels. If there was one thing she had learned in almost forty years of being a widow, it was that the "If Only" road led to no place good. Wishing and worrying served only to make an idol of the past, and her life was in the present. There was no point in looking back. She tore her eyes from the mirror and focused on the road ahead, doing the only thing she knew to do when the valley of the shadow of death rode her tail. It was the thing the sainted Reverend Gardner had told her to do the first time she'd had to drive home all by herself the Sunday after Dean's funeral.

"Sing the devil away, Arlene."

So she did.

"Hold Thou Thy cross before my closing eyes," she belted. "Shine through the gloom, and point me to the skies. Heav'n's morning breaks, and earth's vain shadows flee—" Her voice broke on that last word, but she took a breath and sang out even louder and stronger, fixing her eyes on Jesus, her one true light in the darkness. "In life, in death, O Lord, abide with me" (*LSB* 878:6).

Chapter Five: A Few Bumps along the Way

|||||||||||||||||||||||||||||||||||||||||||||||||||||||||

Emily Duke sat cross-legged on the floor of Rebecca Jones's living room. She was leaning over her best friend's right foot like a surgeon over an operating table, meticulously painting Rebecca's toenails a cheerful shade of coral pink.

"You really don't have to do this," Rebecca objected a bit too unconvincingly. She was lounging in an overstuffed recliner with a glass of cold sweet tea resting on her protruding belly. "I can't even see my feet at this point."

"But everyone else can," Emily responded without moving a muscle. "It's August. Friends don't let friends wear sandals without pedicures."

"Not that my boat-feet can fit into any of my sandals," Rebecca sighed.

"They *are* pretty swollen."

Emily and Rebecca had long ago passed the point of beating around the bush in their friendship.

"They're not the only part of me that's swollen." Rebecca tossed a significant glance down toward her bosom. "What's a girl to do with these things?"

"You could use them as a chin rest."

"Emily Duke!"

Emily's mouth convulsed into a smile, but she carefully kept her face hidden from view. Rebecca required very little encouragement these days when it came to the matter of maternity rants. Even the tiniest thing could set her off. Emily didn't know if it was because of the hormones or the heat or the madness of the impending birth or what, but Rebecca's filter seemed to be shrinking as quickly as the baby was growing.

"I can't even see my plate on the table anymore. It takes my fork longer to reach my mouth than it took Ferdinand Magellan to circle the globe."

Emily held in her laugh for the sake of the four Jones children sitting quietly on a nearby couch. They appeared to be engrossed in an episode of *Star Wars*, but one could never really tell for sure.

"Why must everything on the front side of my body keep expanding?" Rebecca moaned, rubbing her belly with her free hand. "Everyone's going to think these girls are ambassadors for AT&T. They keep trying to reach out and touch someone."

Emily snorted into her arm, hovering her brush over her free hand so as not to drip any polish on the white carpet.

"What's so funny?" Robbie asked, his face still glued to the television.

"Oh, nothing," Rebecca sang on descending notes, her voice matching Eeyore's, pitch for pitch. "Only that your mother is going to tip over one of these days."

"Huh?" Davie asked.

"Nothing, son. Just ignore me. Wait, not yet. First bring me the box fan from my bedroom, then you can ignore me. Please, and thank you!"

Davie groaned but obeyed his mother. He was under strict orders from his father to do so.

Little Alison grew bored with the lightsaber duel on-screen and slipped off the couch to wander over to the ladies' side of the room. "Paint my feet?"

"Yes, when I'm done with your mommy's," Emily said.

"'Kay. I eggsercise." Alison flopped down onto her back next to Emily and began lifting her legs in the air like she'd seen the pretty lady do on her mother's workout DVD. "See? I eggsercise. Ow!"

"What's wrong?"

Alison sat up and pouted, her hands on her stomach. "I hurt baby in my tummy!"

Rebecca gave Emily a meaningful look. "Someone's older brothers helpfully explained that only girls have babies, so she's convinced she's pregnant."

Emily smiled.

"Her brothers also told her—"

"When baby come out," Alison interrupted, her blue eyes large with wonder, "I feed it with my bumps."

"And there it is." Rebecca smiled wryly at her eldest son, who had just arrived with the box fan. "We can thank Davie for that one."

"They're called chicken breasts, Aly," Robbie hollered from the couch, his eyes still fixed on a galaxy far, far away.

"Thank you, Robert. Let's leave Alison's anatomy lesson to her actual parents, shall we?" Rebecca lowered her voice. "Honestly, I'm surprised the boys don't know more about the whole thing considering the way our schools are devolving these days."

Emily sensed another rant coming on. She bowed her head and picked up her pace with the nail polish.

"Unisex bathrooms, equality in marriage, sexual identity . . . even for our kindergartners! Education can't just be about math and reading anymore, can it? I mean, heaven forbid we tell our children there is no Santa Claus, but to *not* tell them where babies come from the moment they form words into sentences? We must be Amish!"

"Where *do* babies come from?" Robbie asked, turning away from the television for the first time.

Rebecca sighed.

"Mrs. Green says they come from a uterus," Davie helped.

"Uterus!" Alison echoed.

Rebecca gave Emily a "See what I mean?" look before calmly, though a bit tightly, explaining to her children, "When a husband and wife are married, God can bless them with children." She then turned back to Emily with mercurial eyes and lowered her voice. "The government has butted in and begun parenting our children in our place, that's what! We can thank President Obama for that."

Unfortunately, Rebecca had not lowered her voice enough.

"She's cool," Robbie said.

"Who?" Davie asked.

"Obama."

"President Obama's a *boy*, Einstein!" Davie scorned.

"No she's not. And you're the Weinstein!" Robbie paused as if not too sure he'd gotten that last part quite right, but he continued anyway. "She's a girl. Go ahead and look. Her hair's all weird and her face is kinda creepy with that white stuff smeared all over it, but she's wearing a dress!"

Davie's confusion melted into brotherly disdain as he followed Robbie's nine-year-old logic to its conclusion. He rolled his eyes and pointed at the costumed character on the screen. "That's Queen *Amidala*, you moron!"

"Enough!" Rebecca called from her cushioned throne. "We don't use those words in our home, boys. Next time I hear you calling each other something other than the names I gave you in the hospital, you're going to lose television for a week. And don't you know who the president is, Robbie?"

Alison clapped her hands and jumped up and down, apparently forgetting about the baby in her tummy. "Pastor Fletcher! Pastor Fletcher president!"

"No, Aly," Frankie corrected, speaking up for the first time that morning from his corner in the couch. He usually stayed out of all arguments begun by his older brothers, but by conviction, he broke his silence on matters of theological import. "God is president."

"I appreciate your optimism, Frankie," Rebecca said, "but I'm talking about the president of our country. Robbie?"

Robbie frowned in concentration. "Is it me?"

Emily snorted into her arm again.

"You're no help, Emily Duke." Rebecca set her empty glass down on a nearby end table. "Okay. I've got to move. My legs are going numb, and I haven't felt my feet in at least five minutes. How about we all get a snack in the kitchen? Anyone want some ice cream? or Oreos? or both? Yes, both, I think. Who cares if it's ten o'clock in the morning? Who's with me?"

The boys cheered and jumped off the couch, racing into the kitchen. Alison galloped merrily along behind them. Emily and Rebecca followed a bit more slowly.

"Have you decided on a name yet?" Emily asked, helping her friend to her feet.

Rebecca winced as the blood rushed back to her limbs. "Well, Davie thinks we should name the baby Taylor if it's a girl, and Swift if it's a boy."

"How about the others?"

"Alison is smitten with the name Alison, of course. And Dora. And Pastor Fletcher."

Emily laughed.

"Frankie thinks Evan would be a nice name. Isn't that sweet? I think he's taken with the idea of having a grandpa."

"Does Evan know?"

Rebecca nodded. "Evan was having dinner with us the night Frankie announced his idea. It's the first time I've ever seen that man come close to crying. He's been reading Narnia books to Frankie ever since. I have a stinking suspicion Frankie's going to want to spend every weekend in the country with him and my mom."

"What about Robbie?"

"You should ask him."

Emily helped the kids scoop ice cream into bowls and set the open package of Oreos on the table directly in front of Rebecca. "Robbie, what do you want to name the baby?"

"Ben Blaine," he said around his spoon.

"Ben Blaine? How come?"

"'Cause they're the coolest names in the world."

Emily thought she understood Robbie's fascination with the name Blaine—her choir accompanist was also Robbie's piano teacher—but she didn't quite get his choice for the first name. "Why's the name Ben so cool?"

Robbie gave her a look like she was crazy. "Don't you know Ben Schmidt? I thought he mows your lawn and stuff. He's the leader of the 4-H Corn Huskers, and Mom says I can join this year. He's so awesome! You shoulda seen him at the fair. He had sheeps an' chickens an' rabbits an' everything. And he can fix motors and tires and has a blue roll of duct tape. He let me have a piece of it one Sunday at church for my catechism. It was ripped. He's prob'ly a ninja." Robbie sighed happily.

"What if the baby's a girl? What would you name her then?"

The freckles on Robbie's face disappeared behind the curtain of his blushing cheeks.

"I like Emily."

It was not the first time Rebecca had ever seen Emily come close to crying.

CHAPTER SIX: PIECES AND JOY

The evening sky had that fuzzy look that comes when the humidity is high and the sun is low. A breeze tried pushing its way through the thick, soupy air, but a schooner in a bog would have had an easier launch. The entire town of Bradbury steeped in a musky cloud of late summer's cologne—two parts field corn and one part dandelion—and a lone cardinal perching in a sweet gum tree sang "Dido's Lament" to the waning light. Pastor Michael Fletcher, a theologian by trade and a poet at heart, thought the scene was just one lightning bug short of looking like a Norman Rockwell painting of small-town America at nightfall.

Pastor leaned forward in his chair on the front porch of 919 Mulberry Avenue and squinted at the jigsaw puzzle piece cupped in his hand. A bead of sweat slid down his face and dropped onto the card table below. He tried wiping it away before Emily could see it.

"You're hot, aren't you?"

"No, no," he assured, looking up and smiling. The sudden motion caused another bead of sweat to drip tellingly down his temple. "I'm fine. This is nice."

"Liar," Emily teased. "It's too hot to sit out here, I know, but I just can't help myself."

"You enjoy the sensation of melting?"

"No," she sighed happily, leaning back in her chair and openly admiring the dusky view from the stoop of her cozy, red-brick bungalow. Well, it wasn't really *her* bungalow. She was renting it from Alice. "I just can't get enough of the sounds. Summer evenings are a symphony in a small town. I mean, listen to that cardinal. He's trilling his final cadenza before sunset, and then the crickets'll put their bows to their strings. But my favorite is when the cicadas start singing." The corners of her eyes crinkled merrily at the thought. "I always picture them as little drunk Russians, clinking glasses over bowls of borscht. It's glorious music! I could never hear this stuff when I lived in the city."

Pastor leaned back in his own chair, thinking that he would gladly sit in a burning furnace if it meant he could hear Emily talk like this. Not that she was normally secretive or uncommunicative in any way. She simply didn't make a habit of volunteering her thoughts and feelings to others at every turn. In the rare moments that she opened up, Pastor stopped whatever he was doing and listened. Nothing sounded so sweet to him as the trickling of little streams from those deep waters pooling beneath Emily's blonde curls, and it was no secret to the town of Bradbury, nor to the congregation of Zion Lutheran Church, that Pastor Michael Fletcher was enamored with Emily Duke's sweetness.

And he was not the only one.

"There's an angel on line one," Mrs. Scheinberg had hollered from her front-office chair early last summer when Emily had first called the church to inquire about their open choir director position. Pastor had thought Mrs. Scheinberg's comment to be odd at the time—his secretary rarely used words that were positive, let alone ones that evoked images of Precious Moments—but he had found himself humming the angelic

"Gloria!" from a certain beloved Christmas carol when he hung up the phone a few minutes later. An angel, indeed! And one that had a doctorate in musicology, to boot.

It wasn't that Emily was all sugar and no salt. She could be stubborn and, when pushed, display a fiery bit of temper. But she was also kind. And forgiving. And compassionate and smart and lovely and musical and . . . Pastor could go on and on, but the quality he most admired in Emily was her quiet trust in God's tender care, even amidst suffering. In fact, hardship seemed only to increase the perfume of her gentle flower.

"Need more lemonade?"

Pastor snapped to attention. "No, I'm good. But maybe we could flip on the light? I'm starting to have trouble telling the difference between the sky and the water in this puzzle." He squinted at the perplexing piece in his hand and tried fitting it to a short line of blue pieces already interlocked on the table. No luck.

Emily popped up to turn on the outside light and, before sitting back down, snapped three loose pieces of a tree trunk in place. She tapped her fingers victoriously on the vinyl tabletop. Pastor shook his head in defeat.

"I'm so glad we found this table in the basement." Emily sat down and picked up another puzzle piece. "I had forgotten all about it. Peter and I got it from his Aunt Jo, I think. She was quite a character. I only ever saw her once—at our wedding—but I remember that she wore these giant feather earrings with large, gold hoops. They looked like parrots."

"Did she have a peg leg?"

"No," Emily laughed but then suddenly stopped short. Her brown eyes grew serious. "Is it weird for you?"

"What?"

"You know, when I talk about Peter and stuff?"

Pastor shrugged. "Why wouldn't you talk about him? You were married to him. He's a part of your story. Do *you* think it's weird to talk about him?"

"Sometimes." Emily stared at the puzzle on the table. "I guess I never thought I'd meet another Peter."

"I'm not another Peter."

Emily blushed at her obvious mistake. "I'm sorry. I know. I didn't say that right. I mean that I never thought I'd meet another . . . another someone . . . who would be someone to me that I could . . ."

Pastor kept his head down so as not to bring unwanted attention to Emily's fumbling, but he did sneak one quick glance at her pretty face. Her cheeks were red as roses. He felt a tiny thrill.

"Look," he said, "you and Peter were married for almost two years before he died. You loved him. And while I would be lying if I said there isn't a part of me that is jealous at the thought of someone having memories with you that I can't share, I do think your marriage to Peter should be remembered and honored. Even celebrated."

Emily smiled behind her puzzle piece.

Pastor decided that the moment had come. There was something he needed to know—a certain question he'd been waiting for weeks to ask—but subtlety was the rule. Questions about dead husbands tasted brackish on his tongue, and he feared they might sound even harsher to his companion's ear. "Tell me something."

"What?"

He took his time dislodging a puzzle piece that had stuck to the underside of his sweaty forearm. "I've never seen you wear your wedding ring."

"Oh. I guess not."

"When did you stop wearing it?"

"I'm not exactly sure. Years ago. It was sometime when I lived in Kansas City, studying for my master's. This'll sound terribly unromantic, but I had gotten a rash under the ring, some kind of eczema or something. The doctor told me to take it off for a while to allow the rash to heal. I never put it back on, I guess."

Pastor nodded. That was not his money question, but he was intentionally taking a circuitous route to the front door before knocking. "Do you still have it?"

Emily looked up. "What? The ring?"

Pastor nodded.

"Yes."

It was now or never. "Can I see it?"

Emily studied him for a quiet moment before answering, "Okay. I'll be back in a minute."

When she came back outside with a red velvet box in hand, Pastor tried to look nonchalant, but his stomach was churning. She opened the box and handed him what appeared to be an engagement-and-wedding-ring set that had been soldered together. "That's pretty," he said.

It was too pretty, actually. The giant solitaire diamond was encircled by petals of tinier, sparkly diamonds. It reminded Pastor of one of those bedazzled coloring sheets little Alison Jones had made for him at Vacation Bible School. It was definitely bigger and shinier and glitzier than anything a parish pastor could ever afford. He felt his heart sink to his ankles. "You know, I'm feeling really hot all of a sudden. May I have another glass of ice water?"

"Of course. I'll be right back."

As soon as the screen door shut behind Emily, Pastor fumbled in his pocket for the piece of string he had planted earlier. His hands were shaking, he felt so nervous. "Steady, MacGyver," he mumbled. Rebecca had carefully instructed him earlier that day how to size a ring using string. If he just ran the string along the inside of the ring and cut it at the meeting point, then it could serve as a sort of makeshift measuring tape later. He used his nail clippers to snip the string before sneakily shoving it all back into his pocket. Oh, the irony of sizing the ring finger of the woman he wanted to marry by using a wedding ring her first husband had given her. It would be a story to tell their children someday, at least.

"Here you go," Emily said, pushing the door open with her hip and setting two ice waters down on the table. The sun had set minutes before, and the twilight was deepening from periwinkle to purple. Her beloved cicadas were starting to sing.

"Thank you." Pastor took a big swig of the water and almost immediately choked. Idiot! He had shoved Peter's ring into his pocket along with everything else. He eyed the velvet box still sitting on the table. At least it was closed. Emily would assume he had put the ring back inside. If he could just distract her somehow and get that ring back into the box without her noticing, then maybe not all was lost. "I'm kind of hungry. Are you?"

"No."

"Should we move the puzzle inside?"

"Not yet," she said, reaching for the velvet box.

Pastor grabbed it first. "I wanted to ask you how Peter gave this to you." He opened the box and stared at it as if he were studying the missing ring inside.

"You . . . want to hear how he proposed?"

He really didn't. "Yes."

Emily leaned back in her chair and studied him. Her brown eyes were placid pools reflecting those hidden, deep waters. "Why?"

"I want to know you." At least that was true. "Unless it hurts you to tell me."

"No, it's just . . ."

"Weird?"

"I guess."

Pastor's right hand was aching to reach into his pocket. If only Emily would look away for a moment or get up and sit on the front step like she often did when she told him stories. "You don't have to tell me."

Those two pools began to shimmer over a growing smile, and to Pastor's relief, Emily stood and moved toward the front step. She sat down, hugged her knees to her chest, and looked out over the disappearing lawn.

"I stepped out of a practice room one night in college to find a red rose with a note tied to its stem. The note was an invitation to come to the studio where I'd had jazz lab my first semester—that was where I'd first met Peter. When I got to the classroom, there was another rose waiting for me with another invitation tied to it and so on and so on. There ended up being sixteen roses total, one for each month Peter and I had dated, and I kept finding them in places that meant something special to our courtship. I found the sixteenth rose in the university's performance hall. It was resting on top of a piano Peter was playing. He was playing 'The Shadow of Your Smile.' That was the first song we'd learned together in jazz lab. Then, he asked me to marry him."

On the one hand, Pastor was ecstatic to be relieved of Peter's expensive ring. He had successfully returned it to the velvet box without Emily noticing a thing.

On the other hand, he was completely devastated. How was he ever going to compete with a proposal like that?

CHAPTER SEVEN: CHICKEN CLOTHES

Not many nine-year-old boys bothered with making life goals let alone got around to composing a list of them, but Robbie Jones was not just any boy. He was a middle son with a mind to improve his position in life, and since God forbade him from advancing his station by any of the more obvious, ignoble methods, he had to be a bit more enterprising in his climb to the top.

Grow taller than Davie
Run faster than Davie
Stay up later than Davie
Fart louder than Davie
Beat Davie at wrestling and Mario
    Kart and Carcassonne
Sleep in the top bunk
Kiss Kendra Plueth on the mouth
Pray longer than Frankie

Thankfully, there were at least a few life goals he'd already met and checked off his list:

Watch Temple of Doom with Dad (NOT
    Davie) after bedtime on my birthday

Drink root beer in the bathtub
Plant a Christmas tree at Grandpa's grave
Play the piano
Belch the Pledge of Allegiance

But it was the last two goals on his list that consumed his boyish ambition as of late:

Be a ninja
Be Ben Schmidt's best friend

Even Robbie recognized that it would take years of special training with the CIA in Japan and China and probably even New Zealand before he could ever become a true ninja, so he concentrated most of his immediate energies on the goal of becoming Ben Schmidt's best friend. At first, he was afraid that Davie would steal his plan—his older brother always swiped the best things in life right out from under his nose—but Davie made it clear from the start that he wanted nothing to do with Ben Schmidt.

"I don't care how many lawns he mows a week," Davie had said on the way to swim lessons one morning. "He's a Cardinals fan."

That news had pierced Robbie's heart straight through with a dragon sword, for it was no small thing for a Jones to befriend a fan of The Team Which Shall Not Be Named. His parents had groomed him from birth to pledge undying allegiance to the six most important things in life: God, family, church, country, Moose Tracks ice cream, and the Chicago Cubs. To align himself with a Cardinals fan would be like changing his last name to Voldemort or Vader.

Thankfully, his mom's friend Emily Duke had saved him.

"What's wrong?" she'd asked him one afternoon last month while they were baking cookies for his mom's baby shower.

At first, he'd been afraid to tell her, but she was so nice and rosy, and she seemed like someone who could keep a secret. "My best friend's a Cardinals fan."

"Aha." Emily had required no further explanation.

"Whatami gonna do, Miss Emily? I can't betray my parents."

"That's a serious question, Robbie, one that deserves careful consideration. Can you keep a secret?"

Robbie had nodded.

"I'm a Cardinals fan too. And so is Pastor Fletcher and Mrs. Scheinberg *and* Carrots." That last one was Emily's pet rabbit.

Robbie grinned. In the end, he decided that if his parents' best friends bled Cardinal red, then it was okay if his did too. In fact, Robbie took the matter one step further, all in the name of Ben.

"What're you doing?" Davie asked the morning of Robbie's first Corn Huskers meeting.

"Gettin' dressed." Robbie pulled on a T-shirt and closed his dresser drawer.

"Is that a—?" Davie's eyes grew round with dismay.

Robbie turned and faced his brother, giving him the bird. The redbird, that is. He put his hands on his hips and let the cardinal on his shirt say it all. "I'm a Cardinals fan now."

The bond of blood has its limits, and a house divided against itself cannot stand. So it was no surprise when Davie scowled at his younger brother and spat the word "traitor" on the ground before leaving the room.

Robbie was too excited about 4-H and animals and farming and all of the cool things in Ben Schmidt's world he was about to see to be bothered by Davie. He climbed into his family's SUV and buckled himself in a full five minutes before they actually needed to leave, and his right knee bounced up and down as fast as a jackhammer when they finally got on the road.

"Are you sure you don't want me to stay with you this first time?" Rebecca eyed Robbie in the rearview mirror.

"No." The meeting was at Ben's house. He was not about to have his *mom* tag along. He stared uncommunicatively out the window as row after row of soybeans whizzed past.

"You have my phone number, right?"

Robbie's cheeks burned with mortification. Of course he had her number. She had written it directly onto his skin with a black marker. At first, she'd started to write it on the back of his hand, where everyone could see it, but Robbie finally convinced her to at least hide it beneath his shirtsleeve on the underside of his left arm. He subconsciously squeezed his arm to his side at the thought.

"What will you be doing today?"

"Having a meeting," was all Robbie volunteered.

"Will you be learning anything?"

"Yes."

"Like what?"

"Ben said we'd be learning how to put clothes on chickens." Actually, Ben hadn't said. It was Caroline Bradbury, the chapter's secretary, who had called him last night with the location and agenda for today's meeting.

Rebecca's brow furrowed in the mirror. "Chicken clothes? Is that someone's sewing project?"

"No, it's Ben's project. He's gonna teach us how to do it himself."

"Are you sure you don't want me to come with you?"

"No, Mom." Robbie was adamant. This was his chance to show Ben that he was practically grown up.

"Here we are!" Rebecca sang, turning down a quarter-mile-long gravel lane. It looked like a skinny bridge crossing a sea of rolling, green fields and ending at a grassy island dotted with several large buildings. A giant, gray machine shed sporting a "Schmidt Farms" sign winked at Robbie in the afternoon sunlight, and an old, red barn accompanied by a hodgepodge of brick and aluminum-sided outbuildings crowded in to say hello. Planted right in the middle of it all was a charming, two-story farmhouse. Ben's house. Robbie's heart jumped in his throat. Once he and Ben were best friends, he'd probably spend every Saturday at this place. He could barely contain his excitement.

"Now, remember," Rebecca said as she put the SUV in park and turned in her seat to look Robbie directly in the eye, "you are to call me from Mrs. Schmidt's phone as soon as the meeting is over. I will come right away to pick you up. And Robbie—" she called, but he had already hopped out the door, "please use your manners and be a good listener and . . ."

Robbie was knocking at the front door of the farmhouse. A woman with short, black, curly hair and a friendly smile opened the door. He turned around to give one discreet wave to his mother before disappearing inside the Schmidts' home.

Robbie followed Mrs. Schmidt through an enclosed front porch to a comfortable, sunny living room where seven other kids were already lounging on blue-and-white-checkered couches and some mismatched chairs. She proffered him one of the wooden chairs that seemed to have immigrated from the kitchen table for the occasion. Robbie sat and hugged his stomach, suddenly self-conscious to be in a room full of strangers. Well, they weren't exactly strangers. He knew Caroline Bradbury and the Plueth sisters from church—and he'd seen that Koelster girl and the Storm twins around school—but none of them were actually in his class. There was one girl sitting on the floor with a long, blonde braid who looked like she might be his age, but he'd never seen her before. The rest of them were at least a few years older than he was.

"Can I get you somethin' to drink?" a friendly voice asked from the kitchen doorway.

Robbie turned in his seat to look over his shoulder and almost fell out of his chair. There stood Ben Schmidt in the flesh, holding a tray of beverages.

"Y-yes," was all Robbie could manage. He swallowed and, miraculously recalling his mom's final instructions, added a hasty "Thank you."

"What wouldja like?"

Robbie looked at Ben's towering frame. His sandy hair was cropped close to his head in a crew cut, and a horizontal tan line crossed his forehead where his ball cap usually sat. He looked so big, standing in the doorway, and Robbie suddenly felt very small. He wracked his brain for a way to prove his quality. "I'll take some coffee."

One of the Storm boys snorted.

Ben glanced down at the tray he was holding. "Um, would lemonade be all right? Or Sprite, maybe? We don't have any coffee."

Robbie's cheeks caught flame. Surely everyone could see right through him. Why did he always say something stupid when it mattered most? He'd ruined everything, and now Ben would never want to be his friend. Robbie cowered against the back of his chair, tears of humiliation stinging his eyes. All he wanted to do was run into the kitchen and call his mom right then and there, but his inner ninja wouldn't let him. "Sprite," he whispered.

Robbie turned back around in his seat and stared at the wall across the room. Hobby shelves displaying John Deere model tractors lined the wall. He could hear the Storm twins snickering behind their junior-high hands, so he counted the tractors to himself as fast as he could. *One, two, three, four, five . . .*

"Here." Ben stood at his elbow, holding out a plastic cup filled with ice and Sprite. Robbie reached out to take it, and just as he did, Ben spoke loudly enough for everyone in the room to hear, *"I like coffee too."*

The Storm boys immediately ceased their whispering.

"Me too," Caroline chimed in. "My mom lets me get those frosty mocha drinks at The Corner Coffee Shop."

"I've never tasted it," the girl with the blonde braid said, "but my dad drinks it every morning before he goes to work. Most men do."

Robbie's eyes dried in a flash. He grinned at Ben, taking the cold beverage and mentally vowing to leave Ben his favorite pair of red nunchucks in his will.

The meeting was actually kind of interesting. Ben, as the club president, called the meeting to order, and Robbie stood with everyone else to recite a really cool pledge involving body parts and stuff. Then, Caroline called the roll. Instead of having everyone answer with the usual "here" or "present," she suggested that members say the name of their favorite animal. Robbie didn't hesitate when it was his turn: "Kung Fu Panda."

Amanda Plueth gave the treasurer's report next, followed by her sister Kendra's correspondence report—both of which Robbie could have done without—but then everyone took turns reporting on their experiences at the recent Illinois State Fair. Amanda showed the blue ribbons her corn and pickled beets had earned, Caroline modeled the "Best in Show" evening gown she had sewn, and Ben passed around a picture of Bo-Peep, his third-place-winning sheep, as well as another of Cinnabon, his second-place Holland Lop rabbit. Robbie gave his own impromptu report, telling the story of how he and Frankie had eaten sauerkraut for the first time at Ethnic Village and then proceeded to throw it up on the Midway. The Storm boys also gave a report from their time at the fair, but Robbie tried very hard not to remember any of it.

Next, it was time for something called project reports. Bethany Roe, the nice girl with the golden braid, stood and adjusted her blue-rimmed glasses. "I read seventeen chapter books this summer. Ten of them were required by my reading list, but I chose the other seven. The best one was definitely . . ."

Andy Storm rolled his eyes and silently mouthed the word "homeschooler" from his seat on the couch. Robbie didn't know what that meant, but he did know that Bethany was the prettiest girl he'd ever seen. And she was a good cook too. Robbie knew, because Caroline had announced after roll call that Bethany had made Rice Krispies Treats for everyone to eat after the meeting was over. Bethany also seemed smart, but Robbie tried not to hold that against her.

Before long, the moment Robbie had been waiting for finally arrived. Ben rose to give his project report.

"As y'all know," Ben said, "today I'll be demonstrating how to dress a chicken, but I'm gonna need some help. Anyone interested?"

This one was a no-brainer. Robbie's hand shot straight into the air.

"Thanks, Robbie. I'll be needin' someone to hold the chicken for me. My mom can do it if'n you'd rather not."

"I'll do it." Robbie grinned. He'd never held a chicken before, but how hard could it be? He'd helped Alison put lots of clothes on her baby dolls. Other than all of the feathers, a chicken wouldn't be much different.

"Well, we'll be doin' this west of the smokehouse," Ben said, gesturing with his arm toward the back door, "so if y'all'd follow me . . ."

Robbie practically skipped alongside Ben as everyone marched to the northwest corner of the property. He was so happy. Not only was he now in the same 4-H club as Ben, but he was about to be Ben's special helper. They'd be best friends before the day was out.

"Okay, now," Ben said when the whole club had lined up behind the smokehouse. He wiped his brow on his forearm. The afternoon sun was particularly hot here, as the buildings on this side of the property blocked the southeasterly breeze. "This here's where we dress our chickens. Normally, we do thirty-six a day in season—twelve in a batch—but today I'll jus' be showin' you one."

Robbie was still grinning, oblivious to anything other than the fact that he was standing beside Ben on a real-life farm with one of his life's goals in sight.

"After we remove its head—"

Wait . . . *what?* Robbie's own head snapped to attention.

". . . this's where we'll drop 'er." Ben pointed to four rubber tires that were neatly stacked on the ground, one on top of another, forming a makeshift barrel. "Our chickens run about four to five pounds, so they don't bruise like turkeys when they're thrashin' 'round, but we still like to keep 'em contained. Next," Ben turned toward a five-gallon bucket into which his mom was pouring hot water from a steaming kettle, "we'll dip 'er. The water scalds the skin and loosens the feathers for better pluckin'. There'll still be tiny hairs 'tween the feathers, so we jus' roll up a few sheets of newspaper, like so, and light it like a torch ta burn off the hairs."

Robbie started to feel a bit uneasy. Hot water? Fire torches? What was going on? Where were the chicken clothes?

"After that, we cut off the feet and start removin' the legs and the wings and the rest. But it's the innards you have ta watch. If you puncture the bile duct on the liver, it'll release the bird's digestive acid and spoil the meat."

Robbie was not computing. He raised his hand. "Uh, Ben? Where are the clothes?"

"Huh?"

"You said we'd be putting clothes on the chicken?"

Ben eyed Robbie thoughtfully, but Andy Storm laughed out loud. Everyone else simply stared ahead in confusion. Robbie began to feel that embarrassed, sick feeling in his stomach, and his cheeks caught fire again.

"There're no clothes, Robbie," Ben explained quietly. "'Dressin'" means *cuttin' up* a chicken."

Robbie's eyes grew wide with alarm. He looked around—the water and fire suddenly making sense—and he visibly cringed when his gaze finally rested on a shiny, double-headed ax wedged into a nearby railroad tie lying on the ground. "You mean, we're gonna . . . ?"

Both Storm boys were doubled over with laughter now.

Ben stepped closer to Robbie and whispered in a voice only the two of them could hear. "You don't have ta do it, Robbie. I mean it. My mom can hold the chicken."

Robbie looked over and saw, for the first time, the lone, very much alive chicken standing in a wooden crate on the ground next to the railroad tie. He felt his head floating away from his neck like a loose balloon. He fought hard to grab hold of its string and tie it back down to his rubbery spine. "What do I do?"

Ben smiled heartily and patted Robbie on the back. "Jus' hold 'er feet while I swing the ax."

Robbie's knees were shaking, but he followed Ben obediently over to the railroad tie and stood by his side.

"Okay," Ben said, lifting the spring door on the top of the wooden crate with his left hand and reaching into it with his right. In one swift motion, he grabbed the chicken by both legs, turned it upside down in the air, and let the crate door fall shut behind him. Robbie fought every nerve in his body to keep his hands from jumping up to cover his eyes. Surprisingly, the chicken didn't make much noise.

"Now," Ben said, addressing the other members of the club, "it's important to brace the chicken before you swing the ax. As you can see, my dad an' I already hammered two four-inch nails about halfway into this tie—oh, about an inch apart. We lay the chicken's neck between the nails—"

"The nails of *death*," Andy said, winking at Robbie.

Ben ignored Andy completely and continued narrating while he worked. "Robbie will now hold the chicken's feet." Ben motioned with his head for Robbie to lean down beside him. Robbie dropped to one knee and reached for the chicken's legs with his right hand, shivering at the rough feel of its skin.

"Pull a little tighter," Ben whispered to Robbie. "That's it."

"Now," Ben said louder, standing and loosening the ax from the tie, "we've been raisin' straight-run chicks this year, which're a mix of roosters and pullets. This one's a pullet. After I cut off 'er head, Robbie'll turn to his right and drop 'er in the tire bin. Ready?" That last question was for Robbie.

Robbie was definitely not ready, but he tried hard to swallow the fear that was threatening to choke him. It stuck stubbornly to the back of his tongue like a gob of gooey peanut butter. He swallowed a second time, determined. Surely things like this would be a part of his ninja training later in life. Maybe this would even count toward it in the end. Regardless, how could he back out now? All those other kids were staring at him. Besides, Ben would never want to be his best friend if he did. Robbie closed his eyes and nodded his head.

"Don't forget to pull on the feet," Ben quietly reminded. Then, standing tall, he swung his ax high and landed it cleanly through the hen's neck.

Robbie wasn't quite prepared for how quickly the hen would be released from the grip of the nails of death, and the momentum of his own pulling threw him back onto his seat. Unfortunately, the headless pullet went with him. Blood squirted out from the hen's topless neck and onto Ben's boots.

"Put 'er in the bin!" Ben cried.

Robbie, his own blood pumping through his arteries as quickly as the chicken's, swung the bird a little too fast for neatness's sake and splattered blood five feet across the railroad tie and directly onto Bethany Roe's blue shirt. She screamed. Robbie immediately threw the bird toward the bin, but his aim was a bit wide for the shot. The hen bounced off the rim of the top tire and landed directly on the ground on her own two feet.

Then, to Robbie's utter horror and shock, the bloody, headless chicken corpse hopped toward him. Twice.

"It's still alive!" he shrieked, falling back into Ben in his attempt to get out of the way. "It's alive! Run!"

Robbie didn't hesitate to take his own advice. He leapt over the railroad tie, pushed past the guffawing twins, and ran straight for the end of the Schmidts' lane, stopping only twice: once to wretch in a flower bed and, the second time, to use Mrs. Schmidt's kitchen phone to call his mom to pick him up.

CHAPTER EIGHT: SCORING A GOAL

||||||||||||||||||||||||||||||||||||||||||||||||||||||||

Robbie didn't say a single word the entire drive home, and as soon as his mom pulled on the parking brake in the garage, he unbuckled his seat belt, ran straight up to his room, and shut the door.

A few minutes later, there was a knock on his door.

"Robbie, can I come in?"

Robbie didn't answer. Instead, he turned on his side, away from the door, and pulled his covers over his head. He heard the soft swish of the door opening and closing, followed by the gentle pad of his mom's bare feet crossing the carpeted floor. He felt her sit down next to him on the edge of his lower bunk bed.

"Mrs. Schmidt just called me."

Robbie closed his eyes tightly against the world.

"She told me about the chicken. She wanted to make sure that you're okay."

Robbie held his breath.

"She also told me that Ben said you were the only one brave enough to help him."

Robbie opened his eyes.

"It all sounds terribly exciting," Rebecca sighed. "Won't you tell me about it? I've never seen anyone dress a chicken before."

Robbie turned over onto his back and peeked out from underneath his covers. His mom was smiling at him as if everything were fine.

"Where did you and Ben do this thing, anyway? Mrs. Schmidt's kitchen?"

Robbie shook his head. "Outside."

"I guess that makes sense. Was it," she wiggled her eyebrows, "messy?"

A small smile cracked Robbie's face. "Yeah. There was blood squirting everywhere."

"*Blood?*" his mom looked impressed. "Didn't that scare you?"

"Nah!" Robbie sat up and made more room for her on his bed. She scooted in closer, all ears. "I held on even when it started squirting."

"Just like a ninja," Rebecca mumbled, seemingly to herself.

Robbie beamed. He hadn't thought of it that way. "Some of the blood got on Ben and Bethany's clothes."

"That's to be expected in a battle, I think. It's just too bad you didn't get any on your own clothes."

"Oh, but I did!" Robbie held out the front of his shirt proudly.

"Well, would you look at that? There's even a bit on your shorts. You know, I don't think Davie's ever had chicken blood on his clothes before."

Robbie felt himself grow three inches taller.

"So what happened next?"

"I threw the chicken in this tire-thingy, and then she JUMPED at me!"

"What? Without a head?"

Robbie opened his mouth and nodded excitedly. "Yeah! She jumped at me without her head on! And there was still blood squirting out and everything!"

"Wow!" Rebecca exclaimed. "You're probably hungry after all of that. Guess what I'm making for supper?"

Come to think of it, Robbie *was* pretty hungry. "What?"

"Your favorite. Macaroni and cheese and," she gave Robbie a mischievous look, *"chicken* nuggets."

Robbie squealed and pulled the covers back over his head. His mom tickled him mercilessly through the covers until he was laughing hysterically. Then, she stood and stretched her back. "Speaking of food, I forgot to tell you. Mrs. Schmidt also said that someone—Bethany, I think?—wanted to make sure you got a Rice Krispies Treat, so she left one at the farm for you."

Robbie smiled under his covers at the thought of those pretty blue frames.

"She said that Ben's going to bring it by for you tomorrow when he comes into town to mow some lawns."

Robbie sighed happily; his fear and anxiety were things of the past. All he could think about now was telling Dad and Davie and Frankie and Aly all about his bloody adventure over supper. And somehow he needed to find a John Deere shirt to wear before his best friend stopped by tomorrow.

First, though, Robbie had one very important thing to do. He pulled out his list of life goals from under his pillow and put a large, satisfied check next to the words "Be Ben Schmidt's best friend." Then, as an afterthought, he hastily scratched out the words "Kiss Kendra Plueth" and added something much, much better to the bottom of his list:

Marry Bethany Roe

CHAPTER NINE: O MORNING STAR

The first Sunday in September dawned sunny and bright, but it was the balcony of Zion Lutheran Church, not the sky, which boasted the fairest and brightest star in Bradbury's firmament.

"Mrs. Ebner!" Emily Duke called out happily as she crested the top step of the north balcony stairwell.

There, seated in her usual chair in the alto section as if nothing out of the ordinary had happened in the last few weeks, was Alice. Emily's dimples deepened at the welcome sight.

"Emily, you dear girl, come over here and give me a hug!"

Emily set down her bag, climbed over two rows of folding chairs—the choir persisted in cramming twice as many chairs as could actually fit in the tiny space—and wrapped her arms affectionately around her friend. "You are practically glowing, Alice. How was Wisconsin? When did you and Evan get back? Have you seen Rebecca and the kids yet? Are you feeling rested? Boy, you gave us all a fright!"

Alice's muffled reply came from somewhere below Emily's left shoulder. "It's all so embarrassing."

Emily stepped back to give her delicate friend some more breathing room, and Alice sheepishly waved her hands before her face as if to wipe out an unpleasant memory. "It's all my fault, dear," she continued. "Really, it is. Who wears a jacket to a summer wedding?"

"I do," Evan spoke up from his roost on the console bench. Emily almost jumped at the sound. In her rush to hug Alice, she had completely missed him sitting there. Even now, he sat so still that he resembled a snowy owl perched on a high limb, observing the curious humans below. Evan, seemingly wise to her thoughts, tossed a subtle, almost imperceptible wink of welcome her way.

"Yes, you did wear a jacket," Alice conceded, "but you didn't faint in front of everyone."

"Well, I didn't have as far to walk as you."

Alice shook her head, not so easily consoled. "Don't even try it, Ebner. I'm on to your sugarcoating ways. The whole thing was a disaster, and you know it."

"It wasn't a disaster," Evan reassured, his tone hinting at the fact that they'd been through this more than a few times before. "Think of all the good that came of it. We had *two* weddings for the price of one, and you and I received a complimentary escort from the church door. What are limousines to sirens and flashing lights?"

Alice cracked a begrudging smile.

"And Alison got to wear her fancy dress two days in a row," Emily contributed. "That's every princess's dream come true."

"Yes," Evan hummed appreciatively, "and more important, Robbie learned that he can put ice cubes in people's armpits."

Alice laughed outright.

Evan smiled, victorious. His wife's star was aglow again. "And let's not forget that your early exit ensured that our dear, pregnant Rebecca got to sit down much faster than originally planned, and the board of trustees unanimously voted—probably for the first time in the history of the church, wouldn't you say?—to replace *all* of the air-conditioning units in a matter of seconds. See, Al? Your fainting was an act of mercy. Besides, now everyone in the church knows the truth."

"What truth?"

Evan shuffled his music nonchalantly on the stand. "That you fell pretty hard for me."

Alice groaned and swatted playfully at her husband's knee. "You plucky duck."

Oh, how Emily had missed these two! She smiled as Evan leaned down to catch Alice's hand and give it a chivalrous kiss. To think that just one year ago, she had been so afraid of this hoary Romeo. Granted, he had not been exactly warm to her in the beginning, and his razor-sharp wit was known in the congregation to draw a little blood on occasion. But he had softened considerably toward everyone after courting Alice, and the balcony hadn't been the same without him these long weeks of their honeymoon.

Emily suddenly remembered that she wanted to ask him something. "Evan, I need your advice."

Evan turned his attention toward Emily, swinging his legs around the organ bench and dangling his feet over the side. He rested his hands on his knees. It was a familiar posture that Emily recognized as his listening position, one of this quirky musician's many eccentricities. She secretly thought he looked a bit like a meditating monk when he did that. "I've been trying to think of something special for the choir to do this year, and I thought maybe a cantata might be the thing."

Evan appeared unmoved.

Emily's confident smile faltered a bit at the venerable maestro's show of apathy. "I found some old Christmas cantata programs in the filing cabinet—dating from about twenty years ago, I think—and I saw that you directed them." She shrugged nervously, no longer sure of herself. "I thought it might be fun to revive an old tradition."

Alice coughed spastically into her hand.

Evan blinked once but gave no other reaction.

"You think I shouldn't do it?" Emily quickly asked.

"I didn't say that." Evan held his perfectly pious pose, but the toe of his left shoe jiggled ever so slightly. "Sure. Go ahead and do it. Why not?"

Alice spluttered again, this time not so successfully hiding her laughter.

Evan broke his straight posture and gave his bride a look of patient forbearance. "Go ahead and say it, Al. I know you want to."

Alice covered her mouth, closed her eyes briefly, and shook her head.

"It's not exactly a secret at this point. Everyone in the choir already knows about it, so Emily might as well too."

Emily remembered a time when Evan had not been so willing to relay stories from the choir's rather colorful past.

"I feel," Alice gasped, "that it's Arlene's story to tell."

Oh, dear. Emily looked back and forth between the newlyweds. "What is it? You'd tell me, right, if there's a reason I shouldn't direct another cantata here?"

Evan sighed and looked entreatingly toward the ceiling as his wife resumed her tittering. His back was straight as an arrow again. "My first year here, I directed a Christmas cantata, and it quickly became an annual tradition. In fact, it became so popular in the community at large that we invited the other area Lutheran churches to join us in the music making. It became a grand affair, and in an effort to make the whole thing more manageable, the choir directors from the participating churches took turns leading the cantata from year to year. We worked out a system where one church's choir director would rehearse and conduct the cantata, while another participating church would host the actual rehearsals and performance. It was a special tradition, one that was *beloved*," he said, directing that last word as a reprimand toward his hysterical wife, "for many years."

Alice looked as if she were wrestling herself in an attempt to squelch her involuntary snorts and squawks.

"Well," Evan continued, "the final year we had it—when was it, Al? In ninety-three?—I was the director, and Grace Lutheran in Fancy Grove hosted. We had subzero temperatures that week, and Grace's heaters have always been notorious for sucking the moisture out of the air on a normal day, let alone an arctic one. Arlene decided to bring some brandy from home the night of the performance—some nonsense about alcohol warming up the larynx—and she passed it around to the singers in the basement kitchen before the downbeat. It was a harmless gesture, however ignorant, but none of us could anticipate that fourteen-year-old Olive Wagner would take four turns at the bottle."

Emily gasped and covered her own mouth with her hand.

"To make matters worse, Estella Wagner—Olive's mother and the longstanding music director of St. Luke's in Hamburg—did not take kindly to her daughter's bobbing and weaving through the entire first half of the cantata. Nor did she appreciate her daughter's mangling of the words on her first big solo."

"Oh, Evan," Alice giggled, her face red with suppressed laughter. "What was it she sang? I can't remember."

"It was 'Silent Night.'"

"Yes, but what exactly did she *sing*?"

Evan looked toward the ceiling again, and in his best adolescent soprano voice, intoned, "'Round, young virgin, tender and wild.'"

Emily stifled a few squawks of her own.

"Suffice it to say," Evan said, "that Estella let Arlene have it at intermission and then proceeded to pull her daughter from the cantata with threats of calling the police. She left the concert that night in a maternal rage of legendary proportion. When the next year rolled around, I didn't quite know what to do other than to let the cantata die a natural death. Then, of course, Dale was hired to direct the choir, and, well, we all know what happened after that."

Emily and Alice sobered quickly at Evan's last sentence.

"Personally," Alice said, wiping the tears from her eyes, "I think that enough time has passed for Emily to give the cantata a try, don't you, dear?"

Evan turned back toward his pearly white manuals and flipped on the overhead music light. It was time to begin playing the preservice music. "I plead the fifth."

Emily pondered what Evan had said—and not said—on her way back down the stairs. Maybe she should scrap the idea. The last thing she wanted to do, after all, was cause Mrs. Scheinberg any more grief in life. At the same time, a joint cantata might be just the thing her little choir needed to bolster its confidence and rekindle its enthusiasm after the summer break. Sure, there were some risks in resurrecting an old tradition, but church history was on her side. Nothing got Lutherans so excited as something being raised from the dead.

Chapter Ten: The Best of Times

||||||||||||||||||||||||||||||||||||||||||||||||||||||||||||||||||

Today was the day.

Pastor Michael Fletcher snapped his clerical collar into place and slipped his arms into his nicest black suit coat, the one his mother had given him for Christmas. It was still a bit warm outside for such things, but he wanted to look his best today. He had even thought to stop by Bob's Barber on the corner of Second and Main yesterday afternoon to get his neck trimmed, but he knew that no amount of shearing or snipping would make a difference in the end if he suffered a tactical error on the field. Of course, Operation Bling String had been a success—those three tenuous minutes of pocketing Peter's ring aside—but it would be through reconnaissance, not personal grooming, that he accomplished this final, important mission: mobilizing the familial troops under cover without Emily suspecting a thing.

And his covert operator was just the one to help him do it.

"Nicole, Brad, and the kids are flying into Lambert International on Saturday afternoon," he had informed Rebecca on the phone late last week. "Greg and Mary offered to pick them up on their way into town, but I'm not sure where to put them all."

"Nicole and her family can stay at our place," Rebecca had reassured.

"But you're—"

"The size of a tank? Yes, I know, thank you very much. But I'm not officially due for another two weeks, and I always go late. It'll be fine."

That left the parsonage guest room for Greg and Mary, but since the parsonage was just seven houses down the street and around the corner from Emily's house, Pastor gave Emily's parents a special directive of their own. "Be sure to park on South Spring Street, or Emily will see your car on her walk to church in the morning."

Greg and Mary were still sound asleep in the guest room Sunday morning when Pastor opened the parsonage door to leave—they had pulled in quite late the night before—so he quietly left his key on the table as well as a note directing them to bagels on the kitchen counter and a carton of orange juice in the refrigerator. The plan was for all of them to arrive at the church a few minutes before nine o'clock to surprise Emily in the narthex.

Pastor, a bit nervously, followed his usual Sunday morning routine at the church—prayed Matins, printed out his sermon and placed it on the pulpit, made sure the service book and the lectionary were turned to the correct pages, double-checked the numbers on the hymn boards, updated the congregational prayer list, and went over his notes for Sunday School—but today he included an extra-special task in his weekly regimen. He opened his leather-bound journal to a poem he had penned more than a year ago, just three weeks after having met Emily, and hand-copied the verses onto a separate piece of paper. Then, he carefully folded the paper and tucked it into the left breast pocket of his suit coat.

He couldn't help but smile now at the thought of that awful, wonderful day when he had first set the poem to paper. Emily had just moved into Alice's Mulberry Street property and had begun to establish herself at the church and in the community, and Zachary Brandt, a colleague of Emily's at Bradbury College—and a sickeningly handsome one at that—had followed her to church one Sunday morning. At the time, Pastor's insides had practically rotted out with envy at the sight of the prepossessing English lit professor following his choir director around the pews, but Zachary turned out to be no more than just a good friend in the end. Still, Pastor had been none the wiser at the time, and he had sat in his study after church on that wretched Sunday, pouring his silent sufferings onto the page in poetic verse. For even then, he had known that he wanted to marry Emily Duke.

At eight-thirty, Pastor rose from his desk to vest for the Divine Service, but he stopped short at the sight of a familiar, curly head peeking around his study door. His heart skipped a beat.

"Good morning." Emily smiled in that rosy, schoolgirl way of hers.

Pastor's hand flew involuntarily to his left pants pocket. The little velvet box was still there, safe and sound. "You're early this morning."

"I wanted to catch Evan in the balcony before the service." She stepped into his study and threw her bag onto one of his chairs. "Are you still coming over for lunch?"

"Of course." Their weekly tradition was to eat lunch together at Emily's house every Sunday noon. "I'm bringing dessert, right?"

Emily nodded. "Don't forget that the Joneses are joining us too."

They secretly weren't, but the only way Rebecca and Pastor could think to make sure Emily prepared a meal big enough to feed her entire family was to lead her to think the Joneses were coming over for lunch, as well. Pastor felt a sting of guilt, and not just from perpetuating a lie. He wanted to be the one to prepare the meal for Emily today, but he didn't dare suggest a change in their routine. She always insisted on cooking for him on Sundays—his "busy day at the office," as she liked to call it—and Pastor knew she would suspect something was up if he proposed anything different. So he nodded his head and silently repented, fervently praying that all of this sneaking around would be worth it in the end.

"Well, I've got corned beef barbecue cooking in the Crock-Pot and creamed corn baking in the oven. My house already smells like Kansas City. Just wait until you walk through that door, Michael Fletcher," Emily teased. "Your mouth is going to water, and you're going to wish I cooked for you every single day of the—"

In three quick strides, Michael Fletcher crossed the room, grabbed Emily's hand, and pulled her close. He didn't care that it was Sunday morning or that he was standing in the middle of his study or that someone might walk around the office corner at any moment. This was his girl, and this was their day. And it was a beautiful one at that—one that the Lord had made—and he was going to rejoice in it, come rain or come Mrs. Scheinberg.

Everything ran like clockwork after that. When Emily descended the balcony stairs a few minutes before nine o'clock, her family was waiting for her in the narthex.

"What?!" she screeched, running over to her sister and fiercely hugging her neck. "What are you guys doing here?"

"Well," Nicole laughed, winking at Pastor over Emily's shoulder, "Brad and the kids had Labor Day off, so we thought we'd come and surprise you. We have to leave tomorrow morning, though, but at least we'll have today together. It's a bit last minute, I know. I hope you haven't made any plans."

"Where are you staying?"

"With you, I hope."

No one breathed a word about having already stayed in Bradbury the night before.

Emily laughed, clapped her hands, and hugged her brother-in-law, niece, and nephew each in turn, blabbering the whole time. "When did you fly in? I could have picked you up from the airport. How did I not know about this? You should have flown in Friday night, so we'd have more time together."

"Tanner had a game on Friday night," Brad quickly covered.

"And Brooklyn had gymnastics yesterday morning," Nicole added. "She's getting ready for a big competition in October, so we didn't dare miss."

"Can I get a hug too?" Mary Heath smiled, her eyes brimming with happy tears. The apple apparently didn't fall very far from the tree, for Emily's own eyes immediately watered at the sight of her mother.

"I just can't believe you all are here at the same time!" She hugged her mother hard and then immediately turned around to point an accusing finger at Pastor. "You knew about this, didn't you?"

"We called him last week," Greg Heath hastily explained, "to make sure you'd be home this weekend."

"And to ask if we could stay in his guest room," Mary added.

That was all true, thankfully, though it wasn't exactly the whole truth. Pastor silently marveled at the dexterous way the Heaths and Johnsons bobbed and weaved around Emily's questions without ever fumbling. As he watched Emily bear hug her father, he made a mental note never to play football—or Balderdash—with any of them.

After church was over, Jeremy Jones came onstage to play his part, though he went a bit off script.

"I'm afraid we can't make it for lunch, Emily."

"Oh, I'm sorry to hear that. Is Rebecca not well?"

"She's all right—a bit tired—but it's Frankie and Alison who're under the weather this morning."

None of them had planned for the kids being sick, but the illness did seem to be rather serendipitously timed.

"Rebecca stayed home with the younger two," Jeremy explained, running a weary hand through his fiery red hair, "so I need to get the other two boys rounded up to go relieve her."

Emily's joy went undaunted by the shift in plans. She bubbled and yakked the entire walk home, turning first to her sister and then to her parents and so on until she had heard every last detail of their trip. Pastor followed behind, hands in his pockets, grinning with satisfaction at the happy scene. He so wanted to make Emily happy.

Emily continued to chatter through the whole meal, but as they finished their dessert of chocolate-covered oranges, Pastor's specialty, Nicole deftly steered the conversation—as planned—toward the operation at hand. "The kids have been practicing a little something just for their Aunt Em."

"Oh?" Emily raised her eyebrows, curious.

"Tanner," Nicole said, turning to her ten-year-old son, "go wash your hands for me in the kitchen." Then, turning back to Emily, she asked, "Do you mind if the kids use your piano?"

"Of course not." Emily pushed back her chair and set her napkin on the table. "In fact, why don't we all move into the living room? Carrots'll get lonely if we stay in here."

Pastor couldn't have planned the transition more perfectly if he'd orchestrated it himself.

Thirteen-year-old Brooklyn jumped up and linked her willowy arm through her aunt's, escorting her to the living room. It was hard keeping such a big secret at such a young age, but Brooklyn was bearing up under the weight like a champ. "I've been practicing my singing," she said, "and I've asked Mom for a rabbit like yours. She said no."

Emily winked at Nicole, letting go of Brooklyn's arm to open the piano lid. "Rabbits are inexpensive, and they're caged. Plus, they don't require any shots," she continued, extolling the virtues of her dear Carrots. "You'll never find a more affordable pet, Nicole."

"And Carrots's favorite food is dandelion greens from Emily's yard," Pastor contributed. "Just think, you could have a groundskeeper on the cheap who moonlights as a foot warmer."

"Yeah," Nicole said, "but then I'd have to hire a maid to keep up with all of the bunny hair. Oh, don't even try to deny it, Em. You were just complaining to me over the phone last month that Carrots sheds every time you turn around."

"Not as often as that," Emily murmured, scratching behind the ears of her favorite broken tort buck. He was stretched out on the floor of his cage near the front window. "It's probably more like every third time I turn around."

"Ooh, can I hold him?" Tanner asked, rushing into the room from the kitchen.

"Not until after you play," Nicole checked.

Pastor smiled to himself, watching as Emily sat on the couch between her parents and Nicole rested on the arm of the overstuffed chair her husband, Brad, was already inhabiting. He leaned against the wall in the background, suddenly feeling very emotional.

Tanner positioned himself on the piano bench and played a simple homophonic introduction. Then Brooklyn, standing in the crook of the black baby grand, began to sing.

Emily turned to look at Pastor, seemingly recognizing the song. She smiled curiously. Pastor smiled back, pleased that things were going so well.

In May, he had secretly mailed the Johnsons a copy of the song Emily had written last Advent using one of his own published poems as a text. He had asked Nicole if the kids could learn it and play it for their aunt when they came to visit. He was happy to discover that they had done more than that. They memorized it for the occasion.

"That was beautiful!" Emily clapped heartily when the kids had finished. "Your posture on the bench is perfect, Tanner, and your voice is maturing nicely, Brooklyn. I think you're ready for something higher."

Next, Nicole stood and took the floor. She had a wrapped package tucked under her right arm. "Emily," she said, looking knowingly at her younger sister. Tears immediately sprang to Nicole's eyes, and she laughed nervously at her sudden show of emotion. She was not usually the sentimental one of the family. She cleared her throat, determinedly pressing on, but her voice wavered. "Ten years ago, you came and stayed with us in Colorado for a month. It was a difficult time." Nicole stopped for a moment, attempting to regain some control of her voice, but it was of no use. The ugly cry had started. "None of us knew what to do. We were all so concerned for you."

Emily covered her mouth with her hand and nodded, her own tears spontaneously spilling onto her cheeks. Pastor shifted, suddenly feeling a bit panicked. He had invited Emily's family to be a part of this day to make it more memorable, but he had not gone so far as to ask what they were going to say to her. Maybe it had been a bad idea, asking everyone to participate like this. Maybe it was all too much and too public for Emily to handle.

"But not all of it was sad," Nicole smiled through her tears, wiping her nose. "You spent hours coloring and painting with Brooklyn, and you sang Tanner to sleep every night. Do you remember what you sang?"

"'I Am Jesus' Little Lamb,'" Emily whispered. Mary took her daughter's hand in her own for support, and Greg put his arm around them both.

"Yes," Nicole nodded, "and your singing reminded all of us to put our trust in Jesus because He promises to care for us even in our sadness. You wrote out the lyrics for me, remember? I was dumb and didn't know the words, and I didn't have a hymnal in my house at the time. Well," Nicole extended the package toward Emily and continued narrating while her sister opened it, "I kept those lyrics in my Bible, and one day a couple of months after you left, Brooklyn got into my Bible with her crayons and proceeded to bless its pages with the colors yellow and blue—your wedding colors. She had no idea they were your wedding colors, but I remember being struck by the irony of that at the time. Needless to say, your lyrics got colored too. I couldn't throw away the sheet after that, especially once I saw what Brooklyn had colored on that paper."

Emily gasped as she pulled out the worn lyric sheet. It had been beautifully matted and framed, and there, covering her handwritten words, was a three-year-old's rendering of a cross in lemon yellow and sky blue.

"I thought you should have it," Nicole sniffed, "you know, to hang in your new home here in Bradbury and to remember everything, the good and the bad, because it's all a part of you. And I love all of you."

Emily stood up and hugged her sister.

"Is this going to make you sad, Em?" Nicole asked, still hugging. "I don't want it to make you sad. I want it to remind you that even the worst of times are redeemed by Christ's death on the cross."

"It's perfect," Emily sniffed.

Greg Heath stood next, taking an envelope out of his pocket.

"What's going on?" Emily said, looking around the room. "Am I forgetting an anniversary or something? It's like you all know something that I don't. Why are you all being so secretive?"

"Here, honey," Mary said, taking her daughter's hand and gently pulling her back down onto the couch. "Come have a seat. We just miss you and want you to know how much you are loved."

Greg cleared his throat and resumed opening the envelope he was holding. "I don't know if you remember, Emily, but you wrote me letters for a few years after you moved to Kansas City for grad school. I wasn't quite up to snuff on the whole email thing yet, so you graciously indulged your old dad in a little snail-mail exchange."

Emily immediately smiled and relaxed. Pastor relaxed too, for he knew that Emily's father, as a rule, always tried to make his daughter laugh rather than cry.

"Well," Greg winked, pulling a piece of blue stationery paper out of the envelope and flapping it dramatically in front of everyone, "I kept all of those letters, and I thought you might enjoy hearing a bit from the Epistle of Emily, chapter 4, verses 6 through 18."

Brooklyn giggled behind her hands.

"'I met a guy named John at the Missouri State High School Solo and Ensemble Contest in Joplin last weekend,'" Greg read. Emily groaned like a teenager and covered her face with her hands. "'We both adjudicated for the small ensembles division, and he asked me out on a date. He was nice enough, but I'm not a fan of guys whose clothes are nicer than mine. It comes across as shallow and vain.'"

"Hear, hear!" Brad cheered. He was a general contractor by trade and rarely changed out of his T-shirts and jeans. Everyone laughed.

"'I politely said no,'" Greg continued reading, "'but it got me thinking. What if God decides to send someone my way again? Please, don't misunderstand me. I can't imagine ever marrying someone other than Peter, but you know how much I like to be prepared.'"

Everyone chuckled knowingly, and Pastor beamed to see Emily join in on the laugh. Victory.

"'After thinking about it,'" Greg read, "'I decided that only "one thing's needful," as Mom's favorite hymn wisely states. I need a man to care more about his church than he does about his clothes or anything else. Well, except maybe me.'"

With that, Greg folded up the letter, put it back in the envelope, and sat back down next to his daughter.

That was his cue.

Pastor, a bit unnerved by the uncanny relevance of the letter Greg had chosen to read, walked to the center of the room and turned around to face the woman he was planning to ask to be his wife. Emily looked up at him with wide, shining eyes. He couldn't read her mind, but he guessed from her expectant posture that she had begun to suspect what was really going on. He reached into his left breast pocket, his heart racing, and opened his mouth to speak, but something happened in the next moment that knocked him completely off his rocker. It was something that—in the hundreds of times he had visualized this very moment—he had never imagined.

His phone rang.

The mechanical trill sounded particularly loud and shrill in this intimate setting, and the effect was about as romantic as an alarm bell reverberating through a school cafeteria. His cheeks burned with mortification.

"I'm so sorry," he said, reaching into his right pants pocket to properly silence the little beast. His vocation demanded that he keep his ringer on at all times, but surely this was one occasion when a pastor could be forgiven for ignoring it. "My phone has the absolute worst manners in all of Bradbury," he joked, laughing nervously.

The Heaths and the Johnsons chuckled politely, and Emily, her beautiful brown eyes radiating kindness and patience and a bit of wild anticipation, nodded to him encouragingly. Pastor cleared his throat and reached for the poem once more, but no sooner had his fingertips brushed the starchy paper than his blasted phone began to vibrate and dance in his pocket for all the world to hear.

Pastor's shoulders slumped in defeat. He fought the urge to chuck his boorish phone out the front picture window, and instead—like a good pastor—checked the caller ID.

Jeremy Jones

Pastor frowned. That couldn't be right. Jeremy knew what was going on this afternoon. There was no reason he would call repeatedly like this, unless—

"I'm sorry," he said, "I need to get this." He spun around on his heel and answered the call. "Jeremy?" He froze at the sound of the panicked voice on the other end and listened for one moment longer before saying, "I'll be right there."

When he turned back around, Emily was already standing, her face mirroring his grave expression. "What is it?"

Pastor honestly wanted to cry. His heart was breaking, but his vocation was crystal clear. He knew what he needed to do. He took both of Emily's hands in his own and gazed earnestly into her probing eyes. "I'm so, so sorry, Emily. Will you please forgive me? I really do have to go." He kissed her hands tenderly before breaking the horrible news. "It's the Jones baby. Something's wrong."

Chapter Eleven: The Worst of Times

||||||||||||||||||||||||||||||||||||||||||||||||||||||||||||||

They were calling it a cord accident.

Emily couldn't quite follow everything the doctor was saying, but she caught the terms "entanglement" and "anoxic."

"Anoxic?" she asked Pastor in a whisper.

"It means the baby is without air," he answered quietly at her side. "There seems to be a knot in the umbilical cord."

They were standing in a private room in the maternity ward of Bradbury Regional. Rebecca was lying in shock on the hospital bed, and Jeremy stood guard like a centurion at her side.

"Is the baby—?" Emily couldn't even finish her question.

Pastor nodded, his face gray.

"We don't always know what causes an intrauterine fetal demise," the doctor was saying, "but we do know that she needs to come out."

"She?" Jeremy asked, his voice hollow.

"Yes," the doctor said gently. "Your baby's a girl."

Rebecca's bewildered eyes suddenly registered acute pain, and her mouth opened in a tortured, silent wail. Her throat reverberated with the seismic rending of a mother's bereaved heart, and the terrible, soundless sight was haunting. Eventually, a strangled moan escaped from between her lips. Emily covered her own mouth with her hand. She recognized that sound. She had made it herself the day Peter died.

Rebecca was inconsolable. She rocked back and forth on the bed, moaning as if in labor, only she wasn't in labor. Jeremy tried soothing her with gentle shushes and tender touches, but nothing registered as comfort.

"What do we do?" he finally asked, turning toward the doctor in defeat.

"I recommend we induce labor," the doctor said.

"I can't, I can't, I can't . . . ," Rebecca repeated over and over again, her eyes closed tightly against the double-crossing world.

"Rebecca," the doctor's calm, kind voice cut through the chorus of grief, "you don't have to do anything right now. This is a time to rest. I'm going to get you something to help you relax."

Rebecca's moans were coming at an even rate now, one perfect *messa di voce* after another. Jeremy tried wrapping his arms around his wife once more, and she ultimately succumbed to her husband's hold, collapsing against his chest in a hum of exhaustion.

Emily, as if guided by an unseen wisdom, stepped forward and sat on the edge of the hospital bed next to Rebecca's feet. She took hold of her friend's left ankle and held onto it as a lifeline. She did not know what it was like to lose a child, but she did know loss. And her particular brand of mettle had been purified by the Refiner's fire for such a time as this. She opened her mouth and began to sing her favorite hymn:

> *Why should cross and trial grieve me?*
> *Christ is near*
> *With His cheer;*
> *Never will He leave me.*

Who can rob me of the heaven
That God's Son
For me won
When His life was given?

Emily's voice was sweet and soothing to the ear, but her song was a sword of the Spirit that pierced through the cosmic powers darkening the room. Pastor stepped forward to join his voice—and his shield of faith—with hers.

When life's troubles rise to meet me,
Though their weight
May be great,
They will not defeat me.
God, my loving Savior, sends them;
He who knows
All my woes
Knows how best to end them.

God gives me my days of gladness,
And I will
Trust Him still
When He sends me sadness.
God is good; His love attends me
Day by day,
Come what may,
Guides me and defends me. (LSB 756:1–3)

Rebecca's moans had ceased. She was watching Emily from behind swollen eyelids that were red from their saltwater bath. "My baby's a girl," she said, her voice nasal and hoarse.

"Yes," Emily squeezed her ankle even harder.

"We decided on names last week. Henry Philip for a boy," Rebecca's lower lip quivered, "but our baby girl's name is Emma. Emma Leigh."

Emily's heart swelled with an indescribable joy and then immediately burst with unspeakable pain. She scooted forward on the bed and enveloped her best friend in a mournful hug. The two sat and wept.

Rebecca finally pulled back and confessed, "I couldn't feel her last night. It was awful. I thought maybe I hadn't eaten enough for supper or that I was a little dehydrated, but nothing worked. Not even caffeine. I drank coffee this morning, and she still wouldn't move. She's still not moving." Rebecca's voice diminished into another airless cry.

Emily said nothing. There was nothing to say.

"Pastor?" Jeremy asked, his voice sounding far away. He had moved to a chair beside the bed, his shoulders bent under the weight of the world's brokenness, his head between his hands. "Is Emma in heaven?"

Rebecca and Emily turned expectantly to Pastor, both desperate for some hope.

Pastor opened his Bible to the Book of First Timothy. "Hear this promise from the Lord: God 'desires all people to be saved and to come to the knowledge of the truth.'" He looked directly at Jeremy. "That includes Emma. And in the Book of Second Peter," he quickly flipped forward several pages, "we read that the Lord does not wish 'that any should perish, but that all should reach repentance.'" Pastor looked up again and spoke with resolve, "Our heavenly Father does not desire the death of anyone—especially Emma, whom He loves—but instead, wants her to be saved. He wants her salvation as much as He wants salvation for you and for me. She inherited Adam's sin at conception, just like us. That's why He sent Jesus to die on the cross for *all* sins, even hers.'"

Jeremy wiped the tears from his cheeks.

"And we know from Scripture," Pastor continued, "that God's 'steadfast love endures forever' and that the children of mankind take refuge in the shadow of His wings, so we will believe that Emma is residing in the shadow of her loving heavenly Father's wings."

"She died without Baptism," Rebecca whispered, her eyes wild with mortal fear.

"Baptism is not a work that we do to save ourselves," Pastor said. "It is a gift of God—a promise of salvation that He attached to simple water—but His promise of salvation isn't restricted to just that. God promises that His Holy Spirit will work through His Word to grant faith to His people, and Emma heard the Word even in the womb, both in church and in your home."

Jeremy and Rebecca contemplated this in silence.

"Hear another promise from the Lord." Pastor now opened His Bible to the Psalms. "'The eyes of the LORD are toward the righteous and His ears toward their cry.' That's you, Jeremy and Rebecca. You are the righteous, and God hears your prayers." Pastor turned several pages and continued reading, "'For You, O LORD, are good and forgiving, abounding in steadfast love to all who call upon You. . . . In the day of my trouble I call upon You, for You answer me. . . . Great is Your mercy, O LORD.'" Pastor looked up from his Bible. "Both of you, as Emma's parents, were praying for her daily that God would preserve her, and you were planning on bringing her to the baptismal font. God knows this, and our faith trusts in His promises to hear and answer your prayers."

"Why did God let her die?" Rebecca's inaugural pain was still too present to make room for anger, but the seeds of it were there.

Pastor's nostrils flared at the sting of his own sadness. "I don't know."

Jeremy and Rebecca bowed their heads in grief.

"We may never understand why God in His wisdom chose for Emma to die," Pastor continued, "but God has given us promises in His Word that we can understand: He is merciful, and He desires *all* to be saved. We trust in God's mercy for Emma even as we trust in His mercy for each of us. We rest on the promises of God, always."

Pastor stepped forward and took Rebecca's and Jeremy's hands in his own. "Let us pray together now, that God would give us faith which trusts in His promises."

CHAPTER TWELVE:

THE GOSPEL ACCORDING TO ZION

‖‖‖

Emma Leigh Jones was stillborn at 7:35 Sunday evening, and the women of Zion wasted no time in mustering the troops to defend their wounded.

"I'll take the grandkids for a couple of days," Candice had told Alice over the phone earlier that day. "They can spend the night in our renovated attic. They'll love it. We'll pop popcorn and play Ping-Pong and watch movies, and Thomas and I'll take them to Six Flags tomorrow. It'll be a good distraction. You should be with Rebecca right now."

Candice, whose own mother had died while giving birth to her, knew a thing or two about a daughter's need for her mother during times of distress. What she did not know was when to stop talking.

"The baby probably had a deformity of some kind," she yammered on. "I once read in a magazine that miscarriages are God's way of protecting the human race from genetic weakness. It's probably for the best that the baby died."

Mrs. Scheinberg and Bev were a bit more sensible—and tactful—in their administering of care.

"Here are two pans of lasagna," Mrs. Scheinberg said to Evan Sunday night, consulting her itemized list while setting the bulging plastic grocery bags on the Joneses' island counter, "as well as two pans of mac and cheese, a box of corn dogs, and Knox Blox from me. The blue are for Robbie and the yellow for Alison. And the vegetable soup, beef and noodles, and brownies are from Bev. It's brownies that Frankie likes, right? Oh, and the Koelster sisters wanted me to tell you that they're bringing over a tuna casserole and a cobbler after tomorrow's lunch rush. None of us could remember what Davie likes, so here's a five-dollar bill for him to pick out his favorite kind of ice cream from the store."

All in the all, the women provided fourteen meals, only half of which could actually fit in the Joneses' freezer, but it was Nettie's gift that made the biggest impression on Rebecca.

"Everyone needs a pretty dress," she said, her eyes large and luminous as she handed Rebecca a package at the hospital.

Rebecca unwrapped the pink-paper-covered box and pulled out a handmade white gown with exquisitely crafted tatting around the collar and sleeves. Her heart—what little was left of it—froze in horror. Nettie, it seemed, had tragically misunderstood the situation.

"It's for Emma," Nettie said. "I made it from the same pattern as Colleen's."

Rebecca had no idea who Colleen was, and she really didn't care. Today was not a day she could suffer Nettie's foolishness. She dropped the dress unceremoniously back in the box, covered it with the lid, and bit her lower lip to keep from speaking.

"It's a baptismal gown," Nettie explained. "This one's bigger, of course. Colleen was much smaller."

Rebecca couldn't even look up to meet Nettie's eyes, her fury was so hot.

"She looked like one of those play dolls, she was so tiny," Nettie chattered, seemingly oblivious to Rebecca's pain. "I held her for two hours. Then they took her from me. I still hate them for doing that."

Rebecca looked up, startled by that last admission. Nettie was staring out the window. Her loose mind—prone to wander—seemed to have settled in some faraway place.

"Thirty-five weeks is a long time when you're pregnant, but it wasn't long enough, I guess. I insisted Colleen be buried in white. Emma should be buried in white too."

Rebecca's eyes were stinging now, both from shame and sadness. She lifted the lid of the box anew and cradled the sweet dress close to her heart. She would treasure Nettie's kindness to her daughter forever. "You lost a baby?"

Nettie looked at Rebecca with dry eyes, though Rebecca sensed they had been crying for many, many years. "I lost five."

|||||||||||||||||||||||||||||||||||||||||||||||

Emma was indeed buried in white, right next to her grandfather.

Pastor Fletcher carried her tiny casket himself, walking the five blocks from Zion Lutheran Church to Bradbury Cemetery, a small procession of mourners following closely behind. There was no motorcade, but Officer Plueth still waited respectfully at the corner of First Street and Bradbury Drive to ensure the funeral procession's safe passage across the street and into the cemetery. He blew his whistle sharply as the somber parade approached and stepped into the intersection, signaling for two oncoming cars to stop.

"Baby Emma dead!" little Alison called out to the idling cars by way of explanation. No one could actually hear her, but she still felt quite proud to be playing the part of the informant. With three older brothers in the family, she rarely got to talk, let alone with any authority. "Not worry! She rise again!"

Davie tugged at her hand to move her along.

At the grave site, Pastor set Emma's casket gently on the ground and poured earth on top of it in the shape of a cross.

"'It has pleased our heavenly Father in His wise providence to call this child to Himself,'" Pastor read aloud from a burgundy-colored book in his hand. "'We now commit Emma's body to the ground; earth to earth, ashes to ashes, dust to dust, in the sure and certain hope of the resurrection to eternal life through our Lord Jesus Christ, who will change our lowly bodies so that they will be like His glorious body, by the power that enables Him to subdue all things to Himself.'"

"Amen," everyone answered.

"'May God the Father, the Son, and the Holy Spirit keep these remains to the day of the resurrection of all flesh.'"

"Amen."

Frankie made the sign of the cross along with Pastor, remembering that God's holy name had first been put upon him in his Baptism.

"'Taught by our Lord and trusting His promises, we are bold to pray . . .'" Pastor bowed his head, leading everyone in the Lord's Prayer. "Our Father . . ."

"Who art in heaven," the small group joined in.

Little Alison, still feeling quite grown-up and self-important, scrunched up her face in concentration and shouted out a sanctimonious "Hollywood by Thy name!"

Alice, who, even in her deepest grief, was not completely immune to the comical cuteness of her adorable granddaughter, coughed spontaneously into her hand; and Mrs. Scheinberg, feeling particularly loopy after organizing and executing the meal train on such short notice as well as producing a perfectly typed funeral bulletin for the occasion, bit down on a rumpled tissue in order to muffle a few choking sounds of her own. The two tired women managed to keep from laughing for the rest of the prayer, but all levity soon fizzled at the sight and sound of Rebecca's sobbing.

"'Almighty God,'" Pastor raised his hands in the air, his own voice quavering with emotion, "'by the death of Your Son Jesus Christ, You destroyed death and redeemed and saved Your little ones.'"

Rebecca dissolved against Jeremy. Robbie hugged his mother's waist fiercely from the other side.

"'By His bodily resurrection You brought life and immortality to light so that all who die in Him abide in peace and hope. Receive our thanks for the victory over death and the grave that He won for us. Keep us in everlasting communion with all who wait for Him on earth and with all in heaven who are with Him, for He is the resurrection and the life, even Jesus Christ, our Lord.'"

"Amen."

Emily then opened the hymnal she was holding and began to sing:

> *Jesus, priceless treasure,*
> *Fount of purest pleasure,*
> *Truest friend to me,*
> *Ah, how long in anguish*
> *Shall my spirit languish,*
> *Yearning, Lord, for Thee?*
> *Thou art mine,*
> *O Lamb divine!*

I will suffer naught to hide Thee;
Naught I ask beside Thee.

In Thine arms I rest me;
Foes who would molest me
Cannot reach me here.
Though the earth be shaking,
Ev'ry heart be quaking,
Jesus calms my fear.
Lightnings flash
And thunders crash;
Yet, though sin and hell assail me,
Jesus will not fail me.

Hence, all fear and sadness!
For the Lord of gladness,
Jesus, enters in.
Those who love the Father,
Though the storms may gather,
Still have peace within.
Yea, whate'er
I here must bear,
Thou art still my purest pleasure,
Jesus, priceless treasure! (LSB 743:1, 2, 6)

After a few minutes of quiet murmuring and hugging, everyone eventually dispersed. Pastor, Emily, and Mrs. Scheinberg headed back toward the church, where the Davises and

Schmidts were preparing a light funeral luncheon for everyone. The Joneses, however, lingered by the open grave with the Ebners so that the siblings could lay flowers on Emma's casket.

"Baby Emma rise now?" Alison asked.

"No, Aly," Frankie said somberly. "Not until the Last Day."

"I ready now. I hold her."

"You can't hold her, Aly."

Alison crossed her arms in front of her chest and turned to pout at her father. "You said I hold her."

"Yes, but that was—" Jeremy sighed. He reached down and picked up his daughter, holding her close. "You can't hold her now, Aly. Baby Emma's with Jesus."

While Alison contemplated things eternal, Robbie turned his attention toward things temporal. He backed stealthily toward his grandfather's grave and pulled a shiny red globe out of his pocket. It was an old Christmas ornament he had snuck from a box in the basement the night before. He quickly hung it on a branch of the young cedar sapling he had planted at his grandfather's grave two years before. The sudden act of arboreal embellishment didn't escape the notice of eagle-eyed Evan, but the new grandpa prudently turned away and pretended to be none the wiser.

Alice was busy watching her daughter. She knew that Rebecca was in no shape to be standing for long periods of time, let alone walking all across Bradbury County in the late-summer heat, and her daughter's face was growing whiter by the minute.

"I think we should go now, dear," Alice prodded, nodding meaningfully to Evan and simultaneously corralling the kids toward the cemetery entrance. Rebecca didn't argue, but she did fall a few steps behind everyone else, bending down at the end of a row to wordlessly rest a small bouquet of purple asters—picked fresh that morning from her own garden—against a little head-stone that read:

Colleen Annette Schmidt
beloved daughter
April 14, 1963

On the walk back to church, Emily tried her best to contain her grief. Committals brought back memories of another casket buried in a little cemetery in the heart of St. Clair County. Death may hold no sting for the Christian, but it sure did its best to leave a scar.

"I'm so sorry, Emily," Pastor interrupted her thoughts.

"Hmm?"

"About leaving you on Sunday," he explained.

"Oh. It's okay."

"No, it's not. I mean, I *had* to leave," Pastor took her right hand in his own. Mrs. Scheinberg was hobbling ahead of them about twenty feet—hastening to assist in the kitchen, she'd said, though they both suspected she was giving them some much-needed privacy. This was the first time they had been alone since his phone had so sadly interrupted them Sunday afternoon. "I should have at least called you, but I couldn't leave the hospital until late Sunday night. Jeremy was really struggling, and I didn't dare leave him. And then I was afraid I'd wake you, so I went home and crashed for a few hours. But then Jeremy called me again in the morning to come back to the hospital because Rebecca was having a hard time—"

"Really, Michael." Emily stopped short on the sidewalk to face him. She smiled kindly. She was sad and disappointed and confused about the recent turn of events, but she was also understanding. "You don't need to apologize. You're a pastor. Your job is to serve your people."

"But you're one of those people. I want to serve you too."

Emily felt a tiny thrill in spite of her sadness. She had been waiting two days for him to revisit the conversation he had started on Sunday. Maybe this was the moment. She looked up at him expectantly and squeezed his hand just a little.

Pastor, unaware of the brown-eyed expectations staring him squarely in the face, simply turned and resumed his walking, casually swinging her hand at his side. "What time did your family finally leave?"

Emily's face fell with disappointment. Of course he wasn't proposing to her right after a funeral! What was she thinking? "My sister and her family left Monday morning, and my parents left yesterday afternoon."

"I didn't even tell them good-bye. They must think I'm a schmuck."

Emily bit her lip to keep from crying. She didn't have the emotional energy to deal with this right now.

"I'm going to make it up to you, Emily Duke. I promise."

But Emily didn't want a promise. She wanted a proposal. "We should get back to church. Bev and Nettie and Arlene'll be needing my help."

Chapter Thirteen: Attila the Honey

‖‖‖

Everyone returned to life as usual, but nothing seemed usual. The golden sunshine of early September that Rebecca adored appeared lackluster outside her bedroom window, and the rich aroma of harvest turned sour in Nettie's nose. Even the regular comforts disappointed. Evan's favorite herbs tasted bitter in his tea, and Alice's sewing machine sat lifeless on the table next to the flannel baby blanket she had started the week before. Jeremy returned to work, but the numbers on his computer screen kept blurring before his eyes. Emily threw herself into her fall-semester classes, but she couldn't remember any of her new students' names. Only Mrs. Scheinberg seemed able to keep on task.

"Arlene, do you have the bulletin ready for next Sunday?" Pastor Fletcher asked the following Thursday afternoon.

"It's warm on the copier, waiting for your review," she quipped from the comfort of her leather chair. "I even printed and trimmed more thank-you notes on some cardstock for you. I noticed you were getting low. They're sitting in your mailbox, and a new box of envelopes should arrive tomorrow morning, as well. Oh, and I ordered some more letterhead from that company you found on the Internet. They gave us a discount for opening a new account."

Pastor leaned against the doorframe of his study and considered the silver head of his church secretary. She wasn't usually so productive from day to day, but he had noticed a pattern of increased activity in Arlene directly following every funeral. Everyone had their own way of processing grief. He bowed his head and offered up a silent prayer for his pasture's surprisingly tenderhearted herd dog.

For her part, Mrs. Scheinberg didn't like to wallow in any kind of emotion, let alone painful ones. She preferred to put her hand to the plow. For this reason, she found herself sitting in the most uncomfortable of plastic chairs the following Tuesday night. She sat as upright as she could in the bucket seat, but no amount of shifting or maneuvering could keep her substantial polyester-shrouded hips from bulging over the sides of her chair like yeast bread in a loaf pan.

"Must *every* chair in this miserable place be fitted for only children and supermodels?" she groused.

Blaine Maler, who was reclining easily in his own bucket chair just to her left, eyed her silently.

"Don't even say it."

"I didn't say anything."

"You said it with your eyes."

Blaine looked nonplussed. "And what exactly are my eyes saying?"

"That I shouldn't have eaten that second piece of apple pie." Mrs. Scheinberg had served ham loaf, creamed peas, and buttered rolls to her young friend for supper, but she had also baked two apple pies for dessert. She was a firm believer that any and every meal should end with a bite—or two—of something sweet. "You have to realize, Mr. Skinny Pants, that not all of us have the metabolism of a black panther."

"They're called skinny *jeans*. And you're calling me a black panther? Really?"

"What? It's a perfectly respectable animal." Mrs. Scheinberg critically eyed Blaine's black T-shirt and jeans. "Maybe if you'd wear an actual color for a change, I'd consider upgrading you to a peacock or a red panda or some other exotic skinny animal."

"Black's a color. When's your doctor's appointment, anyway?"

"I don't have a doctor's appointment."

"What? Then why are we here?" Blaine glanced around Bradbury Regional's clinic and settled his gaze on a placard near the door that read "CPR for Sitters." He pointed to the sign and teased, "Are you opening a day care or something?"

Mrs. Scheinberg didn't answer.

Blaine stared at her. "We're not here for this course, are we?"

Mrs. Scheinberg allowed her gold-rimmed glasses to dangle freely from the knitted chain hanging around her neck and busied herself digging through her quilted bag for her Blistex.

"Oh, no." Blaine shook his head emphatically, standing up and grabbing his hoodie. The long, metal chain that looped from his belt to his back pocket clanged noisily against the plastic chair. "When you asked me to come with you to the hospital, I thought maybe you needed a ride home after a checkup or something. You said nothing to me about taking a class."

Mrs. Scheinberg looked around the room. There were only three other people currently imprisoned in bucket seats, and she was determined to make it through the entire evening unnoticed by any of them. Blaine's extroverted chain, however, had already drawn their attention. "Sit down," she entreated.

Blaine was quiet, but he was resolved. "I'm a college student, remember? I take classes every day. I don't have the headspace for this."

"*Please*, sit down."

"You can't be serious, Arlene. A course for babysitters?"

Mrs. Scheinberg tried a different approach. "I'll make you cinnamon rolls tomorrow if you stay."

Blaine held his hoodie at the ready, but he did plop back down into his seat with a metallic clunk. "I thought you were cracked last month when you talked me into using that post-hole-digger thing in your pasture, but this is certifiably crazy. No one in this town's ever going to ask me to babysit their children." He gave her an impish look. "I'm a black panther, remember?"

"Every man should know how to dig a good post hole." Mrs. Scheinberg pulled two knitting needles out of her bag and began click-clacking her way through the fourth row of a green-and-yellow cotton dishrag. She always had an easier time talking to yarn than to people. Yarn never argued back. "Besides, this course is for me, not you. I just didn't want to come here alone."

"What do you mean?"

"Now, don't go breathing a word of this to Bev or Candice," she murmured, "but I'm getting certified in CPR."

"Why? You live alone."

"I didn't *always* live alone, you know," she muttered.

Blaine did know. "I'm sorry. That was dumb."

Mrs. Scheinberg tossed her needles down into her bag after completing only one row. "Oh, maybe you're right."

"About what?"

"I'm too old for this."

"I never said that."

"Your eyes did."

Blaine sighed. "Stop putting words in my eyes—mouth—whatever."

Mrs. Scheinberg slung her bag over her shoulder and began rocking back and forth to build enough momentum to push herself out of her chair.

"I think you *should* get certified," he said.

Mrs. Scheinberg abandoned her unsuccessful rocking routine and, instead, tried scooting herself over the front edge of the stubborn chair.

Blaine monitored her lack of progress. "What if I choke or something at your house? You should learn how to deal with that kind of stuff."

Mrs. Scheinberg put her hands on either side of the chair to get more lift.

"I'll get certified too, if you stay."

Mrs. Scheinberg sank back down into the scoop of the chair. She tried looking disgruntled, but she couldn't keep the telltale happy color from creeping up her neck. "This *insidious* chair is going to be the death of me."

"No, it won't," Blaine grinned, "because I'm about to learn how to resuscitate you."

Mrs. Scheinberg cracked a smile.

Just then, a short woman with curly red hair bounced into the room. She was toting a blue bag on her back that was half the size of her petite frame. "Good evening, everyone! I'm Anna Cecilia Martin. I'm your instructor for this evening."

Blaine quickly leaned over. "And I want cream cheese frosting on those cinnamon rolls," he whispered.

Mrs. Scheinberg's smile grew even wider.

"On behalf of Bradbury Regional, I'd like to welcome you to our CPR for Sitters program," Anna Cecilia beamed, her brown eyes reflecting all of the unrealized potential sitting in the room. She pulled out a clipboard and consulted her list. "It looks like we have three youngsters signed up for our course. Kelly Bogel . . ." She nodded to the preteen girl with a long brown ponytail who was sitting next to a mousy, middle-aged woman who must have been the girl's mother. "And Shondra Wilson . . ." A teenage girl in electric-blue leggings raised her hand. "And Arlene Scheinberg."

Blaine pointed his thumb to his right.

"Oh." Anna Cecilia looked confused. "Is this Arlene? Is she your grandmother? Can you hear me, Arlene?"

Blaine covered his mouth with his hand.

"I can hear you perfectly fine, Anna," Mrs. Scheinberg answered for herself.

"Anna *Cecilia*, please," the instructor corrected.

"Excuse me, Anna *Cecilia*." Mrs. Scheinberg cleared her throat. The very sound of the Tinkerbell-woman's high-pitched voice flooded her system with cortisol. She felt her face growing red and splotchy in the way that it did whenever her blood pressure spiked.

Anna Cecilia looked down at her clipboard and frowned. "I don't understand. This course is for babysitters seeking certification for CPR."

"Yes."

"Are you a babysitter?" She looked skeptical. "Oh, you must be here on behalf of a grandchild at home or something. Well, I'm afraid that all individuals seeking certification must be physically present for the training. Or did you actually mean to register this young man here? I suppose the forms can be confusing for some people."

Mrs. Scheinberg coolly eyed the little twit standing at the front of the room. She resembled one of those furry, yappy dogs that jump two feet off the ground and nip at people's knees, barking as if they are the biggest dogs in the yard, but weigh no more than a cloud.

"Young lady," she began.

Blaine sank deeper into his chair.

"I am certainly *not* confused," Mrs. Scheinberg continued, "and I most definitely am not so senile as to misrepresent myself on a registration form. The kind operator named Wanda who spoke to me on the phone this morning assured me that I was more than welcome to participate in this class, varicose veins or not."

Anna Cecilia blinked once. "Well, I honestly have some concerns about your ability to complete the course. I designed this course myself specifically for preteens and teens. We'll be spending a good portion of the class on our knees, and a considerable amount of shoulder strength is required to administer chest compressions."

Mrs. Scheinberg wondered if yappy dog tasted better in the Crock-Pot or on toast. "I have lived by myself on a working farm longer than you or these two young ladies have been alive. My shoulder strength is fine."

Blaine quickly came to the rescue. "My name is Blaine Maler. I have not registered, but I would like to take the course."

Anna Cecilia pursed her lips, clearly not happy to have her carefully laid plans thus thwarted, but she squeezed out a squinty smile for Blaine's sake and took his information while Mrs. Scheinberg silently stewed in her bucket seat.

"All right, then." Anna Cecilia capped her pen when she was finished and unzipped her blue bag. She pulled out the torso of a training mannequin and laid it on a table. "We're going to start with the ABCs of cardiopulmonary resuscitation: airway, breathing, and circulation. I'm going to demonstrate how to use these ABCs to assess our friend here, Little Anne. Everyone say, 'Hello, Anne!'"

Mrs. Scheinberg moved to gather her bag once more.

"Where do you think you're going?" Blaine whispered.

"Choking would be better than this."

"Excuse me?" Anna Cecilia's pinched voice called out across the room. "I must ask that you be quiet, Arlene. Whenever you are *speaking*, I know that you are not *listening*, and you are keeping someone *else* from listening, as well."

Kelly's mousy mom shot a reprimanding look at Mrs. Scheinberg.

"Now," Anna Cecilia continued, "if we may be allowed to continue. Everyone gather 'round Little Anne. Arlene, do you need some help?"

Mrs. Scheinberg mumbled something colorful under her breath, but with Blaine's assistance, she managed to successfully push her frame up out of the chair. Her bloodless feet were too tingly and numb to properly hold her weight, however, so she shambled rather than walked to the front of the room. Anna Cecilia met her halfway.

"Here, honey, let me help you."

Mrs. Scheinberg might have been down, but she wasn't out. She pulled back her proud, matronly shoulders and lifted her chin high. "Only one person in the world has ever called me 'honey,' and he earned that privilege with a marriage proposal. You, young lady," she said, putting her glasses on the end of her nose and peering over their golden rims at the red-haired pixie, "may call me *Mrs. Scheinberg*."

⁓⁓⁓⁓⁓⁓⁓⁓⁓⁓⁓⁓⁓⁓⁓⁓⁓⁓⁓⁓

Two hours later, Mrs. Scheinberg and Blaine walked out of Bradbury Regional with two new CPR certification cards in their pockets.

"Why do I feel like I just flew back from Never Never Land?" Mrs. Scheinberg asked, backing her rear into the driver's seat of her Grand Marquis. "That girl was half fairy, half crocodile, and half pirate."

"That's one and a half," Blaine pointed out.

Mrs. Scheinberg ignored the impromptu audit. "I suppose it's all worth it, but I'm going to need at least one more piece of pie tonight before I fall asleep. All I can taste is Little Anne's recycled air in my mouth." She tried to make a show of being grumpy, but she was secretly pleased with herself. She was now CPR certified for the first time in her life. Dean would have been so proud. She smiled in spite of herself. "Hey, do you mind if we make a quick stop before I drop you off at your dorm?"

Blaine shook his head.

A few minutes later, they pulled up in front of the Joneses' house. Mrs. Scheinberg extricated herself from the driver's seat and rang the doorbell with the second apple pie in hand.

"Mrs. Shinebug!" Robbie cried, answering the door. He was standing barefoot in the entryway in a pair of mismatched pajamas and a John Deere cap. "Mom and Aly're asleep, but Dad's letting us men stay up late. We're watchin' *Iron Man.* Have you seen it? It's awesome!"

Mrs. Scheinberg followed Jeremy into the kitchen with the pie, but Blaine stayed behind in the living room with the three boys. He stuffed his hands into his pockets.

"Is that chain for your dog?" Robbie asked, pointing to Blaine's pants.

"I don't have a dog."

"My best friend Ben has a chain *and* a dog."

"Robbie," Davie rolled his eyes, "no one cares about Ben."

"He has chickens too," Robbie ignored his older brother. "I helped him cut off one of their heads. You shoulda been there. I got blood on my clothes and everything. Didja know my sister died?"

Blaine nodded.

"My mom's sad. She sleeps a lot."

"My mom sleeps a lot too."

"Did your sister die?"

"No."

"Then why does your mom sleep?"

Blaine shifted his weight from his right foot to his left. "She's sad."

"Wait a second!" Robbie turned on his heel and sprinted up the stairs, returning a few moments later with a small, fuzzy lamb. He held it out to Blaine.

"What's this?"

"It's a lamb."

"What for?"

"For your mom. To make her happy."

Blaine's eyes stung uncomfortably. He shifted his weight again.

"Grammy took us to the store one day to pick out something for Emma. That was before she died," Robbie explained. "Emma's with Jesus now, so she doesn't need a lamb. She's already happy. Here, take it."

Blaine took the lamb and glanced over at the two other Jones boys sitting on the couch. They were unnaturally quiet. He reached behind his back and swiftly unhooked his chain from his belt loop and wallet. He held it out to Robbie. "Here."

"What? For me?"

"For all of you. To share."

"Cool!" The other boys immediately jumped off the couch and crowded around the chain.

"We can make a zip line with it in the backyard," Davie suggested.

"Or maybe Dad'll get us a dog to put at the end of it," Frankie dreamed.

"Or we could use it to chain up bad guys in the garage," Robbie grinned.

Blaine didn't really care what they did with it. He just wanted the boys to be happier than he was.

Chapter Fourteen:

A Question of Orientation

∥∥∥

Blaine Maler was in his senior year at Bradbury College, and he still couldn't get over the fact that the college's total student enrollment amounted to less than that of his high school graduating class. Even more baffling to him was the fact that the entire population of the town of Bradbury itself was only half that of the neighborhood in Chicago where he grew up. Transferring from Northwestern University to BC in the middle of his sophomore year had felt a bit like jumping off a speeding train and landing on a tractor. At the time, he had been trying to escape the soap opera of his father's adulterous affair, and his scorned mother's alma mater had seemed like the perfect place to hole up and hide.

For the most part, Blaine enjoyed small-town life. The fresh air was nice, the people were friendly, and the coffee was definitely cheaper, but the silence was sometimes unnerving. He often took long walks in the country after practicing late at night, and on the rare occasion that he heard something other than a reckless trucker jake braking fast at the four-way stop some five miles down the Fancy Grove blacktop, it was usually the spooky yelp of a lone coyote in a nearby field or the creepy squeak of a bat flying overhead. Walking down a Chicago street at night, he never would have heard a truck or a wild animal from miles away.

For Blaine, the biggest difference between small-town living and the hustle and bustle of life in Chicago was that he could go about his days completely unnoticed in the city—just another anonymous face in the crowd—but here in Bradbury, there were barely enough people to make a cluster, let alone a crowd. Blaine couldn't change his shirt or cut his hair or push a different button on the soda fountain in the cafeteria without causing a stir.

"Out of Pepsi, are we?"

Blaine looked up from his tray into a pair of flashy green eyes. "No."

"But you've got orange juice," Martin Green, a fellow senior and music major at BC, astutely observed. He filled his own plastic cup with 7-Up. "I've never seen you drink anything but Pepsi since you migrated from Northwestern."

"My throat is sore."

"Ah, staying out too late, are we?" Martin sang, giving him a saucy wink. "Up to no good?"

Blaine ignored the loaded questions and turned to find a table. He and Martin weren't exactly close friends, but they weren't strangers, either. They'd shared a few classes last year.

"Now, don't you ignore me, Blaine Maler," Martin trilled, shadowing him to a corner table and dropping himself into an empty seat directly across from Blaine. "I know where you live. So spill it. Why haven't I seen you at any of Michelle and Hayden's parties this summer? And don't you tell me it's because you've been practicing. No one practices that much."

"I do." Blaine picked up the burrito from his plate and started eating. "You should too."

"Oh-*ho!*" Martin put his hand to his chest, feigning offense, but his cheeks did burn a bit brighter at the truth. "Well, we can't all be Glenn Gould, can we?"

Blaine chewed and swallowed, not bothering to look up from his plate. He liked Martin well enough, but he thought him a bit of a flake. Maybe if Blaine were in a better mood, he might be more willing to laugh and joke around, but he was feeling too sour today to be teased. His phone suddenly vibrated loudly on the table. He turned it facedown, ignoring it.

"Listen," Martin said, meticulously picking the tiny barcode sticker off of his orange, "I thought you might want to consider a new job opportunity."

Blaine kept chewing.

"Don't you even want to know what it is?"

"I don't have time for another job. Besides, Bronson told me that if I take on anything else, I'll lose my position as Finnegan's studio accompanist. That means you'd have to find another pianist for your recital."

"Tut-tut," Martin clucked. "Point taken, but you'd have more time if you dropped that Lutheranville gig."

Blaine took another bite out of his burrito.

"C'mon, Blaine. We both know those misers pay you squat, and they're bigots to boot. You owe them no allegiance."

"I get to work with Dr. Duke."

"You get to work with her here at school."

"Not on church music."

"Since when do you care so much about church?"

"I don't care about church. I care about the *music.*"

Martin tossed a piece of orange peel onto his tray. "That's all fine and good, Van Cliburn, but the Lutherans'll tar and feather you once they find out."

Blaine looked up. "Find out what?"

Martin winked and rested a hand suggestively on Blaine's arm. "That you're in love with me."

Blaine eyed Martin coolly for a silent moment before standing up and hooking his bag over his shoulder. "I've got to practice."

"Suit yourself, lover boy," Martin sang, "but you know where to find me when you get tired of those Reformation racists. I'm leading Presby's worship team now, and they're looking for a keyboardist. I'll put in a good word for you."

"Don't bother." Blaine secretly loathed praise-and-worship music and all of its mind-numbing repetition. No church could pay him enough to play the same five chords over and over again, song after song, week after week. He picked up his tray.

"Oh, c'mon. You'd love it there, I swear. They pay more." Martin sucked a renegade drop of orange juice off of his thumb. "And they won't judge you for being *you*."

Blaine shook his head and walked his tray over to a receptacle. Martin was always trying to get a rise out of him, but Blaine had to admit that the thought of more money was appealing. *They won't judge you* . . . Martin's words rang in his ears as he trudged through the light autumnal rain toward McPherson Hall. Blaine thought back to last Christmas Eve at Zion, when Evan Ebner had publicly accused him of trying to seduce young Robbie Jones. His cheeks burned at the memory. But then, Dr. Duke had only ever treated him with kindness and respect, and Mrs. Scheinberg had taken a week off of work to drive him all the way to Chicago last spring when he'd had to testify in his parents' divorce trial. And the church secretary had been inviting him over to her house for supper every Tuesday night since. If those two women of Zion were judgmental, they had a strange way of showing it.

Blaine shrugged off his unease. What did it matter, anyway? Everyone was judgmental in some respect, even Martin. Hadn't the self-righteous tenor just trashed a whole sect of the town with his accusations? Besides, if these Bradbury Lutherans were indeed bigots, Blaine was confident he could handle them. He'd noticed that they weren't completely innocent when it came to the topic of personal preferences, for they had some pretty strange predilections of their own.

For example, on more than one occasion, Blaine had witnessed the ladies of Zion Lutheran Church adding bizarre ingredients to their Jell-O, like shredded carrots, chopped celery, and marshmallows—often at the same time. And they had a compulsive habit of grinding meat and unnaturally reshaping it into loaves. They also used gravy as a condiment, cream of mushroom soup as a roux, and Tater Tots as a garnish for practically every casserole. The women even added—horror of horrors—canned tuna to their pizza!

"It's the economical choice," Mrs. Scheinberg had pontificated to Blaine over her gold-rimmed glasses one Tuesday evening as she'd set a homemade pizza before him that reeked of the sea. Blaine hadn't bought into her Bradburian brand of economics at the time, however. He knew pizza apostasy when he saw it. He was a Chicagoan, after all.

Even quirkier than their culinary palette was their strange, secret-order language. It took Blaine three full months of working as Zion's choir accompanist before finally realizing that "Page 15" was actually a reference to a liturgical service found on page 184 of their burgundy-colored hymnal. He was also surprised to learn that "Walther League" was the name not of a local baseball team but of some cherished youth group from generations past, and that "Lutheran beverage" was code for beer. And it seemed that the word "Concordia" was to Lutherans what "Philadelphia" was to Quakers. They pasted it on every book, magazine, building, city, and educational institution they could, and they made sure the lettering was displayed in either burgundy or gold.

The quality that most likely ruffled Martin's feathers, however, was not the Lutherans' propensity for weird salads and hot dishes but their stubborn, unbending—maybe even ruthless—worldview. Just last month, the women of Zion had practically put a man named Karl Rincker in the stocks for eating two doughnuts in the fellowship hall while paying for only one. But then five minutes later, those same women turned their purses inside out to pool money for one of their own whose hospital debt was unpaid. One minute they were tyrants, the next they were saviors. Blaine shook his head. However perplexing, these Lutherans seemed to be a considerate people, and he liked them. In just a few months, he had learned that they were sincere in their affections, loyal in their allegiances, and devoted to their doctrine—even when they didn't always understand it. For instance, that old lady Nettie Schmidt had once made eye contact with him over her strawberry jam–filled doughnut in the fellowship hall one Sunday after church and whispered, "Babies have faith, don't you think?"

Blaine hadn't known what to say in response to her bizarre question, so he'd just done what he'd seen other people do when Nettie singled them out. He nodded his head and backed away slowly.

There was one area of personal taste where Blaine happened to be in full agreement with the Lutherans. He'd heard other churchgoers around Bradbury accusing members of Zion of being "liturgical nazis" because of their persistent use of the historic Ordinary and Propers, but repetition and routine made sense to a musician such as Blaine. Practicing was how anyone got to really know anything. As a pianist, he'd never be able to perform any of the great composers if he didn't take the time to learn their works and then replay them often to keep them fresh in his mind. If Lutherans truly believed Jesus to be the "Author and Perfecter" of their faith, like the pastor kept saying during their church services, why wouldn't they set His words to music and then sing them week after week for the same reasons?

Blaine's phone buzzed annoyingly in his pocket, yanking him back to real time. He pulled it out and scowled at the text:

It's Dad. Call me.

"Hell, no," Blaine muttered. He shoved his phone back in his pocket and dropped his bag on the floor of his chosen practice room, the one with the Steinway upright. He opened the lid of the black lacquer piano and ran his fingers over the worn keys. BC's music department could only afford Baldwins and Yamahas for their practice rooms, but a rich alumnus had donated this Steinway years ago. Blaine had come to think of it as his own.

His phone buzzed again.

Please. I want to talk.

Blaine felt his blood begin to boil. His father had been texting him several times a day, every day, all summer long. Earlier in the year, the charlatan had been perfectly content to ignore him completely, but ever since his parents' divorce had been finalized last spring, his father hovered over him like a pesky, blood-sucking fly. At first, Blaine had tried blocking him from his phone, but he couldn't afford the fee his cellular company charged for such discrimination. Then, Blaine seriously considered powering off his phone during the day, but if his

mom ever called, she did it in the late morning or early afternoon. He didn't want to miss any of her calls. They were so rare.

Blaine sat on the bench and took a deep, calming breath.
This afternoon, it was going to be just him and Rachmaninov.
His cheat of a father could rot in hell. Blaine rolled his shoulders
backward and down and stretched his back before resting his
hands on the keyboard and digging into his scales. There were
a couple of modes in particular that he wanted to work into his
fingers before tackling the third movement of the sonata.

Buzz.

```
Come on, son. This is ridiculous.
You can't ignore me forever.
```

"Yes, I can," Blaine mumbled under his breath, jumping up
from the bench and ripping open his practice room door. He
chucked his phone as hard as he could against the far wall, almost hitting a cleaning lady who happened to be emptying a
trash can in the hallway. She flinched, ducking her head defensively. The phone bounced off the wall just above her neck and
landed with a dull thud on the floor beside her right foot.

Blaine rushed over to apologize. "I'm so sorry. I wasn't
looking."

The lady straightened up, and Blaine was surprised to see
that she was much younger than he'd originally thought. *She
must be a student worker or something.* She picked up the phone, still
in one piece thanks to its protective case, and silently handed it
over to Blaine.

"It . . . slipped out of my hand," he mumbled, knowing his
excuse sounded as lame as he felt.

The student worker adjusted her black plastic eyeglasses on
her nose and tucked a lock of dark, chin-length hair behind an
ear. "I hate it when that happens."

"Yeah. Well. Thanks."

The girl nodded and returned to her task.

Blaine stood there for a moment, watching her work. Then, before he could stop himself, he spoke. "Hey, I haven't seen you before. Are you a music student?"

She shook her head.

Blaine thought he knew everyone on campus. "Did you just transfer in?"

"No."

"Why haven't I seen you?"

"I take night classes." She shook out a new plastic liner for the trash can.

Blaine studied her profile thoughtfully. Night classes at BC were usually reserved for adult students, and he couldn't think of a polite way to say that she looked way too young to be in any adult learning program.

His phone began buzzing obnoxiously again in his hand. He squeezed it tightly at his side, eyeing the freshly emptied trash can hungrily.

"Hold onto that phone," the girl smiled, her dark, almond-shaped eyes flickering with a quiet humor. It was almost as if she could see exactly what he was thinking.

"Yeah. Sure. I'll do that."

CHAPTER FIFTEEN: WITH ANTHEMS SWEET

IIIIIIIIIIIIIIIIIIIIIIIIIIIIIIIIIIIIIIIIIIIIIIIIIIIIIIIIIIIIIIII

"Now, I'm not saying that Glenda and Brenda *shouldn't* sit by each other, but those old gals have been best friends since they were schoolgirls, and they'll chit-chat back and forth the whole time as if choir rehearsal were no different than the county fair. It's always 'How're your pickles?' and 'Did you finish that table runner?' and 'Have you seen Iris's tomatoes?' from downbeat to cutoff. I once heard them talking about breakfast cereal. Can you imagine? *Breakfast cereal!* While rehearsing John Rutter's *Gloria!* I'm telling you, they'll distract everybody and drive you absolutely mad before the evening is out, so you might as well save yourself the headache and sit them on opposite ends of the soprano line. Now, Simon and Shelley Hopf won't give you a lick of trouble, and their daughter Mary is an absolute doll—she was adopted, of course. But it'll cost you the entire rehearsal if you sit Gina Probst next to my Olive. Gina is a clinical gum-smacker, and Olive simply can't abide the sound of loose saliva sloshing around inside of someone else's cheeks. If Olive gets nauseous, she'll up and leave, and there goes your soprano section."

Emily's eyes glazed over like a Casey's doughnut. Estella Wagner, St. Luke's longtime choir director and resident queen bee, was giving her the buzz on every singer in Hamburg whether she wanted to hear it or not.

"Now, Forest Reynolds is an okay guy, but he sometimes comes to rehearsal with a few too many in his system, if you know what I mean. The good news is that when he's drunk, he sings like an Irish Dean Martin, but when he's sober—well, let's just say that his pitch could sink the Titanic faster than an iceberg. I suggest you sit him next to Dwight Holley. Dwight is a rock—always has been and always will be—and he knows how to handle Forest, sober or not. And then Pastor Douglas will sit on Forest's other side. Pastor's actually a bass, but he and I have an unspoken understanding that he'll travel depending on which way Forest's leaning. Oh, I almost forgot about Joe and the Kull sisters. . . ."

Emily did her best to maintain an interested expression on her face, but inside she was dying. Estella had been talking nonstop since the moment she had first arrived on the scene twenty-five minutes before, and the forceful, chatty matron was showing no sign of running out of steam.

"Now, I'll keep Charlene and Betty in line, like always—you don't mind if I sit in the alto section, do you? I can sing soprano if you insist, but a woman's voice does tend to settle at my age, if you know what I mean, and we already have enough sopranos, unless you bring too many altos from Zion." Estella ran an authoritative, bejeweled hand along her remarkably long neck. She was a stately woman, taller than most men Emily knew, and she was considerably leaner in her shoulders than in her hips, making her look a bit like a decanter of Burgundy in her maroon pantsuit. Her hair was dyed an unnatural shade of black, and her nails, impeccably trimmed and polished, were painted to match the roses in her floral chiffon scarf. She was an impressive, imposing figure, and she seemed to know it. "Anyway,

Louise is the one you should worry about. She has always re-fused to listen to anything I say. For years I've tried explaining to that woman that she's not really a tenor, but she simply won't listen. She just smiles at me and says that she wants to sing the tenor part because—" Estella's voice suddenly took on an unat-tractive tone as she attempted to imitate poor Louise. "'That's the part my grandfather always used to sing.' Well, what can a musician do? I can't *force* her to be sensible, and it's not like I can dock her pay, can I? That's just part of the cross we directors bear in working with volunteers, don't you think?"

Emily silently prayed for deliverance.

"Now, you're the director, of course, so by all means, please, do what *you* think is best. I just thought you should be prepared, if you know what I mean. Of course, I'm not trying to tell you what to do. I wouldn't *dream* of it, but I do think it would be best if you used a seating chart for the cantata. Oh, and that reminds me. I suppose you'll want to use my music stand, won't you? Now, you should know that it sometimes gets stuck when the humidity is high, but if you just . . ."

Emily thought that perhaps she had made a mistake in asking St. Luke's to host the cantata this year. She had hoped her offer would serve as an olive branch of sorts—something to smooth over that awkward, sloshy blip from the last cantata at Grace Lutheran in Fancy Grove seventeen years before—but Estella seemed quite recovered from any scandal. In fact, the woman appeared unflappable. Emily's only concern was wheth-er or not Estella could sit through a rehearsal that she herself wasn't directing.

"'Though rosy lips and cheeks,'" a deep, Shakespearean voice merrily quoted somewhere behind Emily's left ear, "'with-in his bending sickle's compass come.'"

Zachary!

Emily, rosy as a sonnet, spun around and grinned at her colleague and friend. She could have hugged the English lit professor for all of the joy and relief she felt at his timely arrival. "You came!"

"Of course I came," Zachary Brandt laughed, his sandy hair perfectly framing a pair of dark eyes, "and I brought your pianist with me."

Blaine put his phone in his back pocket and gave a small wave.

"I thought you weren't going to be able to make it all the way out to Hamburg for rehearsals on Thursdays. Aren't you teaching a night class this fall?"

"Well, 'the man that hath no music in himself,'" Zachary quoted the Bard again, "'is fit for treasons, stratagems, and spoils.' That, and my class didn't make."

"Is it bad that I'm glad?" Emily smiled sheepishly. "I can't tell you how happy I am that you'll be singing with us for the cantata. Well, it's really going to be more of a festival of lessons and carols than a cantata, but we'll get into all of that later. Tell me. How was your summer across the pond?"

"Wordy," Zachary said. "I got the bits I needed for my book at least, so that was good. How about you? Anything exciting happen here in good ol' Bradbury?"

Emily caught Zachary not-so-discreetly glancing down toward her ringless left hand. "No," she said, self-consciously hiding both hands behind her back. "I just taught some private lessons and worked in my garden."

Estella cleared her throat.

"Oh, excuse me." Emily stepped aside and gestured toward the grand lady-in-waiting. "Mrs. Wagner, this is Dr. Zachary Brandt. He sings bass in my choir at Zion, and this is Blaine Maler, my accompanist."

As Estella succumbed to Zachary's inevitable charms and narrowed her eyes critically at Blaine's quiet quirks, Emily turned to welcome the other singers trickling into St. Luke's nave. Most of them were people she didn't recognize, and the majority, judging by their familiarity with Estella and the space, were from St. Luke's. The handful of politely distant singers milling about at the edge of the group were from Fancy Grove, Emily assumed. She couldn't help but wave excitedly as some familiar faces came through the door. Evan and Alice walked in first.

"Rebecca's not coming," Alice was quick to explain. "She's just not ready yet. Too tired, I think."

Emily thought Alice looked a bit too tired and worn down to be rehearsing herself, but she was careful not to say as much.

Candice and Caroline Bradbury entered next, followed by Marge Johnson, Zion's resident warbler. Lois Kull, having car-pooled with Irv and Bev Davis, caused quite a scene with her entrance. Opal and Teresa—"the Kull sisters," as Estella had called them earlier—happened to be Lois's grown nieces, and they squealed and clapped and hugged their aunt as if they were little girls. Lois, never having had any children of her own, practically glowed at the show of affection.

"We tried picking up Phyllis and Irene along the way," Bev explained, "but they decided to sit this season out. Neither of them likes to be out after dark, you know."

Emily nodded. "And the Koelster sisters said they'll be coming late each week, after the dinner rush. Otherwise, our whole lot should be here."

Emily noticed, however, that Mrs. Scheinberg was conspicuously absent. Alice seemed to notice too.

"She'll be here, dear. I'm sure she's on her way."

Emily looked out over her large choir, thirty-three in all, not counting herself, Blaine, and Zion's missing few. Everyone in attendance was sitting clustered together in a section of pews situated perpendicular to the nave. St. Luke's, as a whole, was cruciform in shape. The nave, lined with red-cushioned pews, made up the majority of the length of the cross, while the chancel sat at its head. Two arms extended to the right and left of the nave just where the front row of pews gave way to the chancel steps. The open area extending to the right of the pulpit was packed with boom stands, monitors, a drum set, a veneer-covered Clavinova, and various other electronic instruments and amplifiers well suited for St. Luke's eleven o'clock contemporary service. The open space extending to the left was filled with four pulpit-facing pews, an organ console, and an upright piano. The members of St. Luke's, not having a balcony with a choir loft, referred to this area as their choir nook. It was here that the cantata choir was meeting to rehearse from week to week.

Emily clapped her hands lightly to get everyone's attention. "Welcome! My name is Emily Duke. Most of you probably don't know me, but I'm the new choir director over at Zion in Bradbury. I'll be directing this year's joint cantata."

The singers quickly settled down and faced their blonde director expectantly.

"It's a joy for me to see this musical tradition being reestablished among our communities, and I'm hoping our weeks spent making music together will be as much of a blessing to all of you as it is sure to be to me and to everyone else who comes to hear you sing in December. I'd like to take a moment to thank Estella Wagner and our hosts here at St. Luke Lutheran Church—"

"Thank you!" Estella jumped in, standing up from her seat at the end of the alto section and extending her arms like Luciano

Pavarotti at curtain call, soaking up the applause of her adoring fans. Only, there was no applause. "We are truly honored to be hosting you here at St. Luke's, and I am certain that all of you are going to *love* the acoustics of our refurbished space. In case you missed them, the restrooms are in the narthex, just off of the main entrance, and the water fountains of old have been moved to the new Sunday School wing. I must remind you that this is a *dry* campus, so no alcohol may be brought onto the church property at *any* time." Apparently, Estella couldn't help getting in at least one small dig.

"Now," the matron continued, looking first to her right and then to her left while gesturing blithely toward Emily in the front, "I know what you all are thinking. How can such a young director possibly have enough experience to lead us cantata veterans?"

Make that two *small digs*, Emily thought.

"Well," Estella continued, "I'd like to remind you what the apostle Paul said to young Timothy: 'Let no one despise you for your youth.' Let's not despise the youth of Miss Duke—"

"*Dr.* Duke," a masculine voice interrupted from somewhere within the bass section.

Estella turned sharply toward the basses in search of the miscreant, her lips pressed in a thin line from the effort of restraining a scowl. "I see. *Dr.* Duke, then. Yes. Thank you, Evan. Well, I am sure we will all do our best to support Dr. Duke in her first year of directing the cantata. I know I will."

With that, Estella sat back down, leaving everyone else to marinate for a few uncomfortable moments in her awkward sauce.

Emily, unsure of how to recover from that mess of an introduction, took a calming breath and continued from where she had left off. "I imagine that most of you probably already know one another from singing together in years past, but I thought it might be nice if we started this evening by going around and introducing—or reintroducing—ourselves. Irv," Emily said, looking with pleading eyes toward her faithful bass, "would you please start? Tell us your name, where you live, and where you go to church."

Irv nodded and obediently began the introductions. Evan went next, and so it continued until everyone had taken a turn. Emily did her best to memorize each face as it was presented to her, but she knew that it was going to take some time for everyone's names to stick. That, and she was still reeling from her encounter with Hurricane Estella.

Nevertheless, in spite of all the chaos and stress, Emily was pleased to find that there was at least one face in the crowd that was going to be easy for her to remember. With a heart-shaped chin line, short black hair, and a warm complexion distinct from all of the Anglo-Saxons bobbing around the choir nook, this memorable young woman also shared Emily's mother's name.

"I'm Mary," she said, her voice as sweet as her face. "I'm a member here at St. Luke's, and I'm a soprano."

Emily couldn't help but notice from the corner of her eye that Blaine, ducking his head behind the soundboard of the Yamaha upright, was turning as red as one of the nearby pew cushions. He wordlessly reached up a lone hand to remove his phone from the top of the piano and set it somewhere out of sight.

"Well," Emily smiled at the eager faces before her, "I know that you have followed a cantata format in the past, but I thought we'd try something a little different with the program this year."

Estella's face immediately clouded with concern.

"Don't worry," Emily quickly assured, "we're going to sing lots of everyone's favorite Advent and Christmas tunes—'The

Night Will Soon Be Ending,' 'E'en So, Lord Jesus, Quickly Come,' 'Of the Father's Love Begotten,' and so on—but we're going to intersperse some Scripture readings between the songs to give the program more of a festival of lessons and carols feel. I chose songs that all of you can reprogram in your own church services on various Sundays throughout Advent and Christmas. . . ."

Emily's voice faltered. Her singers were no longer looking at her, but instead were focusing somewhere beyond her left shoulder. Emily turned to find Mrs. Scheinberg, chin held determinedly high, standing behind her, just beyond the choir nook.

"Arlene!" Emily called out a little too loudly, panicked that her friend might turn hightail and run if she didn't act fast. "Come on in! We've got room for you right here in the tenor section. Excuse me . . . um . . . Louise, right? Yes, I thought so. Do you think you could scoot a bit to your left? That's right, then Arlene can squeeze in at the end of the pew and—"

Emily stopped short, suddenly realizing that she was placing Arlene at the end of the tenor section, directly behind Estella. Everyone else noticed too.

"Arlene," Estella acknowledged coolly.

"Estella." Mrs. Scheinberg eyed her maroon nemesis evenly.

Emily felt like she was a child again, watching with anxious trepidation as her sister turned the handle of their antique jack-in-the-box. At any moment, a scary figure was going to jump out.

"You're tardy, as usual," Estella breathed.

"You're charming, as usual."

"Punctuality is close to godliness, you know."

"That's not exactly how the saying goes."

"Well," Estella sat tall in her seat, not even bothering to turn and watch as Mrs. Scheinberg lowered herself onto the pew directly behind her, "you missed my announcement earlier that St. Luke's is a *dry* campus."

Mrs. Scheinberg rolled her eyes behind Estella's back. "Then it's a good thing I left the booze at home."

"Right, then," Emily jumped in. "I think we should begin, don't you? Let's start with a word of prayer. Evan, would you please—?"

But Emily was interrupted once again. Another tardy singer came running up the side aisle to the choir nook, this one smaller and younger than Mrs. Scheinberg but just as spunky.

"I'm so, so sorry, everyone!" she sang. "I was teaching a class at the hospital and couldn't get away until my husband brought me my sweet Beatrice—that's our daughter—for her six o'clock feeding. Breast is best, you know."

Emily watched as Mrs. Scheinberg's already sour expression turned positively rancid. What in the world was going on?

"Have I missed anything? Oh, are you the director?" The tiny, vivacious woman with curly red hair extended a confident hand toward Emily, then turned to address the entire choir. "I'm Anna Cecilia Martin from Fancy Grove. I'll be singing alto. Where are the altos sitting? Over here? Well, would you look at that! Arlene! Do you sing too? Bless your heart, I had no idea that you were into music. Well, don't you worry, honey. I studied music in college before earning my nursing degree, so I can help you with the difficult parts."

Alice coughed spastically into her hand.

Mrs. Scheinberg's face turned yellow, then green, then gray as Anna Cecilia squeezed her minute frame into the small space between Estella—who refused to budge even an inch—and the end of the altos' pew, directly in front of Mrs. Scheinberg.

Anna Cecilia smiled encouragingly at Emily. "Please, go on."

Emily, openmouthed, did just that. She motioned silently for Evan to pray and then folded her hands and bowed her head to fervently petition that Jesus would hurry up and come again.

Tonight.

CHAPTER SIXTEEN: BY ANY OTHER NAME

"Is that really necessary?" Mrs. Scheinberg asked, watching as Bev meticulously unrolled a paper napkin from around one of the sets of silverware that had gone unused at the Ebner wedding dinner.

"These napkins are perfectly good, still," Bev defended. "It'd be a waste to throw them away."

"We're reusing them?"

"Technically, we never used them in the first place."

"Technically. But they're wrinkled. They look used."

"Well, that's what the iron is for."

Nettie waved happily from her spot in the back corner of the church kitchen. She was standing next to the ancient, rickety ironing board the Zion Lutheran Church Ladies Aid Society had purchased many years before for such a frugal time as this. "They'll be good as new, Arlene," she promised cheerfully. "Smooth as a baby's bottom."

"Thank you, Nettie," Mrs. Scheinberg said. "A baby's bottom is exactly what I want to picture every time I wipe my mouth." She turned back to Bev. "Don't you think this is all a bit labor-intensive when we have six new packages of paper napkins waiting to be used in the cabinet?"

"We're a mission society, Arlene," Bev reprimanded. "The more money we save, the more money we can give away."

Mrs. Scheinberg sighed deeply and shook her head, but in deference to her friend's altruistic heart, she said no more.

"Help me with these, will you, Arlene?" Candice asked. She was hugging eight plastic cottage cheese containers from the kitchen freezer against her bosom.

Mrs. Scheinberg reached out and helped Candice set the frozen containers onto the island counter where Alice, standing at the ready, began opening lids and dipping each of the containers, one at a time, in a bowl of steaming-hot water. Then, with a little bending and twisting, Alice prodded homemade blocks of ice out of the repurposed containers and into a large plastic tub.

"We could just buy bags of ice at Casey's, you know," Mrs. Scheinberg suggested, begrudgingly picking up a nearby ice pick and hacking at the frozen blocks until they broke into delicate, frosty shards.

"Now, where would be the fun in that?" Alice winked.

"You know as well as I do that we're all getting too old for this, Mrs. Ebner."

"Speak for yourself, Arlene," Alice smiled good-naturedly. "I happen to be in the prime of my life."

Even Mrs. Scheinberg, in all of her grouchy glory, couldn't argue with Zion's golden girl. Alice had a special way of turning even the prickliest of pears into something palatable. Mrs. Scheinberg acquiesced a wry smile.

"I'm telling you, it's a mistake," Candice quipped, taking the empty containers and refilling them with water from the tap.

"What's a mistake?" Bev asked. "The ice? Remember, we're a mission society—"

"No, no, no," Candice cut her off, clearly irritated that Bev wasn't keeping up. Candice had an annoying habit of beginning conversations midstream as if everyone else were already aware of what she was thinking. "Pastor Fletcher should never have scheduled a Baptism so soon. It's a mistake."

Mrs. Scheinberg frowned. "Baptisms are never a mistake."

"It's too soon, I'm telling you," Candice shook her head. "It's going to break Rebecca's heart."

"Rebecca's heart is already broken," Nettie reminded everyone from her post at the ironing board. She picked up another wrinkled paper napkin from Bev's pile and dutifully straightened it with her iron.

"Well, I think Rebecca's going to be thinking of her dead baby the whole time Yvonne's grandchild is at the font."

"We're all going to be thinking of *Emma*." Alice made a point of calling her granddaughter by name. "But at the same time, we'll be rejoicing with Yvonne in God's adoption of her grandbaby into His family. Arlene's right. Baptisms are never a mistake."

"Well," Candice clucked, "I think the whole thing shows a want in human decency!"

Mrs. Scheinberg rolled her eyes. Here it came.

"I mean, look at us!" Candice waved her hands dramatically around the room. "We're all *devastated* at the loss of Jenna—"

"*Emma*," Mrs. Scheinberg tersely corrected.

"Yes, Emma." Candice blinked innocently and then yammered on, quick to forgive her own bungles. "The Bible says there's a time for everything under the sunshine, right? Well, this is a time for mourning, not for celebrating. And we're not mourning like we're supposed to! Instead, we're standing in the church kitchen on a Sunday morning, getting ready to throw a party for another *baby*, of all things!" Candice pursed her lips. "Yvonne probably planned this whole luncheon thing on purpose. She just wants everyone to celebrate *her* family's good fortune."

"That's usually why we have luncheons, Candice," Mrs. Scheinberg pointed out. "We did the same for your family when your children were baptized."

"Yes, but that was the proper time for celebrating," Candice reasoned.

Mrs. Scheinberg shook her head in an attempt to stop the madness.

"Did you hear the baby's name?" Bev quickly changed the subject.

"No," Alice said. "What is it?"

"*John Wayne* Roe."

"How lovely!" Nettie smiled.

"How tacky." Candice stuck her nose in the air. "I suppose I should have bought the child a cowboy hat instead of a cross."

"Oh, there's no need," Nettie answered brightly, forever obtuse to sarcasm's subtleties. "I already knitted little Johnny a baptismal cap."

"He'll be dressed in camo and hunter orange, no doubt," Candice scoffed.

Mrs. Scheinberg immediately set down her ice pick and looked around the kitchen with feigned excitement. "Did Geraldine just walk through the door? I thought for sure I heard her voice just now."

Candice frowned at the church secretary. It was not a compliment to be compared with Miss Geraldine Turner, a particularly prissy former member of Zion.

"Well, Robbie made the flower arrangements for the altar today," Alice beamed, swiftly moving the conversation in a different direction.

"Oh, how nice!" Bev smiled. "What do they look like?"

"I haven't actually seen them, but—" All of a sudden, Alice backed away from the plastic tub on the counter and coughed politely over her right shoulder. She cleared her throat a couple of times and swallowed before turning back around to continue. "Excuse me. I'm so sorry. Is it just me, or is the pollen count atrocious this year? I told Evan the other night that I may have promised to marry him 'for better or for worse,' but I never said anything about 'in country or in town.' That man has more plants in his yard than there are cornstalks in the entire county of Bradbury. I can barely walk through his garden without coughing up a storm."

Bev handed her a tissue.

"Thank you, dear." Alice blew her nose before continuing. "Anyway, Robbie's taking flower arranging in 4-H, the dear boy, and he came out to the house yesterday to pick some flowers. You should have seen him and Evan with their pruners and buckets. They picked Queen Anne's lace and cockscombs and asters and mums and everything else they could find that was still blooming. Evan's never looked so happy. That man has really taken to being a grandpa."

"Mmm, it smells good in here." Pastor Fletcher stuck his head in the kitchen. He was already fully vested for the Sunday service. "Green bean casserole?"

"Meat loaf and mac 'n' cheese," Bev corrected, nodding toward the ovens.

"Even better! Anything I can do to help you ladies? Need a taste tester?"

Alice walked over to her pastor, her blue eyes suddenly watery with tears. "You can go baptize that precious baby."

Pastor reached out his arms and gave the grieving grandmother a long hug while the other ladies hung their heads in a respectful silence. They were all thinking about the precious baby who was no longer with them. Then, Pastor quietly slipped out of the kitchen to prepare for the service. Nettie folded the ironing board and returned it to the closet. Bev put the tub of freshly chipped ice back in the freezer, and Mrs. Scheinberg—with tears glistening in her eyes—listened as Alice generously explained to Candice, "See, dear? You were right. There is a time for everything. Only, this is one of those special times when we get to share in Yvonne's joy and Rebecca's sorrow all at the same time."

"'The Lord giveth, and the Lord taketh away,'" Mrs. Scheinberg murmured under her breath. "'Blessed be the name of the Lord.'"

The Baptism itself was beautiful. Pastor Fletcher, as always, choked up as he cradled the chubby baby in his arms, and as he leaned over the baptismal font, the crucifix he was wearing around his neck swung out and dangled enticingly over John Wayne's head. The baby boy—dressed in baptismal white, much to Candice's surprise—promptly reached out a chubby hand, grabbed hold of the image of his Savior's corpus, and held on with all of his might.

Bev's breath caught in her throat at the sight. She had no idea whether Rebecca's mourning heart would be able to rejoice in the poetic significance of the moment, but hers certainly did. She leaned over and nudged Irv with her elbow, whispering a line from her all-time favorite hymn: "'Nothing in my hand I bring; Simply to Thy cross I cling'" (*LSB* 761:3).

||||||||||||||||||||||||||||||||||||||||||||||||||

After the service, Mrs. Scheinberg found Robbie Jones hiding behind the guest book stand in the narthex.

"I heard you arranged the flowers for today."

Robbie tried to smile, but he couldn't quite get the corners of his mouth to turn upward.

"What's wrong?

Robbie shrugged.

Mrs. Scheinberg grew alarmed. Something was terribly wrong if Robbie Jones couldn't manage to speak a single word. That boy hadn't stopped talking since the moment the two had first bonded over her homemade cinnamon applesauce in the church office during Vacation Bible School last year. She bent her heavy frame forward to look the sensitive boy straight in the eye. "You can tell me."

His lower lip quivered. "I don't want anyone to know 'bout the flowers."

"Why?"

"Davie says it's gay."

Mrs. Scheinberg stood up straight and gave her young red-headed friend a stern look. "So what if it is? Why do you or Davie care so much?"

At the sight of Robbie's wounded tears, Mrs. Scheinberg softened a bit. But just a little bit.

"Now, listen to me, young man. Three quarters of the men in this congregation spend their waking hours working the ground, cultivating life out of the cursed soil, just so you and your older brother can eat cereal every morning and so your mama can have beauty outside her window to cheer her when she's sad. My own husband died trying to take care of our fields, and I've never known a stronger man. There's nothing so manly as working with plants, do you hear me?" Mrs. Scheinberg gave a definitive nod, glad to have that matter settled. "Now, tell me about your flowers."

Robbie obediently stepped out from behind the guest book stand, his mouth finally curling upward in a smile. He really did want to tell someone about his arrangements. "I used all kinda plants, Mrs. Shinebug. Pretty ones and manly ones and kid ones too. My new grandpa let me pick anything I wanted to out of his garden. There were chrysanthemoms—"

"Chrysanthe*mums*."

Robbie nodded. "Yeah. And cocksbrushes—"

"Cockscombs."

"That's what I said. And asteroids and goldenbars and . . ."

Mrs. Scheinberg shook her head, bemused. The boy was getting every single flower name wrong, but he was obviously so happy in his ignorance that she decided to let him talk without correction. What did it matter, anyway? Flowers—and Robbie Jones, come to think of it—by any other name would still be as sweet.

Chapter Seventeen: Ablaze!

"Emily, dear," Alice coughed over the phone, "I was wondering if you could come by the house this afternoon?"

"Are you sick?"

"No, dear, I'm fine. It's Rebecca."

"Is Rebecca sick?"

"Not exactly. She's— oh, I think you'd better just come and see for yourself."

Emily was knocking on the Ebners' door in eleven minutes flat.

"Thank you for coming," Alice hacked again, opening the red front door of their large Cape Cod–style house.

"Alice, I'm worried about that cough."

"Oh, don't be." Alice waved her hand dismissively, ushering Emily into the foyer and closing the door behind her. "I'm fine, dear, really. It's the harvest. It does this to me every year. My allergies can't take all of the field dust and," she said, lowering her voice significantly, "all of Evan's gardens."

"I heard that!" Evan hollered from somewhere within the kitchen.

Alice gave Emily a conspiratorial smile. "It'll all pass once the first freeze hits. Besides," and now she turned her face and hollered down the front hallway toward the kitchen, "Evan brews me the *best* medicinal teas in the world, morning, noon, and night! I've never had it so good!"

"That's more like it," Evan grinned, sticking his head around the kitchen doorframe and waving at Emily. "Speaking of tea, can I pour you a cup, Emily?"

"Maybe later, dear," Alice said, steering Emily toward the rear of the house. "She's here to see Rebecca first."

Alice led Emily over to a bay window that faced the back of the Ebners' sprawling property, where segments of luscious, green lawn could be seen interspersed with flower beds, vegetable gardens, a grove of fruit trees with a shade bench, and a trellised gazebo covered with Virginia creeper that was just beginning to turn red. Alice pointed to the remotest corner of the yard—near Evan's enormous compost pile—where Rebecca stood all by herself. She appeared to be ripping pages out of a book and tossing them into a nearby burn barrel.

"What's she doing?"

"That's the question, isn't it?" Alice said, absently brushing her fingers against the vibrant leaves of a nearby potted hibiscus. "I honestly have no idea, and I'm afraid to ask. She's a little sensitive to my pushing these days." Alice turned her bright eyes up toward Emily's pink cheeks. "I was hoping you could ask her."

A few moments later, Emily let herself out the back sliding door of the Ebner home and slowly made her way across the lawn toward Rebecca's agitated frame, stopping every so often to admire a fading aster or to brush her fingers against a feathery cedar bough or to monitor a bumblebee bobbing and weaving its way across the yard in the long shadows cast by the setting sun. She was taking her time, watching her friend from a respectful distance, being careful not to trespass too suddenly on what was most likely a private date with grief. Emily was all too keenly aware of the fact that Alice, not Rebecca, had invited her to this impromptu garden party.

"Hello."

Rebecca started, turning her face toward Emily for a brief, confused moment before returning her attention to her obsessive ripping. "My mother called you, didn't she?"

Emily didn't risk a lie. "Yes."

Rebecca bent over and picked up another book from the cardboard box at her feet. Up close, Emily saw that it was not actually a book but a notebook, a journal of some kind.

"Mother's worried that I'm going crazy." Rebecca tore out a fresh page, wadded it up, and tossed it toward the barrel. "I supposed you're worried too."

"I don't know yet. I'll tell you in a minute."

That caused a smile to flicker across Rebecca's face, but it faded quickly. "I don't really want to talk."

"Okay."

Emily lowered herself down onto the cool grass. Her arms ached to reach out and hug her suffering friend, but it was still too soon. She wrapped her arms around her own knees instead.

Grief's wrecking ball was making fast work of Rebecca's fortified defenses, that much was certain. The metaphysical attack was noiseless, but the country air practically quivered from the impact. Unspent emotion crackled from Rebecca's every pore, and she seemed unable to stand still. She ripped page after page out of her book, puckering her strawberry-blonde brow in fierce concentration, a fighter to the end, but grief had a way of wearing down even the strongest and firmest of human resolves. Emily watched and waited in silence.

"It makes me so angry, you know?" Rebecca caved just a little.

"What does?"

"Everyone's pity and concern."

Emily imagined that Alice's wrinkled, concerned face was peering at the two of them through her bay window that very moment.

"I already feel like I'm going to die." That last word sounded like it got caught on Rebecca's tongue. Her voice shook. "How can everyone expect me to bear their worries and concerns and sympathies on top of everything else? It's too much. I can't do it."

Emily didn't bother trying to explain away the whys and hows of everyone else's thoughts, words, and deeds. She simply hugged her knees and listened, letting the hard things in life be hard.

Rebecca, empowered by the silence, lifted her chin high in a final show of stubborn resistance, but her shoulders instinctively braced against grief's next big blow. "Did you get angry when Peter died?"

"I still get angry."

"Will this feeling ever go away?"

"Probably not today."

Rebecca's proud chin fell in utter defeat.

Now was the time for a hug. Emily stood and walked over to her friend, and Rebecca, exhausted from dodging and deflecting grief's relentless blows, dropped her book to the ground and crumbled against Emily's comforting shoulder.

"What did she look like?" Emily asked.

"She was perfect," Rebecca blurted.

"Red hair?"

"No, it was blonde. More like Aly's."

"And her face?"

Rebecca, safe in compassion's embrace, openly sobbed. "Just like my dad's."

Emily squeezed harder.

"I-I killed her," Rebecca confessed.

"No, you didn't. Sin and the brokenness of this wretched world killed her."

"I should have gone in sooner."

"There was no reason to go in sooner. You did exactly what you were supposed to do."

"She died inside of me."

Emily took a deep, steadying breath. "Yes. She did."

"My womb was her tomb!" Rebecca wailed like a child.

Emily alternately hugged and then held and then rocked her friend, humming hymns in her ear as she would to soothe a restless child. Eventually, Rebecca's weeping turned to sniffling, then her sniffling turned to sighing, and then her sighing—as so often happens in moments of extreme distress—turned to hysterics.

"Oh, Em!" Rebecca lifted her matted head from Emily's shoulder and snorted. "Look at you! I got snot all over your pretty blouse."

Emily released her friend and stepped back to properly assess the situation.

"It looks like you hugged a slug," Rebecca squawked.

"It's okay. I ruined a shirt or two with my own crying back in the day."

Rebecca rubbed her eyes hard with her hands and then swatted at her cheeks to try to sober up a bit. "Ugh, I'm a mess, Emily Duke. A big, slimy mess."

Emily bent over and picked up the book Rebecca had been holding. "What are you doing with all of these, anyway?"

Rebecca's cackles began anew. Suddenly, everything was very funny. "Oh, it's so dumb!"

"What is?"

"Well . . ." Rebecca took a deep breath, trying again to regain some control. "I was down in the basement this morning, putting away Emma's baby toys and clothes, and I came across this old box."

"What are they?"

"They're my old journals. Oh, don't give me that look, Emily Duke! You don't even know the half of it."

Emily grinned, happy to see her friend's usual spunk somewhat restored.

"There were twenty-two journals total—yeah, I know. Can we say *narcissistic*? I had originally kept them because I thought they'd make a nice record of my life—you know, something for the grandkids to read someday—but when I started flipping through them this morning, I was appalled to read what I'd written. I don't want anyone to read these. Ever. They're beyond embarrassing. I must have been the most vain, dramatic, emotional, overwrought teenager ever to walk the face of this earth. Everything was about how everyone else was so terrible and how I was so wonderful and how no one understood me, blah, blah, blah. I bear false witness on every page of these things, so I decided to burn them. All of them. Well, not *all* of them. I kept the ones where I wrote about Jeremy."

"So we're having a book burning?"

"You think I'm crazy, don't you? You think I shouldn't do this?"

Emily turned to her friend, wiggled her eyebrows, and ripped a gigantic handful of pages out of a hapless journal. "Oh, we're so totally gonna do this!"

Rebecca giggled, then chuckled, then threw her head back and guffawed.

Twenty minutes later, when all of the stripped journals were ablaze in the bin, Rebecca stepped back and stared at the dancing flames. The jovial mood had passed, and the tortured thoughts waited hungrily along the edge of the flickering light.

"I was going crazy in my head," Rebecca reflected. "When I saw that box in the basement this morning, something in me kind of snapped. I was tired of feeling so much. I just wanted to *do* something, you know?"

Emily did know. She picked up a big stick and poked at the fire, feeling a special kinship with Rebecca in her suffering. "I don't think I ever told you. When I stayed with Nicole and Brad for a while after Peter died, they kept *whispering* all of the time. They didn't even realize they were doing it, but whenever I sat with them on the couch or helped them in the kitchen, they always lowered their voices. It was like all of life had suddenly become a perpetual wake. I know they meant well, but it drove me crazy."

"Yes!" Rebecca said. "I know exactly what you mean. Everyone's been tiptoeing around me like we're still at the funeral. I know they're all trying to be sensitive or whatever, but it makes everything so much worse. It makes me remember that—" Rebecca swallowed. Some things were so hard to say out loud. "—that Emma is dead to this world."

Emily nodded thoughtfully.

"I'd much rather remember that she's alive in Jesus, you know?"

"Yeah," Emily said, staring at the dying flames. "I know."

For a short, delicious second, Rebecca almost forgot her pain. She smiled at Emily and watched as her best friend reached out to stoke the fire with her gigantic stick, but it was then that Rebecca caught sight of Emily's decidedly naked left hand.

Where was the engagement ring?

With a sudden, sickening jolt, Rebecca realized the terrible truth: *Pastor must not have proposed.* In mere moments, the entire, awful scene played out in Rebecca's mind. *Pastor was going to propose that Sunday afternoon, wasn't he? . . . But Emma stopped moving . . . and then they were all at the hospital, weren't they? . . . And Emma was . . . and then there was the funeral . . . and now . . .* Rebecca almost threw up, she felt so sick with guilt, but she was a fighter. She took a deep breath and straightened her shoulders, firmly resolved. She might not be able to do a single thing about the fact that her daughter was dead, but she sure could do something about her sweet friend's naked left hand.

CHAPTER EIGHTEEN: THE CROSS BE BORNE

▬▬▬▬▬▬▬▬▬▬▬▬▬▬▬▬▬▬▬▬▬▬

October blew its way onto the calendar. At first, only field dust and corn shucks rode the windy waves, but a squall the size of Bradbury County eventually pushed in and settled its humid haunches directly over Town Hall, rattling the floor-to-ceiling windows of the historic Bradbury House for two days straight. Most of the county's crops were already safely in the bins, but a few unlucky farmers, Irv Davis included, were still out in the fields, discing stalks into the ground.

"Tractor's down," Irv announced, stepping through the kitchen door of the Davis home at six o'clock sharp the first evening of the storm. His hat and jacket were dripping rainwater onto Bev's shiny linoleum floor, but he was careful to keep his muddy work boots firmly planted on the old rag rug. "Hydraulic pump failure."

"Which one?" Bev asked, wiping her hands on a dish towel.

"My 4020."

"Oh, no!" A broken-down tractor meant serious delays if not flat-out disaster in the fields. Bev walked over to plant a commiserating kiss on her husband's soggy lips. "And you're going right back out into that mess to try and fix it, aren't you? Can't you eat a bite of supper first? I made goulash."

Irv shook his head. "Hank Schmidt's on his way to the field right now. I've got to scoot. Just wanted to come and tell you first."

Irv and Bev were still not in the habit of using their new cellular phones to call each other. Decades of face-to-face communication couldn't be replaced so easily.

"Won't be making it to choir practice, either," Irv added. "You all right driving yourself tonight?"

"I'll take the truck."

"Watch the Crawford Road. It always floods."

"I'll take the Fancy Grove blacktop instead. Are you sure you can't eat something before you leave? That sandwich I packed for your lunch has got to be long spent. Here, take this corn bread." Bev wrapped a slice of the crumbly, golden goodness in a paper towel and handed it to her hungry husband. "I'll be sure to leave a plate for you in the fridge. Just heat it up in the microwave when you get back, and don't forget to put a paper towel over it this time. It took me twenty minutes to scrub that petrified tomato sauce off the roof of the machine last time you reheated something."

Irv's eyes twinkled under the brim of his seed corn hat. He kind of liked being chastised by his favorite girl. He leaned over for one more quick peck on the lips before turning to leave.

"Aren't you going to say anything?"

"About what?"

"My hair."

Irv dripped a few more raindrops onto the floor and shrugged. "What about it?"

"I changed the color. Do you like it?"

Irv's eyes twinkled even brighter. "I like you."

Mrs. Scheinberg's eyes were not so twinkly when she caught sight of Bev's new raven-colored coif an hour later in the women's restroom of St. Luke's.

"For the love of Elvis and Priscilla, Bev! What on earth did you do to your hair?"

Bev was standing in front of the mirror, self-consciously combing and scrunching her short, dark, sopping locks. Since Irv hadn't been along to drop her off under the portico as usual, she'd had to park the truck herself and trot on foot through the driving rain to the church door. And she'd left her umbrella in the back of her car at home. "I-I colored it."

"You mean you did that on purpose?"

"Estella thought a little color might—"

"Estella? Since when do you listen to a word that old leather handbag says?" Mrs. Scheinberg untied the plastic scarf from around her second chin and fluffed her own gray, permed curls with both hands. "I didn't realize the two of you were so cozy."

"She invited me over to see her genealogy papers last week," Bev hastily explained. "She thinks we might be related. I've a Wagner on my mother's side, you know. I've a Scheinberg too, but that'd be Dean's side of the family, wouldn't it? So you don't like it, then?"

"What? You and Estella? You're a grown woman, Bev. You can be chummy with anyone you like."

"No, no. I mean my hair."

Mrs. Scheinberg sighed, weary to the bone. Sometimes, it was difficult being the only honest person left in the world. "Well, I'm not gonna lie. You look like an old lady with American Girl doll hair, and contrary to what Estella the Great and every other princess in America may try to tell you, the two were never meant to go together."

Bev sucked in her breath.

"The truth stings, I know." Mrs. Scheinberg resigned herself to always being the responsible parent at the potluck who dishes vegetables onto the child's plate full of fluff salad. "But no one looks good with dyed hair. It makes the skin look older. And this all-black thing is, well," Mrs. Scheinberg eyed Bev's hair like a piece of modern art at a museum, "it's two-dimensional, that's what. It's all shade and no depth, like a dull matte paint. I miss your natural shimmer and shine."

Bev's eyes looked confused, as if they didn't know whether to cry from the sting of being insulted or from the sweetness of being missed.

"Your silver hair was lovely, much lovelier than mine's ever been. It had all of these different shades of white and gray and black in it. It was curly and colorful. It was *you*. Oh now, stop that, Bev," Mrs. Scheinberg reprimanded. "C'mon, now. Don't cry. Not over *hair*, and certainly not over Estella. Why is that woman trying to make you look like her, anyway? She's not exactly an upgrade, you know. Next time you have the itch to copy someone's look, at least have the good sense to pick Alice or Emily or someone prettier than you."

The toilet in the far corner stall flushed just then, and Mrs. Scheinberg and Bev—startled to realize they were not alone as they had originally assumed—held their breath in horrified unison. Then, as if in slow motion and accompanied by the cinematic swell of woodwinds and strings, Estella Wagner, commanding as any diva making a grand entrance onto the screen, sauntered through the stall door and posed before a sink.

Mrs. Scheinberg honestly didn't know what to say. Estella, however, did.

"It would appear that *some* people never change," she clipped, intentionally looking at no one but seemingly looking at everyone. She turned on the tap, washed her hands for what felt like an eternity and a day, and then reached for a paper towel. Then, she turned to give Bev a wan smile, opining, "Beverly, dear, your hair looks lovely no matter what anyone *else* says."

Estella then tossed her towel into the trash receptacle and stood shoulder-to-shoulder with Mrs. Scheinberg, still look-ing only at Bev. "Unfortunately for Arlene, however, no amount of hair color will ever be able to improve what's graying on the inside."

With that, Estella the Great, showing off her emerald green blazer to its best advantage under the fluorescent light, paused for her close-up and exited the scene.

Bev was simply unable to contain herself. As soon as the door shut behind Estella's imposing frame, she blurted out, "Oh, Arlene, how awful! I thought I was going to die. I'm sure she—"

"Nope!" Mrs. Scheinberg held up a silencing finger. "We will not talk about it."

"But—"

"I mean it," Mrs. Scheinberg warned. Her chronic honesty was acting up again, and hers was that rare strain which didn't balk at a little self-criticism. "I hate to admit it, but Estella is right. It was distasteful of me to talk about her like that, and I stand properly corrected. I'm sorry, Bev."

Bev was about to answer with a word of friendly absolution when Mrs. Scheinberg cut in to clarify, "I mean, I'm sorry for the gossip. Not the hair. I'm right about that, of course."

⸻⸻⸻

The ladies returned to the choir nook to find Anna Cecilia holding court. Mrs. Scheinberg tried not to vomit. Estella had already put her on edge, and she was one egocentric Lutheran short of losing it.

"I think it's appalling, the amount of hormones and antibiotics that are being injected into our local herds," Anna Cecilia was postulating to the small cluster of singers sitting in the pews, "not that it affects me directly. I used to eat meat, but now I'm a vegan. Well, I do eat eggs on occasion, so I guess I'm about 98 percent vegan—"

"Then you're not actually a vegan," Mrs. Scheinberg snapped. Nothing irritated her more than a twenty-something know-it-all. At least Estella's age warranted some respect. Was the woman a narcissistic clown? Yes, but even the incompetent Wizard of Oz hiding behind the smoke and curtains could be called upon for a little knowledge and experience in the end. Anna Cecilia, however, was little more than a yapping Toto—an inconsequential pooch that barked more to get attention than to contribute anything of significance to the plot—but the red-haired smarty-pants was convinced she was the ruby slippers themselves.

"Arlene, honey, I was hoping you'd make it! Here, let me help you sit down." Anna Cecilia popped up from her seat and took Mrs. Scheinberg by the elbow to escort her the remaining two feet to her seat in the tenor section. Dwight Holley—by far Mrs. Scheinberg's favorite singer in the tenor section and owner of Bradbury County's largest drove of swine—gave Mrs. Scheinberg an entreating look. She softened a bit at the sight of the slighted pig farmer. Judging from the redness rising from the collar of his plaid flannel shirt, she wasn't the only one who was allergic to Anna Cecilia's personal brand of pixie dust.

"Anyway, as I was saying," Anna Cecilia continued, sitting back down next to Estella in the front pew and twisting herself a bit so as to better include her entire audience, "I first tried eliminating gluten and soy from my diet, but it wasn't until I eliminated dairy that I noticed a huge improvement in Beatrice's stools."

Dwight looked like he might actually start banging his head on the pew in front of him. Forest Reynolds, however, smelling a bit like he had recently preserved himself from the inside out with a bottle of bourbon, leaned forward in his seat next to Dwight and slurred, "Well, missy, I haven't had a proper stool for three years."

Bev hid her face behind her choir folder, her shoulders shaking with laughter, and Emily Duke, standing beside the conductor's stand up front, quickly turned to admire the stained glass window above the altar in the chancel.

Anna Cecilia was not to be deterred. "Of course, a mother's diet is *key* to the health of her child. I made sure to eat an avocado every day while I was pregnant with Beatrice, and," Anna Cecilia added, beaming her brightest smile around the nook, "her brain developed beautifully. I even started homeschooling her this past month. She can't speak, yet, of course, but we already communicate through sign language. It's obvious that she's ready to learn."

"Sorry we're late!" Alice panted, leading Rebecca up the side aisle with Evan bringing up the rear. The entire choir breathed a sigh of relief at the interruption. "The Crawford Road *and* a small section of Route 11 are currently under water. I imagine anyone else coming from Bradbury will be late."

"Oh, dear," Emily said, glancing around at the faithful few. It was already ten minutes after seven, and at least ten people were still missing from the pews in the nook. "That explains why Candice, Caroline, and Zachary aren't here yet. Oh, and Zachary was supposed to bring Blaine. I suppose we should assume they aren't going to make it, at this point. Hmm. Estella, do you feel like sitting at the piano tonight?"

Estella rose majestically from her seat, adjusted her shimmery blazer, and turned to address the choir. "I would be happy to serve in this way. Before we begin, however, I'd like to take a moment to welcome Rebecca Jones to the cantata *ensemble.*" She intentionally used the French pronunciation of the word. "This is Rebecca's first year to join us, and as the director of St. Luke Lutheran Church's choir and the official host of this year's cantata, I would like to be the first to offer my condolences."

Anna Cecilia giggled behind her hand.

Estella's eyebrows shot up to the edge of her dull hairline. "What, may I ask, is so funny?"

"Well," Anna Cecilia teetered, "I think you just insulted Rebecca."

"I most *certainly* did *not.*"

Mrs. Scheinberg hung her head. Although she usually delighted in a good foible—especially one made by Estella—this was one in which she took no pleasure.

"Now, I'm sure you didn't mean to, Estella," Anna Cecilia was using her best mothering voice, "but you technically offered sympathy to the choir for Rebecca's joining."

"I wasn't offering my condolences to the choir. I was offering them to *Rebecca.*"

"Oh, are we that bad at singing?" Anna Cecilia winked conspiratorially around the room.

Steam leaked from Estella's ears. "My condolences, young lady, are for the death of Rebecca's child."

Nothing could be heard but the sound of the rain pouring on the roof of the church.

Anna Cecilia blinked, looking first at Estella, then at Emily, then settling her inquisitive gaze on poor Rebecca. "I'm sorry. I didn't know. I suppose that's because I'm new too. That, and we don't get the Bradbury news much in Fancy Grove. How did your child die?"

Rebecca's stone-white face turned blood red in a matter of seconds. She was pressing her lips together in a straight line and staring fiercely at her choir folder.

"It was a cord accident," Alice quietly explained.

Emily swiftly stepped in. "Now, I think it's time for us to—"

"Ah, an intrauterine fetal demise," Anna Cecilia persisted, her voice tinged with just the right amount of authority but not nearly enough concern. "My cousin suffered one of those, but she did *not* eat an avocado every day. She also wore antiperspirants with aluminum. Do you wear antiperspirants, Rebecca?"

"Okay," Emily practically shouted, her knuckles white from the tension of squeezing the sides of her music stand. She appeared desperate to silence Anna Cecilia. "Evan, would you please lead us all in prayer? We're ready to begin. Now."

Rehearsal was touch and go. Between Estella's backseat conducting from the keyboard, Anna Cecilia's generous advising of Mrs. Scheinberg on how to sing high notes, and Rebecca's painfully somber expression, everyone was quite relieved when Alice suggested, "I'm wondering if it wouldn't be a good idea for us to call it a night? The Mason Road bridge is out now. As far as I can tell, the blacktop's still clear, but our Fancy Grovers are going to have a tough time making it home as it is."

Rebecca, mostly recovered from Anna Cecilia's misguided inquisition, leaned forward from her seat in the soprano section to better see her mother. "How do you know all of this?"

"I receive updates from the county, dear." Alice held up her phone.

"What? They call you?"

"They text me."

"The county texts *you?*"

"Mm-hm," Alice said, blinking innocently. "I signed up for road updates on their website before we left this evening.

It's a handy little feature. They send me weather updates too. I suppose some may prefer the weather app for such things, but I prefer to 'buy local,' if you know what I mean."

Rebecca shook her head, baffled.

"What, dear? I told you I'd read the manual." Alice coughed gently into her hand. The rain still hadn't quite yet washed all of the allergens out of the air. "Well, it wasn't a manual, exactly. More of a quick-start guide, but the young man at the Apple store—Danny was his name, wasn't it, Ebner? Anyway, he directed me to these really helpful videos online. You'd be *amazed* at the things this little phone can do, dear. I've been able to track the storm this entire rehearsal!"

Rebecca was still shaking her head. "It's just that . . . you're . . . texting."

"Oh, she's texting, all right," Evan tattled, standing to help Alice into her jacket. "If your mother's in the living room and I'm in the kitchen, she'll text me if she needs something."

"Well, it's a large house, Ebner," Alice defended, "and you know I don't like to shout."

"I'll remember you said that," he grinned.

"Oh, look! Another update!" Alice's eyes lit up as brightly as the screen on her phone. "We're expected to get another two inches within the hour. We'd better hit the road." She started moving down the aisle, her face fixated on the electronic glow emanating from her cupped hands.

"She's worse than a teenager," Evan said, shaking his head. "I'm going to have to start imposing nonscreen hours in our house. That, or I'll have to take away her charger."

Rebecca giggled, slipping into her rain jacket. Evan was good at making her laugh.

"I'll have you know," he said, "that wretched device dings morning, noon, and night. It's the most monotonous, mind-numbing music in the world."

"I'm so sorry. I had no idea she'd take to the phone like that."

"It's okay." Evan winked, holding his arm wide for her to step ahead of him down the aisle. "But be forewarned. Paybacks are rough."

"What do you mean?"

"I'm getting the boys a drum set for Christmas."

||||||||||||||||||||||||||||||||||||||||||||||||

As everyone else trickled out of the nave, Mrs. Scheinberg lingered next to her pew. She took her time tying her plastic scarf underneath her chin, building up the nerve to address the emerald green–shrouded elephant in the room. "Estella," she cleared her throat, "I would like to apologize."

Estella busied herself shuffling music at the piano. They were the only two left in the entire nave.

"I said," Mrs. Scheinberg repeated, raising her voice, "I'd like to apologize."

Estella looked up and stared down her nose at her declared nemesis. "For what?"

Mrs. Scheinberg swallowed her pride, willing her eyes not to roll. She opened her mouth to take another big bite out of her humble pie. "I'm sorry for what happened in the bathroom."

"Only for that?"

Mrs. Scheinberg pursed her lips. She assumed Estella was referring to that unfortunate incident involving her bottle of brandy and Estella's gluttonous fool of a daughter, but one of the side effects of Mrs. Scheinberg's chronic honesty was that she never took responsibility for someone else's sin. She deflected, "I should not have called you an old leather handbag. And other things."

"And what about my daughter?"

"What about your daughter?"

"My Olive was publicly shamed in her youth because of your . . . your . . . dipsomania!"

"Olive was shamed because she threw that bottle back more times than the rest of us could count!"

"*You* brought the bottle!" Estella pointed an accusing finger over the top of the piano.

"I brought the bottle for sipping, not for swigging! Who could expect she'd guzzle the whole thing?" Mrs. Scheinberg's face was growing splotchy. She took two deep breaths and then looked the green giant in the eye. "Look, Estella, I am sorry for what happened to Olive. In hindsight, I probably did not *need* to bring the bottle of brandy to the performance, and I *suppose* none of what happened later would have happened if I'd left it at home." She forced herself to keep looking Estella in the eye, even though it was getting harder by the second. "It's just that I wanted to feel a little closer to my husband that night. I was missing him, and I thought—well, I thought it would help me feel close to him."

Estella's nostrils were still flaring unattractively, but her crow's feet had softened just a smidgen. She was a widow twice over, and she understood a thing or two about missing dead husbands. "Was he a drunk or something?"

"No!" Mrs. Scheinberg looked offended at first, but then she started laughing. It was a belly laugh, one that started deep inside of her gut and rumbled out of her mouth like an echo of thunder. "No, Dean was not a drunk, but he did get a bottle of brandy from his oldest brother each Christmas, and we'd use it to warm our throats every Christmas Eve before caroling to the shut-ins. Since we didn't have children of our own, it was easier singing to the sick than staying at home."

Mrs. Scheinberg immediately clammed up after that last, very personal admission. She had never voiced such a thing aloud to anyone, let alone to a nemesis.

Estella, while proud, was not entirely unfeeling. "What would you sing?"

"I suppose we sang all of the usuals, but I mostly remember Dean belting 'What Child Is This' at the top of his lungs."

Estella, looking remarkably like Liberace in the low light, lowered herself back down onto the piano bench and played a flourish of an introduction with her bejeweled hands. Then, pausing to give Mrs. Scheinberg a slightly less patronizing look, she said, "I'll take the top part, of course."

Then, the two adversaries sang together in perfect harmony, the taller one swaying dramatically at the piano, the rounder one standing still with her hands folded.

> *What child is this, who, laid to rest,*
> *On Mary's lap is sleeping?*
> *Whom angels greet with anthems sweet*
> *While shepherds watch are keeping?*
> *This, this is Christ the king,*
> *Whom shepherds guard and angels sing;*
> *Haste, haste to bring Him laud,*
> *The babe, the son of Mary! (LSB 370:1)*

Mrs. Scheinberg, in spite of all of her best attempts, was sniveling like a baby by the end, but her crying didn't last for long.

"I tell you what, Arlene," Estella said, shutting the piano lid over the keys and giving Mrs. Scheinberg one of her queenly looks, "I may have been wrong."

"About what?"

"About the dry campus policy. Perhaps you should bring that bottle of brandy to rehearsal next week." She winked. "I think I'm going to need it if I have to sit next to Anna again."

"Anna *Cecilia*," Mrs. Scheinberg grinned.

CHAPTER NINETEEN: THE LIVING DEAD

The gray rain pelted miserably against the windshield of Blaine's Dodge Neon. He was driving north on Interstate 55, a route he'd traveled so many times in the last two years that his brain went into autopilot every time he passed the Sherman exit. Every Friday afternoon, like clockwork, he turned north out of Bradbury to visit his grandmother, mother, and sister in Lincoln, and whenever he could, he left early enough to be there in time to pick up his younger sister from school. His grandmother, however, had warned him away from such chivalry a few weeks ago.

"Shelby doesn't want you to pick her up from school anymore."

"Why?"

"Some of her classmates have been making fun of her."

"For what?"

Grandma Joyce had sighed over the phone. "For you."

Well, he was taking his time getting home this week. Blaine turned up the volume on the disc player and tapped his fingers on the rim of the steering wheel in perfect synchronization with Laurence Hobgood's piano solo. He listened only to jazz in the car anymore. The white noise of the engine always canceled out the more subtle nuances of symphonic music. He pulled over at the Walmart Supercenter in Lincoln to get his mother some flowers, and then he moseyed across town to his grandmother's two-story Victorian. The rain was coming down hard now, so he bypassed the front door altogether and let himself in the back of the house with his key.

"I'm home," Blaine called.

"We're in here, honey."

Blaine dropped his bags by the kitchen table and walked into what once upon a time had most likely served as the one-hundred-year-old house's front parlor. Now, the simple room housed only Grandma Joyce's sewing machine, a floor lamp, a couch, and Shelby's TV.

"Come here, honey." Grandma Joyce held out her arms over her sewing basket to better hug Blaine. "Shelby, turn that non-sense off. Your brother's here."

Shelby only muted the television. "Hi."

"Hi yourself," Blaine smiled. "Where's Mom?"

"Where do you think?" Shelby promptly unmuted the television.

"You really should read a book instead of watching that junk," Blaine couldn't help but advise.

"You really should wash your face."

Blaine held his tongue. He usually did when it came to his sister. Shelby had her own anger to manage, and Blaine noticed that it was getting more and more difficult for her to do so with each passing year. Blame it on the divorce or the hormones of a teenage girl or whatever, but Shelby's anger toward her mother rivaled Blaine's toward his father. And he really couldn't blame her. Their mother had mentally checked out on them shortly after their father's affair became public, and the move from Chicago to Grandma Joyce's house in Lincoln had only worsened her depression. Blaine imagined that losing a mother's attention and affection would be hard on any girl, let alone one whose father had abandoned her at the start of her most volatile season of life. He shook his head and grabbed the bouquet of flowers and his smaller bag from the kitchen, ascending the back stairs two at a time.

"Hi, Mom," Blaine murmured, simultaneously knocking on the bedroom door and pushing it open.

Ellen Maler, wickedly thin and sallow of complexion, was lying in bed on her right side, staring blankly at the rain-soaked window. An afghan was haphazardly strewn over her legs, and Blaine surmised from his mother's wrinkled pajamas that she hadn't bothered getting dressed at all that day.

"I brought you these." Blaine held out the flowers, but his mother didn't move. She looked at the flowers without turning her head but then blinked and looked back toward the window, blurry with rain. He set the flowers on her nightstand, making a mental note to bring up a vase of water before he left. "I started working on the *étude* you love so much. 'Tristesse.' It's the one you played in your senior recital, remember? Dr. Bronson agreed to let me program it for my recital too. I can't play Chopin as well as you, of course, but it feels good in the fingers. Would you like me to play it for you now? I brought the music home. Or how about you play it for me?"

His mom turned to look at Blaine, her eyes startlingly vacant as though she was devoid of any thought or feeling.

"How about it, Mom?" Blaine pleaded, leaning in closer to stare into her empty eyes. He was certain that his mom was in there somewhere.

She blinked. "Not now, Blaine. Maybe tomorrow."

That's what she always said.

"C'mon, Mom. You love music. Come downstairs. I want to play for you."

She closed her eyes and turned her face back toward the window. "I'm too tired. Maybe tomorrow."

Blaine felt some of his sister's frustration and anger creeping into his heart, but he quickly banished it with a deliberate kiss on his mother's cheek. He would not hate the woman who had been cheated and abandoned into this awful state.

"Okay. You rest. Oh!" Blaine suddenly remembered Robbie's gift. He reached down into his bag and pulled out the white lamb. "Here. My friend wanted you to have this."

His mom kept her eyes closed, so Blaine simply set the stuffed animal next to her cheek on the pillow. "It's so you won't be sad."

Then, Blaine straightened, closed the door, and went downstairs to sit at the piano in the darkened room adjoining the parlor.

"I'm trying to watch my show!" Shelby hollered from her throne.

Blaine hesitated. He really did feel bad for Shelby. Sure, she was insufferable, but at least he got to escape to Bradbury every week. His sister had to stay in Lincoln and face their mother's depression day after day.

"Ignore her, honey," Grandma Joyce said, following Blaine into the side room and turning on a light. She settled herself into her favorite rocking chair. "Now, play me what you've been working on at school."

Blaine pulled out the *étude* from his bag and set it on the music stand, fighting back tears of frustration. Before tragedy had struck their family, his mother had been his biggest supporter. A student of the piano herself, she had made sure that he was tutored by the finest teachers in Chicago. In fact, she had handpicked Dr. Douglas Hemmingway for Blaine's undergraduate work. It must have come as a terrible shock to her when the teacher for whom she had advocated so strongly and whom she had admired so greatly ended up having an affair with her husband. Now, his mom wouldn't even listen to music, let alone play it herself.

Never mind, Blaine thought. He would play it for the both of them.

CHAPTER TWENTY: TAKE TWO

Rebecca had it all planned out.

They would eat first, then play a few rounds of cribbage while munching on Pastor Fletcher's chocolate-covered fruit. Then, using the excuse of being too tired to continue, Rebecca would call it an early night. Everyone would be too polite to keep playing without her, of course, so Pastor Fletcher would stand up, like he always did, and escort Emily outside to her car. Then, Rebecca would turn off the front porch lights like she had done that first cribbage date night so long ago, and Pastor would propose, right then and there. Rebecca would then flip the lights back on, throw open the front door, and usher everyone back inside to celebrate the happy occasion with some champagne. It would be nostalgic and romantic and wonderful, and her dear friend—finally!—would have that blasted ring on her finger, once and for all.

Rebecca took a deep breath. The truth was that she felt responsible for the fact that Pastor's first proposal attempt went wonky, and she was desperate to make things right.

"Here, Em. Take these, will you?" She pushed a plate of lettuce wraps into her friend's hands.

"Hey," Emily smiled, "these are what you made to eat the very first time we played cribbage together. Remember that night?"

"Huh. You're right," Rebecca said, trying to sound nonchalant. Emily had noticed. She smiled, pleased with herself. "What I remember about that night is how you almost ran straight out the back door once you realized Pastor Fletcher was going to be your cribbage partner."

Emily giggled. "And I distinctly remember that you bullied me into staying."

"Well," Rebecca winked, "at least you knew what kind of friend you were getting from the beginning."

The two linked arms and walked into the dining room just as Alice and Evan arrived.

"Hello, dear! I brought deviled eggs. Where should I put them?"

"On the buffet," Rebecca said, kissing her mother on the cheek.

"Oh, Alice, these look divine!" Emily admired.

"Ironic, isn't it, considering their name?" Evan smiled, uncorking a bottle that was chilling in a bucket of ice on the buffet. "Riesling, Al?"

"Yes, dear."

The doorbell rang just then, and Jeremy could be heard welcoming Mrs. Scheinberg and Blaine at the front door.

Emily picked up one of the eggs to inspect its smooth underside. "How'd you get them to come out of their shells so perfectly? Every time I try peeling an egg, it ends up looking like I've shot it through with a shotgun."

"Your eggs are probably too new, dear."

"Too new?"

"Mm-hm." Alice took a sip from the glass of Riesling Evan handed her and immediately sputtered. "Sorry," she coughed. "Down the wrong tube."

Evan patted her on the back.

"You should never pat the back of a choking person," Mrs. Scheinberg reprimanded, trudging into the dining room with Blaine and a giant bowl of homemade caramel corn in tow. "It can cause the object to further lodge in a person's airway."

"I'm not choking," Alice explained, clearing her throat, "just drowning."

Rebecca elbowed Emily good-naturedly and nodded her head toward the sullied egg. "You'll have to eat that one now, Em. There's no putting back what's been touched."

"What a shame." Emily opened her mouth and took a big, happy bite.

The doorbell rang again.

"That'll be Pastor," Jeremy whispered excitedly to Rebecca.

"How can eggs be too new?" Emily was intent on cracking the case of the ugly egg. "You want them to be fresh, right?"

"Well, you don't want to use *rotten* eggs," Rebecca explained, "but the older the eggs are, the easier they'll peel."

"Why?"

"They just are." Mrs. Scheinberg popped open a tab on a can of Diet Dr. Pepper, poured it into a glass filled with ice, and handed it to Blaine. "I think it has something to do with the acidity level. The older the eggs are, the less acidic they are and the more loosely the protein bonds with the membrane. Or something like that. Regardless, it makes for easier peeling. Hot-starting them will help too."

"Hot-starting?"

"Get the water boiling before you add the eggs. Nine times out of ten, they'll peel better."

"And add some vinegar to the water," Alice suggested.

"Or some salt," Rebecca chimed in.

Emily stared at her friends. "Where'd you all learn this stuff? Martha Stewart?"

"Martha Stewart?" Mrs. Scheinberg scoffed. "Please! I've been hard-cooking perfect eggs on my 1947 GE stove longer than she's been rich enough to pay her minions to do it."

Emily shrugged. "It just sounds like something from her blog, that's all."

"Ooh, I've read that blog," Alice waved her phone in the air, "though I prefer the one by that pioneer lady."

Rebecca held out her hands in amazement. "Mother, since when do you read blogs?"

Emily still wanted an answer. "So where did you all learn these cooking tricks? City girls want to know."

The other three women in the room turned simultaneously toward Emily and answered in perfect unison, "4-H."

"See, Emily?" Evan put a consoling, fatherly arm around the city girl's shoulders. "The conspiracy theorists have been right all of this time. There really is a secret society that works behind the scenes to keep civilization from collapsing."

"The chocolate is here," Jeremy sang, leading Pastor Fletcher and a tray of chocolate-covered fruit into the dining room. "Now, the party can begin."

The banter that bounced across the dinner table that night was particularly lively, and riotous laughter spread among the friends like a communicable disease. Even Blaine couldn't help but catch the hoot-and-holler bug, though no one at the table laughed harder or longer than Rebecca. The hostess, weary from her forty days of crying, discarded her veil of tears for a party hat with almost reckless abandon. Emily watched her friend's transformation with bright eyes, silently offering thanks to God for lifting Rebecca out of the miry bog and setting her feet firmly on a rock. Pastor Fletcher, too, seemed particularly happy that evening, and when he and Emily won the final cribbage match with his killer twenty-two-point hand, his grin was unparalleled.

"Well, folks," Rebecca stood from the table, trying her best to look tired, "I'm sorry to put a damper on the party, but I feel like I need to lie down."

"Are you all right?" Pastor Fletcher asked, rising to take her elbow. His left eye twitched her way ever so slightly.

"Oh, I'm fine, really. Just tired."

"Maybe we should all leave, dear," Alice suggested, genuinely concerned, "and let you get some rest."

God bless her!

"Yes, I think that's a good idea," Pastor nodded, turning to Emily, his cheeks suddenly flushed. "Can I walk you to your car?"

Everyone chatted easily as chairs scraped against the dining room floor and plastic wrap was dutifully applied to dishes. Evan told Emily and Mrs. Scheinberg about his new venture in wine-making, Jeremy and Blaine debated which pizza joint in Chicago was the best, and Rebecca whispered to Pastor that the champagne was currently chilling in the fridge. Only when Alice leaned over her chair in a coughing fit did everyone in the room grow quiet.

"You okay, Al?" Evan asked, turning to place his hands lightly on her shoulders.

"Yes, dear, I'm—" but Alice dissolved into another fit of coughs. When she finally stood back up, her right hand held a tiny pool of blood.

"Mother!" Rebecca cried, running around the table with a napkin. "What happened? Did you knock out a tooth? Let me see your mouth." Then, as she would with one of her children, she put a hand on either side of Alice's face to tilt it up for better inspection. "Dear God."

"What is it?" Evan asked.

"Jeremy, get a towel." Rebecca's voice was solemn.

"What is it, Rebecca?" Evan repeated, still standing behind Alice.

"It's . . . " Rebecca shook her head. When she looked up, her eyes were wild with fear. "I honestly don't know."

Alice coughed again, blood spurting from her mouth.

"I'm taking you to the hospital." Evan was resolute. He took the towel from Jeremy, held it to his wife's mouth, and wrapped his other arm around her waist, quickly steering her toward the front door.

"We're coming with you," Rebecca said, running to the kitchen for her purse.

Pastor took one look around the room, registered the obvious fear and concern on everyone's faces, and made up his mind. The proposal would have to wait. "We all are."

CHAPTER TWENTY-ONE: THE SHEPHERD'S STAFF

When it rains, it pours, and the deluge rushing down life's drainpipe threatened to whisk poor Rebecca away.

"I just don't understand," Rebecca said, shaking her head as if to clear it of some foreign matter. "You want to do a what?"

It was all happening too fast for her to process. Just three days ago, they had rushed her mother to the emergency room, and the ER doctor, after determining the heart and lungs were fine, sent her home with a strong urging to consult with her primary care physician as soon as possible. Then, after running some preliminary blood work early Monday morning, Dr. Benson had referred her mother to a GI specialist in Champaign, and here it was, Tuesday afternoon, and the gastroenterologist wanted to perform an esophagoscopy the very next morning.

The doctor patiently explained the situation again. "Your mother is exhibiting symptoms consistent with having an esophageal stricture—"

"What do you mean by 'stricture'?"

Alice laid a quieting hand on her daughter's knee as if she were only eight years old.

"We don't know at this time," the doctor continued politely. "That's why we'd like to perform an endoscopy, to take a closer look at the situation and, if needed, perform a biopsy."

"A biopsy? Wait, that sounds like cancer!" Rebecca almost rose out of her chair. "Are you saying my mother has cancer?"

"All the doctor is saying, dear," Alice's voice was remarkably calm, "is that he would like to look down my throat to see what's causing me to cough so much."

Rebecca turned toward her mother. "But you said you were coughing because of allergies."

"Apparently, I was wrong."

Evan reached a consoling arm around Alice's shoulders. His face was almost as white as his hair.

Rebecca was normally steady as a rock when it came to life's little blips, but the death of her daughter had left her unusually shaken and unstable. She was dangerously close to falling apart as the three of them exited the doctor's office. There was only so much any one person could take, after all.

"Well, I'm glad we packed bags, just in case," Evan said.

"You packed bags?" Rebecca asked. "For what?"

"In case we needed to spend the night in town somewhere," Alice answered.

"You two thought you might need to spend the night? Why didn't you tell me? I didn't pack a bag."

"We didn't want to worry you, dear."

"You coughed up blood, Mother. I think we're past the point of me not worrying, don't you?" Rebecca's voice was tight with stress. "Besides, we came in the same car. I go where you go."

"Evan and I thought you could drop us off at the hotel and then drive our car home. We can take a cab to the hospital tomorrow morning, and then you can come back later in the day, after you've rested and hugged the children a bit."

"Well, it sounds like you two have this all planned out, don't you?"

"We are married, dear." Alice's voice was kind but firm.

"I just don't understand why you packed bags in the first place. It's like you knew something was wrong and didn't tell me."

"We don't know any more than you do, Rebecca," Alice sighed, leaning a little closer to Evan. She looked tired. "You sat in on the same consultations that we did. We're just facing the facts, that's all."

"The facts? What facts? No one told me there were facts."

"Well . . ." Alice glanced at Evan. She looked like she was unsure of just how far she wanted to go down this road. "The weight loss, the fatigue, the coughing—"

"The fainting," Evan added.

"Oh, yes," Alice nodded, pulling out her phone to add that one to her list. She typed on her screen with amazing speed and dexterity. "I hadn't even thought of that. And I've been having some trouble swallowing."

"What?" Rebecca practically screeched. The receptionist looked up from her desk and gave them a reprimanding look. Rebecca dutifully lowered her voice. "For how long? Why aren't you telling me these things?"

"I didn't think anything was wrong."

"But now you do, apparently?"

"Well," Alice said, pulling up some bookmarked websites on her phone and hastily scrolling through them, "several sites we've been looking at suggest these symptoms are consistent with esophageal cancer."

Rebecca grabbed the phone and determinedly turned it off, dropping the rejected device into her own purse. She crossed her arms like a security guard and stared her mother down.

"Rebecca, that's my phone."

"Yes, Mother, but I think it's time you listen to your doctor, not the Internet."

"While I hear what you're saying, Rebecca," Evan said diplomatically, "we were planning on using that phone to look up a hotel room."

Rebecca held her stance. Then, while still maintaining constant eye contact with her mother, she reached into her purse and handed the phone to Evan. "Fine. But Evan should hold on to this for a while. I think you need to take a break from your device for a bit."

Evan quickly stepped away to look up area hotels and let the women in his life work out their differences on their own.

"Rebecca," Alice warned, "you're behaving like a child."

"No, Mother, you are. You've been sick for how long now? And you haven't once said a thing to me about it."

"I didn't know I was sick."

"But you thought you might need to pack a bag?"

"I only just put everything together in my head this weekend," Alice explained. "You have to understand, dear, that I'm not a spring chicken, and older people get used to living every day with aches and pains of some kind or another. I'd never get out of bed if I took every one of them as a sign of cancer."

Rebecca winced at the sound of that word. She tried desperately to discipline her wayward lips into submission, but they still quivered.

Alice reached out a mothering hand. "Sweetheart, I really didn't mean to leave you out of anything. This is all new to me and to Evan, I promise you."

"You can't have cancer," Rebecca whimpered. "I simply can't take it."

Alice wrapped her arms around her troubled daughter. "Well, we don't know for certain that I do. Let's take it one day at a time, okay?"

"Daddy had cancer."

Alice sighed. It really was an awful word.

"Why would God do this to us again?"

Alice hugged Rebecca tightly and silently prayed for her daughter's faith. She had a feeling it was about to be sorely tested. Again. "Remember what Jesus said to Peter in the Upper Room? He said, 'Satan demanded to have you, that he might sift you like wheat, but I have prayed for you that your faith may not fail.' Jesus is praying for you now, Rebecca. He sits at the right hand of God, interceding on your behalf. Satan will not have you."

"Nor will he have you," Rebecca sniffed, stepping back and wiping her eyes. "God will never give us more than we can handle, right?"

"That's not exactly true, dear."

Rebecca looked up, surprised.

"People are always saying that, I know," Alice hastily explained, "but God never promises such a thing. In fact, I suspect He *always* gives us more than we can handle, that we might turn to Him again and again and again. We're sheep prone to wander, dear, and the Good Shepherd bops us with His staff to keep us in the fold."

"I'm beginning to fear that staff."

"Don't fear the staff, Rebecca," Alice warned. "Fear the wolf that would lead you astray."

Chapter Twenty-Two:

Good Christian, Fear

<hr />

"It's cancer," Bev whispered.

Candice's eyes grew wide. "What? Where?"

"In her squamous cells," Mrs. Scheinberg said.

"In her what? Is that in her backside or something?"

"No," Bev shook her head. "In her esophagus."

The three women were standing on the outskirts of St. Luke's choir nook before cantata rehearsal, their heads bent together.

"Well, I'm sure she's going to be fine. They can just cut that out, right?" Candice looked from Bev to Mrs. Scheinberg and then back to Bev again, desperate for some hope. "One of Thomas's colleagues had part of his intestines cut out just last month, and that's pretty close to the esophagus."

Mrs. Scheinberg shook her head. "The cancer's already spread to her stomach and lymph nodes. It's too advanced for surgery."

"What are you saying?" Candice was getting worked up rather quickly. Alice was the closest person to a mother she had in this life. When Candice had moved to Bradbury as a young bride seventeen years before, it was Alice who had first knocked on the big, solid oak door of Bradbury House and handed her an apple spice cake, welcoming her to the community and inviting her to be a part of the life at Zion Lutheran Church. Then, when she had been pregnant with her son, it was Alice who had organized a baby shower and come to the hospital and checked in on her at home to make sure she and Thomas Jr. were getting along all right. And ever since, Alice had made a point of attending every one of her children's special events, easily stepping into the role of grandmother in place of the mother Candice had lost so many years before. Candice tried to swallow the panic that was quickly rising in her throat. She simply couldn't tolerate the thought of her beloved Alice being ill. "Something's being done about this, right?"

"The doctor's putting in a stent."

"In her heart?"

"No," Mrs. Scheinberg clarified, "in her esophagus, to make swallowing easier."

"And she'll do chemo and radiation, of course," Bev added.

"Who will?" Anna Cecilia asked. The young redhead had snuck up behind them unnoticed.

Mrs. Scheinberg sighed.

Bev looked around uneasily, unsure of whether or not she should say anything.

Candice, however, found comfort in numbers. "Alice Ebner."

"Alice has cancer?" Anna Cecilia clicked her tongue. "Well, that explains why she was so skinny. What kind?"

"It's in her squatting cells," Candice said.

"*Squamous* cells," Bev corrected, her face turning the color of a summer tomato. Discussing the news of Alice's condition with Candice and Arlene felt all right—they were church family—but answering Anna Cecilia's questions made her feel dirty for some reason, as if she were somehow breaking a precious confidence.

Still, it would better for Anna Cecilia to learn the truth from her than a mottled variation from Candice. "Alice has esophageal cancer."

"Oh, dear." Anna Cecilia's tone sounded like a death toll. "That's a highly lethal disease."

"What do you mean?" Candice's eyes were wild.

"Alice might die."

"We all might die," Mrs. Scheinberg snapped. "All our days are numbered, so let's leave the accounting to the Lord, shall we?"

With that, Mrs. Scheinberg turned and pushed her way toward the tenor pew, and a penitent Bev and Candice, heads bowed, dutifully followed behind.

The mood of rehearsal was particularly somber that evening, what with Alice, Evan, and Rebecca gone, but Emily did her very best to revive the troops.

"Pull out your hymnals."

"We're going off-book?" Estella asked, her right eyebrow raised to the high heavens.

Emily winked at the woman, and Estella, completely clueless as to Emily's intentions, interpreted the gesture as a secret handshake shared between fellow directors. She immediately winked back and reached for the burgundy book in the nearest rack.

"Open to hymn 372, 'O Jesus Christ, Thy Manger Is.'"

"Ah, yes," Estella hummed appreciatively. She actually had never sung the hymn before in her life, but no one else in attendance knew that.

"We've had a huge, devastating blow delivered to us this week," Emily continued, looking out at her singers with a mixture of sadness and compassion. "Alice is a personal friend of mine, and every time I take a deep breath to sing tonight, my lungs keep coming up against this giant ball of fear right in the middle of my stomach." Emily pointed to a spot just below her ribcage. Several singers nodded in agreement. "Even if you feel like you don't know Alice very well, at least three of our sections are feeling the absence of Alice and her husband and daughter this evening."

Emily looked down at the open hymnal in her hand, her inner teacher coming out. "At times like this, I often turn to the wise poets of the Church and their profound words set to song for comfort. I find that no matter what I'm going through, these wordsmiths can take all of the chaos in my mind and soul and order it neatly according to Christ and His cross. Hymnwriter Paul Gerhardt, especially, does this so well. As a pastor who suffered persecution for his faith and endured the death of his wife and even some of his children, he understood the tension of the life of the Christian: that having been baptized into Christ's death and resurrection, we will share both in His suffering and His glory. Listen to this first stanza."

Emily nodded at Blaine over the piano. He instinctively played three measures of an introduction, and Emily began to sing:

> *O Jesus Christ,*
> *Thy manger is*
> *My paradise at which my soul reclineth.*
> *For there, O Lord,*
> *Doth lie the Word*
> *Made flesh for us; herein Thy grace forth shineth.*

"Would someone please sing stanza two for us?" Emily asked. Estella nodded her head and took off before Blaine was even ready.

He whom the sea
And wind obey
Doth come to serve the sinner in great meekness.
Thou, God's own Son,
With us art one,
Dost join us and our children in our weakness.

"How about stanza three, Caroline?"

Emily's young voice student immediately blushed, but she obediently sang:

Thy light and grace
Our guilt efface,
Thy heav'nly riches all our loss retrieving.
Immanuel,
Thy birth doth quell
The pow'r of hell and Satan's bold deceiving.

"Stanza four is actually my favorite," Emily admitted, "and I find it particularly comforting today. Mary, would you please sing it for us?"

Mary looked up, taken aback to be singled out in such a way. Her cheeks burned with introversion, but she nodded respectfully, took a deep breath, and opened her mouth to sing:

Thou Christian heart,
Whoe'er thou art,
Be of good cheer and let no sorrow move thee!
For God's own Child,
In mercy mild,
Joins thee to Him; how greatly God must love thee!

Blaine, along with everyone else, found himself watching Mary more than his music while the young woman sang. Something in her sweet voice moved him deeply. Her tone was pure—untouched by the machinations of training—and her every note floated on the breath like a dandelion seed on a soft summer breeze. Everyone in the choir was openly gaping at her when she finished, but Mary didn't notice. She was focused only on the open hymnbook in her lap.

"Thank you, Mary," Emily said and looked next at her friend and colleague. "Zachary? Stanza five?"

The English lit professor smiled and nodded, his rich bass filling the entire nave.

> *Remember thou*
> *What glory now*
> *The Lord prepared thee for all earthly sadness.*
> *The angel host*
> *Can never boast*
> *Of greater glory, greater bliss or gladness.*

"Stunning poetry," Zachary murmured upon finishing.

"Isn't it?" Emily agreed. "It's a difficult truth to understand, but it is truth, nonetheless: in Christ, we share in both the 'sadness' and the 'gladness.' It helps me to remember this as Alice suffers. Whatever's ahead for her, we always have the hope of Jesus' victory on the cross over sin, death, and the devil. There is no greater glory. There is no greater joy, for her or for us." Emily took a deep breath. "Let's all sing the final stanza together."

> *The world may hold*
> *Her wealth and gold;*

But thou, my heart, keep Christ as thy true treasure.

To Him hold fast

Until at last

A crown be thine and honor in full measure. (LSB 372)

As the choir cadenced on the final note, Anna Cecilia raised her hand. "I think we should add this hymn to our cantata program. Even if Alice never makes it to another rehearsal, we can sing it to her at the actual performance. Maybe she'll find it comforting like we do."

Mrs. Scheinberg's eyebrows raised in pleasant surprise. She had not realized that either dogs or fairies were capable of such mature thoughts and feelings. "I agree with Anna Cecilia."

Everyone else quickly murmured their approval, and Anna Cecilia, pleased as any fairy in the company of true believers, turned around in her seat and smiled.

"Now, I think we should pray for Alice," Dwight suggested.

Emily nodded, and everyone bowed their heads to petition the help of the Great Physician on behalf of their dear fellow singer.

꧁꧂꧁꧂꧁꧂꧁꧂

As Zachary, Blaine's ride back to Bradbury, lingered next to the director's stand after rehearsal, Blaine found himself moving toward the soprano section like a piece of driftwood caught in a swift-moving current. The pew was empty except for Mary, who was still seated, patiently waiting for her parents to finish talking with Estella at the end of the alto pew.

"Nice singing."

Mary looked up and then immediately looked back down. "Oh. Thanks."

"What's your major?"

"Library science."

"You should be studying music."

Mary shrugged.

Blaine plopped down onto the same pew, sitting sideways to better watch Mary's face. He didn't usually initiate conversations with anyone, but something about Mary's shyness made him feel safe, maybe even bold. "Seriously. Why aren't you studying music?"

"There's no music degree in the adult learning program."

"I don't get it," Blaine shook his head. "You can't be any older than me. Why are you in the adult program?"

Mary stared at her knees. "I can't drive."

"Does that matter?"

"It does when your ride works during the day." Mary ran her fingers along the outside rim of her choir folder. "I have to wait until one of my parents gets home from work to drive me to Bradbury. That leaves me only night classes to take."

"Why don't you take the Metro?"

Mary eyed Blaine out of the corner of her right eye.

"Oh," Blaine suddenly remembered. "That's right. We're out in the boonies, aren't we? Can't you hire a tractor or something?"

Mary's face cracked into a smile.

"But I've seen you on campus during the day sometimes."

"My mom's a speech pathologist, and she runs an after-school program at Bradbury Elementary on Tuesday and Thursday afternoons. I sometimes come with her to study or work on campus."

Blaine nodded, staring openly at Mary's profile. Her skin, even though they were months away from the summer sun, was still a beautiful golden brown, and her black hair shone in the lamplight like his favorite Steinway on the third floor of

McPherson. He also liked her quirky glasses. They were her only adornment. "You could just live on campus like the rest of us."

Mary's cheeks deepened to a red-brown. "No, I can't."

"Why not?"

She unexpectedly turned her face to look Blaine squarely in the eye. "Why do you throw phones?"

Blaine held his breath. Mary's look unnerved him, and he was suddenly, uncomfortably aware of the gaudy black eyeliner he'd traced around his own eyes that morning. Makeup seemed clownish next to her natural glow. "My dad's a jerk."

It felt good to tell someone. He expelled the air from his lungs.

Mary smiled. "I have epilepsy."

Blaine couldn't help but smile back at her, not because of what she said but because of what she didn't. "Want to get a coffee sometime?"

"Want to pick me up first?"

CHAPTER TWENTY-THREE: HOW BAZAAR!

‖‖‖

The following notice ran in the November issue of the *Bradbury Times*:

The Zion Lutheran Church Ladies Aid Society

will be hosting a bazaar and silent auction
in support of

Alice Ebner

on Saturday, November 12th, from 2:00 to 8:00 P.M.

Tickets cost $20 per person and include food
and beverages.

Choir will be sinning at 7:00 P.M.

When Bev read the announcement over her morning cup of coffee, she sprayed her Folgers clear across the kitchen table. Irv wiped at his left eye with a hanky from his back pocket.

"Sorry, love," Bev tittered, dabbing at his face with her napkin. "It's just . . . well, Arlene did it again."

Candice did not find the situation quite so amusing. She stormed into the church office, waving the paper in her right hand as if it were on fire, her purple handbag swinging recklessly from her dimpled elbow.

"*This* is the final straw, Arlene!" she hollered, holding the object of offense just a few inches from Mrs. Scheinberg's face.

"Calm down, Candice." Mrs. Scheinberg carefully removed the folded paper from the incensed woman's clutch like a gun from a perpetrator. "You'll have a heart attack."

"How *could* you?"

"How could I what?"

Candice's face was blooming veins. "You soiled the reputation of our church."

Mrs. Scheinberg didn't know whether to be amused or offended. "I think you mean *sullied*, though I have no idea how."

"This!" Candice poked a manicured finger at the advertisement. It had already been marked with a red permanent marker. Mrs. Scheinberg looked down and scanned the familiar text, her neck growing splotchy when she got to the end.

"Everyone will think we're fools. It's already difficult enough for me to hold my head high in this community as a Lutheran."

Mrs. Scheinberg rolled her eyes. Leave it to Candice to claim minority status whenever it suited her cause.

"Is it too much to ask, *for once*, that you actually proofread something? I mean, I know you and the spell checker are sworn enemies, but—"

"Technically," Mrs. Scheinberg pointed out, "every word in that ad is spelled correctly."

Candice gathered her plentiful self and stood as tall as her five-foot-two frame allowed. "At a time such as this, when our dear sister in Christ needs our help the most, you pen an ad that reads like a smutty book! We were hoping to attract families to this fund-raiser. I just hope your *egregious* error doesn't cost us the patronage of the Baptists."

Thankfully, the Fancy Grove Baptists loved Alice just as much as the Bradbury Lutherans, and they turned out in droves. In fact, so many people attended the Ebner fund-raiser that the Meat Shot Quail Club ran out of brats and raisin pie by six o'clock, and the Koelster sisters had to bring in pork burgers and cherry cobbler from their restaurant on the square in order to sufficiently feed the masses. The children's games that Nettie arranged were also a hit, what with Alice's own grandsons serving as barkers. They sold tickets to tots at a quarter apiece, and Nettie's gallon-size sun tea jar was practically overflowing with coins by the end of the evening.

It was the bazaar and silent auction, however, that brought in the biggest returns. Candice, a natural procurer, gathered items for the silent auction, pulling in donations from her long list of local celebrities. Emily and Blaine both offered packages of private music lessons, Ben Schmidt donated one free month of mowing, the Cornhuskers went in together to provide one dozen cupcakes every month for an entire year, and Candice donated a homemade Italian meal for eight served in Bradbury House, all to the highest bidder. The item that brought in the highest bid of the night, however—sold to Thomas Bradbury's law firm for $350—was not a free service or a fancy meal of any kind. It was a basket of silk flowers arranged by Robbie Jones.

Mrs. Scheinberg organized the bazaar portion of the event. Zion Lutheran, while modest in membership, was not short on resourceful women, and the entire west side of the fellowship hall was decked out with a myriad of colorful displays featuring homemade soaps, family cookbooks, handmade Christmas decorations, greeting cards, lawn ornaments, and cloth diapers. Irene Rincker's seasonal place mats and table runners went like hotcakes, and Evan Ebner's assorted teas, sold by a friend-ly Pastor Fletcher and a delightfully engaging Alison Jones, completely sold out in two hours flat. Even Lobelia Alwardt, Bradbury Public Library's effervescent librarian, rounded up donations of used books from the community to resell at the benefit, and Lois Kull built two pyramids of perishable items on a corner table, one made out of bricks of her homemade cheeses and the other built with pounds of butcher paper–wrapped butter.

Perhaps the most unique item for sale at the bazaar was the quilting circle's commemorative calendar, *Still Stripping: 100 Years of Tradition at Zion Lutheran Church.* Each month of the cal-endar featured a different image of a quilt sewn by a particular generation of women who had served on the circle at one time or another. The calendar even contained a picture of the orig-inal quilting circle sitting on the lawn of the converted coun-try schoolhouse that had served as the congregation's original meeting place before a tornado wiped it out in 1922. While many men stopped at the table to give the calendars a curious flip-through, very few committed to the final purchase.

"No one appreciates local history these days," Bev lamented to Phyllis Bingley, who was helping her manage the table. Their effort was not a complete waste, though, for Estella Wagner, who had carpooled to Bradbury with the Hopf family for the event, purchased ten calendars before the evening was out.

"They'll make perfect gag gifts for Christmas," she whis-pered into sweet Mary Hopf's ear.

It was Mrs. Scheinberg's table, however, that drew the largest crowd. Her assortment of knitted and crocheted accoutrements displayed across the table looked like a giant yarn rainbow. She had baby blankets and eyeglasses chains neatly arranged on one side and bonnets and tea cozies on the other, but the middle of the table was devoted entirely to what appeared to be a stack of acrylic dickies.

"What are these, Arlene?" Estella asked, holding a blue-and-orange one up for inspection. "They look like bibs."

"They are," Mrs. Scheinberg confirmed, demonstrating how the straps fastened efficiently behind the neck by slipping the button through an eyelet.

"Aren't they a bit big for babies?"

"Oh, these aren't for babies."

"For the elderly, then?" Estella looked confused.

"No, the stitch I used is entirely too porous for catching food bits. I mean, I suppose you could use them that way, but I designed these specifically for teenagers."

Estella blinked, trying to picture it.

"They're Boob Bibs," Mrs. Scheinberg explained. "You know, coverings for cleavage? Nothing's worse than walking into church and coming face-to-face with the exposed bust of a sixteen-year-old girl or—even worse—her sagging mother's. It's like staring at a plumber's crack from the front."

Estella stood with her mouth hanging open, utterly speechless.

"And our poor pastors!" Mrs. Scheinberg ranted. "To think what kinds of canyons they have to stare into these days whenever they offer the Lord's Supper! The shirts keep dipping lower and lower, and the bosoms keep getting pushed higher and higher. Some women are turning the communion rail into a Hooter's. I'm starting a campaign at Zion for the ushers to hand Boob Bibs out to families along with the kiddie bags, and I'm giving each of our female confirmands one for Christmas this year."

Estella, fully recovered, needed no more convincing. She bought five.

At seven o'clock on the dot, as advertised, the Zion Lutheran Church sanctuary choir made an appearance, though their contribution to the event was not the sin-fest as promised but, instead, a robust hymn sing. They sang a few of their favorites—"What God Ordains Is Always Good," "Lord, Thee I Love with All My Heart," and "Entrust Your Days and Burdens"—before leading the crowd in a rousing version of "Great Is Thy Faithfulness," at the end of which no eye was dry in the entire place. Then, Evan stood to offer a word of thanks.

"I cannot express how much your love and support mean to both Alice and me," he started, "and Alice wants more than anything to be here with all of you this evening. However, her aggressive treatment plan has considerably weakened her immune system, and her doctors have insisted that she avoid large crowds for the time being. Still, as you all know, Alice is not an easy woman to keep down—"

Everyone chuckled affectionately.

"—so she gave me a special tutorial this morning on how to take a video with her new phone. She thought seeing all of your faces on the screen would be the next best thing to being here herself. So if you'll be patient with an old man unused to these contraptions . . ." Evan fumbled with the iPhone.

"Allow me," Pastor Fletcher said, stepping forward and quietly taking the phone from Evan. He stood on a folding chair against the wall to get more height, then said, "Get ready, everyone. On my count, say hello, and then I'll pan the entire room. Ready? Three, two, one . . ."

||||||||||||||||||||||||||||||||||||||||||||||||||

Before Evan went back home to his wife that night, Phillip Rincker, treasurer of the congregation, handed him a check for $27,328. Evan stared at the check. "I don't know what to say."

"We only wish it could be more." Phillip patted him sympathetically on the shoulder and stepped away. Evan turned to leave for his car, but Mrs. Scheinberg caught him before he got to the fellowship hall door.

"Here," she said, thrusting a brown paper bag into his hands. "It's not much, but I thought it would keep Alice warm in the months ahead."

Evan peeked inside the bag and saw a knitted blue stocking cap. He looked back up, his eyes serious. "Alice laughed out loud for five minutes straight when she read your ad in the paper this week," he said.

"She and everyone else, apparently," Mrs. Scheinberg scoffed.

"No, Arlene," Evan's tone was sincere, "I don't think you understand. Alice hasn't laughed like that since the doctor told her she has cancer. I'm thanking you."

Mrs. Scheinberg swallowed.

"I know you take a lot of flak from people all the time for things like that ad," Evan continued, his eyes shining with gratitude, "but don't you doubt for one second that you are needed and loved in this church."

Mrs. Scheinberg, moved by Evan's words, drove home in complete silence. It had been almost forty years since a man had paid her such a tender compliment, and she had forgotten how nice it felt. She would bake a pie—no, two pies—for Evan tomorrow morning, the poor man. He had a hard road ahead, and he was in need of a patron saint. Or a sister in Christ with a good oven, at least.

Chapter Twenty-Four: A Hairy Situation

"Now, kids!" Rebecca raised her voice over the sound of the engine so that all of her children could hear. "Grammy may look a little different today."

"Why?" Frankie asked.

"The medicine she's been taking causes her hair to fall out."

"Cool!" Davie grinned.

Robbie scrunched up his nose in mild disgust. "That prob'ly doesn't look very good on an old woman."

"First of all, Robert Douglas, that is the last time you will ever refer to your grandmother as 'an old woman.'" Rebecca's voice betrayed just how short her fuse was this particular afternoon. "And second, even if Grammy does look terrible, no one is going to say a single word about it, am I right? Robert?"

"Yes, Mom."

"Actually, I want to hear *all* of you promise."

"Yes, Mom," the others sang.

Rebecca pulled up to the four-way stop at the intersection of Bradbury Drive and Second Street and eyed the Chevy Silverado idling noisily to her right.

"Are we taking the longcut to Grammy's again?" Robbie asked.

"Yes, son," Rebecca answered absently, tapping her fingers impatiently on the steering wheel. They had only one hour in which to pop by her mother's house for a quick visit and then get back home to eat supper before Davie's club basketball game. "C'mon, fella," she mumbled, edging her SUV forward inch by inch. "If you're not gonna go, then I am."

"I'm pretty sure you have the left-of-way, Mom," Robbie reassured.

Rebecca needed no further encouragement. She gunned the SUV and pulled out into the intersection, waving politely at the scruffy driver as they passed.

"Hey," Robbie said, looking out the window, "that man's really nice. Look, he's trying to wave back. He can only get one finger up, though."

"It's the middle one," Davie explicated.

|||||||||||||||||||||||||||||||||||||||||||||||||

Evan answered the door when the Joneses arrived. "She's in the living room," he said, ushering them into the large, open room at the back of the house. Alice was reclining in a cushy chair next to the bay window, her emaciated frame wrapped in a felted wool blanket. The children stopped short at the sight.

"Children," Alice smiled, clearly pleased to see them. Her blue eyes looked like two faraway planets encircled by dark, shadowy rings, and her white head was bald but for a few matted wisps. "Come here and give me a hug."

Aly immediately turned away and buried her face in her mother's waistline.

"Alison Louise!" Rebecca worked to disengage herself from her daughter's fierce embrace. "Don't turn away from Grammy like that. Give her a hug."

"No, no!" Aly resisted, stubbornly hiding her face.

"It's all right, Rebecca," Alice said. Her voice was tired.

"No, it isn't, Mother." Rebecca knelt to look her daughter in the eye. "Alison, stop this. Go give your grandmother a hug."

Aly started whimpering.

"Really, Rebecca," Alice assured, "it's perfectly fine. I don't blame her. My appearance must be alarming. I haven't quite got my scarf collection built up yet. What do you think, boys? Do you like my new haircut?"

Rebecca held her breath, giving Robbie a look that clearly threatened death by quartering should her command be disobeyed.

"Where'd it all go?" Davie asked.

"Most of it went down the shower drain."

"All at once?"

"In clumps."

Davie nodded his head, clearly impressed. He was smack-dab in the middle of the blood-and-guts phase of every boy's life. He walked over and gave his grandma a proud hug.

"What about you, Robert?" Alice asked, her arms extended.

Robbie held back a bit. He turned to his mother and whispered, "Will I catch it?"

"No," Rebecca shook her head.

Robbie moved in to hug his grandmother, but he kept a watchful eye on her bald head the entire time.

"Looks pretty bad, huh?" Alice said.

"At least you won't have to buy shampoo for a while," Robbie justified. "That's good, I guess."

Alice laughed.

Robbie immediately grinned and wrapped his arms around his grandmother. "I've missed your fun, Grammy."

"I've missed yours too, dear." Alice patted his back. "Now, where's my Frankie?"

Frankie had been standing back with his Grandpa Evan.

"Hi, Grammy," he waved from a safe distance.

Alice smiled at her youngest, most serious grandson. "What do you think of my hair?"

"It looks like Emma's."

Rebecca sucked in her breath. Frankie was right, but she still wasn't expecting to hear Emma's name at that particular moment.

The doorbell rang just then.

"It's Candice," Evan said moments later, escorting the first lady of Bradbury into the room. She was carrying a large paper gift bag.

"Hello, Alice," Candice breathed, smiling brightly at the reclining chair and then nodding coolly across the room. "Rebecca."

Rebecca nodded back. For some reason, Candice always behaved like a jealous older sister around her.

"How are you feeling?" Candice murmured, tucking Alice's blanket more tightly around her legs and motioning for Evan to refill her water glass. Rebecca half expected Candice to pull out a clipboard and begin taking vitals.

"I've been better," Alice admitted, "but I'm happy to see you, dear."

Candice rearranged the books and phone on the side table to make room for the gift bag. "I brought you something."

"Oh?" Alice looked in the bag.

"Now, it's just a little something," Candice yammered, clenching and unclenching her hands in an uncharacteristically awkward fashion, "and it should fit. At least, I think it should.

I had to guess at the size, of course, but I can always return it if you don't like it."

Alice carefully lifted a wig out of the bag, one with shoulder-length locks of white hair that were almost identical to the ones she had just lost.

"There's a wig head in there too," Candice continued, this time clicking her violet fingernails rapidly together. "That's how you should store it."

Alice studied the wig, touching the silky hair and letting it fall through her fingers.

"I got it from my favorite shop in St. Louis. It's where I get mine." Candice's voice petered out on the last word.

Alice looked up, her eyes shining. "It's beautiful, Candice. Absolutely perfect. And so thoughtful of you. It must have cost a fortune. I can't thank you enough."

Candice looked pleased.

"I'll need you to show me how to put it on, but maybe at another time? I'm feeling pretty tired this afternoon."

Robbie climbed onto the arm of his grandmother's chair and straddled it like a horse. "Will your hair grow back, Grammy?"

"Maybe," Alice answered, carefully lowering the wig back into the bag, "but I'm going to wear this beautiful wig from Candice until it does. After I get better, who knows? Even if my hair does grow back, I'm thinking about keeping it short like this."

"Why?"

"To show solidarity with Blaine," Alice said with a wink. At Robbie's quizzical expression, she explained, "To show others that I like him."

Robbie grinned. His grammy was so fun.

Candice thought about Alice's statement long and hard as she sat before her vanity's mirror that evening. She had no interest in showing solidarity with the likes of a sodomite like Blaine Maler, but she did want to show support for her stand-in mother. Besides, some strange, foreign sensation was pushing against her heart—empathy, maybe?—and she felt moved to do something special and meaningful in the face of this awful situation. Candice removed a couple of pins from her own wig and then lifted it off her head, staring at the thin wisps of gray-brown hair she usually tried to hide from the world. She sighed. Her real hair was the part of herself she liked the least, that much was certain, and she would rather die than show it to anyone else. But then, Alice might *really* die.

Yes, she would do it. She would do it for Alice.

Chapter Twenty-Five: Such Mean Estate

||||||||||||||||||||||||||||||||||||||||||||||||||||||||||||||||

"Sorry I'm late," Candice mumbled, sneaking into the choir nook from behind Emily's director stand. She slipped into a seat at the far end of the soprano pew, but no one even noticed. They were all too busy making the silent transition in their heads from the key of D-Major to the key of D-flat Major. Emily, her eyebrows lifting simultaneously with her hands, took a deep breath in perfect time with her preparatory beat and cued the sopranos and altos for their *a cappella* entrance.

"'Peace be to you,'" they sang together in ascending notes, but several of the women scrunched up their noses at the sound. A handful of the singers were at least a quarter tone apart in pitch.

"Ugh!" Estella groused, giving up. She let her music folder crash down onto her lap in a dramatic show of disgust. "That was worse than the last time."

Emily's hands fell to her sides in defeat.

"The sopranos need to think just a bit higher," Anna Cecilia coached, leaning forward in her seat and smiling brightly down the line.

Olive Wagner, whose temper was fully ripened after having endured four previous failed attempts at the tricky transition, was prompt in her prickly reply. "The altos were hanging too low on the pitch."

The other sopranos nodded and murmured their agreement.

Emily held up her hands before the two sections could offer any more helpful suggestions. "Let's just try it one more time. Blaine, roll us a D-Major chord, please, and everyone start again at the pickup to the final line of 'O Jesus Christ, Thy Manger Is.'" Emily took a deep, cleansing breath and smiled encouragingly. "Now remember, sopranos and altos, *think* a minor third up to find your starting note for 'E'en So, Lord Jesus, Quickly Come.' Ready?"

Blaine rolled the chord to tonally acclimate everyone to the land of D-Major.

"'A crown be thine and honor in full measure,'" the choir sang in four-part harmony, the altos ascending in quarter notes on the final word to resolve the chord. They ended in perfect unison with the sopranos. It was as close as the two sections had come to being united the entire evening.

Emily smiled at the sonorous sound, gently cutting off the choir but keeping her right hand poised in the air to maintain everyone's focus and attention. Then, with her left hand, she tapped her ear, noiselessly reminding the sopranos and altos to silently audiate their starting pitch for the next song. Everyone looked to the ceiling in quiet, thoughtful concentration, but Marge, like an overeager musket pointed across the green of Lexington, fired off with a warbling hum.

Estella snapped her music folder shut. "That's it. I've lost the pitch."

Anna Cecilia sighed, all cheeriness and gentleness gone from her voice. "The dramatic effect will be lost if the sopranos try finding their pitch *out loud* before the actual entrance."

"Maybe this is too much to expect of everyone this late at night," Emily suggested, chewing on her bottom lip. The altos, especially, were getting a bit tired and testy.

"Oh, we can do it." Estella revived her weary arms and lifted her folder resolutely to her chin. "Just not if the sopranos refuse to wait for the proper cue."

The nook erupted into a cacophony of high-pitched explanations and accusations and justifications.

"Y'all should use a pitchfork," Forest hollered over the din from the tenor pew.

Everyone quieted at the absurd suggestion, staring at one another in confusion.

"I think he means a pitch *pipe*," Mrs. Scheinberg interpreted.

"He means a *tuning* fork," Estella corrected, turning in her seat so that the entire choir might better hear her. "That's what we use here at St. Luke's, though I'm not sure *everyone* in attendance would be successful in using one. The sopranos would still have to find their starting note from an A, and that's not any easier than finding it from the D at the end of the hymn."

The sopranos narrowed their eyes at their tall target.

"Yes, thank you, Estella," Emily quickly intervened, staving off a treble insurrection. "I do think it would be powerful in the performance to go straight from 'O Jesus Christ' to 'E'en So, Lord Jesus' without Blaine giving a starting pitch, but it's not the end of the world if we don't. My biggest fear is that we might accidentally start a bit too high at the beginning, and then our sopranos' high B-flat on page six would launch from the stratosphere up into outer space—"

"We can manage." Marge proudly threw her shoulders back and shot a heated look down the pew toward the altos.

"Yes, I'm sure you can," Emily smiled, "but I'd rather you not have to. You know, come to think of it, we could insert a reading in between the two songs. Yes, that's what we'll do. 'E'en So, Lord Jesus' is based off of Revelation 22. We'll have Pastor read the Scripture citation before we sing the actual song."

Emily scribbled a hasty note on a pad of paper on her director's stand. "Now, let's pull out the Hildebrand 'Angels We Have Heard on High.' Simon, you said that you can play trumpet on this one, right? And Candice, Thomas Jr. is still available to play trombone for the performance?"

"Yes."

"Good, good," Emily nodded, looking down at her music stand and making another note on her pad of paper.

Anna Cecilia was leaning forward in her seat again. "Why, Candice," she said, "you got a new haircut, didn't you?"

"Um, yes."

Mrs. Scheinberg instantly looked up from her own folder, alarmed. Candice's answer was uncharacteristically short. The woman never passed up a chance to talk about herself, especially when the inquiry was about something as frivolous as her appearance.

"Well," Anna Cecilia continued, her tone careful but still betraying a touch of criticism, "do *you* like it?"

"What?"

"Do *you* like your new haircut?"

"Oh, well, I . . . I . . ."

Mrs. Scheinberg craned her neck to get a better view of Candice, but Leota and Letha—the eighty-three-year-old twins from Fancy Grove—were effectively blocking her view with their shoulder pads and permanents.

"I'm just wondering if maybe you should try a different stylist next time," Anna Cecilia suggested.

Mrs. Scheinberg couldn't actually see Candice, but she could see Emily's face. The director's brown eyes grew large and round with concern, like a silent-film star who couldn't quite figure out how to save the damsel in distress from the oncoming train.

Something stirred at the end of the soprano pew, and Mrs. Scheinberg finally caught a glimpse of Candice as she scurried past the choir nook, hugging her plum-colored coat to her chest and wiping at her eyes. Mrs. Scheinberg sighed.

"Did I say something wrong?" Anna Cecilia asked innocently, her ringlets bouncing against her cheeks like little pendulums as she swung her head from left to right in search of affirmation. No one said a thing.

"I was trying to be helpful," she explained, her voice gaining in momentum and volume, the usual music that so often accompanies self-justification. "I'm a firm believer in honesty. I think we can all agree that it doesn't help anyone to tell a lie."

Emily was staring at her music stand, her cheeks burning a bright red. She looked as if she were seriously considering whether or not to help out Anna Cecilia with a bit more honesty.

"The truth stings, I know—"

Mrs. Scheinberg sucked in her breath, suddenly recalling her bathroom conversation with Bev.

"—but I happen to think it's nicer in the end to tell people the truth than not." Anna Cecilia's ringlets were swinging again. "Candice will thank me later."

Mrs. Scheinberg rose from her seat, gathering her things one at a time. She methodically buttoned her coat and slung her quilted bag over her arm.

"Arlene, honey," Anna Cecilia called over her shoulder, "are you upset too?"

Mrs. Scheinberg maneuvered her swollen feet out of the nook and turned to face the redheaded wise apple. "No, I'm not upset. I'm grateful."

Anna Cecilia's lightbulb of a smile plugged into Mrs. Scheinberg's words and grew painfully bright. "I'm glad you agree."

"I didn't say that I agree."

Anna Cecilia's lightbulb flickered ever so slightly.

"I said that I'm grateful, and I am. I really am. I'm grateful because I have friends sitting in this room who are quick to forgive an old truth-teller like me." Mrs. Scheinberg gestured around the room, smiling penitently at a tearful Bev and winking at a grinning Estella. Her voice was remarkably free from sarcasm. "And I hope they'll be just as quick to forgive a young one like you. Now, if you'll excuse me, I think one of those friends needs me now."

ıı

Mrs. Scheinberg knocked on the solid oak door of Bradbury House, her old knuckles stinging from the cold. Thomas Jr. opened the door.

"Mom's in the kitchen," he answered, closing the door behind her and leading her to the back of the house. Mrs. Scheinberg motioned for him to scoot before they got to the kitchen.

"What are you making?" Mrs. Scheinberg asked, standing in the doorway.

Candice was leaning against the kitchen counter, a rubber spatula streaked with something dark and smooth poised before her open lips. She was dressed in her yellow bathrobe, and her eyes looked like she had been crying. "Brownies."

"Shouldn't you bake them first?"

"Not these." Candice unabashedly licked the spatula and took the mixing bowl over to the kitchen table. She pulled out a chair and sat down. "I left out the eggs so I wouldn't have to bake them."

"Nice." Mrs. Scheinberg walked over to the counter, opened the drawer where she knew the tablespoons were located, and pulled one out. "Should I get my own bowl, or do you want to share?"

Candice didn't answer, but she did scoot the mixing bowl closer to the center of the table. Mrs. Scheinberg took that as an invitation and pulled out the chair across from Candice, moaning with blessed relief as she sat down. Her feet were killing her tonight. Mrs. Scheinberg dipped her spoon in the batter and looked around the red and yellow farm-style kitchen, pleased by what she saw. While the other furniture Candice had chosen for Bradbury House looked as if it belonged in Disney's Magic Kingdom rather than in a small town in south-central Illinois, the woman was entirely sensible in her kitchen design. The room was charming but functional, colorful but tasteful, clean but pleasantly cluttered. Built-in cabinets lined the east wall and reached all the way to the ceiling, interrupted only occasionally by some necessary modern appliance. A cheery, re-purposed pie hutch held court at the north end of the kitchen while a warped, arthritic Hoosier cabinet bowed its headboard at the south. Rows of open shelving lined the west wall and supported Candice's eclectic collections of cookbooks, chicken figurines, and Pyrex, and a handmade butcher block the size of a football field and a wooden serving cart stood at the ready next to the dining room door. Sitting at Candice's kitchen table was like visiting the set of some Food Channel cooking show.

"You left rehearsal pretty quickly."

Candice's cheeks pinched.

"Why aren't you wearing your wig, Candice?"

Candice set down her spatula and buried her face in her hands. Her shoulders shook with a fresh wave of tears.

"What's the matter?"

"I-I," she hiccuped, "c-can't wear it."

"Why?"

"Because Alice is baaaaald!" she cried.

Mrs. Scheinberg sat back in her chair, mildly surprised at Candice's confession, but then, not really surprised at all.

Candice hid her face in the crook of her fuzzy yellow elbow. "I know my real hair looks terrible," she said, her voice muffled, "but at least I *have* hair, you know?"

"Your hair doesn't look terrible."

Candice looked up with accusing eyes. "Don't lie to me, Arlene!"

"Oh, Candice," Mrs. Scheinberg slapped her spoon onto the table in irritation, "when have I ever lied to you?"

Candice didn't answer. She sniffed noisily and pulled a used tissue out of her robe pocket.

"I didn't say your hair looks great. I just said that it doesn't look terrible."

Candice looked anything but comforted.

"Why do you wear a wig, anyway?"

Candice blew her nose into the crumpled tissue, then stuck it back into her pocket. She stared at Mrs. Scheinberg for a long moment, her eyes untrusting. "I have alopecia."

"What?"

Candice lifted up the top layer of hair to reveal two large balding spots on the right side of her head.

"Oh. Will it grow back?"

"It has before, but then it just falls out again."

"Will it always fall out?"

Candice sighed and picked up her spatula. "I don't know. It's been falling out like this ever since I gave birth to Caroline. Doctor says it's my immune system attacking my hair follicles."

"Well, I like your natural hair color."

"What little there is of it."

"No, I'm serious. The mix of gray and brown softens your face a bit."

"No one looks at my face when they see my hair," Candice sniffed. "Anna Cecilia is right. My hair looks like someone made a mistake. I look like a freak."

"Well, yeah," Mrs. Scheinberg grinned, "but not because of your hair."

A bit of Candice's old fire returned. "You should talk, Arlene."

Mrs. Scheinberg laughed, relieved.

"I just want to do something for Alice, you know?" Candice dipped her spatula in the brownie batter and took a bite. "She can't eat anything I make, and she's too ill to be visited very often. I just thought that, well, if Alice has to be brave while losing her hair, maybe I can be brave while losing mine. She still looks beautiful, though, and I look so terrible."

"Oh, Candice." Mrs. Scheinberg shook her head, overwhelmed by a strange sense of liking. "To be perfectly honest, you've never looked so beautiful."

CHAPTER TWENTY-SIX: THE WIDOW'S MITE

The church office was a war zone on Friday afternoon.

"She's not getting any younger, you know."

Pastor Fletcher pressed his lips together and turned his back on the cherrywood desk. Mrs. Scheinberg was behaving like a Boeing B-52, rumbling around the church office in her executive chair, strategically dropping conversational bombs on him right and left.

"I'm telling you, it's a mistake to wait too long."

Pastor's nostrils flared with irritation, but he determinedly held his ground. He would not engage in open warfare with the church secretary, not when it meant abandoning his defenses and leaving his personal life vulnerable to attack. Instead, he feigned indifference, innocently flipping through the afternoon mail and lightly humming the Kyrie.

"You do realize, don't you," Mrs. Scheinberg said, taking careful aim from her leather cockpit, "that Zachary Brandt's been to choir practice practically *every week*."

That caused him to raise his guns. "Arlene, this is none of your business."

"Of course it's my business!" she exclaimed. "I pretty much got the two of you together in the first place. Now, be sensible and ask the girl to marry you before she up and leaves us all."

"Leaves us? What are you talking about?"

Mrs. Scheinberg gave him a look of consternation over the top of her glasses. "I'm talking about the fact that Emily's the catch of Bradbury, and you're over here hemming and hawing like she's going to wait around for you forever. If you were smart, you'd give her a reason to stay."

Pastor, agitated, fumbled the mail and dropped it noisily onto the floor.

"And for heaven's sake, cut your hair. Are you trying to grow a mullet? I never can tell. Whatever you're doing, this in-between thing is unattractive *and* unprofessional."

Pastor bent over wearily to pick up the scattered pieces of mail, eventually managing to balance the precarious stack on the edge of Mrs. Scheinberg's desk. His face felt hot. "I'm not talking about this with you."

Mrs. Scheinberg effectively ignored his sentiment. "It's like you *want* her to marry someone else."

"That's not true."

"Then what are you waiting for, man?"

"It's not that simple."

"It is that simple."

"I'm a pastor."

"What on earth does that have to do with anything?"

"I can't just—" Pastor's hands suddenly took flight as if to communicate what his brain was failing to compute. "I can't just ask her to marry me when everything is . . . when so much is . . . Alice is family to her."

Mrs. Scheinberg narrowed her eyes. "You think Alice's being sick makes Emily want to be married any less? You're more of a fool than I thought."

"No." Pastor ran his hands through his hair. "I just think that it would be good to wait for a happier time, is all."

Mrs. Scheinberg shook her head disapprovingly. "You'll be waiting forever then, and so will Emily. No time is ever truly happy. Besides, the girl's in her thirties. Must I remind you that every day you cower in the corner and wait to pop the question is another big, loud tick of the proverbial biological clock? Emily'll be of advanced maternal age by the time you ever find that happy day of yours, and—"

Pastor Fletcher didn't wait for her to finish. He marched back into his study and swung his coat off the back of his door, stirring a tiny breeze that fluttered the pages of his Greek New Testament and the Matthew commentary lying open on his desk. He frowned. His sermon still needed finishing. Well, he would come back later—much later—long after Mrs. Scheinberg had gone.

"You forgot your mail!" Mrs. Scheinberg hollered after him as he pushed through the front office door.

"It can wait."

"So can Emily, apparently," he heard her grumble as the door shut.

Pastor Fletcher expelled the sour office air from his lungs and took in a deep, frosty breath of the November draft. The sting of cold did him good. He turned west and walked as briskly as he could, his dress shoes scuffing slightly on the rough pavement. He was hard on shoes. They never seemed to last him more than a year or two.

Pastor didn't know exactly where he was going, but his feet seemed to be heading straight for the Mulberry property of their own volition. Emily wouldn't be there, of course—it was still too early in the afternoon for her to be home—but Pastor didn't know where else to go. The parsonage had begun to feel unbearably lonely, especially with Emily living just a few houses down the street, and he certainly couldn't remain in his study while Mrs. Scheinberg was bent on using him for target practice. He trotted easily up the front steps of Emily's bungalow and lowered himself onto her porch swing.

What a mess! He leaned back in the swing and stuffed his hands into his coat pockets. Maybe Mrs. Scheinberg was right. Maybe he should go ahead and propose to Emily, but the morbid events of the last few months had all but consumed both of their lives. Every conversation they'd shared since Emma's death and Alice's diagnosis had centered around the topic of how to better care for their dear friends. When exactly, in all of that grief and lamenting, was he supposed to have pulled out a ring? Pastor sighed and leaned his elbows on his knees, burying his face in his hands. If there had been an appropriate moment in which he could have proposed, he'd missed it.

"Then *make* an appropriate moment," he could almost hear Mrs. Scheinberg chastise him.

Pastor sat back and crossed his arms over his chest, pushing the swing with his right foot and allowing himself to sway back and forth. The chains creaked above his head. It wasn't that he *wanted* to wait so long to ask Emily to marry him. He'd have said "I do" months ago and carried her over the parsonage threshold already if it were all up to him, but it wasn't. He was a pastor, and his time wasn't necessarily his own. Parish life had a stubborn habit of elbowing its way into his personal life and pushing things around in order to make more room for itself. Honestly, he'd begun to have serious doubts as to whether or not he should even ask Emily to share such a life with him.

Pastor stood and eyed the empty space where Aunt Jo's card table and chairs had sat that hot summer evening back in August. That was another thing. How could he possibly compete with a guy whose memory was stamped even on Emily's furniture? And Peter had already won Emily over with the proposal of a lifetime. Pastor couldn't now just pop the question willy-nilly without at least a little bit of pomp and circumstance.

His phone rang. Pastor dug in his pants pocket for the little pest and answered, "Hello?"

"Pastor Fletcher," a dreamy voice floated on the other end of the line, "this is Nettie Schmidt. I called the church, first, but Arlene said you'd stepped out of the office to have a street fight with your conscience and that I should call your cellular phone. Can you hear me all right?"

"Yes, I can hear you just fine, Nettie."

"Well, you never can tell with those cellular phones. Hank Jr.'s phone drops me all the time, though I've no idea how a phone can drop a grown woman. It can't even hold me in the first place, but Hank says it's because of the water tower reception and there being too many people using the same pipes. I haven't noticed any problems with my water pressure, though. Just a minute, Pastor." Nettie made sounds as if she were lowering the phone against her shoulder. "I'm talking to him now, Harold . . . I don't know. I haven't asked him yet." Nettie got back on the line. "Sorry, Pastor. That was Harold. He wants to know if you need a hatchet."

"A hatchet?"

"Yes, a hatchet. Harold found one at an auction outside of Mason yesterday, and he already has three."

"No, thank you, Nettie. I don't need a hatchet."

"He doesn't need a hatchet!" Nettie hollered, forgetting to lower the receiver.

Pastor winced. Talking with Nettie on the phone was a bit like sitting in the woodwind section of an orchestra. Even though you knew the entire brass section was sitting right behind your ear, the blast of the trumpet still shocked you every time.

"What about a box of Louis L'Amour books?"

"Um, no. Thank you, Nettie."

Pastor heard the deep, muffled rumblings of Harold in the background.

"He said no, Harold. . . . Well, I don't know why. . . . Of course he reads, but I don't think he reads Westerns. . . . No, he doesn't want your old shirts, either. . . . I know I didn't ask him, but I don't need to. I already know he doesn't want them. . . . There's nothing wrong with your shirts, Harold. They're perfectly fine, but he's not your size, that's all. . . . I don't know what size his father wears." Nettie's voice suddenly got louder. "Pastor, what size shirt does your father wear?"

Pastor sucked in his breath. "My father is dead, Nettie."

"Oh."

Harold's voice could be heard growling again.

"Let it rest, Harold," Nettie whispered rather ineffectively. She was still holding the receiver close to her mouth. "Pastor's father's dead. . . . No, not fled. *Dead.* The man doesn't need your shirts. He doesn't need your hatchet, either."

Pastor sighed and kicked his toe against the concrete floor of the porch. There went another scuff. The Schmidts were so generous. They were always buying him stuff at auctions and moving things out of their home into his own—the whole church was generous that way—but sometimes their generosity felt a bit as if they viewed the parsonage as no more than a glorified dumpster. Just last year, the Jepson family had dropped off three boxes of children's clothes even though he had no wife, let alone any children, and Yvonne Roe had handed him a bag of queen-size bedsheets from the 1970s.

"Your bed is smaller than a queen, I'm sure," she'd quipped, "but these are perfectly good sheets. Better quality than anything you'll ever find in the stores these days, that's for sure. Just hem them up a bit, and they'll be fine."

"If they're so great," Mrs. Scheinberg had mumbled after the church office door had shut behind Yvonne's cashmere suit, "then why isn't she still using them herself?"

Sometimes, though, the generosity of his congregation was nothing more than God's faithful fulfilling of His promise to provide his daily bread. For example, the Kulls wordlessly filled his deep freeze with a quarter of a cow every Christmas, and sweet Alice always bought him a new clerical shirt and a bag of black socks at the beginning of every Lent. The Joneses were continually slipping gas cards into his church mailbox, and Irv and Bev paid for any mechanical servicing of his car. The Koelster sisters insisted every week that he eat Saturday supper at their restaurant for free after his afternoon visit to their shut-in mother, and Candice made him a Sacher torte every year on his birthday. It was Mrs. Scheinberg's show of selfless care, however, that always moved him to tears. In spite of all of her public prickling toward him, she stood up at every voter's meeting to defend his reputation, and he knew that she prayed for him daily. He had seen her handwritten prayer list sitting on her desk more than once, and his name was always at the top.

"How about a table and chairs, Pastor?" Nettie stirred him out of his stupor.

"No, thank you, Nettie. I still have the dining set you and Harold gave me when I first moved into the parsonage."

"Oh, but these are red, Pastor."

Definitely not.

"And they're romantic and sweet, like something you'd see in one of those French paintings."

Most definitely not.

"Why don't you come on by and take a look at them before you decide? Then you can take a peek at these books too. You never know, Pastor. You might enjoy Westerns. They're a lot like those stories you like so much in the Old Testament. Lots of wandering and wilderness and lynchings and stuff."

"I'm full-up on books right now, and I really don't have room in the parsonage for another table."

"Oh, no, Pastor. The table and chairs aren't for inside. They're for outside."

"Thank you, Nettie, but I don't really need—" Pastor stopped short, his eyes on the empty spot on Emily's porch floor where Aunt Jo's table and chairs had previously sat. "Wait, what color did you say they were?"

‖‖‖‖‖‖‖‖‖‖‖‖‖‖‖‖‖‖‖‖‖‖‖‖‖‖‖‖‖‖‖‖‖‖‖

When Emily got home later that afternoon, she found a darling table-and-chair set sitting on her front porch. The iron furniture had been painted a cheerful shade of red, and a bright blue ceramic teapot with a festive bow sat welcomingly on the tabletop. She reached for the card tucked under the pot and opened it to read:

Tables are red,
Teapots are blue,
I'd sure like to work
On a puzzle with you.

No offense to Aunt Jo, but I thought it was time we had a spot to call our own.

Love, Michael

Emily's happy smile lasted the entire evening.

Chapter Twenty-Seven: A Hardened Heart

The sky was gray with low-hanging clouds, and a sharp, cold wind whipped at Blaine's hooded sweatshirt. He stuffed his hands into his jeans pockets and leaned into the blustery gale.

"It feels like my face is freezer-burned," Mary said, pulling her scarf up around her ears. They had just left The Corner Coffee Shop on Main Street—for the third time that month—and were cutting across the parking lot of Wesleyan Methodist on their way back to the college. The relentless northwesterly wind slapped at her chapped cheeks.

"This is nothing," Blaine said. "You should come with me to Chicago sometime. Then you can feel a real wind."

"Or you could just come with me to the library right now, and we can bypass the wind altogether."

"I've got to practice."

"Again? I thought you already practiced this morn— What is it?"

Blaine had stopped dead in his tracks. He was staring straight ahead at McPherson Hall, his face graver than a mausoleum.

"Blaine, you're scaring me. What's wrong?"

His skin had turned a chalky white. Not even the wind could tease the color back into his cheeks, and his voice was just as pallid. "It's my dad."

Mary looked across the street to see a man of about Blaine's height and build sitting on a bench by the front entrance to the music building.

"He knew I'd be here today," Blaine growled, apparently working it all out very quickly in his head. His mouth and nostrils were the only parts of him that were moving, and neither of them communicated peace and goodwill toward men. "What should I do?"

Mary was taken aback by the question. She looked up at Blaine over the top of her scarf and studied his dark eyes. They were two black cauldrons of emotion, swirling with equal parts anger and resentment, but there was something else in there too. Something vulnerable and uncertain and frightened and— her heart grieved at the sight—completely broken. "I think you should talk to him."

"That's exactly what he wants."

Mary chose her next words very carefully. "I think, maybe, that's what you want too." She then lowered her head respectfully. She felt terrible for Blaine, but she didn't know how to help him other than to give him some privacy. "If you need me, I'll be in the library."

"Wait," Blaine said, grabbing her arm. The desperation in his voice anchored her to the spot. "Don't go. Please."

Mary stood still, studying his face. A large part of Blaine's personality and life was still a mystery to her, but she instinctively sensed that his asking her to stay was a big deal. "You want me to stay with you?"

He nodded.

"Okay," Mary whispered. She walked elbow to elbow with him across the street, stepping up onto the curb. Blaine's father seemed to have spotted them, for he was already standing, his hands shoved into his pockets just like his son's. Mary quietly observed the man's clothing—black corduroy slacks, a gray wool coat, and a ribbed orange scarf—and noticed how the splash of color set off his salt-and-pepper hair attractively. Mr. Maler was definitely a handsome man. In fact, his face was the spitting image of Blaine's—or vice versa—minus the makeup and piercings, of course.

"What are you doing here?" Blaine asked abruptly, not even bothering with a greeting.

"I wanted to see you."

"Please, go."

Mr. Maler's face fell. Mary looked down at her feet. This was too painful to watch. Blaine's father hesitated for one more awkward moment before flashing his white teeth in a cheerful smile toward her and extending his hand. "I'm Tony Maler, Blaine's father. You must be one of his friends?"

Mary snuck a sidelong glance at Blaine before accepting the handshake. "I'm Mary."

"I told you to leave," Blaine spoke directly to his father.

Tony sighed. "Blaine, we need to talk."

"No. We don't."

"C'mon, son. I've put up with this long enough. We're family."

"We *were* family," Blaine corrected. "You exchanged our family for another one, remember? Douglas is your family now. Go talk to him."

"Douglas cares about you too, you know." Tony ran his hands through his hair, visibly unnerved. "We both do, and we're worried about you. I mean, look at you. You're obviously confused." He tossed a significant look toward Mary. "We just don't want you to be afraid. You don't have to hide who you are on account of your mother or your grandmother or any other woman you happen to meet."

Blaine looked like he had been shot in the chest.

"We've always been so much alike," Tony continued. "You used to borrow my sweaters all of the time and iron your slacks before school and, well, take care of yourself, but now . . . You've really let yourself go, Blaine. It's like you've stopped caring."

"You think *I'm* the one who's stopped caring?"

"And I don't even know where to start with these piercings on your face. You're mutilating your body."

"You mutilated my *family*!"

Tony stared at his son. "What do you want me to do? Do you want me to pretend? Do you want me to go back to your mother and lie about who I am?"

Blaine shook his head, clearly disgusted. "You keep insisting on playing the part of the martyr in all of this, but you're the one who lied."

"I never lied!"

"Yes, you did."

"When did I lie?"

Blaine stared coldly at his father. "You lied to Mom when you said 'I do.'"

"That wasn't a lie."

"Then what would you call it?"

Tony expelled the air in his lungs. "Look, I meant it when I said it. Things changed, that's all."

"Yeah, see, this is where we'll never agree, and this is a perfect example of why I don't want to talk to you. You change the meanings of words to fit your feelings in the moment."

"What does that even mean?"

"It means that you think a vow is only worth keeping as long as you *want* to keep it." Blaine's breath was coming shorter every moment. "But a vow is a promise, period, and you broke your promise to our family. Your word means nothing now."

"I'm gay, all right?" Tony threw his hands out to his sides.

Blaine indulged in an ugly laugh. "Yes, Dad. Thank you. You've made that perfectly clear to the world. Yet, once again, you think this is about your feelings or preferences or whatever, but it's not. It never has been. It's about the fact that you broke your word to all of us, and you won't admit that it's wrong."

"I can't apologize for being who I am."

Blaine shook his head. "You're unbelievable."

Tony stepped forward. "I can't change who I am, Blaine."

"Nobody's freaking asking you to!" Blaine clenched his hands into fists and pounded them fiercely against his knees in a sudden burst of rage. "When will you get it through your selfish head that this is not about how you *feel* or who you *think* you are? This is about what you *did*."

"What did I do other than love you enough to tell you the truth?"

Blaine suddenly doubled over, hugging his sides and dry-heaving all of his unspent emotion onto the sidewalk in alternating gags and coughs. Tony reached out to touch his suffering son, but Blaine blocked his hand with his elbow and with his stream of words. "The truth? Here's the truth, Dad. You love yourself more than you've ever loved me or Mom or Shelby. You willingly tossed all of us aside just so that you can *feel* good, and now," Blaine stood up, wiping his mouth, tears streaming down his face, "we all feel like we're going to die. That's the truth."

Tony stared, first at Blaine, then at the sidewalk. After a few moments of agonizing silence, he cleared his throat and said, "Look, Douglas and I want you to come for Thanksgiving this year. That's all I came here to say. So if you can find it in your heart to spend the holiday with your fathers, you're always welcome in our home. Even if we're never welcome in yours."

With that, Tony Maler turned and walked away.

Mary held her breath and watched Blaine struggle under some heavy, invisible weight. He looked a bit ghoulish with his makeup running down his cheeks, but she didn't dare say a thing about it. She suddenly understood all of the eyeliner and the piercings and the black clothes and everything else. Blaine was doing his best not to look so much like his dad.

Blaine lowered himself down onto the curb and buried his face in his arms. Mary sat next to him, the cold of the concrete seeping through her jeans. She'd wait out a blizzard if it would only offer her new friend some comfort.

"Pianos are so much easier than people," Blaine finally spoke, his voice muffled by his clothes.

"I suppose," Mary said, "but pianos won't love you back."

"Neither will people, apparently."

"Some people will love you back."

"Not my dad." Blaine looked up and wiped his face on the sleeve of his hoodie. "He's a real piece of work, isn't he?"

"I guess I can see why you keep wanting to throw things."

Blaine snorted.

Mary desperately wanted to make Blaine feel better, to smile again. "Did you really used to iron your pants?"

"And sometimes my undershirts."

"Why?"

"I guess I wanted to be like my dad."

"But not anymore?"

Blaine sighed and let the cold wind have its way with him. "Not anymore."

Chapter Twenty-Eight:

The Iniquity of the Father

‖‖

Rather than head back to his dorm, Blaine cut across campus and walked the six windy blocks to Zion Lutheran Church. That was the one place in Bradbury—and on earth, for that matter—he knew his father would never look for him.

"Here to practice?" Mrs. Scheinberg looked up from her desk in surprise.

"Um, yeah."

The church secretary looked like she wanted to say more, but Blaine didn't give her a chance. He kept his head down and walked straight past her desk, on down the darkened hallway to the narthex, and up the north stairwell, stopping only when he was safe in the balcony.

Except he wasn't alone.

"Hello, Blaine."

Blaine froze at the sound of Evan Ebner's voice. Of all the people in the world, Evan was the only other person he wanted to see less than his father. Blaine turned around to walk straight back down the stairs.

"Don't leave on account of me," Evan called out. He was sitting on a folding chair in the alto section, bent over his feet and tying his street shoes. "I'm on my way out."

Blaine stopped, but he kept his back to the man, staring instead at the army of organ pipes lining the east wall.

"I suppose you're here to practice."

Blaine remained silent.

"I remember preparing for my senior recital. The agony and the ecstasy, it was."

Blaine heard a drawer of the filing cabinet being opened, and he knew that Evan was tucking his organ shoes in the top drawer like he always did.

"What have you programmed for your recital?"

Why was the old man being so chatty? Blaine sighed, finally turning around but keeping his eyes averted. "Um, the usual. Chopin, Bach, Rachmaninov, you know the gig."

"Any original works?"

"Bronson doesn't allow unpublished compositions on his studio recitals."

"Ah, yes. I imagine not."

Blaine crossed his arms and looked at the floor, pulling out every nonverbal cue he knew to communicate his desire to be alone. But Evan had never been one to be bullied by others' wishes.

"Have you considered taking organ lessons?"

Blaine shrugged.

"Bronson's a piano purist, I know, but Clarence Mitchell still gives private organ lessons, I'm pretty certain. Not every pianist can find his feet, of course, but you seem to be a natural. You did a fine job at our wedding."

Blaine looked at him then. "How is Alice?" He was too sensitive a person not to at least ask.

Evan's eyes suddenly looked old and tired. "She's fighting." He sat back down in his chair. "How's your mother?"

"What?"

"Your mother, in Lincoln."

Blaine felt his stomach lurch. How did Evan know about his mom? Did Mrs. Scheinberg—?

"I know Dr. Douglas Hemmingway," Evan explained. His voice was matter-of-fact, as if the mention of that loathsome name wouldn't inflict a thousand wounds upon Blaine's heart. "I once gave Douglas a few organ lessons. Of course, he wasn't a doctor then but just a scrawny undergraduate with bad posture. I've followed his career ever since." Evan looked pointedly at Blaine. "I've followed everything else too."

Blaine dropped his gaze back to the floor, trying desperately to process this bit of news. Evan knew. He knew everything. "How do you know my mom?"

"Well, I don't know her personally, but I do empathize with her situation."

Blaine felt a crazy impulse to swing out at the pompous little man and his perfect posture. "She doesn't need your pity."

"I don't pity her, Blaine. I said that I empathize with her."

Blaine was unmoved.

"Ah, I see." Evan nodded his head, pragmatic to a fault. "You do not know. Yes, well, I was previously married, but my first wife left me years ago and ran away with the choir director here at Zion. As you can imagine, I am not immune to the particular pain your mother feels. Hence, I ask, how is she?"

Blaine retreated a bit. "She's depressed."

"No doubt. Does she still play the piano?"

Blaine shook his head.

"Now, *that* is a pity," Evan sighed. "The sin of adultery steals more from us than the world wants to admit. Is your dad still living in Chicago?"

"Yes."

"With Douglas?"

There was that sting of pain again. Blaine instinctively tightened his arms across his chest as if to protect his aching heart. He had never before been on the receiving end of such direct questions about his family. He had left everyone he'd known before his parents' divorce behind when he transferred from Northwestern. And since then, he had been careful to avoid talking about them with anyone in Bradbury—even Mrs. Scheinberg to an extent—so no one knew enough to ask any questions. Still, Evan's straightforwardness, though a bit unnerving, was strangely freeing. "My dad came to see me today."

"Did he?" Evan raised his eyebrows. "Did you invite him down for a visit?"

"No."

"I see. How'd it feel to see him?"

Blaine unfolded his arms, dropped his bag to the floor, and sank into a chair at the end of the tenor section. "I don't know."

Evan nodded thoughtfully. "I've often wondered what it would be like to see Shirley again—Shirley's my ex-wife—but she's never once come back to Bradbury. I imagine it would be painful and wonderful to see her again. Sure, she betrayed me, but she was my wife, you know?"

Blaine nodded.

"Is it hard to forgive your father?" Evan asked.

"Forgive him?" Blaine scoffed, his voice sloshing with sarcasm like an overfull pint. "For *what*? The man's a god, didn't you know? He can't do anything wrong. It's the rest of us who're cracked."

"I see."

"He ruined my mother, and he won't even admit it," Blaine spat.

"Unrepentance is the ugliest of traits," Evan nodded, "especially in a father."

Blaine's mask was dangerously close to fracturing. He suddenly needed to know something. "Have you forgiven Shirley?"

"I have."

"Why?"

If it was even possible, Evan seemed to grow more serious. "I am compelled to forgive her."

"Why?"

"Because I am forgiven by Jesus."

"Forgiven of what?"

"Of hating Shirley."

Blaine was quiet, his own conscience pricked.

"I suppose that may sound bizarre to the non-Christian ear, but mercy and forgiveness are at the heart of our beliefs. If I don't forgive Shirley of her sins, then I am in essence preaching a sermon to her and to you and, ultimately, to myself that there are sins which are unforgivable, and that is simply not true. Jesus died on the cross to atone for every sin, even Shirley's. Even mine. To forgive her is to be forgiven by God. To be forgiven by God is to forgive others. They go hand in hand."

Blaine chewed on this. It was all a bit heady for him, but then, Evan was a clever guy. "My dad thinks his leaving us is justified. He thinks it was okay to divorce my mom just because he's . . ."

"Because he's gay?"

Blaine's breath came short. He was not used to such forward talk, especially in a church balcony with an old, conservative, Christian man.

"What do you think?" Evan asked.

Blaine knew exactly what he thought. "I think my dad broke his word to my mom and to Shelby and me. Who cares if he's gay?"

"Are you gay?"

Blaine eyed the man warily. "Is that what people are saying?"

"Of course," Evan smiled. "This is Bradbury. You're the most exotic thing to hit these cornfields since iced mochas. The question remains. Are you gay?"

Blaine lobbed the ball easily back over the net. "What if I am? What would you say to that?"

Evan, who had always had a strong backhand, quickly volleyed, "I would say that a man is more than just music and makeup, whatever he wants people to think."

"That's not an answer."

"Maybe," Evan shrugged, "but some questions aren't for me to answer. Some have already been answered by God, and you would do well to ask Him yourself. I just hope He doesn't visit the iniquity of your father upon you and your sister. Thankfully, the Lord 'is slow to anger and abounding in steadfast love,' and Alice and I pray for you daily, Blaine."

Blaine wasn't sure what to think of that. Part of him was afraid he had just been insulted by the quirky Lutheran organist, but another, wiser part of him suspected he was actually being loved.

"Now," Evan stood up, "never mind about Mitchell giving you organ lessons. I've decided. I'm going to teach you myself. I'm free on Wednesday afternoons and Thursdays before choir. How about you?"

Chapter Twenty-Nine:

That You May Believe

||||||||||||||||||||||||||||||||||||||||||||||||||||||

Alice was in great pain, but not so much as to put down her phone.

"Come on, Mother." Rebecca held out her hand like an impatient schoolmarm. "Give it up."

"Just a second, dear." Alice swiped at the tiny screen with her right pointer finger. Her left hand was hooked up to an IV. "I'm almost to Level 6."

Rebecca turned and gave Evan and Pastor Fletcher a tolerant look. "I think the pain meds have kicked in."

"Indeed," Evan grinned.

"Forgive me for ignoring you, Pastor," Alice said, her voice raspy and her eyes still glued to the screen of her phone, "but I'm trying to beat Robbie's score. I'm . . . so . . . close."

"Oh, for Pete's sake, Mother! You're worse than the children." Rebecca leaned over the hospital bed and snatched the phone from her hands. She was shaking her head in a silent reprimand, but her eyes sparkled mischievously underneath the brim of her Cubs ball cap. "Let's give the birds a rest, all right? They'll be just as angry tomorrow, I promise."

"But I was going to check my email next." Alice gave Pastor a feisty wink behind Rebecca's back.

"You've already had your one Internet session for the day," Evan teased.

"You see how it is, Pastor, don't you?" Alice asked.

"Yes," Pastor smiled, "I see."

"Don't let my mother's sad song fool you. She's never had it so good." Rebecca walked swiftly over to a chair across the room and dropped the phone into her bag. When she came back, she gave her mother a tender kiss on the top of her bald head. "I'm sorry that I forgot your wig in all of this hubbub. Want me to go home and get it?"

"No, dear." Alice smiled tenderly. "We can get it tomorrow."

Rebecca returned her mother's affectionate smile. "I'm going to slip out for a few minutes and chat with Dr. Jacobi while you visit with Pastor, all right?"

Alice nodded.

"She takes good care of you, doesn't she?" Pastor asked as Rebecca left the room. He took Alice's right hand in both of his own.

"Too good," Alice agreed. "I have the best daughter in the world, Pastor. Evan knows it too."

Evan nodded from his seat in a nearby chair. The man looked weary, but it was clear that he was doing his best not to show it.

"So you fell, huh?" Pastor turned back to Alice.

"Doctor said I was dehydrated," Alice's voice sounded like it was being rubbed against sandpaper, "and the nausea makes me dizzy."

"What now? Will you stay in the hospital?"

Evan's deep exhale sounded suspiciously like a sigh. "Perhaps," he answered for Alice. "We're waiting to hear whether the doctor recommends a feeding tube or a port."

"I see."

"It's so hard for me to swallow," Alice explained.

"Of course," Pastor nodded, studying her sweet, familiar face. Alice's blue eyes were as bright as ever, but her frequent smiles and jests couldn't hide a deep, underlying fatigue. Her cheekbones were also more prominent than he remembered, and her eyebrows were completely gone. Still, her gentle, quiet spirit was her crown, and it shone as beautifully as ever.

"Evan and I have been talking, Pastor," Alice began, but her words soon turned into coughs.

Evan leaned forward to continue. "Alice will be buried next to David."

"Okay."

The three sat in a reflective silence for a moment.

"Does Rebecca know?"

"We haven't discussed it with her yet." Evan and Alice exchanged significant looks.

"How is Rebecca?" Pastor asked carefully.

"She's determined," Alice smiled.

"But?"

"But she's in denial."

Pastor nodded. "Do you think it's time to bring her into this conversation?"

"We do," Evan said. "It's just a matter of how. She doesn't seem to want to even consider that Alice might die, let alone talk about it.

"It's time, I know." Alice shifted her position on the bed. "I've done my best all of these years to teach Rebecca how to live, trusting in God's promises," Alice stopped to try to swallow, "but I have one last thing to teach her."

"What's that?" Pastor asked.

"How to die trusting in those promises."

Pastor's eyes stung with tears. His heart was conflicted. He was so sad to see the suffering of his dear sister in Christ, yet he also rejoiced in the full measure of faith that God had given her. He wanted to be more like Alice.

Rebecca suddenly blew back into the room, her hands full of pamphlets.

"Mother, I was just talking with Dr. Jacobi about a new clinical trial they're running at Barnes-Jewish, and I think you should apply. It would require relocating you to St. Louis, and I know how you feel about that, but I think it would be well worth it in the end to—"

"Rebecca, dear," Alice interrupted, closing her tired eyes for a moment. "We need to talk about my funeral."

Rebecca stopped in her tracks. She looked like she'd just been slapped across the face. "Don't say that, Mother. It's like you've already given up."

"I haven't given up, dear," Alice's voice was calm, "but I'm having more and more trouble swallowing. I don't expect to be able to talk this easily with you forever."

"You have given up." Rebecca's face turned red.

"It's time, dear."

"I'm not doing this." Rebecca shook her head and hastily opened one of the pamphlets. "If you'd just read about this new trial, I think you'd see that—"

"Rebecca." Alice reached for her daughter's hand. "Listen to your mother."

Rebecca hesitated for one long moment before obediently sitting on the edge of Alice's bed and taking the outstretched hand. She seemed unable to look her mother in the eye, but she sat still to listen.

"Even if God saves me from this cancer, I am still going to die."

Rebecca's shoulders registered sadness and defeat.

"All cancer survivors eventually die of something or other. Even Lazarus died again after Jesus called his dead body from the tomb." Alice's raspy voice was heavy with battle fatigue, but she persisted. "Our hope has to be in something other than just living on this earth, dear."

Rebecca's head fell gently against her mother's lap. She wept softly. Pastor stepped to the side to give them some privacy.

"Death is awful. Believe me, dear, I know. First, I watched your father die, then Emma died, and now you are going to have to watch me die."

Evan was now crying quietly in his chair.

"There's nothing good about death, dear," Alice continued, her hand resting on Rebecca's head, "but Christ has made it good. He went to the grave before us and cracked it open from the inside out with His victorious resurrection. Now, we don't need to fear death's prison. Jesus has set us free! He has opened the tomb! He really is the resurrection and the life, and we who believe in Him will live, even though we die. Did you hear that, my precious daughter? I will live, even though I die."

Rebecca nodded, her face still buried in the bedsheets.

Alice tenderly ran her fingers through her daughter's pony-tail for a quiet minute, her eyes shining in that singular way of hers. "I get to confess the truth alongside Job. Though cancer destroys this body, yet in my flesh, I will see God."

"Amen," Pastor whispered.

Rebecca sat up, her face wet and her hat askew. She looked her mother in the eye this time. "Are you scared?"

"Terrified," Alice admitted, "but I'm also comforted. We do not grieve as those who have no hope, Rebecca. We wait on the Lord in all things. Even in the grave, we wait on Him. We wait on Him to raise us."

||||||||||||||||||||||||||||||||||||||||||||||||||

Later that evening, Pastor sat at the parsonage kitchen table and wept. He buried his head in his arms, his shoulders shaking and his stomach vomiting moans. For twenty exhausting minutes, he lamented the suffering of Alice, his beloved daughter in the faith and his cherished mother in the Church. He grieved the failing of her flesh even as he rejoiced in God's preserving of her faith, crying out to the divine ear for mercy and strength on behalf of Alice's family and his congregation. Only when his tears had subsided and his moans had ceased did he finally pick up his poet's pen. The words were burning on his conscience, and he dared not wait a moment longer, lest he forget.

I am the deaf that heareth
The calling of the Lord.
My ears, unstopped, now listen
By water and the Word.

How sweet the sound of washing,
Which cleanses me from shame,
And drowns the voice of Satan
With God's own holy name.

I am the lame that walketh,
No more my stride to thwart:
In sin, a paralytic;
In faith, a leaping hart.

What stumbling block can fell me
With crooked paths made straight?
He walks in perfect freedom
Who lives as Christ's estate.

I am who sits in darkness,
In dungeon dark and cold,
My sin, a prison barring;
My grave, a jail of old.

Yet, Christ has gone before me,
His Gospel promise plain.
He cracked the crypt which holds me.
I do not wait in vain.

I am the dead who riseth,
To greet my Savior fair.
Though worms destroy this body,
I meet Him in the air.

With breath anew I praise Him,
With beating heart, I sing:
"I live in You, Lord Jesus,
My Prophet, Priest, and King."

CHAPTER THIRTY:

LET LOVING HEARTS ENTHRONE HIM

‖‖

Alice was not able to attend the cantata as everyone had hoped.

"Well, we may not be able to sing 'O Jesus Christ, Thy Manger Is' *to* her," Bev cheered in the choir room of St. Luke's a few minutes before the performance, "but we can still sing it *for* her."

"Yes," the singers all agreed, nodding their heads and murmuring their approval. Well, Mrs. Scheinberg wasn't nodding. She stood at the rim of the gathering with her arms locked protectively around her choir folder and her lips pressed firmly together. It wasn't that she disagreed with Bev's sentiment. No, she was in favor of singing the hymn, but she didn't trust her tongue to speak anything good, right, and salutary at the moment. For the past five minutes, she had been eyeing the inch-wide strip of gray running along either side of the part in Bev's hair, and the effect was positively irritating. It was all Mrs. Scheinberg could do to keep her scrupulous self from shouting "I told you so!" across the sea of heads.

"I know, I know," Bev mumbled penitently as she resumed her place next to Mrs. Scheinberg, "I look like a skunk."

"I didn't say a thing." Mrs. Scheinberg continued staring straight ahead.

"Your mouth didn't, but your eyes sure did."

"That's not fair, Bev," Mrs. Scheinberg scolded. "My eyes don't talk. Besides, if I had said anything, it wouldn't have been that you look like a skunk. It would be that you should try for a broken line next time, so people know they can pass you on your left."

Bev gasped and swatted Mrs. Scheinberg's arm with her choir folder.

"Oh, now, don't be so hard on Bev," Anna Cecilia interrupted, her squeaky voice sounding about as pleasant in Mrs. Scheinberg's ears as the screech of a braking train. "She's simply giving us a literal picture of the figurative."

Mrs. Scheinberg sighed. Leave it to Anna Cecilia to ruin a good joke with some kind of hipster hogwash. "We don't know what you're talking about, Anna Cecilia."

"Bev's a walking metaphor." The young woman winked, nudging Mrs. Scheinberg with her right elbow. "Every dark cloud has a silver lining, does it not?"

Mrs. Scheinberg was slow on the uptake, but once the thought took root, her belly erupted with a volcanic laugh. Anna Cecilia couldn't have looked more pleased. Bev couldn't have looked more exasperated.

"What's so funny?" Estella asked, scooting in on the small party.

"Nothing," Bev said, going against her very nature to keep this conversation as short and sweet as possible.

"Anna Cecilia," Mrs. Scheinberg choked, "said the funniest thing!"

"What?" Estella asked.

"Nothing!" Bev gave Mrs. Scheinberg a pleading look.

"Oh." Estella suddenly noticed Bev's hair. "Honey, your roots are showing. You need a touch-up. Why don't you come by my house tomorrow, and I'll fix that for you."

"I'm letting it go natural again."

"What? Did Arlene bully you?"

"Yes," Bev nodded, "she did."

"I did no such thing!" Mrs. Scheinberg wiped her eyes. "I simply let good reason run its course. Bev has finally realized that a crown of silver better suits a lady than a cast iron helmet."

"Well, suit yourself, Bev," Estella crowed, "but gray hair ages you by ten years. By the way," she added, pushing a gift bag into Mrs. Scheinberg's hands, "this is for you."

"What is it? It's not a bottle of Garnier Nutrisse, is it? For the last time, I'm not coloring my hair, Estella."

"Just open it."

Mrs. Scheinberg reached inside the bag and pulled out a bottle of brandy.

"A little something to remember me by," Estella winked. "Well, me and Dean. Open it on Christmas Eve, and sing a carol for the both of us."

Mrs. Scheinberg's eyes misted over at the sweet sentiment. "Hey, this has been opened."

"What?" Estella grabbed the bottle and closely inspected it. "It sure has," she said, mystified.

"You didn't by any chance ride here with Olive, did you?" Bev asked.

"I did not!" Estella grumped. Her mouth immediately puckered defensively, but her forehead grew two inches as realization dawned on her face. "But I did pick up Forest on my way into church."

Anna Cecilia succinctly grabbed the bottle, put it neatly back in Mrs. Scheinberg's bag, and nodded across the small circle. "Let this be a lesson to you, Estella."

"What?" Estella asked, her mouth puckering again.

Mrs. Scheinberg's own mouth twitched. She felt a good one coming.

"Only *you* can prevent Forest fires."

Mrs. Scheinberg blinked, a bit disappointed. It wasn't nearly as good as she had hoped. Really, it wasn't even that funny. She reached out to pat Anna Cecilia consolingly on the shoulder. "Keep trying, honey. We can't all start at the top."

〰〰〰〰〰〰〰〰〰〰〰〰〰

Estella was right. The acoustics of St. Luke's refurbished sanctuary did serve their singing well. From the moment Blaine first rang the E-flat and B-flat handbells to cue shy Mary to float the opening chant line of "Of the Father's Love Begotten" across the nave, the audience sat in a chilled silence. Song after song the choir sang, retelling the story of God's promise to send a Savior to His fallen people and of the fulfillment of that promise in the birth of the child Jesus. From "O Come, O Come, Emmanuel" to "What Child Is This"—at which point Estella threw a knowing wink over her shoulder to Mrs. Scheinberg—the choir marched alongside the Israelites in the wilderness and ran with the shepherds to the manger, marveling at the wonderful things the Lord had done.

The only crisis moment of the entire program was when the choir attempted the tricky *a cappella* transition from "O Jesus Christ, Thy Manger Is" to "E'en So, Lord Jesus, Quickly Come." (Emily had decided to take a risk and forgo the additional reading, after all.) "Peace be to you," the sopranos and altos sang, but their singing sounded anything but peaceful. Marge Johnson, a bit distracted after having said a quick prayer for dear Alice at the end of the previous number, overshot the starting pitch by an entire whole step, and the choir looked around at one another in nervous alarm. Thankfully, Olive—determined to redeem herself after the embarrassing cantata foible of her youth— heroically sang out even louder, anchoring their tenuous ship against Marge's warbling waves. It took a couple of measures for the capsizing vessel to right itself and set a solid course for the land of D-flat Major, but the choir eventually did it and set sail, all the more confident because of it.

The sopranos practically shimmered on their high B-flat, and there was not a dry eye in the room at the end of the song. It was Zachary's *pianissimo* B-flat, however—sung a good four octaves below the sopranos' soaring note—that caused Emily's neck hairs to stand on end. His low, rumbly hum was like a peaceful benediction at the end of an eventful season, and she couldn't help but whisper a grateful "Amen."

After the cantata was over and everyone had departed, all of the singers headed to Estella's house for an impromptu celebration, but Emily slipped quietly away, unnoticed. There was something she needed to do—something she was compelled to do—and the strength of her conviction had been pulling at her gut the entire length of the cantata, from downbeat to cutoff. She pointed her Honda toward a certain big white house in the country and geared herself up for the heart-wrenching sight she was about to see.

"Come on in," Evan said, letting her in the front door. "How was the cantata?"

"It went well. How are *you*?"

"I'm tired."

Emily took his hand in her own and squeezed it. She wished there was something more she could do for him, something wise she could say, but her own experience with suffering reminded her that simply being present was enough. "How is Alice?"

"She's been in and out the entire day." Evan rubbed wearily at the stubble on his chin. "She's started hallucinating a bit, so don't be afraid if she babbles or moans while you're here. The nurse said that's to be expected."

Emily nodded, and Evan guided her to the hospital bed set up in the middle of their family room. Alice had deteriorated significantly over the last few weeks, and the family had opted for in-home hospice care.

Emily looked down at Alice's emaciated frame. She could make out every one of her friend's bones under the thin bed-sheet, and her delicate head looked so small on the large white pillow.

"Hello, Alice." Emily smiled and sat in the chair next to the bed.

Alice didn't respond. Her sunken eyes remained closed, and her lax jaw hung open as she labored to breathe.

"It's the dyspnea," Evan explained. "I can't decide which is harder: listening to her struggle to breathe or watching her struggle to breathe. Both tear my heart out of my chest."

Emily bit her lip to keep from crying. "Can I hold her hand?"

"Please, do."

Emily reached out for Alice's right hand and tenderly cradled it in her own. It was so cold.

"Is Rebecca here?"

"I made her go home for the night. We have a nurse on duty, so there's no point in her losing sleep again."

Emily hesitated to ask her next question for fear of insulting him. "Would you mind leaving us alone for a bit?"

Evan didn't seem the least bit offended. In fact, he looked as if he understood her desire perfectly. "I'll be in the kitchen."

When Evan had left the room, Emily leaned in closer to her friend and studied her face, memorizing every line, every shadow, every angle. It was the thing she'd wished she'd done the day Peter died, but she had not been wise enough to do so at the time. Now, she knew better, and this was her friend and mother, the woman who had taken her in and sheltered her in this strange little town. She did not want to forget a single thing about her.

"Thank you, Alice," Emily whispered, gently kissing her cheek. Then, she let go of her friend's hand and did her duty—that simple, necessary thing she had been born to do: she sang. She reached into her bag, pulled out her hymnal, and gave flight to those precious rhyming words of faith in Christ Jesus. She sang Mary's Magnificat and Simeon's song, joining her voice with the saints of old on behalf of her dying friend, and chanted psalm after psalm, proclaiming directly into Alice's ears God's faithfulness to His people through all the ages.

Even when her voice began to break with fatigue, Emily kept on singing, for she had once heard a nurse say—years ago—that a person's hearing was one of the last things to go. Emily had resolved right then and there never to abandon her family in Christ in their hour of need, and Alice—in her weakness—was in great need. Emily turned in her hymnal to "O Sacred Head Now Wounded," folded her hand once more over Alice's, and sang a final, parting prayer:

> *My Savior, be Thou near me*
> *When death is at my door;*
> *Then let Thy presence cheer me,*
> *Forsake me nevermore!*

When soul and body languish,
O leave me not alone,
But take away mine anguish
By virtue of Thine own!

Be Thou my consolation,
My shield, when I must die;
Remind me of Thy passion
When my last hour draws nigh.
Mine eyes shall then behold Thee,
Upon Thy cross shall dwell,
My heart by faith enfold Thee.
Who dieth thus dies well. (LSB 450:6, 7)

Then, Emily kissed Alice's cheek one last time, made the sign of the cross upon her dear friend's forehead, and said, "I commend you into the hands of a loving God."

Then she let herself out the front door and drove home to the little red brick house that God—through His servant Alice—had provided for her.

CHAPTER THIRTY-ONE: FOR YOU ARE DUST

||||||||||||||||||||||||||||||||||||||||||||||||||||||||||||||||||

There was no parting of the clouds when it happened. No chorus of angels majestically appeared to carry Alice away—at least, none that could be seen by any human eye—but that was okay. Faith is the hope and conviction of things unseen, after all, and the Ebners and the Joneses were a convicted, faith-filled people. They did not need to see something in order to believe it.

Alice died as most Christians do, with scandalous simplicity. Her breaths grew shorter and shorter and farther and farther apart until they ceased altogether. The only change in the room when she finally died was that her life stopped while everyone else's kept moving forward, and Rebecca suddenly grew wise to an age-old panic. For with each passing second, time—that cruelest of companions—whisked her farther and farther away from the life of her mother.

Evan stood at the bay window that looked out onto his back lawn. He did not need to observe the corpse of his wife. Her body, while created by God and marked with the promise of the resurrection, was already decaying. His Alice was gone, never to return until the Last Day, and so he watched the snow falling onto a sagging cypress tree and listened to the music of Rebecca's sobs—the melismatic *crescendos,* the diminuendoing *glissandos*, the haunting melodies marked with frequent *fermatas* and *marcato* cries. He listened and tried to remember what it felt like to be looked at by Alice, to be noticed and loved by those bright blue eyes. He never wanted to forget.

Bev rocked back and forth in a kitchen chair, hugging her stomach, while Irv took the call from Mrs. Scheinberg. She felt suddenly strange. Empty. Nervous. Afraid. It was not right for Alice to be dead. It was an error that could never be undone, and the bleakness of this new reality threatened to make her sick. But soon, Irv was hugging her close and kissing her hair, and his familiar scent restored her senses and calmed her fears and made firm the ground under her feet. Irv was here. Irv was the same. They would go on together. And Bev wept for shame, for she was indulging in the very comfort which Evan now lived without: the physical presence of a beloved spouse.

Mrs. Scheinberg set her phone down and stared at her refrigerator. Evan would be waiting right now. He would be waiting for the family to come, then the pastor, then the undertaker. Then he would wait for the funeral, then the committal. Then he would start seeing Alice in crowds, hearing her voice on the phone, feeling her embrace in his dreams. Then he would wake up and wait for things to return to normal, only to remember that nothing would ever be normal again. Not his mail, not his phone bill, not his prayers, not his sleep, not his thoughts, not his days, not his nights. Everything would be new and laced with pain, simply because it wasn't the old which he had loved. Mrs. Scheinberg knew this all too well, so she reached determinedly for the refrigerator door and pulled out the milk and eggs. She would make Evan a pie today and then a cake tomorrow. And then she would make him a casserole, the one with the green beans that he liked so much. And then she would plant flowers at Alice's grave and sit in the balcony during the church service for a month or two, just so that he would know that some things, like the love and support of his church family, would remain the same even while the comfortable old changed into the awful new.

Pastor drove straight to the Ebner home and let himself in the front door. He found Rebecca sitting by her mother's body and Evan standing at the window, one hand caressing an exotic bloom on his wife's favorite potted hibiscus. Both were calm and still, keeping silent vigil with their thoughts. When Rebecca turned to greet him, her eyes were empty of tears but still resonated intense sadness. But there was relief there as well. "Peace be with you," he said, taking her hand in his and reaching out for Evan's. "Let us pray: 'O God the Father, fountain and source of all blessings, we give thanks that You have kept our wife and mother Alice in the faith and have now taken her to Yourself. Comfort us with Your holy Word, and give us strength that when our last hour comes we may peacefully fall asleep in You; through Jesus Christ, our Lord.'" When they had said their amens, he let go of their hands and opened his Bible, turning to the Gospel of John and reading, "Jesus said, 'I am the resurrection and the life. Whoever believes in Me, though he die, yet shall he live, and everyone who lives and believes in Me shall never die.'" Rebecca teared up then, most likely recalling her mother's reciting of those very same words in the hospital not too long ago. Pastor reached for her hand again and held on while she cried. Then he asked, "Are you ready?" Rebecca and Evan nodded, and Pastor slipped out to ask the nurse to call the funeral home.

Emily arrived shortly thereafter, walking straight toward Rebecca with arms open wide. She stroked her friend's hair while Rebecca wept on her shoulder. She thought of Alice and Emma and Peter and all of those she loved now resting in Jesus, but she said nothing of her thoughts. She was not there to talk, only to put a shoulder under Rebecca's cross and to help bear the weight of it for a bit. When Rebecca's well had once again run dry, they turned together to view the body and behold God's wrath upon sin, even while they clung to His promise of mercy and forgiveness and salvation for His people. The Resurrection Day couldn't come fast enough. Then they sat on the couch and remembered and talked and even laughed, recalling apple cakes and rainbow chicken and orange suits and motherly hugs. Then a man from the funeral home arrived, and they all—the living and the dead—left the house together.

Robbie sat on the couch next to his brothers. His dad was explaining and reexplaining that Grammy was dead, that she was now with Jesus, just like Emma. He looked at Davie's face—his older brother was crying—and he watched as Frankie held Aly's hand and whispered things in her ear. Robbie's stomach felt dizzy, and his arms felt uncomfortable, like his skin no longer fit his bones quite right. He hugged them to his chest to keep them from falling off. His eyes began to sting. He blinked twice and tried to swallow. If only Grammy were here. She'd let him try on her wig and make him laugh. She'd hug him too, until his skin fit his arms again. She would make everything better. "I want Grammy," he said, but she didn't come. She stayed with Jesus.

CHAPTER THIRTY-TWO:

ROBBIE JONES, NINJA WARRIOR

He was stealth, as always. No one noticed when he took it, and no one missed it when it was gone.

He crept along the wall. The room was teeming with people, all of them hovering in tight clusters and talking in muted tones. Most of them were adults, and he figured that worked to his advantage. They wouldn't notice a kid, especially one wearing dark sunglasses and a black suit. He was so close. All that remained was for him to safely deliver the package. Then, his mission would be complete.

"Hi, Robbie." Caroline Bradbury suddenly appeared out of nowhere. A lesser ninja would have faltered, but he had been training for this moment his whole life.

"Hi."

"I'm sorry for your loss," she said, handing him a homemade card.

"Thank you." He took the card and gave one curt nod of his head. He wondered if he should lean in and kiss her. That's what most of the heroes in the movies did whenever a pretty damsel entered the scene, but Caroline was Ben's girl. He settled for a hero's line instead. "I think you like me because I'm a scoundrel."

"What?"

"You don't have enough scoundrels in your life."

"Are you okay, Robbie?"

"I'm only trying to help you, your worship."

That last line didn't work quite as he had hoped. Caroline was looking at him as if he were bonkers, not Han Solo. That's what he got for mixing ninjas with starships. He gave her one more curt nod of his head and dodged safely to his right behind a grown woman.

"Robert Jones, are you okay?"

Robbie's heart froze in his chest. He looked up into the eyes of Mrs. Nettie Schmidt. The wrinkly woman had recognized him. He would have to make a difficult choice now: stay and fight, or flee? Honestly, he couldn't fight Mrs. Schmidt even if she were a threat—nothing was keeping her from blowing his cover—for she was Ben's grandma, and he had taken a ninja vow just last night to devote his life to protecting all of the grandmas of the world. He gritted his teeth. He would have to flee.

"Honey, you don't need to wear sunglasses in here. Oh," Nettie's eyes suddenly grew large, "I see. You're trying to hide your tears, aren't you? Dear, sweet boy! Here," she reached into her black purse and pulled out a pack of gum, "chew this. It will help you keep from crying. That's what I do in church every Sunday."

Score! Robbie took the proffered gum and politely nodded his thanks, careful to keep a smile as far away from his mouth as possible. He didn't want to blow this new, awesome cover Mrs. Schmidt had concocted. He unwrapped the gum, handed her the wrapper, popped the gum into his mouth, and then ran to the nearest wall. He crouched behind a chair, taking a moment to catch his breath. He was just ten or fifteen feet away from the drop-off point now, but his greatest obstacle—the receiving line—still lay ahead.

His mom and dad and Grandpa Evan were all standing next to the casket like sentinels, tall and strong and totally in the way. Thankfully, though, Robbie had come to this mission prepared. He stood on his tiptoes to peer over the shape-shifting crowd and made eye contact with his decoy. Frankie nodded in return, and immediately led Alison by the hand to the front of the receiving line.

"Mommy," Robbie heard Frankie say, "Aly needs to go potty."

Rebecca looked down at her two children and then at her husband.

"I'll take her," Jeremy said.

Drat! That wouldn't do. Robbie gave the signal to his decoy using his right palm and left elbow. Frankie sighed in disappointment but obediently complied. He reached over and grabbed Tilly Willy from Alison's arms, promptly causing his little sister to scream as if her very arm had been removed.

That was his cue. It was now or never. Robbie rolled on the ground and jumped to his feet, then ran toward the casket from the other side while his parents knelt to calm the shrieking banshee. He swiftly pulled the package from his pocket and shoved it down into the casket somewhere around Grammy's hip. Then, completing a smooth 180 on his right heel, he immediately ran back the way he had come, pushing through the front door of the funeral home and victoriously jump-kicking off the edge of the wheelchair ramp onto the frozen ground below.

||||||||||||||||||||||||||||||||||||||||||||||

Later that evening, when everyone else was asleep, Robbie stole across the hallway to the bathroom to find Frankie already waiting for him there.

"Did you bring it?"

"Yeah," Robbie said, pulling a book out from under his shirt and handing it to his younger brother. "Just be careful with it. Davie thinks it's still on the shelf."

"I'll be careful," Frankie whispered, tracing his finger along the edge of the Lonely Mountain pictured on the cover.

"You could always check that out from the library, ya know."

"I know," Frankie said, "but it's not the same."

Robbie shrugged. He didn't quite get Frankie's obsession with books, but he wasn't complaining. It made for easy bargaining with his younger brother. "Good work out there today, soldier."

"Thanks," Frankie said, hugging the coveted book tightly against his chest. "Hey, what did you put in Grammy's casket, anyway?"

"Some secrets must be taken to the grave, grasshopper."

Robbie clasped his fists in front of his chest, bowed, and went back to bed for some much needed ninja sleep.

CHAPTER THIRTY-THREE:

TO DUST YOU SHALL RETURN

Evan, of course, was in no shape to play the organ for Alice's funeral, so Mrs. Scheinberg spent half of the preceding week trying to find an appropriate substitute to cover the service. Clarence Mitchell—her usual go-to guy on the rare occasion that Evan was ill—happened to be out of the country that week for some weird music theory conference in Finland, and Blaine was already holed up in Lincoln with his family for Christmas break. That completely exhausted her list of competent players in Bradbury.

"There's always Nina Himmel," Estella Wagner suggested over the phone.

"Absolutely not," Mrs. Scheinberg said. "She's agnostic."

"Does that matter?"

"It does when she's evangelical about it. The one and only time we ever asked her to play at Zion, she tried skipping over the entire Service of the Sacrament."

"Really? She did that?"

"Oh, yes, she did. That bumper sticker–wielding broad accused all of us of being cannibals and debated the issue, right then and there, in front of the entire congregation. She stood at the balcony railing and hollered down to Pastor Gardner while he stood in the chancel. It was a complete disaster."

"I don't believe it. Nina's always so pleasant at the organ guild meetings."

"That's probably because you don't serve Communion at those meetings."

"Well, how about Teddy Brick?"

"Nope." Mrs. Scheinberg shot that suggestion down like a bird in the air. "He calls out random hymns from the console. *During* Communion."

"So? I sometimes have to do that whenever we run out of hymns during distribution."

"Oh, we didn't run out of hymns," Mrs. Scheinberg clarified. "He just wanted to play 'America the Beautiful' and other patriotic fluff over 'At the Lamb's High Feast We Sing.'"

"What about Patricia Morgenstein?"

"She plays too fast."

"Vivian Fricke?"

"Too slow." Mrs. Scheinberg suddenly had a bright idea. "Estella, what about you?"

"Me? Oh, no," Estella said, "I can't."

"Why not?"

"Well, it just wouldn't do, would it? I'm the music director at St. Luke's. I can't possibly play at Zion."

"Why not?"

"It would be like batting for the other team."

Mrs. Scheinberg rolled her eyes. "Thank you, Estella, for reminding me why I drive into Bradbury for church instead of Hamburg."

"Oh, come on, Arlene. You don't come over here to sub for our secretary, do you? Besides, I can't play a service that morning. I teach a handbell class at the senior center. Call Grace Pryce."

"Who?"

"Grace Pryce," Estella spelled out her last name. "She's ELCA, but she grew up LCMS. She knows our services, and she's got loads of experience. She's been playing for decades."

"It looks more like she's been playing for centuries," Mrs. Scheinberg mumbled the morning of the funeral as Grace Pryce, hunched over her aluminum cane, shuffled across Zion's narthex toward the north stairwell.

"What?" Bev asked at her elbow.

"Oh, nothing." Mrs. Scheinberg sighed, making a mental note never to take advice from Estella Wagner ever again. She nodded toward Grace. "I'm not convinced the old gal can make it up the stairs."

"Should we offer to help?" Bev asked.

"No," Mrs. Scheinberg shook her head, resigned to whatever lay ahead. "Let her be. You know what they say. Never insult the driver before climbing into the passenger seat of a car—and we've got a long drive ahead of us with Miss Daisy at the wheel."

Surprisingly, Grace proved to be quite proficient on Zion's 1939 Kilgen organ. At least she didn't hesitate to literally pull out all of the stops. The first chord of the opening hymn practically launched the entire balcony into outer space, and Nettie Schmidt, sitting just a few pews in front of the smoking launchpad, reflexively felt around her pew for a seat belt.

"Lord, help!" Mrs. Scheinberg shouted from the narthex, pushing her shoulders up to her ears in order to better block the tsunami sound waves pouring out of the nave. She desperately wanted to cover her ears with her hands, but she couldn't. They were already occupied with two corners of the funeral pall. Her wild gaze settled on the new, young funeral director standing meekly along the wall, two service folders held defensively before his ears. She reached out an elbow and hit him squarely in the ribs. "Vonnie, run upstairs and tell Grace to turn that thing down!"

"You can't turn down a pipe organ, Arlene," Pastor Fletcher mouthed, the sound of his words drowned out by the deafening music.

"Well, then," she shouted back, "pull down some pipes or shoot the organist or something. Just make it stop!"

Vonnie rushed up the stairs and must have worked his directorial magic, for by stanza two, the organ was a little less offensive, and by stanza three, the volume was registering at a good, solid, bearable loud.

"Are my ears bleeding?" Mrs. Scheinberg mouthed to Bev at the end of the hymn. She was standing several feet away, holding the other end of the pall.

"What? I can't hear you!" Bev answered loudly, her face frozen in a permanent wince.

Pastor began the service. "In the name of the Father and of the Son and of the Holy Spirit," he spoke from the back of the nave, facing the congregation. He was standing at the foot of Alice's casket, and Evan and the Joneses stood at the head. A crucifer holding the image of Christ's corpus high above everyone's heads stood ahead of them all.

"In Holy Baptism," Pastor continued, "Alice was clothed with the robe of Christ's righteousness that covered all her sin. St. Paul says, 'Do you not know that all of us who have been baptized into Christ Jesus were baptized into His death?'"

Mrs. Scheinberg and Bev stepped forward to lay the silken, white funeral pall over Alice's casket.

"'We were buried therefore with Him,'" the congregation confessed as one, "'by baptism into death, in order that, just as Christ was raised from the dead by the glory of the Father, we too might walk in newness of life. For if we have been united with Him in a death like His, we shall certainly be united with Him in a resurrection like His.'"

Grace let loose with an introduction to the entrance hymn—the very same hymn that had served as the processional for Alice and Evan's wedding—and the congregation wiped their eyes as Alice once more was led down the aisle. The organ volume was still a bit too loud to best serve the needs of the small congregation, but no one complained. They were all just so happy to no longer be in blast-off mode.

Now let all the heav'ns adore Thee,

Let saints and angels sing before Thee

   With harp and cymbals' clearest tone.

Of one pearl each shining portal,

Where, joining with the choir immortal,

   We gather round Thy radiant throne.

No eye has seen the light,

No ear has heard the might

   Of Thy glory;

Therefore will we

Eternally

Sing hymns of praise and joy to Thee! (LSB 516:3)

Pastor Fletcher's sermon was based on 1 Peter 1:3–8.

"'Blessed be the God and Father of our Lord Jesus Christ!'" he read from the pulpit. "'According to His great mercy, He has caused us to be born again to a living hope through the resurrection of Jesus Christ from the dead, to an inheritance that is imperishable, undefiled, and unfading, kept in heaven for you, who by God's power are being guarded through faith for a salvation ready to be revealed in the last time. In this you rejoice, though now for a little while, if necessary, you have been grieved by various trials, so that the tested genuineness of your faith—more precious than gold that perishes though it is tested by fire—may be found to result in praise and glory and honor at the revelation of Jesus Christ. Though you have not seen Him, you love Him. Though you do not now see Him, you believe in Him and rejoice with joy that is inexpressible and filled with glory.'"

Pastor looked up from his Bible and tenderly smiled down upon Evan and the Joneses sitting in the front pew below. "Grace, mercy, and peace to you from God our Father and from our Lord and Savior, Jesus Christ. Evan, Rebecca, Jeremy, children, dear brothers and sisters in Christ." He then took a breath to speak the first line of his sermon, but a cacophonous crash—the sound of which nearly made Mrs. Scheinberg regret her decision not to wear a pull-up that morning—rattled the rafters of the nave and the teeth of the congregation.

"What in the—?" Mrs. Scheinberg turned around in her seat just in time to witness Grace Pryce pushing herself up from the manual onto which her torso had fallen. The elderly woman, just as shocked as everyone else, adjusted her wonky eyeglasses and looked around the nave in confusion, mistakenly interpreting the stunned silence of Pastor and the congregation as the end of the sermon. She cleared the register and immediately started in on the Nunc Dimittis.

Pastor eventually found a way to weave the sermon back in after the prayers of the church, but Sherlock Scheinberg couldn't listen to a single word the good reverend preached. She was too busy trying to work out in her head what exactly had happened in the balcony and whether or not the situation warranted docking Grace Pryce's pay. She might have been a bit more merciful in the moment had she known that the whole noisy ordeal was, in fact, the direct result of the most unfortunate and tiniest of blunders. For earlier that morning, Grace had mistakenly opened the PM box of her pillbox and swallowed her evening medications along with her breakfast. As usual, her Ambien worked like a dream.

Alas, the organist's self-induced sleep was not the final foible of the funeral, for just as Mrs. Scheinberg and Bev were reverently removing the pall from Alice's casket at the end of the service, the electronic bleat of someone's cell phone went off, underscoring the usually silent ritual with the most ridiculous of sounds. The scale-like ringtone was muffled—no doubt buried in some careless infidel's purse—but that only enraged Mrs. Scheinberg all the more. The coward was letting the wretched device keep ringing rather than turning it off and risk revealing her identity. It was all Mrs. Scheinberg could do to keep from patting down the funeral attendees one by one and searching for the phone herself. She had a mind to silence it forever in a nearby toilet.

|||||||||||||||||||||||||||||||||||||||||||||||

On the short drive to the cemetery, Rebecca dug around in her purse for a clean tissue and suddenly called out, "Where is Mother's phone? Jay, have you seen Mother's phone?"

"It's not in your purse?"

"No."

Jeremy glanced over at his wife, his hands still on the wheel. "Are you sure?"

"I can't find it. Try calling it, will you?"

Jeremy reached into his pants pocket with one hand while keeping the other on the wheel. He made the call, but nothing happened.

"I don't understand," Rebecca said, digging around in her purse once more.

"When was the last time you saw it?"

"I used it to check Mother's voicemail Monday night," Rebecca said, withholding the fact that she had then sat on her bed and replayed the recording of her mother's greeting over and over again for three minutes straight.

"Did you leave it charging by the bed?"

"No, I distinctly remember putting it in my purse before the visitation. You don't suppose someone stole it, do you? Who would do such a thing?"

They had pulled into the cemetery and parked. It was time to get out.

"I'm sure it will turn up," Jeremy reassured, unbuckling his seat belt and taking his wife's hand. "I'll help you look for it later."

Rebecca nodded thoughtfully, still staring at her open purse. Then, she opened her door and stepped out into the bitter cold. Robbie quickly jumped out behind her, tucking his hand inside hers and leaning against her arm as they walked side by side.

"Mom?"

"Yes, Robbie?"

He paused for a moment. "What if we can't find Grammy's phone?"

"What do you mean?" Rebecca was distracted by the sight of the crowd gathering at the burial site.

Robbie was annoyingly lagging behind. "Am I going to go to jail?"

"Jail?" Rebecca suddenly stopped short and looked down at her son. "Robert, is there something you want to tell me?"

Robbie's eyes filled with tears. Rebecca knelt down to his level and held her son by both of his arms. Her grip was firm, but it wasn't unloving. "Do you know where Grammy's phone is?"

Robbie swallowed.

Rebecca's voice softened. "I'm not angry, Robbie. I'm just confused. If you know where it is, please tell me."

"It's with Grammy."

Rebecca processed this news. "It's with Grammy, right now?"

Robbie nodded.

"You mean you put the phone in her coffin?"

Robbie nodded again.

"Why?"

"Because it was hers, and she liked it."

Rebecca stared thoughtfully at her son. "But she doesn't need it anymore."

Robbie started to cry. It was the first time Rebecca had seen her middle son cry since his grammy's death, and she could barely stand the sight of his grief. She reached out and folded her soggy ninja into her arms and held on for dear life.

"I don't want to go to jail!" Robbie wailed.

Rebecca couldn't help but smile a bit at the ridiculousness of it all. Of all the stunts for Robbie to pull! She chuckled against his thick hair and kissed him behind his ear. It was kind of perfect, really—just the kind of thing that would have made her mother laugh, and Robbie so loved to make his grammy laugh. Rebecca's eyes leaked tears. Poor boy. He would need to find someone else to laugh with now. "You're not going to jail, son. At least, not for this."

Robbie pulled back and sniffed. "Really?"

"Really." She wiped his cheeks dry, took his hand again in hers, and resumed walking.

"What are you going to do?"

"I'm not going to do anything," Rebecca said. They were almost to the tent.

"You mean, Grammy can keep it?"

Rebecca sighed, resigned to the situation. It was just a stupid phone, after all. What did it really matter? "Grammy can keep it."

Robbie's face broke into a happy grin. "Awesome! Now, I can give her a call whenever I want."

Rebecca looked down at her son, appalled. But then she noticed the telltale crinkling around his eyes. He was joking. It was a morbid joke, but then, it was Robbie.

And the laugh bubbled instantaneously from her mouth. She threw her head back and shook all of the cackles out of her gut—just like her mother used to do—and stood for one happy moment, abandoning her sorrow to delight in the bright, sparkly charm of her funny, thoughtful, sensitive, ornery son.

Chapter Thirty-Four: Like Father, Like Son

‖‖‖‖‖‖‖‖‖‖‖‖‖‖‖‖‖‖‖‖‖‖‖‖‖‖‖‖‖‖‖‖‖‖‖‖‖‖‖

Blaine played with the top button of the red shirt his grandma had sewn him for Christmas.

"I know it's not your usual style, honey," Grandma Joyce had apologized Christmas morning, "but you've always looked so good in red. Besides, the material was seventy-five percent off. It practically bought itself."

Shelby's skirt had been made from the same bolt of fabric.

"How beautiful!" she'd said, lifting it out of the box to better view it. She held it up to her waist and winked at Blaine, a wicked gleam in her eye. "You can borrow it any time you want, Blainey."

Shelby was growing more obnoxious with each passing day, so Blaine didn't exactly complain when she decided to leave Lincoln for a few days to spend New Year's Eve in Chicago with their dad. Still, the thought of the two of them—three of them, counting Douglas—jaunting around town as if everything were hunky-dory on the home front made him sick to his stomach. He played nervously with the top button of his new shirt again.

"Can I make you some hot chocolate, honey?" Grandma Joyce asked from behind her sewing machine.

Blaine shook his head. He ran his finger along the big black Bible sitting on the edge of her sewing table. He usually avoided religious talk of any kind, but Shelby's being gone made him want to pick his grandma's brain. He had a few questions to ask, especially concerning Evan Ebner's mysterious comment made that crazy afternoon in the balcony: "the iniquity of your father."

"Grandma," Blaine asked, careful to keep his voice nonchalant and his gaze downcast, "is homosexuality a sin?"

The needle on the sewing machine promptly stilled. "Who's asking?"

"Me."

"For your father or for yourself?"

Blaine shrugged.

"I guess it doesn't matter either way," Grandma Joyce murmured to herself. She looked up at Blaine. "God says it's an abomination."

"How do you know?"

"It says so in the Bible."

"Where?"

"That's a good question for that pastor friend of yours."

"I don't have a pastor friend."

"What about the pastor at that church you go to?"

"I don't go to church."

"But I thought you played piano for a church in Bradbury."

"That doesn't count. That's work."

"Oh." Grandma Joyce resumed her sewing, but then she stopped again. "Why are you asking?"

Blaine shrugged. "Someone I know called it a sin. And Mom said something to Dad the night he left. She told him he was going to hell."

Grandma Joyce remained silent.

"Is that true?"

"All I know," Grandma Joyce said, pulling out the length of fabric she had been stitching and giving it a careful look-over, "is that all of us deserve to go to hell, even your father." She looked up pointedly. "Even your mother."

Blaine flinched.

"It's true, honey. We're all lazy and selfish and covetous. We're all gluttons and liars and thieves and murderers and adulterers—if not because of the work of our hands, then because of what's in our hearts. All of us would go to hell except for the fact that Jesus died on the cross to pay the debt of our nasty sins and give us His abundant righteousness. If your father goes to hell, it'll be because he doesn't believe that he needs saving from his sins."

"Then homosexuality is a sin?" Blaine looked up.

Grandma nodded. "It is."

"But none of the Ten Commandments mention it."

"Oh!" Grandma Joyce looked at him over her material, surprised. "You've been studying the Commandments, have you?"

Blaine's face grew hot.

"Homosexuality is included in God's command not to commit adultery."

"How do you know?"

Grandma Joyce set down the material and leaned back in her chair. "I'm not a smart woman, honey. I've never been good with books and words. I'm much better with a needle, but even I know that a male and female were created to complement each other, to marry each other, to be one with each other. Their parts can be physically joined together, and God can bless that joining with children. And the Bible says that 'what God has joined together, let not man put asunder.' Any kind of sex that puts asunder God's joining together of a man and his wife is adultery."

Blaine chewed on this in silence for a minute. Evan's words still echoed annoyingly in his mind. "Grandma?"

"Yes, honey?"

"What does it mean for the sins of the father to be visited upon his children?"

"Such questions!" Grandma Joyce exclaimed. "I honestly don't know very much about that kind of thing. Where is all of this coming from, honey?"

Blaine leaned his elbows onto his knees and stared at the floor. Some things were simply too hard to say aloud, even to his grandma.

"Blaine, what is this all about?"

Blaine's eyes were seeping. He suddenly felt confused and scared and so very alone.

Grandma Joyce abandoned her sewing project and walked over to the couch. She sat next to him and put an arm around his shoulders. "You can tell me, honey. What is it?"

Blaine's face felt pinched from the effort of trying to hold back his emotions. He felt like his head might literally pop. He whispered, "I don't want to be like him."

Grandma Joyce squeezed him tightly and put her mouth close to his ear. "Blaine, I don't know much about a lot of things, but I do know this. Whatever Shelby or your father or anyone else says, you are *not* your father."

Blaine did take that cup of hot chocolate, after all. He sipped it slowly at the kitchen table, and after he had swallowed the last drop, he confessed to his grandma, "I don't want to be selfish like Dad."

"Then don't. Be different from your father."

"How?"

"Live for something other than how you feel. Live for the good of others instead. Help your father. Pick up your phone and call him."

"What do I say to him?"

"Tell him the truth. Tell him that Jesus doesn't want him to commit adultery, and if he'd just believe it, Jesus forgives him. It's good for him to be forgiven and loved by Jesus."

Blaine hesitated.

"It's good for your father to be forgiven and loved by you too, Blaine."

"But he doesn't believe any of this stuff about Jesus and adultery and sin. I'm not sure I do, either."

"That doesn't change the fact that it's true. It's loving and respectful to tell your father the truth, to give him a chance to believe. Whatever happens after that—well, you can't control him, honey. All you can do is love and respect him."

Blaine took his phone from the pocket on his pants and stared at the keypad.

"Go ahead," she nodded.

He felt like he might throw up, but he knew his grandma was right. Evan was right too. Forgiveness, however impossible, was necessary. It was good, and he so wanted to be good. He dialed the familiar number.

I am not my father, Blaine reminded himself as the phone rang. *I am not—*

"Blaine? Is that you?"

He took a deep breath and swallowed the lump hovering at the back of his throat.

"Hi, Dad."

Chapter Thirty-Five: That Year

||||||||||||||||||||||||||||||||||||||||||||||||||||||||||||||||

It was the longest winter in Bradbury that anyone could recall, but eventually, the frozen farmland thawed and the bleak barrenness of winter gave way to the pregnant promise of spring. Soggy fields snuggled comfortably under warm green blankets of early wheat, and the swollen red buds of the yawning maple trees gave distant groves an illusive pink hue. Even the sky threw off its gloomy pall in exchange for a mantle of regenerate blue, and the bright golden sun threw revitalizing rays from east to west, resuscitating even the most dormant of souls. Young Robbie Jones, especially, seemed revived by the sun.

"How long will it take for these peons to bloom?" he asked, dropping to his knees to better dig his gloved hands into the loose, dark soil. He was helping Ben Schmidt transplant starts from the Schmidts' yard into Emily Duke's front flower bed.

Ben grinned. Robbie was always getting the names of the flowers wrong. He handed his young shadow a clump of the red-tipped shoots dug fresh this morning from his mom's garden. "*Peonies* usu'lly bloom in the early summer, but these here may not bloom at all this first year."

"Well, I like cocksbrushes. They look like little brains on stems. I always wonder what they're thinking of me."

Ben liked Robbie Jones. The kid had a knack for seeing things in a way that he never did. He was a hard worker too. Ben lifted a wooden crate of annuals off the front porch step and set them on the grass next to Miss Emily's new red table. The seedlings were from the nursery in Hamburg. Mrs. Jones had brought them this morning along with two large pots for Miss Emily's front steps. He would start working on those.

"What're these?" Robbie pointed to a nearby cluster of slim, green fingers pushing through the ground.

"Daffodils. No, wait. Narcissus, I think." Ben cocked his head, trying to remember what he and Miss Emily had planted there last fall. "Yeah, narcissus. They look sim'lar to daffodils at the start, but narcissus have a pretty white skirt to their bloom."

"Oh, yeah," Robbie nodded. "We have narcissists at our house too."

"Hey, guess what?" Ben was practically bursting open like a peony to share his news. "My dad took me to the dealership last weekend."

Robbie didn't need to ask what kind of dealership. Everyone knew the Schmidts bled John Deere green and yellow. "For a new tractor?"

"Nah," Ben shrugged. His chest swelled with a young man's pride. "I saved up money to buy me a ridin' lawn mower."

"Whoa! Really?" Robbie's eyes grew round with excitement and with a touch of envy. "Is your old push one busted or something?"

"Nah, I just need somethin' faster, that's all. Business is boomin'. I'm up to mowin' seventeen yards a week." He handed Robbie another clump of peony starts.

"I wish I could mow. Mom'll barely even let me ride my bike on the street by myself."

"Have ya ever string-trimmed?"

Robbie shrugged, patting dirt around the roots of the baby peonies. Ben thought he looked like he didn't really know what string-trimming was.

"Don't be afraid to pack the dirt a littler harder," Ben reminded. "Lean into it. That's right. We want ta make sure the dirt's snug up against those roots."

"What are you gonna do with your old push mower?" Robbie dug another hole in the dirt. "Sell it?"

Ben smiled behind Robbie's back. He'd already asked his dad's permission, and the way was all clear. "I was thinking 'bout givin' it to you."

Robbie jumped to his feet and turned around, all in one giant bound. Dirt scattered across the nearby sidewalk. "What? You mean it, Ben?"

Ben laughed, stepping back a foot from Robbie's eager face. "Hold on, now. I'll only give it to you on one condition. Like I said before, business is boomin', an' I've got more yards scheduled fer this summer then I can handle. I'm in need of a partner, someone who can push a few of the smaller yards for me in town while I mow the bigger ones with my new rider."

In a flash, Robbie leapt onto Miss Emily's front porch and tore through the door, not bothering to catch the screen after him before it slammed noisily shut. Ben shook his head, bemused. Whatever case Robbie was about to make before his mother, slamming Miss Emily's screen door and dropping dirt all over her shiny, clean floor was not a good way to start. He figured he'd better follow behind for moral support.

"Mom, I can do it, I know I can!" Robbie was pleading desperately before his mother by the time Ben stepped into the kitchen. Mrs. Jones was seated in a chair near the counter, snuggling Carrots on her lap, and Robbie stood before her like a mud-caked hoodlum. Miss Emily, standing at the counter with flour all over her hands and apron, winked subtly at Ben.

"Slow down, Robert," Mrs. Jones calmed. "Take a deep breath and start again. Ben asked you to do what?"

Robbie's shoulders rose up to his ears in a show of obedience, and then he started in again. "Ben asked me to be his partner. He got a new riding mower, and he'll give me his pusher if I can help him this summer. Please, Mom, please? I know I can do it. I'm really good at mowing!"

"When have you ever mowed a yard?"

"I helped Grandpa Evan trim his bushes last fall."

"That is a far cry from pushing a large engine that's attached to rotating blades."

"I'll help 'im, ma'am," Ben asserted.

Mrs. Jones looked up at Ben. Her eyes were weary and a little bit scared.

"I won't let 'im push by hisself 'til you say it's all right, ma'am. I'll teach him just like my dad taught me, real slow and careful like."

"How will he transport this push mower?"

"Well, he can pull it in a wagon on his bike like I do—"

Mrs. Jones's eyes grew wide with motherly fear.

"—or you can come with 'im and watch 'im while he mows. It'll only be three yards a week, ma'am. It won't take no more than a coupla hours a week."

Ben held his breath. He was doing his darnedest to win this gig for his young friend. Robbie Jones had endured more heartbreak in the last year than Ben had in his entire life. And since mowing in the sunshine always helped him feel better about things, he thought Robbie could use a little more sunshine too.

"Please, Mom?" Robbie pleaded. "I'm strong, and I'll be real careful. You can come with me, and maybe . . ." Robbie swallowed hard. "Maybe Davie can help me if he wants."

Mrs. Jones's eyes softened immediately. She seemed to recognize a true sacrifice and compromise when she saw one.

"Well," she said, "I suppose we can try anything for *one* summer, at least."

Ben smiled at Miss Emily.

Robbie hooted and hollered like the hoodlum he was, scaring poor Carrots off of his mom's lap, and the terrified rabbit hightailed it back to the safety of his cage in the living room.

"Now, get back outside before you trail more dirt onto Dr. Duke's kitchen floor." Rebecca shook her head, but her lips were twitching with a persistent smile. She turned to Emily once Robbie and Ben had made it safely back outside. "Can you believe that boy?"

"Don't worry," Emily assured her. "Ben's a good role model for Robbie. This'll be good for him."

"Where in the world am I going to put that mower?"

"Keep it here," Emily said. "I'm most likely going to be one of the smaller yards Robbie'll be push-mowing. This property is technically yours now anyway. Stick the mower in a corner of the garage, and make it easier for everyone."

"Well, I'm not convinced you'll be staying here much longer," Rebecca teased. "I fully expect you to be moving into the parsonage within the year."

Emily blushed. "I don't know. The way things are going, I might be in this house forever."

"He still hasn't proposed?"

Emily shook her head. Her eyes looked like they were going to pop out of their sockets from all of the pressure building up inside. "I don't understand. Is it me?"

"No, Em." Rebecca shook her head. She wanted to shout, "It's *me!*" but she didn't. Instead, she made a mental note to talk some sense into that pastor of hers. "I think he's just been distracted. What with Emma and my mother dying, I think he's just been, you know, helping a lot of us through a tough time. I know he wants to marry you."

Emily stuck a spoon in the jar of solidified coconut oil. "Well, I'm not getting any younger. Oh," she stabbed at the blobby white substance with irritation, "this stuff is impossible to work with!"

Rebecca stood and walked over to the counter to better assess the situation. "Don't try pressing the oil into the measuring cup like that. That'll take forever. Here," Rebecca picked up a measuring bowl and handed it to Emily. "Fill this with water at the sink. Make sure it's *cold* water, and only fill it to the two-cup line. That's it . . . now drop spoonfuls of coconut oil one at a time into the water until it rises to the two-and-a-half-cup line. Then, pour the water out, and you've got the perfect measurement of fat."

"Of course," Emily murmured. It all made such good sense.

"It only works when your fat source is solidified, but it's kind of a handy trick."

Emily sighed. "I feel like there should be a 4-H club for adults who grew up in the city."

"It's called the cooking channel."

"But I don't have a TV, remember?"

"I keep forgetting." Rebecca leaned against the counter. "But didn't you take home economics in school?"

Emily shook her head. "You had to choose between home economics and business economics at my school. They were offered the same hour."

"Business economics? No TV? You're such a progressive, Em," Rebecca teased.

Emily laughed, but she sobered quickly. "How's Evan?"

Rebecca smiled. "He's loving being a grandpa. He's insisted on paying for music lessons for all of the boys, and he wants to take them on a camping trip."

"Evan likes camping?"

"I don't think so," Rebecca said, "but Frankie read *The Hobbit* this winter, and now he's obsessed with the art of survival. Davie and Robbie went through the same phase at his age. What is it with boys?"

"What is Evan like with Alison?"

"He's sweet," Rebecca's eyes misted over. These days, she cried at the drop of a hat. She had hit one of the monsoon seasons of life. "I don't know if it's because Aly looks so much like my mother or if it's her name, but all that girl needs to do is hold her hand out to him and he comes running."

Emily smiled as she pictured Evan chasing that little strawberry-blonde cloud, and she marveled at the mercy of God in granting Evan the gift of a family to love and to cherish.

"Did you hear what Blaine gave Evan?"

"No," Emily looked up curiously. "What?"

Rebecca washed her hands at the sink, dried them on a towel, and stuck them in Emily's pie dough to demonstrate how to knead it properly. "Blaine got him tickets to hear Bach's St. Matthew Passion in Chicago this summer."

"Oh, wow!" Emily raised her eyebrows. A thoughtful gift indeed, especially for a church musician such as Evan. Blaine was full of surprises. She stepped to the side and watched as Rebecca expertly pinched and pressed and rolled the dough. "And how are you, my friend?"

"I'm all right."

Emily let Rebecca's words stand on their own and quietly took over working the pie dough. Rebecca moved on to the sink to wash her hands again.

"I'm not sure I can take another year like this one anytime soon, though," Rebecca laughed wryly.

Emily kept kneading and listening.

"I have a feeling," Rebecca sniffed, another spring shower popping up on the radar, "that whenever you and I talk about this year in the future, we're going to refer to it as '*that* year.'"

"'*That* year,'" Emily repeated. "Yep. That sounds about right. I think I'm ready to move on from *that* year. How about you?"

Rebecca held her silence for a moment. When she spoke again, her voice was little more than a squeak. "Jeremy and I haven't been able to get pregnant again since Emma."

Emily's heart sank in sympathy for her hurting friend. She had wondered as much. She closed her eyes and offered up a quick prayer.

"What if we can't?"

Emily opened her eyes again. "What if you can?"

Rebecca nodded and wiped at her eyes. She sniffed determinedly and dried her hands on her pants. "Okay, I'm done with crying for today."

Emily wasn't entirely convinced.

"Do you know what we should do?" Rebecca drummed her hands on the countertop. "We should have another one of our old tea parties. Get the girls together, bake some delicious things, you know the drill. It's been too long, don't you think?"

"Way too long."

"I could host it this time, maybe make some of Mother's chicken salad." Rebecca's eyes immediately clouded over again. Emily knew that it was just going to be touch and go for a while until the rainy season had passed.

"You should definitely host," she said, walking over to Rebecca and hugging her tightly, ignoring the mess on her hands, "and you should make your mother's chicken salad, for sure. All of us will want it. And Candice'll probably want to make a cake, and Bev'll bring pigs in a blanket. And Arlene'll bring two pies: one for the party and one for your fridge." Rebecca couldn't help but laugh at that. Emily squeezed her friend once more for good measure. "Your mother won't be there, but the rest of us will."

Rebecca sighed. It wasn't a happy sigh, but it wasn't a sad one, either. "Thank you, Emily."

"For what?"

"For being there."

CHAPTER THIRTY-SIX:

THE CHOIR IMMORTAL

||||||||||||||||||||||||||||||||||||||||||||||||||||||||

Emily wasn't surprised to find Evan kneeling at Alice's grave the following afternoon. What surprised her was the sight of the four ruddy-haired children crowded around him on the ground.

"We're planting a hibiscuit for Grammy—" Robbie started to explain.

"Hibiscus," Evan amended, giving Emily a half-exasperated, half-amused look over his shoulder. That boy!

"It's Grammy's favorite," Frankie informed, smiling from his seat next to Evan on the greening grass. The boy was leaning contentedly against his grandpa, making the two appear as if they were literally joined at the hip.

Evan brushed the loose, black soil from his gardening gloves, gestured to Frankie to scoot to the side a bit to make some more room, and leaned back on his heels. "Go ahead now, Davie. Lower it in."

Davie, who was balancing the hibiscus's substantial root ball between his preadolescent hands, glanced up at Emily and gave her a shy smile. The boy had grown up so much in the last year. Maybe it was turning twelve or finally recognizing a lady when he saw one or—more likely than not—losing two family members in one year, but whatever the reason, Davie's tongue had softened considerably and his demeanor now emanated a quiet maturity. Emily smiled warmly back at him and watched with appreciation as he gently lowered the plant down into the hole Evan had dug to the left of Alice's headstone.

"Now," Evan nodded toward Robbie and Frankie, "pack in the dirt, boys. And Alison, get that water jug ready. It's your turn next."

Alison jumped up to grab the plastic jug sitting a few feet away, but she immediately took a detour straight toward Emily.

"I lost a tooth!" she announced proudly, opening her mouth wide to give Emily a front-row seat to the gaping hole in her mouth where her upper right central incisor should have been.

"What?" Emily exclaimed. "Already?"

"I had an allergy."

"She means an accident," Frankie translated.

"What happened?" Emily asked.

"Well . . ." Evan gingerly pushed himself up from the ground—Emily offering him a steadying hand—and removed his gardening gloves. There was laughter in his eyes. "A certain ninja was taking a certain sister of his prisoner in my backyard last week. The prisoner naturally resisted having her hands tied behind her back, but she did agree to bite down on the ninja's rope to be led away to my gazebo—"

"Jail!" Robbie interjected.

"Pardon me," Evan gallantly nodded his head toward the offended ninja, "to *jail*. What you see before you now, Dr. Duke, is the result of a very unfortunate meeting of Robbie's right toe with one of my landscaping stones. Our ninja—however capable!—" he was quick to assure the reddest head in the bunch, "tripped and fell to the ground, bringing his rope and his prisoner's tooth along with him."

Emily winced. "Ouch."

"It did not hurt!" Alison assured.

Emily smiled down at not-so-little Alison and marveled at how much all of the Jones kids had grown over the winter. Where was the little toddler with the strawberry-blonde pigtails? She had been replaced with this lively, spunky kid. "Are you sure it didn't hurt? Not even a little?"

"I'm four," Alison said. No other explanation, apparently, was needed.

Frankie gave an explanation anyway. "She thinks that's old."

"Wait until you're double digits like me, Aly," Robbie puffed. "Then, you'll *really* be old." The freckled ten-year-old promptly stood and grabbed the abandoned water jug.

"No!" Alison screeched.

"Robbie, that's your sister's job," Evan monitored. "Let her do it."

Emily smiled at the sight, tickled to see Evan in such a role. Who would have ever thought?

Alison hefted the sloshing jug of water to her chest with both of her hands and then, tilting a bit off-center, proceeded to spill the majority of its contents onto Frankie, the only Jones boy unfortunate enough to still be seated on the ground.

"Aly!" Frankie cried, jumping to his feet.

"On the bush, Alison," Evan sighed, shaking his head. "Frankie doesn't need any watering to grow."

All of the children giggled.

"Hey, look!" Robbie said, pointing to something lying on the other side of the headstone.

"What?" Davie asked. Every Jones—double and single digits alike—promptly gathered around the back of the headstone.

"It's a dead bird," Robbie said.

Alison reached out a finger to touch it.

"Stop!" Evan called, quickly shooing the children back to the other side. "Come away from there."

"Why?" Robbie asked.

"It's dead."

"But we're in a cemetery," Frankie reasoned. "Everything's dead in here."

"Yes," Evan said, "but everything dead in here is properly buried. This bird is not, and it could have lice or be carrying some kind of disease or—"

"How did it die?" Robbie interrupted.

"Probably of natural causes," Davie said thoughtfully. "Old age, I think."

"Nah," Robbie said, clearly disappointed with that answer. "Looks like a car came by and hit him and then caught him up in its wheel and then spun him into the cemetery."

"Over a thousand feet?" Davie looked skeptical.

Robbie pondered this miracle in a brow-furrowed silence.

"It ate a pois'nous apple," Alison postulated.

"I think an eagle got it." Frankie's voice seemed to be coming from some faraway place, most likely Middle Earth. "It was already dead when the eagle found it, but the eagle rescued it anyway. It picked it up in its beak and flew it here to rest forever in peace."

Robbie scrunched up his nose. "More like an eagle took a bite out of it with its beak and then threw the rest of it away in here. Or maybe a snake got it."

Alison screamed and jumped into Davie's arms.

"What do you think, Dr. Duke?" Frankie asked.

Everyone turned expectantly toward the quiet choir director.

"Well . . ." Emily immediately blushed, taken aback. She glanced around at the precious faces staring up at her and carefully weighed the consequences of her answer. "Perhaps

Davie is right about the natural causes. Maybe the bird was sick."

"You mean, like with cancer? Like how Grammy died?" Frankie asked.

Robbie's face fell.

"No, no!" Emily backpedaled as fast as she could. "Not cancer. Um . . ." She stepped closer to the bird as if to examine it. It had flies buzzing around its eyes and mouth. Her hand involuntarily flew to her nose. "You know, the more I look at it, I think it probably got caught in an ambush."

"Is that one of those flowering bushes you like so much, Grandpa?" Frankie turned and asked.

"An ambush is not a plant, Frankie." Robbie's chin lifted with the authority of a well-seasoned botanist. "It's a surprise attack. Like from behind a tree or a grave or something."

"Exactly," Emily said, lowering her hand and willing it to stay at her side. She was fully aware of Robbie's watchful eyes on her, so she feigned interest and leaned down for one last peep at the carcass. She hoped she looked like one of those movie detectives investigating a crime scene.

"Is the bird black?" Evan asked from a healthy distance.

Emily nodded.

"Then it was probably one of Maleficent's spies." Evan reached out to tickle one of Alison's pink cheeks. The princess giggled and buried her face in Davie's shoulder.

"Or," Emily countered, "maybe it was delivering a secret message to Saruman."

Frankie's eyes lit up. Davie shook his head to show he was wise to the game, but he smiled nonetheless.

"Regardless," Emily confirmed," I think we can safely say that a ninja got it."

Robbie's grin almost outgrew his face.

"Okay, crew," Evan announced, "let's start loading up the car. Your mom said she'd have supper ready as soon as we get home."

"But we haven't sung yet," Frankie pointed out.

Evan's hand instinctively reached out for Alice's headstone. "You're right. We haven't. How foolish of me." Evan turned to Emily, his hand still protectively gripping the sandblasted granite bearing his wife's name. He looked as if he might never let it go. "Won't you join us, Dr. Duke? The children and I have made a habit of singing Grammy's funeral hymn every time we visit her grave."

Evan then nodded to the children, and they all gathered in song around the radiant throne of God, joining their voices with the choir immortal—their beloved Grammy included.

When everyone finished singing, Evan and the Jones children dutifully carried trowels, gardening gloves, empty pots, and the miscreant water jug to the car. Emily hung back for a moment to study the epithet on Alice's headstone.

**Jesus, said,
"Whoever believes in Me,
though he die, yet shall he live."
John 11:25**

Emily reached into her pocket and pulled out a worn red strip of material and rubbed its smooth, silky surface one last time between her fingers. Then, she lovingly tied it to a branch of the newly planted hibiscus.

As she turned to walk away, Robbie sidled up next to her and slipped his hand in hers. Apparently, boys who are double-digits old are still young enough at heart to hold the hands of curly-haired choir directors.

"Hey, Miss Emily," he said, leaning against her arm. "What was it you left at Grammy's grave?"

"Something special," Emily murmured, her mind wandering back in time to her very first Sunday at Zion. Alice's singular smile shone across the pews in Emily's memory, those familiar blue eyes as warm and welcoming as ever. "It was the very first thing your grammy ever gave me."

"What?" Robbie looked up into her face eagerly.

Emily smiled at the thought. "A red ribbon tied to the key of what was to become my new home."

CHAPTER THIRTY-SEVEN: BLESS HER HEART

‖‖‖‖‖‖‖‖‖‖‖‖‖‖‖‖‖‖‖‖‖‖‖‖‖‖‖‖‖‖‖‖‖‖‖‖‖

Emily walked the block and a half to Zion Lutheran Church in what appeared to be a snowstorm, only there wasn't a single cloud above in the pristine sky. Thousands of snowy white crab apple petals, plucked from a nearby tree and swept up by a rather gregarious gust of wind, billowed and swirled around Emily in an aromatic cloud. She threw back her head and laughed, spreading wide her arms to embrace the serendipitous sight. She absolutely loved Bradbury, Illinois, and she never, ever, ever wanted to leave.

"There's a letter for you," Mrs. Scheinberg announced as Emily entered the front office door. "It's from Indiana."

"Oh?" Emily smiled and dropped a tiny, blooming crab apple sprig on Mrs. Scheinberg's desk as she made her way to her mailbox. She pulled out the yellow envelope with a white gardenia embossed on the front flap. The shimmery piece of cardstock inside read:

Ms. Geraldine Alexandria Turner
and
Mr. Theodore Jonathan Wright

request the honor of your presence
at their marriage

Saturday, the ninth of June
at three o'clock
First United Methodist
Cicero, Indiana

"What is it?" Mrs. Scheinberg asked, leaning back in her chair to get a better view of the piece of paper in Emily's hand.

"It's a wedding invitation," she murmured. "For Geraldine Turner."

"Geraldine?" Mrs. Scheinberg spurted.

Miss Geraldine Turner had left Zion in a bit of a tizzy last Easter over the silliest of mistakes in the bulletin, and other than the letter that had come through the church mail the following month requesting a release of membership from Zion, no one in the congregation had heard from her since.

Mrs. Scheinberg pushed herself up onto her feet, peering nosily over Emily's shoulder. "Well, would you look at that? Geraldine finally found someone to marry her, bless her heart. Makes you wonder about the mental state of the man, though, doesn't it?"

Emily stared at the invitation. "Did you get one?"

"An invitation? Nope," Mrs. Scheinberg shook her head. "Pastor Fletcher didn't either. At least, I haven't seen another envelope like this come through the office mail. Imagine," she ruminated aloud, clearly enjoying herself, "Geraldine's going to be Mrs. *Wright*. I suppose she picked the man based on his name alone."

Emily kept her silence. She felt flustered by the whole thing. There was no doubting the fact that she had never been Geraldine's favorite person back when the woman had lived in Bradbury, and it now seemed oddly intimate to be receiving an invitation to her wedding. Emily flipped the paper over in her hand. "Oh, there's a handwritten note on the back!"

"What's it say?"

Emily's eyes quickly scanned Geraldine's perfectly even script:

Dr. Duke,

I heard that you are still unmarried. That's too bad. Everyone had such high hopes for you and Dr. Brandt. I guess not every man can be as wonderful and devoted as my Teddy. Have you considered Pastor Fletcher? I hear that he's still available.

Geraldine

Emily hastily stuffed the invitation back into its envelope, but it was too late. Mrs. Scheinberg had already read it.

"Why, the malicious cow!" Mrs. Scheinberg hissed through her teeth. "I take back my 'bless her heart' of earlier. That woman has a forked tongue, I know it."

But Emily was already out the door.

"What just happened?" Pastor Fletcher asked, sticking his head out of his study in time to witness Emily's fleeing the scene.

Mrs. Scheinberg pulled out her best frown for the "available" clergyman. "Nothing good, thanks to you."

||||||||||||||||||||||||||||||||||||||||||||||||

Emily no longer felt any joy at the sight and smell of the crab apple blossoms. In fact, she ignored them completely, walking straight to the college with her head down, her eyes fixed on the pavement. She knew that it was silly, getting worked up over Geraldine's ridiculous note, but the uppity woman had hit a raw nerve. Emily was trying to be patient; she was trying to be understanding. But Pastor Fletcher's persistent silence on the proposal front was beginning to make her angry. Did he expect her to wait around forever? She loved the man, but either he wanted to marry her or he didn't. And even if he was indeed trying to be sensitive to everyone else's grief as Rebecca had said, surely he could at least understand that life was always going to be difficult and wonderful and horrible and beautiful and full of grief. Wasn't the point of getting married so that they could share all of those experiences—the good and the bad—*together* rather than apart? Emily stormed into her office in McPherson Hall and dropped her bag on the floor, but no sooner had she shut her office door than someone knocked three times on the outside of it.

Emily sighed and silently prayed that it wasn't one of her music students standing on the other side of that door. There was no possible way she could appear cheerful and welcoming right now. She was desperate to be alone with her thoughts, so she stood still and, for one naughty moment, considered not answering the door at all. Maybe the person on the other side would assume she wasn't there and would go away. Emily's vigilant conscience soon intervened, however, and she wrestled her sour face into a smile, took a deep breath, and opened the door. "Yes?"

Lauren Basset, the head of BC's music department, was standing in the hallway. "Have a moment to chat?"

Emily nodded and stepped back, allowing her blonde, spiky-haired boss to enter the room. "Come on in."

"I have new W-4s for everyone to fill out," she chatted easily, walking over to Emily's desk and setting the tax worksheets on top of a stack of choral octavos, "and I saw you walk by my office window and thought it'd be more fun to deliver them in person." Basset suddenly turned around and caught sight of Emily's red face. She stopped in her tracks. "What is it?"

Emily immediately buried her face in her hands and began to cry.

"Good heavens," Basset mumbled, effectively directing a blinded Emily to a nearby chair and helping her sit down. "I know taxes are a drag, but we have to 'render unto Caesar,' you know?"

Emily laughed through her tears and wiped her sloppy nose.

"Here." Basset grabbed a tissue from a box on Emily's desk. "What's the matter? Did something happen in one of your classes?"

Emily shook her head and blew her nose. If only it were as simple as that.

"Did something happen with Michael?"

Emily started to cry even harder. Basset grabbed her another tissue and waited for the tears to subside. The nice thing about Lauren Basset was that not only was she the world's best boss, but she was also a pretty great friend.

"Did he say something stupid?"

"That's the problem," Emily moaned. "He hasn't said a thing. For a long time."

"I don't understand."

Emily held up her left hand and wiggled her naked ring finger.

"Ah, I see. Well, the guy must have his reasons, surely. Have you told him how you feel about it?"

"I never get a chance." Even as Emily said it, she realized how dumb and immature she sounded. Still, her inner five-year-old had been released, and there was no reining in the little rascal. "He's just so busy all of the time! There's always someone at church who needs him. I never *see* him, let alone talk to him."

That last statement was a bit of an exaggeration, but then, five-year-olds—especially inner ones—excel at hyperbole.

Basset sat in a chair across from Emily. "Emily, men can't read minds like us women. They need us to tell them *exactly* what we want and need from them. Michael needs to hear that you are hurting."

Basset was being entirely too sensible in all of this. Emily fought the childish urge to cross her arms over her chest and throw out a champion pout. "But how do I tell him that I want to get married without actually proposing to him myself?"

Basset shrugged. "I don't know. I've always been better at theory than application. But I do know that miscommunication is a wimpy foe, one that's easily defeated by a few honest words."

Emily sighed. Basset was right. Her inner child obediently submitted to the calm, reasonable woman and sat in the corner for a good long time-out. "I'm being a baby, I know," Emily admitted, "and I need to talk to Michael, I do. But I still want *him* to be the one to bring up the subject of marriage. I think I'd have trouble submitting to him if he didn't."

Basset stood and winked. "I understand. We're expected to take their names, aren't we? Seems the least they could do is be polite and offer it to us in the first place."

‖‖

What Emily couldn't have known was that, just a few minutes before, a certain English lit professor of the male, sandy-haired persuasion had been sitting in his own office rereading *A Tale of Two Cities* and—upon spotting a particularly vibrant dogwood blooming outside his window—dropped his book on his desk and jaunted over to McPherson Hall with the intent of inviting his pretty church choir director out for a personally guided tour of the flowering campus. The sound of the female voices floating out from behind Emily's ajar office door, however, kept him at bay. For over a year, he had been harboring a small vessel of hope that she would turn out to be the Lucie Manette to his Charles Darnay—and that hope had only grown with each passing week that Pastor Fletcher neglected to propose. But Emily's last statement broke his mainmast clean through. Engaged or not, she had her heart set on the good reverend, and no amount of walking around campus in the lusty spring air would change her mind. Zachary Brandt was crushed, but he was not without purpose. He lifted his chin and did what any self-respecting Sydney Carton would do. He quietly vowed to the fair lady sitting behind that door, "'I would embrace any sacrifice for you and for those dear to you.'"

Chapter Thirty-Eight:

Sydney Carton's Sacrifice

‖‖‖

Everyone was excited for Blaine's recital. The women of Zion, especially, fussed and fretted over their pierced pianist, even offering to throw him a reception the likes of which Bradbury College had never seen. After Blaine shyly accepted the offer from his seat at the upright before choir practice one night, the quilting circle spent the next two Tuesday mornings talking over menu ideas ad nauseam and deciding and redeciding upon linen colors and napkin brands and flower arrangements.

"I'll bring rhubarb custard bars, of course," Candice declared from her usual spot at the south end of the quilt. "They'll look perfect against my lavender tablecloths."

"I thought we'd decided on green cloths for the reception." Bev looked confused.

"Oh, no. It was lavender, I'm sure of it. I remember, because I specifically picked out my dessert with that fabric in mind." Candice, who had decided to give up her wig altogether the week after Alice died, now wore her graying locks in a stylish pageboy, and she'd managed to lose a few pounds around her middle. She was feeling really good about herself, and this newfound confidence seemed only to magnify her natural charm. Where

Candice was headstrong and tenacious before, she now was obstinate and immovable.

"I think lavender's a mistake," Bev wrinkled her nose. "It's too schoolgirlish for a college student like Blaine. I've never seen that boy ever wear a pastel."

"He's never worn green either," Candice pointed out.

"Irene Rincker already offered her ivory cloths for the reception, and I said yes." Mrs. Scheinberg settled the matter with a nod of her head. She was Blaine's guardian angel, so she had the final say in all reception matters. That's how she saw it, anyway. "Now, don't worry, Candice. Marge is bringing lilacs, so your beloved color will be on the table. Nettie, are you still making sugar cookies?"

Nettie nodded her head enthusiastically. "I found the most adorable cookie cutters at Hobby Lobby last week. They're in the shape of musical notes, and they were half off. I went ahead and bought two sets. I was planning on making a double batch anyway."

Bev opened her mouth as if to say something but then appeared to think better of it.

"What are you making, Rebecca?" Nettie asked kindly.

Everyone turned to look at the newest and youngest member of the quilting circle.

"I'm making Mother's coconut shortbread and dipping it in chocolate," Rebecca replied, her head bent studiously over a corner of the quilt. She had been sewing with the ladies for at least three months now—she had joined the circle exactly one month after her mother had died—but she still kept pretty much to herself at the frame.

"Well, those will go well with my banana slush punch," Bev smiled. She, too, was sporting a new hairdo. She had been so excited to get rid of those oppressive black locks that she had splurged and paid to get her hair cut at the fancy salon in Hamburg. She felt like the atrocious amount of money had been worth it the moment Mrs. Scheinberg had leaned over at the next choir practice and said, "You look like a young Judi Dench."

"Do you need my punch bowl?" Candice asked Bev.

"No, I'm borrowing my Aunt Jessie's crystal bowl and ladle for the occasion. Oh, that reminds me." Bev turned toward Mrs. Scheinberg. "Emily wanted me to pass along that she's making Viennese walnut cookies with buttercream frosting."

"Good," Mrs. Scheinberg approved.

"What about you, Arlene? What are you making?"

Mrs. Scheinberg rethreaded her needle. "I'm making snickerdoodles, seven-layer bars, mint marbled brownies, and chocolate chip meringues." She was also making a pan of cinnamon rolls with cream cheese frosting for Blaine to take home with him after the recital, but the other ladies didn't need to know about that.

IIIIIIIIIIIIIIIIIIIIIIIIIIIIIIIIIIIIIIIIIIIIIIIIII

The evening of the recital, the ladies arranged bouquets of lilacs and trays of decadent treats on three ivory-draped tables in the foyer of McPherson Hall. By the time they were done, the space looked more like a wedding reception than a student recital.

"Look at all of this!" Grandma Joyce exclaimed as she stepped into the foyer, her arm linked proudly through Blaine's. The elderly woman was wearing a corsage of red roses on her left shoulder. Shelby followed closely behind, sporting the handmade red skirt she'd gotten for Christmas. It was Blaine's red button-down shirt, however, that caused a few jaws in the room to drop wide open, for the church ladies had never before seen

Blaine wear anything but gray or black. Even more astounding was the fact that his face was washed clean of any trace of makeup, and the young man's self-conscious blush warmed the entire room.

"Blaine, you look so handsome," Rebecca smiled.

It was true. The red of Blaine's shirt set off the shine in his black hair, now grown out a couple of inches and conservatively trimmed around his ears and along his neck. The dark brown of his eyes, free of their circular black prisons, seemed to better reflect the softness of the women standing around him, and his long lashes lowered modestly toward the floor. He still had his piercings, but they seemed so much a part of him at this point that the women hardly noticed them anymore.

Candice, whose alopecia had made her sensitive to the open stares of others, stepped forward to relieve Blaine of the unwanted attention. "You must be Blaine's grandmother and sister. I'm Candice Bradbury. My husband is Thomas Edison Bradbury. His family founded this town five generations ago. . . ." Candice suddenly began to falter, no longer feeling completely comfortable with her usual script. The historical importance of her familial ties just didn't seem to be the most important thing right now. She found herself wanting to be connected more with the people standing in this very room than with a list of names in a genealogy book sitting on her shelf at home. She bit her lower lip, took a breath, and opted for an entirely different introduction. "We," she gestured to the other women, "are Blaine's family at Zion Lutheran Church here in Bradbury, and we're so proud of him and his music!"

Mrs. Scheinberg grinned.

Grandma Joyce squeezed her grandson's arm and smiled at the assembly of ladies. "We are proud of him too."

Mary Hopf and her parents arrived just then, and Blaine became occupied with introducing his friend to his family.

"Who's that?" Nettie asked, moving closer to Mrs. Scheinberg.

"That's Mary."

"She's really sweet," Bev smiled, keeping her voice low. "She's a member at St. Luke's in Hamburg and sang with us in the cantata. I think Blaine likes her."

"We all like her," Mrs. Scheinberg said.

"Is she Blaine's girlfriend?" Nettie asked.

All of the women looked to Mrs. Scheinberg for an answer. Hope practically gushed from their eyes.

"She's Blaine's friend who is a girl." Mrs. Scheinberg honestly didn't know what else to say. Blaine had never said anything to her about Mary, though it was obvious he sought out the girl's company more than he did any other student's at the college. He seemed drawn to her for some reason. Mrs. Scheinberg suspected the attraction had more to do with Mary's calm and considerate demeanor than with her being a girl.

Tony Maler arrived next with a tall, bespectacled man wearing a sharp gray suit and pink and green bow tie in tow.

"Is that . . . ?" Nettie's voice drifted off.

"Yes," Mrs. Scheinberg answered.

"And is he with . . . ?"

"Yes."

The ladies watched in curious silence. Blaine shook his father's hand and nodded politely to Douglas Hemmingway, but he was not as warm in his welcome as Shelby. The teenage girl threw herself into her father's open arms and then wrapped an affectionate arm around Douglas's waist. Blaine turned to chat a bit more with Mary, kissed his grandmother on the cheek, and then excused himself to go backstage.

The church ladies quickly scattered to find good seats in the auditorium, but Mrs. Scheinberg stayed behind to guard the refreshment tables from the curious college students wandering through the hall. She didn't trust these starving artists to wait until the end of the recital to start sampling the goods. That, and she needed a moment to herself. Seeing Blaine all dressed up and looking spiffy in his new red shirt made her feel suddenly proud and sad all at the same time. Blaine wasn't her son, of course, but she felt like his mother, especially since his own mother wasn't there. Mrs. Scheinberg sighed. She'd met Ellen Maler only once—back last spring when she had driven Blaine to Chicago for his parents' divorce trial—but even then, she could tell that Blaine's mother struggled with depression. Still, she had hoped the woman would rally and make the effort to come to her son's recital. Some wells were simply too deep to climb out of, apparently. *God, help her. And God, help Blaine.*

Blaine's recital was spectacular, of course, unparalleled in the history of student recitals at Bradbury College. His J. S. Bach was perfectly precise, his Rachmaninov was appropriately moody, and his Gershwin was positively symphonic, but it was his Chopin, the "Tristesse" *étude*, which brought down the house. No one but Blaine, Tony Maler, and Grandma Joyce understood the familial significance of the song, but it didn't matter. Blaine's sensitive, masterful interpretation of the piece moved even the most musically illiterate of souls, and after Blaine released the sustain pedal on the piano for the last time and rested his hands humbly in his lap, the hall erupted in explosive applause. Douglas Hemmingway threw a bouquet of roses at Blaine's feet, and Robbie Jones ran to the foot of the stage to hand his piano teacher the cluster of white tulips he and his grandpa Evan had picked that afternoon. Mrs. Scheinberg blubbered like a baby in the back row while Emily hugged a consoling arm around her shoulders, and the other church ladies quietly slipped out the door to man the refreshment line.

Bev took up her post behind the punch bowl, but before ladling punch into the little plastic cups, she tossed back one of Mrs. Scheinberg's chocolaty meringues. Her toss was a little too assertive, however, for the crusty sugared ball shot all the way to the back of her throat and planted its sticky roots in her soft palate. She tried her best to cough it out, but the meringue wouldn't budge. Bev's eyes grew wide with panic, and she gripped spastically at her neck with her hands.

"Aren't those good?" Nettie asked.

Bev shook her head emphatically, her face quickly turning the color of Blaine's new shirt.

"You don't like them? But they're light and airy. Like a bunny's nose."

Bev blinked wildly and pushed past Nettie, bumping into a red-eyed Mrs. Scheinberg.

"Good grief, Bev! Watch where you're—" but Mrs. Scheinberg stopped midsentence, immediately recognizing Bev's universal sign for choking. "Dear Lord! Bev, turn around!"

Mrs. Scheinberg got behind Bev and wrapped her arms around her friend's waist, tucking her right fist snugly against her diaphragm and holding it in place with her left. "I'll try not to break a rib," she whispered in Bev's ear, and then she thrust her fist inward and upward, administering the Heimlich maneuver over and over again until—what seemed like an eternity later—Bev finally wretched a slimy piece of meringue onto the carpeted floor. By that time, a rather large group of onlookers had circled around the women, and the audience burst into the second standing ovation of the evening.

Bev, shaky and emotional from her airless minute, collapsed against Mrs. Scheinberg's shoulder. Mrs. Scheinberg quickly directed her toward a chair along the wall, and when Bev was safely sitting down, she called out to Pastor Fletcher, "Get Irv on his cell phone. He's in the field with his planter, but he'll want to know what happened."

Then, Mrs. Scheinberg turned back around to assess her friend's coloring and state of mind. Bev was still crying, but her eyes now looked more relieved than scared. She even had a small smile on her face.

"What is it, honey?" Mrs. Scheinberg asked, concerned. She wasn't exactly sure just how long Bev had been without air. "Does your head hurt?"

Bev shook her head and grabbed Mrs. Scheinberg's hand, pulling her close enough to speak shakily into her ear, "You did great, kiddo."

||||||||||||||||||||||||||||||||||||||||||||||||||

Emily took over serving the punch so that Mrs. Scheinberg could properly look after Bev, and Zachary Brandt was first in line. "Two, please," he smiled, keeping one for himself and handing the other to Pastor Fletcher, who was standing just a few feet away, putting his phone back in his pocket.

"I've been meaning to ask you something," Zachary started.

Pastor smiled amicably and took the cup. "What's that?"

Zachary sipped at his punch and watched as Emily smiled and chatted easily with Blaine's sister and grandmother. "Are you and Emily no longer dating?"

Pastor almost spit out his punch.

"I couldn't help but notice that she spends a lot of evenings working late in her office these days," Zachary pointed out, innocently taking another sip of his punch and looking sidelong at his floundering companion. "That, and her left hand is still unadorned."

Pastor's face grew red. Whether it was from embarrassment, anger, or jealousy, Zachary didn't know, but he figured any and all of those reactions would work to his Lucie's—Emily's—advantage.

"A fellow wonders," Zachary calmly continued. "Is Emily now available?"

"She is *not* available," Pastor muttered.

"Oh, then you've proposed?"

Pastor's face might have been a beet. "No, not exactly."

"'Not *exactly*'? What does *that* mean?"

"It means," Pastor said, turning to look Zachary in the eye, "that I have every intention of asking Dr. Duke to be my wife."

Good. He used her professional name. He was getting territorial. "But you haven't yet?"

"Well, no." Pastor looked like he might explode. "There hasn't exactly been a good moment."

Zachary gave the flustered man a tiny, knowing smile. "Really? I find that hard to believe. I, for one, would have no trouble finding a good moment to propose to that divine creature."

Pastor stood an inch taller. "What are you saying?"

Zachary immediately dropped the macho act and, smiling kindly, laid a friendly hand on his pastor's shoulder. It was time to embrace his sacrifice. "All I'm saying—from one friend to another—is that it would be wise not to wait too long. She's worth it, Pastor, and I think she's ready. Find a good moment. Soon."

With that, Sydney Carton walked away, a peaceful smile on his face. "'It is a far, far better thing that I do,'" he whispered, "'than I have ever done.'"

After the reception dwindled to just a few lingering students, Blaine asked Mrs. Scheinberg to follow him out to the parking lot across the street from McPherson Hall.

"These are for you," she said, taking advantage of the moment to hand him his personal pan of cinnamon rolls.

Blaine smelled them and grinned, unlocking his dad's black Lexus and storing the prized pan safely on the backseat of the car. When he stood back up, however, he wasn't empty-handed. He returned to Mrs. Scheinberg's side, holding a bundle of wiggly fluff in his arms.

"What's this?" Mrs. Scheinberg asked, frowning at the sight.

"It's a dog."

"Your dad bought you a dog?"

"Not exactly." Blaine shifted his feet. "He, um, bought the dog for you."

"What?" The line between Mrs. Scheinberg's eyebrows deepened considerably. "Why on earth would he do that?"

"I asked him to."

Mrs. Scheinberg stared at Blaine, careful not to let her true feelings show. The boy had been through a lot. But still. "I don't need a dog," she said evenly.

Blaine shrugged. "I think you do."

"What in the world will I do with him?"

"Well, you can take care of *her*."

"Take care of her?" Mrs. Scheinberg scoffed. "I already take care of hundreds of people every day in this rotten town. I don't have time to take care of anyone—or any*thing*—else!" She nodded meaningfully at the ball of fluff.

"Yeah, but none of those people live with you. You're lonely."

"I am not!"

Blaine pushed the dog off into Mrs. Scheinberg's arms. "She can keep you company."

"Young man, in case you've forgotten, I live on a farm. Coyotes will make a snack of this little squirrel before the sun even rises."

"Then you'd better keep her in the house." Blaine seemed pleased with himself. He was actually smiling.

Mrs. Scheinberg sighed, staring at him and wondering who had finally convinced him to wipe off all of that ridiculous makeup. Was it his father, his grandmother, or Mary? "I hate pet hair."

"See, that's the good news. She's a Shih Tzu—"

"A what?"

"A Shih Tzu, so she doesn't really shed."

Mrs. Scheinberg looked down into two black eyes surrounded by a cloud of reddish-brown hair. The little thing weighed no more than a cat. Mrs. Scheinberg stubbornly resisted the cuteness, but she felt the inevitability of defeat ahead. "What did you call it again?"

"A Shih Tzu."

Mrs. Scheinberg rolled her eyes. "Really? You got me a dog that sounds like feces?"

"It does not."

"Everyone's going to think I'm sneezing whenever I tell them its name."

"Shih Tzu's not her name. It's her breed."

"Why couldn't you get me something respectable, like a German shepherd or a collie?" The tiny dog wiggled and licked Mrs. Scheinberg's face with her paper-thin tongue. "Ugh! Oh, for crying out loud, Blaine Maler!"

Blaine laughed, clearly enjoying himself. "She'll keep you company when I'm gone."

Mrs. Scheinberg immediately sobered. She honestly hadn't allowed herself to fully consider the fact that Blaine would ever leave. He was graduating in a few weeks, she knew, but she'd always secretly hoped he would decide to stay in Bradbury forever. She looked at the boy she had grown to love as a son and felt her throat tighten with emotion. "You got into Berkeley, didn't you?"

Blaine nodded.

"Of course you did," Mrs. Scheinberg tried to smile. "They'd be idiots not to accept you. When do you leave?"

"First week of June."

Her shoulders slumped, and she somewhat unconsciously hugged the dog closer to her heart. That was so soon. "Well, you're not going to pay those liberals anything, are you? I once heard Dr. Duke say that a musician should never pay a dime to go to grad school. The school should pay you."

"I'm on full scholarship."

"That's my boy," Mrs. Scheinberg whispered, looking down at the fuzzy bundle in her arms. She was dangerously close to crying. "Well, fine. I'll keep this rat on one condition."

"What's that?"

Tears were now falling freely down her cheeks. She wanted to wipe them away, but her arms were too full of Blaine's puppy love to move. As if on cue, her furry companion reached out a sympathetic tongue and politely erased the salty evidence. Mrs. Scheinberg's heart warmed ever so slightly toward the sensitive creature. Maybe having a dog around wouldn't be so bad after all. "I'll keep her if you promise to visit this old lady now and then."

Blaine stuffed his hands into his pockets and shifted his weight onto his other foot. He wasn't much of a hugger. "I'll come every winter break and summer."

"And letters. I want letters. And not the electronic kind, either. I want letters in your own handwriting, telling me how and what you are doing. Every month."

Blaine gave her a rueful smile. "I'll have to practice sometime, you know."

"Family before practicing, young man," Mrs. Scheinberg scolded. "That piano will never love you back."

Blaine looked as if he'd heard that before. "Fine. But only if you ship me cinnamon rolls with cream cheese frosting in return."

Mrs. Scheinberg smiled. "Deal."

Blaine tossed his chin toward McPherson Hall. "I heard what you did in there tonight, by the way."

"What?"

"You saved Bev from choking."

"Oh." Mrs. Scheinberg's gaze fell humbly to the ground, but she stood at least two inches taller. "If I hadn't done it, someone else would've."

"But you did do it, and I'm proud of you."

Mrs. Scheinberg's smile was beaming brighter than the lamplight at the corner of the parking lot. "I guess it's a good thing we took that CPR class, huh?"

Blaine nodded and reached out to scratch the little dog behind her velvety ears. "What're you going to name her, anyway?"

The Shih Tzu immediately barked two high-pitched yelps, as if to give her own answer to Blaine's question. An ornery smile dawned on Mrs. Scheinberg's face. "I'm going to call her Anna Cecilia."

Blaine threw back his head and laughed.

Mrs. Scheinberg grinned happily, her reward complete. She looked down into the pair of soulful canine eyes, and the dog's entire backside wagged in appreciation. "But we'll call her Ceci for short."

Chapter Thirty-Nine: Third Time's a Charm

The next day, Mrs. Scheinberg called Emily from the church office.

"Emily? It's Arlene. I know it's the middle of the day, but could you hop over here for a second? I need your signature on the invoice for the new choir folders before I stick it in the mail."

"I'm on campus right now. Can I come by in an hour?"

"As long as it's by two fifteen, I'm fine. That's when Walter picks up the mail."

At 1:58, Emily blew through the church office door on a spring breeze that smelled of sunshine, earth, and lilacs. Her honey-colored curls, disheveled from the brisk bike ride across town, housed a few rogue crab apple petals, and her pink, happy cheeks bore the marks of the wind's merry kisses. In her hurry, Emily had accidentally misbuttoned her white sweater over her favorite yellow sundress, but her senses were too full of April's lustrous bouquet to notice or care. "Where's that invoice?"

"Right here." Mrs. Scheinberg held out a clipboard and a pen from the comfort of her own chair.

Emily quickly scribbled her signature on the paper, humming cheerfully the entire time.

"Sorry to call you away from work like that," Mrs. Scheinberg apologized. A sudden, friendly bark offered its own apology from somewhere beneath the cherrywood desk.

Emily's eyes grew wide. "Arlene? Is that a—"

The happy bark answered for itself.

"Be quiet, Ceci," Mrs. Scheinberg shushed at her feet. "The lady wasn't talking to you."

Emily hurried around the desk to find a tiny ball of hair lounging in a cushy dog bed at Mrs. Scheinberg's feet. Emily was astonished. "Arlene Scheinberg! Did you get a dog?"

"*Blaine* got me a dog."

"Well!" Emily leaned down to rub the dog's belly, which was on display for proper inspection. "She's a sweet little thing. Aren't you, cutie-pie?"

"Careful," Mrs. Scheinberg warned. "She'll get a big head, and she can barely hold it up the way it is."

Emily smiled at the distinct note of pride in Mrs. Scheinberg's voice. *Who would have ever thought?* "Well, she's beautiful, and Ceci is the perfect name. Cecilia is the patron saint of music, did you know?"

Mrs. Scheinberg's neck grew splotchy for some unknown reason.

"Does Pastor know?" Emily whispered.

"He does," a deep voice answered.

Emily turned around to find Pastor Fletcher leaning against the doorframe of his study, his hands in his pockets, a smile playing on his lips. His gaze was particularly appreciative. Her heart skipped a beat.

"You rode your bike here, didn't you?"

"How can you tell?"

"I know you, Emily Duke."

"That wall was built to hold up the ceiling, not the pastor," Mrs. Scheinberg griped. She primly removed the invoice from the clipboard and stuck it in a preaddressed manila envelope, her nose flared in righteous agitation. "Besides, you're going to ruin your back, standing like that. Some people have to live with scoliosis their entire life, you know. It's a shame that you abuse your posture the way you do. It's an insult to those who truly suffer."

"You're always thinking of others, Arlene." Pastor's smile was a tease, but he obediently stood straight. He looked at Emily. "Want to put a puzzle together tonight? We should finally break in that new red table of yours."

"Sure," Emily agreed readily.

"Wow," Mrs. Scheinberg's voice was dull with understatement. "You two really paint the town red, don't you?"

Emily smiled behind a blush. "I get done with my vocal lit class at 4:30."

"Then I'll pick up sandwiches from The Corner Coffee Shop for supper and bring them by your place. Shall we say 5:30?"

"Yes. And I'll pick up stuff for milkshakes."

Normally, Pastor would have reached out to Emily for a proper good-bye, but Mrs. Scheinberg's watchful eye kept his farewell to a simple nod. "I'll see you, then."

Emily turned toward the front office door.

"Before you go," Mrs. Scheinberg said to Emily with a wave, "there's something in your mailbox."

Emily glanced over to the west wall behind Mrs. Scheinberg's desk where the open mailboxes for church staff hung. She spied a brown paper bag in her box and smiled knowingly. It had been a long time since she'd seen one of those. "Well, I wonder who put that there?"

"I've no idea," Mrs. Scheinberg shook her head and turned back to her desk to shuffle some papers.

Emily seriously doubted that. She walked over to her mailbox, smiling the whole time, and retrieved the bag.

"It was there when I got here this morning," Mrs. Scheinberg overexplained, not even bothering to turn around and watch. That's how Emily knew she was in on it.

The bag was very light. Emily reached inside and found a simple envelope with only the words "Will you marry me?" written on the outside. She immediately sucked in her breath, her heart thumping wildly. She fumbled with the envelope, her hands trembling, and unfolded the starchy paper inside. With tears blurring her vision, she read the familiar script:

Would thou be mine
That I might love thee?
Forsaking father, mother, hearth,
Commending all my life, my worth,
I'll hold thee fast till from this earth
The Lord in mercy calls me.

Would thou be mine
That I might serve thee?
My very life and name reside
To cover thee, my holy bride,
And make thee spotless, sanctified,
Before the great assembly.

Would thou be mine
That I might save thee?

As Christ Himself upon the tree
Did spend His final breath for me,
So, too, I'll perish willingly
To guard thee and protect thee.

Would thou be mine
That I might keep thee,
Flesh of my flesh, bone of my bone?
My health, my wealth, all that I own,
I freely give to thee alone,
My wife, my rib, my only.

Emily, tears running freely down her face, hugged the precious poem to her chest and ran to the open study door. Pastor was waiting for her there, his lanky frame down on bended knee, an open ring box extended in his hands. "I'm over a year late in giving you that poem, Emily. I wrote it three weeks after I met you, and I've wanted to give it to you every day since. I've been a fool to wait so long. Will you please forgive me?"

"Yes," Emily whispered, openly crying now.

"Then marry me, Emily Duke. Please?"

Emily opened her mouth to answer, but a noisy hiccup escaped instead.

"Say yes!" Mrs. Scheinberg hollered from her hideout around the corner of the study door.

Emily laughed through her tears and nodded her head, holding out her left hand for Pastor to slip the sensible solitaire diamond onto her ring finger. "Yes!" she cried loudly enough for anyone of interest to hear.

"Hallelujah!" Mrs. Scheinberg shouted, the sound of her hooded double-wheel casters squeaking unromantically back across the office floor toward her desk.

"It's nothing fancy," Pastor apologized.

"It's perfect!" Emily admired her ring and then her groom-to-be. "Everything's perfect."

Pastor's eyes overflowed with joy and contrition. "At first I thought you wouldn't want someone like me," he explained, pulling Emily onto his knee, "and then I was convinced that I needed to do something special for you like Peter did, and, well, I was an idiot, and I'm sorry—"

Pastor tried his best to finish his apology, but he never got the final words out. Emily Duke made sure of it.

Mrs. Scheinberg, smiling to herself and wiping away a few renegade tears of her own, used the edge of her desk to push herself up from the comfort of her leather chair and waddled slowly toward the study. Her blasted feet had fallen asleep again, but there was a job to be done and she, as always, was the only one qualified to do it. Pastor Fletcher, young and paranoid, persisted in leaving his door respectfully ajar a few inches when meeting alone with a woman, but finally—the good Lord be praised!—there was a woman alive in Bradbury for whom the study door could be shut.

DISCUSSION QUESTIONS

1. This book's title, *The Choir Immortal*, is taken from the hymn "Wake, Awake, for Night is Flying" (*LSB* 516), specifically the line in stanza 3, "Where, joining with the choir immortal, We gather round Thy radiant throne." How is the "choir immortal" represented in this book?

2. Which member of Zion Lutheran Church has grown and changed the most since *House of Living Stones*?

3. Why is Evan the perfect person to talk to Blaine about forgiving his father?

4. How does Geraldine's being gone affect Candice's life at Zion Lutheran Church?

5. What are Rebecca's strengths and weaknesses as a mother? as a daughter?

6. Grief is compounded in this story by the piling up of suffering upon suffering. Can you identify which stages of grief the characters experience in their suffering?

7. How are Anna Cecilia and Mrs. Scheinberg alike? How are they different?

8. Do you think Blaine is a Christian?

9. How is Emily well prepared to be a pastor's wife?

10. What is it that Alice wants to teach Rebecca?

11. What do you think Robbie will be when he grows up?

12. With which character in this book do you most identify?

13. What does Jesus mean when He says, "I am the resurrection and the life. Whoever believes in Me, though he die, yet shall he live, and everyone who lives and believes in Me shall never die" (John 11:25–26)?

14. For whom is the Christian funeral—the dead or the living?

ACKNOWLEDGMENTS

Thank you to . . .

Peggy, Elizabeth, Holli, and Rev. McCain for publishing a little made-up story about Lutherans; Jamie for jake braking commas and keeping Bradbury's word traffic from jamming; Lucy for talking to me for hours on end about people who aren't even real; Braden, Via, Zeke, Jack, Olivia, Mary, Lily, David, Abby, and Lydia for the great ideas; Dad and all of my aunts and uncles for schooling me in the art of dressing a chicken; Dad, Uncle Russell, and Josh for the farming tips; Dad, again, for making sure all of my plants are growing in the correct seasons; Kahra for the medical advice; Adriane for patiently fielding my organ query texts; Jane for the gum smacker; Rebekah for the sinning choir; Mrs. Jeanne Korby for commending me into God's loving hands; Sue for the organ; Carol for teaching me how to make a flaky pie crust; my focus-group readers: Mom, Grandma, Addie, Steve, Nora, Julia, Lauren, Sheryl, Lena, Margy, and Teresa; and Michael, my husband and pastor, for tirelessly reading every chapter aloud to me at night and for giving words to Pastor Fletcher where a pastor's wisdom and authority are necessary.

Soli Deo gloria.

House of Living Stones

A whimsical and touching story about small-town life, misconceptions, and the power of forgiveness.

In the small Illinois town of Bradbury, change doesn't come often, and it certainly doesn't come easily. So when Pastor Fletcher hires Emily Duke as the new choir director at Zion Lutheran Church, he unknowingly sets in motion a chain of events that turns the life of his congregation upside down.

The crusty church secretary, Mrs. Scheinberg, must learn to adjust her curmudgeonly ways. Zion's talented but pompous organist, Evan Ebner, must recognize his shortcomings. Emily must come to terms with her past. Even Pastor Fletcher must face reality when his world is shaken by the baggage Emily brings and by the handsome Zachary Brandt who pursues her.

With its host of lovable and relatable characters, *House of Living Stones* will find a special place on your bookshelf and in your heart.

KATIE SCHUERMANN

House of Living Stones

House of Living Stones

Excerpt from

CHAPTER ONE:

MRS. SCHEINBERG IS INCONVENIENCED

Mrs. Arlene Compton Scheinberg positioned herself advantageously behind the cherrywood desk in the front office of Zion Lutheran Church. The sign out front on the church lawn announced to all the world that the Reverend Michael G. Fletcher was Zion's divinely called shepherd, but every sheep in the flock knew that Mrs. Scheinberg was the self-appointed herd dog, and she did not care for the looks of the two wolves in wrinkled suits sitting expressionless on the chairs along her east wall.

The man on the left with salt-and-pepper hair wore a blue suit coat but no tie. Mrs. Scheinberg scrutinized the exposed top button of the man's shirt over her gold-rimmed glasses while simultaneously editing the bulletin for the upcoming Sunday service. *A man should finish dressing before leaving the house*, she grumpily thought.

The young man on the right appeared to be growing a beard for the first time. The blond hair on his chin, however, was growing much faster than the hair on his red cheeks, leaving him looking oddly like a rooted sweet potato. "A job half done is a job undone," she quipped under her breath. She picked up her red pen and made a large, annoyed check on the bottom of page 2. Pastor Fletcher would expect the bulletin to be finished for printing by four o'clock that very afternoon, and Mrs. Scheinberg was not about to let these two sojourners distract her from her service to the Lord—not, at least, while so many other generous women in the congregation waited in line to steal her blessing.

Just last year, Miss Geraldine Turner, after catching a misplaced appositive in the bulletin announcements two Sundays in a row, made a point of suggesting to Pastor Fletcher that perhaps Mrs. Scheinberg would appreciate some help proofreading the bulletin every Thursday afternoon, between three and four o'clock to be precise.

"As the English teacher emeritus of Bradbury High School," Miss Turner had quipped in that tight, queenly way of hers, "I would be most happy to be of service."

Mrs. Scheinberg had kindly reminded Pastor Fletcher that the trustees had thought to provide only one chair behind the front office desk, and unless he could spare his own chair between three and four every Thursday afternoon, the benevolent Miss Turner would have no place to sit.

Miss Turner hadn't been her only critic. This past December, Mrs. Thomas Edison Bradbury III had dropped by the church office one Monday morning to express her sorrow and regret at the misspelling of her husband's ailing mother's maiden name in the prayer requests. She had even provided her own marked copy of the bulletin for Pastor Fletcher to keep, and she meaningfully handed Mrs. Scheinberg a copy of the Bradbury County Home Extension Office's recent publication, *The Life and Times of Bradbury: A Complete History.*

"Oh, no, I insist you keep it for free," Candice Bradbury had fluttered, her counterfeit smile pushing sideways against her ample cheeks. "You will find it to be a useful resource in the future. The *correct* spelling of every name of every one of my husband's relatives is in there. I know. I edited the book myself."

Mrs. Scheinberg had made sure to tie a festive, red-and-gold ribbon around Candice's miserable book before giving it to Pastor Fletcher as a Christmas present.

Even the sweet widow of the deceased Pastor Gardner had offered her proofreading services just last month. "Arlene, dear," Alice had crooned, "I couldn't help but notice the heading in last Sunday's bulletin about the fund-raiser for the food pantry on Washington Street."

Mrs. Scheinberg had not bothered to look up from the magazine she was perusing. "I double-checked the date and time, Alice. It's correct."

"Well, dear," Alice stumbled, "it's not the date and time to which I'm referring."

Mrs. Scheinberg wondered why a faithful servant of the church could not be allowed even one moment's peace in which to properly view the new line of sport coats featured in the JCPenney summer catalog. She sighed from her hips, put her glasses on top of her head, and gave Alice an eyeful of feigned civility.

"You see," Alice blushed, holding out the bulletin in question, "it says, 'Come and support our tasty food *panty*.'"

Mrs. Scheinberg hadn't missed the masculine chuckle—quickly stifled and masked as a cough—that escaped from behind the door of Pastor Fletcher's study. Even now, she scowled at the memory, her ears taking on the shade of her new, melon-colored blouse. "Everyone's a critic," she muttered aloud, causing the two dark suits to look up expectantly from their perches against the wall. She glared at them over her glasses, daring them to breathe, before slowly returning her attention to her bulletin.

The front door to the office opened just then, letting in a gust of warm air that smelled of sunned boxwood and potting soil. A young woman with rosy cheeks and serious, brown eyes floated in on the breeze. She wore a gray pencil skirt, white blouse, and quarter-length pink sweater. Her dark-blonde locks were cut short and stylishly curled around her forehead and cheeks. The two suits turned curious gazes toward the newcomer, and Mrs. Scheinberg felt oddly grateful to the young woman for the distraction. Uncharacteristic feelings of good-will and hospitality for the ingenue stirred in the older woman.

"May I help you?" Mrs. Scheinberg smiled generously, though a bit unnaturally. She was out of practice.

"Yes, my name is Emily Duke. I have an appointment with Reverend Fletcher, though I think I may be a bit early."

"Won't you have a seat?" Mrs. Scheinberg gestured to the empty chair sandwiched between Neiman and Marcus. The young woman hesitated, scanning the room for an alternative that imposed a little less intimacy upon three total strangers. Mrs. Scheinberg followed her gaze to the rickety, three-step footstool near the floor-to-ceiling bookcase and the brass plant stand supporting an overgrown aspara-gus fern in the corner. Evidently finding nothing more suitable, Emily Duke lowered herself carefully onto the seat that had been proffered and hugged her elbows to her ribs in an obvious effort to keep from touching the two men.

Mrs. Scheinberg creaked back comfortably in her executive leather chair and resumed her editing, though not before taking note of the fact that the young woman now seated in the waiting room appeared refreshingly modest and pressed for a woman of her generation. She even sat with her ankles crossed. And wore hose. *Naked knees are for young children and harlots*, Mrs. Scheinberg thought with satisfaction. As far as she was concerned, Emily Duke's honor and reputation were for-ever secured right then and there by a simple pair of nylons.

The door to the left of her desk opened, and out stepped a man in a clerical collar. He had an ordinary face and an unassuming manner, but his dark eyes were bright with intelligence and looked as if they could crinkle into a smile at any moment, a characteristic that endeared him to everyone in his flock but the church secretary. "Mrs. Scheinberg," Pastor Fletcher said, "would you please invite Mr. Norton into my office?"

As faithful and as nice as Pastor Fletcher might be, Mrs. Scheinberg couldn't bring herself to forgive him for being under forty. It was not his fault, to be sure, but it was a fault all the same. She took off her glasses and rubbed the bridge of her nose, careful not to leave the comfort of her own chair. "Mr. Norton," she called across the room, "the Reverend Fletcher is ready to meet with you."

Pastor Fletcher's mouth twitched and his dark eyes twinkled, a sight that irritated Mrs. Scheinberg to no end. How she wished these young pastors' mothers had taught their sons to smile a little less and to comb their hair a little more! A lesson or two in ironing would have been in order as well. Why, in thirty years of faithful service, she had never once seen Pastor Gardner, may he rest in peace, step out of his home without a starched clerical on his back and a blazing white part in his hair, but this Michael Fletcher barely remembered to cut his mop of curly hair, let alone tame it; and by the end of the day, the wrinkles in his clerical wiggled and squiggled across his back like a sloppy community garden whose rows had been hoed by a five-year-old. What were the seminaries teaching these men anyway?

For the next forty-five minutes, Mrs. Scheinberg wrangled with the third page of the bulletin while simultaneously listening to the muted interviews behind Pastor's closed door, first with the unbuttoned Mr. Norton and then with the half-bearded Mr. Simmons. (She found it satisfying to discover that Mr. Simmons's voice was higher pitched than her own. She had guessed as much.) Then, there was also the matter of Emily Duke, who was patiently waiting for her turn. As hard as Mrs. Scheinberg tried, she could not help sneaking glances at her. The young woman had a curious yet charming tendency to sway her head back and forth ever so slightly, as if listening to music that no one else could hear, and she pursed her lips and furrowed her brow like a little girl who had lost herself in her thoughts. She could not have been a day over thirty, but even from across the room, Mrs. Scheinberg saw that there were faint lines etched around her eyes and mouth as if they were lingering shadows of laughter and smiles from years past. Disarmed by Emily Duke's mannerisms, she caught herself staring at the young woman.

Each in his turn, Mr. Norton and Mr. Simmons exited Pastor's study and, subsequently, the office door. Mrs. Scheinberg celebrated the return of peace to her pasture with a desk picnic of four peanut butter cookies and one canning jar of iced peach tea. She brushed the incriminating cookie crumbs off the front of her blouse just as Pastor Fletcher ambled out of his study on his long legs. "How is the bulletin coming?" His tone was friendly, and his hands were in his pockets. Put off by his casual manner, Mrs. Scheinberg sniffed and made a large, visible check on the third page. "It would go a lot faster if there were not so many people requiring my attention and skill this morning. You *know* Thursdays are my busy days."

"Duly noted, Mrs. Scheinberg." Pastor Fletcher turned to smile warmly at the young woman. "You must be Dr. Duke."

Doctor Duke? Mrs. Scheinberg thought with approval, though she was suitably rankled to be hearing of the young woman's title for the first time. For some reason known only to Pastor Fletcher, she had not been privy to the résumés of the candidates ahead of the interviews. And that was another thing about these young pastors. They locked their filing cabinets every evening. Pastor Gardner never would have done such an untrusting thing.

"Yes," the young woman said, her smile lines blossoming in full glory. She stood and shook the reverend's hand and then walked before him into his office at his gestured invitation.

Pastor Fletcher lingered for a moment next to the secretary's desk. "Mrs. Scheinberg, would you please include a congratulatory note in the bulletin this week for Pastor Douglas? He retires a week from this Sunday."

"But he is not a member of this congregation."

"His grandchildren are."

She made a show of exchanging her red editing pen for the green writing pen in the top drawer of her desk and then looked over her glasses at the clergyman. "It seems to me that the proper place for an announcement regarding Pastor Douglas's retirement would be in his own church's bulletin. Would you like me to go ahead and call the other churches in the county to see if they have anything they would like to add?"

Pastor Fletcher, eyes sparkling, appeared as if he was resisting the urge to plant a patronizing kiss on the top of her gray head, but apparently, even youth has its wisdom. He simply stepped into his study.

"And what exactly am I supposed to say in this congratulatory announcement?" she called loudly into the great wide void.

"How about, 'We wish Reverend Douglas many blessings in his retirement,'" was the faceless reply.

Pastor Fletcher, as was his custom when meeting alone with a woman, left his door respectfully ajar a few inches, and Mrs. Scheinberg, as was her custom when sitting alone behind her desk, angled her chair and scooted a few feet closer to the door of the study to better hear every word. Although she could not see him, she could hear Pastor Fletcher sifting through the open file on his desk.

"Your résumé is impressive, Dr. Duke. I can't help but wonder why someone with your credentials would even want to interview for our part-time church choir director position."

"Thank you. I'm interested because I want to make music in a church."

"Any particular reason why you want to make music in *this* church?"

"I am a baptized Lutheran, and this is the only Lutheran church in town." Mrs. Scheinberg heard, rather than saw, Emily Duke smile.

Pastor Fletcher chuckled. "Actually, it's the only Lutheran church within thirty miles of town. What brings you to Bradbury?"

"Bradbury College hired me to teach their survey of music history courses this year."

More shuffling of papers. "Are you currently living in Bradbury?"

"Not yet. I plan to relocate from St. Louis."

"I see." Pastor Fletcher paused. "Dr. Duke, what exactly do you expect of a church choir? I mean, what situation are you used to in St. Louis?"

"Well, I've served the last three years as the senior choir director at St. Paul's in Crestwood. We average between twenty-five to thirty singers every Sunday, and we sing at both the early and late services three times a month with every fourth Sunday off. We also sing on festival Sundays and midweek services."

Pastor Fletcher's response was honest and matter-of-fact. "We have not had a consistent choir director in our employment for the last fifteen years, and we hold only one worship service every Sunday morning. It's a good week if ten singers show up for a Sunday service. I would understand if you don't find that scenario appealing."

Emily Duke's response was just as matter-of-fact. "I don't know that size is a deal breaker. 'Where two or three are gathered in My name . . .'"

Mrs. Scheinberg heard Pastor Fletcher tap his fingers on his desk, and she knew that meant he was excited. "Have you had any theological training?"

"I took a Bible and Culture class in college, but I think it hurt my theology more than helped it," Emily Duke confessed. She laughed, and the musical sound reminded Mrs. Scheinberg of a favorite wind chime her grandma used to hang on her front porch every summer.

"Honestly," Emily Duke continued, "the best theological training I ever had was in Sunday School. My teachers made sure I knew every article of the Apostles' Creed and their meanings before I finished second grade."

As she listened to the silence, Mrs. Scheinberg knew Pastor Fletcher was digesting Dr. Duke's remark. "Can you tell me a little bit more about the specific role you see the choir playing in the worship service?"

"At St. Paul's, we often sing the Alleluia Verse, sometimes the Gradual, and at other times the Psalm. Personally, I always like having the choir sing a meditative anthem or hymn during distribution or the offering."

"What are your feelings regarding traditional and contemporary styles of worship?"

Mrs. Scheinberg held her breath. One misstep here, and her good opinion of Emily Duke, nylons and all, would go the way of the sewer.

"I try *not* to have feelings on the subject," was Dr. Duke's simple reply.

Pastor Fletcher laughed. "I can appreciate that. However, what do you *think* about it?"

"Well, as a church musician, I appreciate that which promotes good order for the congregation. As a Christian, I want the music to serve the Word."

Mrs. Scheinberg let the air out of her lungs in relief.

"And what do you think as a Lutheran?" Pastor Fletcher asked, tapping away on his desk.

"I think that—"

Suddenly, the phone rang, causing Mrs. Scheinberg to drop her pen on the carpeted floor. She scrambled to pick it up and used the soles of her new Dr. Scholl's to scoot herself and her hooded, double-wheel casters back to the desk. She picked up the phone on the third ring.

"Zion Lutheran Church. This is Mrs. Scheinberg speaking," she panted.

"Oh, good, Arlene, I'm so glad I caught you," was the anxious reply. "This is Beverly. You won't believe what Irv did this morning! He dropped by the church just after breakfast to check on the leaky toilet in the men's bathroom, and he left his wallet on the counter of the sink. He told me that he set it down with his hat before going into the stall and then picked up only his hat on the way out the door. Can you go check for me real quick and see if it's still there? If it is, I can swing by and pick it up on my way to my hair appointment in town this afternoon. Seriously, I don't know what I'm going to do with that man! Just yesterday, he took one of my white dish towels out to the pig barn and . . ."

Mrs. Scheinberg rolled her eyes. Beverly Davis was the Lance Armstrong of windbags: the woman could talk longer and faster than anyone else she knew. This was going to go on for a while, so she laid the receiver down on her desk and made her way to the men's room. "As if I don't have anything better to do today," she grumbled under her breath. Adding to her irritation was the fact that she was missing precious minutes of Emily Duke's interview.

Pushing open the door to the men's restroom with her hip, she could see Irv's wallet sitting on the counter in the dark without even turning on the restroom light. She snatched it up, grumbling to herself about germs, and headed back to her office. She swung a little wide, closer to Pastor Fletcher's open office door, taking time to resituate herself comfortably at her station and rub an ample portion of antibacterial gel on her hands before picking up the phone receiver.

"... and would you believe that he ate half of the batch before I even came back to the kitchen? Now I'm out of butter and have to think of something else to make for the VBS cookie train!" Beverly paused to take a breath, and Mrs. Scheinberg jumped at her opportunity.

"I'll be sure to keep Irv's wallet safe for you to pick up this afternoon, Bev."

"Oh, thank you, Arlene! I knew I could count on you. You're a gem! One of these days, we should—"

"I'll give you a call if there's any trouble," she barreled along. "Otherwise, plan on stopping by before three. Bye, Bev."

She hung up the phone just as Pastor Fletcher and Dr. Duke walked out of the study. Mrs. Scheinberg was so disappointed at having missed the rest of the interview that she seriously considered running Irv's nuisance of a wallet through the paper shredder.

Pastor Fletcher stopped at her desk and picked up the dog-eared church directory. He quickly found a phone number and wrote it down on the pad of paper that was kept at the ready on the corner of her desk. Tearing off what he had written, he handed it to Dr. Duke.

"Here is Alice Gardner's phone number. She owns a small rental house just down the street from here. You'll find her to be an honest and kind landlady. She may even be home this afternoon if you want to see the property before you drive back to St. Louis."

"Thank you," the young woman replied, sticking the piece of paper in her purse. "I appreciate the contact and the interview, Pastor Fletcher. Thank you, both of you." Dr. Duke beamed a sunny smile that fell directly on Mrs. Scheinberg.

"Be careful of the coffee at the Casey's on your way out of town," Mrs. Scheinberg impulsively warned. "I don't trust those teenagers who work the register to make it correctly."

Emily Duke thanked her again, letting in another fresh summer breeze as she opened the door on her way out. Mrs. Scheinberg felt oddly disappointed when the door closed behind her. She swiveled in her chair to face Pastor Fletcher's profile and said, "Please tell me that you're planning on recommending her to the council instead of one of those two gangsters."

"I am," Pastor Fletcher replied, somewhat absently. Mrs. Scheinberg noted that he was still staring at the door through which Emily Duke had left. "I already invited her to come to church this Sunday to meet Evan."

She sighed mightily, quickly regaining her natural optimism as she returned to her work on page 4 of the bulletin. "Well, I guess we can't hide him from her. God have mercy on her soul!"

"God have mercy on us all," Pastor Fletcher said as he stepped back into the quiet of his study and softly shut the door. He did not fully understand what had just happened, but he knew that half of his body wanted to jump up and holler while the other half strangely wanted to sit down and cry. Since Mrs. Scheinberg was sitting just five feet away on the other side of the closed door, he did neither. Instead, he walked over to the window and stared unseeing at the north green lawn of the church property, quietly pondering all things intelligent, brown-eyed, and Emily Duke.